I0527790

The Ballad of Colt Sturgess

A NOVEL BY

FRED TERLING

vestige
press

Copyright© 2023 by Fred Terling

All rights reserved. Except as authorized under U.S. copyright law, no part of this book may be reproduced in any form without written permission from the author.

This book is a work of fiction. Names, characters, places, and incidents either are the products of the author's imagination or are used fictitiously, and any resemblance to actual events or persons, living or dead, is entirely coincidental.

Library of Congress Control Number: 2023910591
Terling, Fred, author,
The Ballad of Colt Sturgess / Fred Terling.

ISBN: 979-8-9874914-3-0

Printed in the United States of America

Cover Image by: Warm Tail Art, Russia

Back Cover Art by: Celena Deng
https://celenadeng.square.site

Cover design and book layout by Banished Rascals Design
www.banishedrascals.com

FIRST PAPERBACK EDITION, JUNE 2023

Visit the author on the web at www.fredterling.com

For friends …

"Each friend represents a world in us,
a world possibly not born until they arrive,
and it is only by this meeting
that a new world is born."

– Anais Nin

Prologue

The woods were quiet. Unusually quiet for the morning. Streaks of dawn's light cut through the dense pine trees in Cooper's Gulch on the edge of the Biggs County picnic area. That part of the park got little foot traffic as it was, according to the last survey, two point four miles from the closest picnic pavilion. This morning, however, a lone angler hoping to get an early morning run on late season rainbow trout had wandered up through the creek.

As he worked his way upstream with his fly rod, a flash of light caught his periphery. Initially, he thought nothing of it, but as he drew closer to the source; it was, in fact, emanating from a stationary point. A vehicle had breached the guardrail, chewed up a good portion of the hill, judging by the tire tracks, finally coming to rest at the base of a large tree. The front of the car was folded up and inward towards the driver's compartment. Without investigating further, the angler made haste back to the closest ranger station to report the finding.

Less than twenty minutes passed when a Biggs County Sheriff Deputy's car rolled slowly above the accident scene. The deputy exited his squad car to gather what would be the best approach route, as the bottom creek path would require additional time, offering no clear path. A direct engagement with the hill below offered the most expedient way to reach the vehicle. He moved with a sense of urgency, not knowing the condition of the vehicle's occupants or how long the car was sitting at the bottom of the embankment.

After setting up two flares on the road, with accompanying safety cones from his cruiser, the deputy removed a cord of climbing rope from the trunk. Fastening one end of the rope to the closest tree, the other to a belay, he swung it around his waist and began his descent.

It was a skill he learned in boot camp when he enlisted in the Marine Corps Reserves four years prior. Rappelling was a make or break for a lot of recruits, as dropping from the one-hundred-foot tower at Parris Island recruit training depot required a modicum of trust in the person serving as the ground anchor during the descent. This deputy not only enjoyed the exercise but maintained an active participation in his civilian time during weekends. The nearby former Kinston Fire Chief, now in charge of the county's emergency response unit, was happy to toss a cord of the rope to his favorite deputy when he asked.

Covering the distance in under a minute, the deputy reached the wrecked vehicle. The angler's assessment was accurate. The front of the vehicle had skidded over through the guardrail, down the hill, eventually crashing into the tree. Next came the aspect that was the worst part of the job. Inside of the vehicle, two bodies lay slumped against the dashboard. The windshield was smashed like an accordion inward, fragmented, but intact. Strangely, the rear driver's side passenger door was ajar.

"Possibly from the impact?" thought the deputy aloud.

Without fear, he tugged on the driver's door, cursing himself for not bringing the pry bar that sat next to the rope in his trunk. Fear wasn't something that this law enforcement officer entertained. He had been at ground zero of the events that unfolded five years ago in the neighboring town of Kinston. In fact, he helped dispatch the foul creatures that left only two-hundred ninety-one of its two thousand, two hundred and forty-four residents alive.

The car door shrieked on its hinges, falling unceremoniously to the ground. Reaching across the bodies, the deputy pushed them each back onto the seats. Two very old people, one male, one female, sat lifeless in the forest's stillness. Examining them closer, the deputy felt something was amiss. Both victims of this horrible accident appeared more than just aged. Their skin was grayish, more crepe paper than actual skin to the touch. Glancing around the dashboard, another peculiar observation. For the violent impact of the vehicle on the tree, there was no blood. Not a drop. Exercising caution as to not disturb the scene until the crime scene investigators could give the car a good examination, the deputy reached into the driver's back pocket. Sure enough, he located the man's wallet. Searching the contents, he found a driver's license. It read, "Mark Richards, 4151 Old Oak Road, Kinston. Born, October 17, 1949."

Stepping back, the deputy did quick math in his head. Today was October 19, 1983. That would make this man, if it is Mark Richards, thirty-four years old. There was no way this dead man sitting less that ten feet away was that young. The deputy stepped in for a closer look. He noticed several dark imprints along the man's neck, in the crease of the internal jugular veins.

Frowning, he said, "That's damned peculiar."

Warranting further investigation, he moved to the passenger side of the crashed car. That door opened with a little less effort. Holding the woman's chin, he moved her head left and then to the right. It, too, had the same marks. Her skin was much more brittle, however. So much so when he released her chin, her head slumped forward, falling from her neck onto the floor. The deputy backed off, turning, emptying the contents of his morning breakfast into a clump of grass the tire unearthed before the car hit the tree.

After wiping his mouth, he turned, embarrassed, towards the front cab of the car. He had seen much, but a head falling off practically in his hands was a new one that his body reacted to, much to his personal dissatisfaction. Glancing down at the head on the floor, dead eyes looked back up at him. Hollow, lifeless eyes, slate gray like both of their skin tones. Beside her head, he spied a purse that he retrieved quickly, not looking back. He decided any further investigation would best be left up to the crime scene unit. Doubling back around the rear of the vehicle with the purse and wallet, he took one last look at that back door. It was open with no damage. The deputy noticed a set of muddy footprints on the floor mat. Bending over to touch the outer edge, again, exercising caution not to disturb the integrity of the prints, the print was damp. Once more, the young deputy frowned.

He returned to the rope, scaling the hill, careful not to disturb the tracks. After reaching the top, he opened the door and sat down in his police cruiser. The deputy paused momentarily before reaching down for the microphone of his in-dash radio. Exhaling, he pressed the transmit button.

"Dispatch, this is Deputy Allen out on rural route twenty-nine responding to a possible 11-80. Accident is confirmed, reporting now a 10-55. Request coroner and crime scene investigator on scene," he said.

"Roger that, Jud. You say a coroner and a CSI team?" a voice answered.

"Affirmative, Molly. I have a weird one out here. A few things don't add up and…"

Deputy Jud Allen nearly forgot to search the passenger's purse for identification following the head incident. He rifled through the purse until he found her identification, a driver's license as well. A young woman, Sarah Richards, by his math, age thirty-one. He cursed himself for not checking for wedding bands.

"And?"

"Two victims. Identities not matching government issued credentials."

"What do you mean, 'not matching credentials?'"

"Just trust me, Molly. This one has a few inconsistencies. You wouldn't believe me unless you saw it."

"10-4, I'll put out the request. Slow day here, so you may just get your wish."

"Roger, that."

Jud placed the microphone on the unit. Looking at the face of the young woman on the driver's license, he hoped that what he just saw was wrong. There had to be an explanation for those two passengers. Then the matching set of shoe marks, and her head. Could the impact had done something to the body to just make the head fall off like that? Not in his experience. The girl in the photo was pretty. Not as pretty as his wife, Rhonda, but certainly not the shriveled-up corpse that looked at least a hundred years old sitting in the front seat of that smashed vehicle. Gripping the top of his steering wheel, he peered out through the glare at the morning sun.

"Damn, shame. If it is Mark Richards, his birthday was two days ago."

FRED TERLING

Chapter One

Nothing is quite as beautiful as a feeder stream gurgling over the rocks on a brisk autumn morning. Beams of sunlight wandered through a cabin window, resting on the oak planks of the kitchen floor. The air was filled with the smell of butter, onions, and freshly caught trout. It was morning breakfast a few hours earlier. The dishes were washed and put away, only the sunlight and lingering odors remained as the inside of the cabin was prepared to welcome visitors. Visitors that hadn't been seen in five years.

Funny thing about time. Too often we ignore it as it slips by, not waiting for a moment to be captured unless we grant some of our own in return. What was a bonding experience in the half decade that passed sped by at breakneck speed. It seemed like the events that took place in roughly the same time period in 1978 just happened yesterday. For immortals, it did.

On the porch of the cabin, music cut into the solitude of its location. Two figures danced, one a jitterbug, the other a more contemporary style. The boombox on the glider spit out the rhythms as the two matched steps, each in their unique way. Individual, yet in perfect synchronization. It was their style. Decades apart, but one was closing in on the other quickly. A little too quickly for both of their liking.

"You're getting better, old man," Emma Adams said, swinging her hips like a pole dancer.

"You too, young blood," Colt Sturgess replied, sidestepping with the occasional kick, ball change.

He reached in, grabbing her hands, spinning her around, then a dip. Breathlessly, Emma laughed.

"Hey now! Are you tossing some new tricks in on me?" she asked playfully.

"You know what they say about old dogs," he answered with a wink.

"If only I were so lucky!" she winked back, laughing.

Colt released her hands as the music stopped, shaking his head. "You're incorrigible."

"And you love it!"

Pushing the cowboy hat back on his head, a new one he purchased for this special occasion, he reached down for a pitcher of lemonade. It was cold enough to cause condensation on the outside of their glasses after he filled them.

"Not bad. Getting better at this. Not too tart, not too sweet," Emma said.

"Kinda like you, Ms. Adams."

She laughed again, spitting an ice cube at him.

They sat down, getting a brief respite from the morning's dance off. Sitting quietly, taking in the morning flurry of activity around the two bird feeders hung on alternating sides of the porch, the two just watched the nirvana before them. Squirrels frolicked in the leaves busily burying buckeyes in the yard in anticipation of winter's freeze. Swallowing down a gulp of lemonade, Emma watched intently.

"How do you think they find those again? I mean, they're all over the yard. I keep stepping on the pits in the ground when I cut the grass. Little fuckers," she asked.

Colt watched them with a similar curiosity. "Not rightly sure. Maybe some sort of nut radar?"

She laughed hysterically at his answer.

"Yeah, that makes sense. In all these years of living, that's the best you got. 'Nut radar?'"

He smiled. "This may come as a shock to you, but I don't know everything about everything."

"So much for that older and wiser saying."

This time he spit an ice cube at her.

She jumped up, crashing down on his lap, tickling him without a response.

"You know I'm not ticklish," he said.

She grimaced mischievously. "So, it's still fun to try. Especially since you refuse to kiss me."

Colt stood, lifting her up, then placing her back in his seat effortlessly.

"Darlin', we've had this discussion a hundred times," he said.

"Yeah, yeah. You're a million years old. I just turned twenty-two and I'm supposed to regard you as a parental figure. But that's a bunch of, what's your word, 'malarky?' Besides, I've been aging way beyond where I'm supposed to be and I'm going to pass you, eventually."

"Let's hope not!"

At that moment, the sound of an approaching car caught their attention.

"Think that's them?" she asked.

"Sounds like one set of them," he answered.

Emma sprang to her feet, retrieved the boombox and rushed inside the cabin. Colt stepped down off the porch to greet his visitors. Well, the first of his visitors.

—◆—

A tan 1972 Oldsmobile Delta 88 pulled up the dirt road, clearing through the dust and leaves of the access road to Colt and Emma's cabin. Sturgess pointed them over to a patch of grass next to the barn he repaired that also served as his workshop. Not merely the barn, which was the only thing left standing when he bought the property, but the entire cabin he built by hand on the twenty-three acres of land he called his homestead. His enhanced strength, among his other gifts courtesy of the elixir vitae, enabled him to accomplish what would have taken a team of builders and machinery to accomplish. Although over the past couple of years, Emma helped renovate the inside of the place with touches that made the lone cabin in the woods of the Allegheny Forest truly a place to call home.

Looking worn, a bit stressed, Kat Ellis was the first to depart the vehicle walking slowly towards Colt. He was a bit surprised by her apparent lack of enthusiasm. As she approached, he noticed the dark circles beneath her eyes.

"Hey, Kitty Kat. How was your drive up?" he asked.

She walked past him towards the cabin. "I hope you have a restroom. I drove through and didn't want to stop."

"Sure. Through the front door, past the living room to the back of the —"

Before he finished with the directions, Emma shot through the front door, running towards Kat.

"Hey, Kat! So glad to see you again. Remember me from that town? I was the one who knocked over the thrift shop. Well, shopped actually, but the same thing. We're so jacked that you guys are visiting. It's usually just me and gramps here," Emma said, unable to contain her enthusiasm for company.

Kat stopped, looking her up and down.

"Do I know you? You look familiar, just older," Kat said.

"Well, la de da! You look like death warmed over, honey. Sure you're sleeping?" Emma responded, not at all pleased with her response.

"I gotta pee," she said, pushing past Emma.

Emma watched every step Kat Ellis took towards the house. After entering, Kat slammed the screen door. Emma turned to Colt, face riddled with confusion over the rude welcome from Ms. Ellis. Colt shrugged. It was definitely not the way he remembered her. In all his years, decades even, people changed, but it typically took a lot longer than a mere five years. He turned to the Oldsmobile to see if Johnny accompanied her on the trip. A person sat in the passenger seat, but whoever it was, wasn't in any rush to depart the car. Motioning Emma to stay, Sturgess walked slowly towards it.

Colt tapped on the passenger side window. John Paul Ellis, rather Johnny, slowly cranked down the window. He looked at Sturgess as if he were an alien invading his space.

"Hey, Johnny, you can come on out. Made some fresh lemonade. Must be thirsty after that long drive," he said.

Johnny just kept staring at him over the rim of his glasses. On top of his head was a mask, but Colt couldn't quite see what it was because of the limited space between it and the roof of the car. The interior cloth had separated from the roof and hung down a bit.

"I can fix that right up," he said.

Before he could get the next word out, Kat bolted out the front door, across the porch to their location.

"Wait! Don't go near him. I got this," she yelled.

Colt stepped back away from the car, walking back up the hill to Emma's side.

"Damn, strange," he muttered.

"You're telling me. Thought these were friends of yours?" Emma asked rhetorically.

"Yup, me too."

"They act like you have the bubonic plague and that girl is lucky she didn't get a fat lip calling me 'old.'"

Colt watched as Kat coaxed Johnny out of the car. They went around to the trunk where Johnny took out three bags and a fishing pole. Before approaching the house, Johnny pulled the mask down over his face. It was a Ben Cooper red devil mask. Without looking at his host, he ran into the house, slamming the screen door like his sister did. She followed not far behind with her own plaid one-piece cloth luggage. Kat stopped in front of Colt and Emma.

"We got our stuff. Can you show me where we'll be sleeping?" she asked.

Colt nodded; Emma reached down for Kat's case to help. She tugged it away from her.

"Okay then, lug it yourself," Emma said, crossing her arms.

Sturgess stepped forward, leading Kat into the house. This time, he held the door to prevent it from slamming.

Out on Rural Route Eight, forty-four miles south of the homestead, a pickup truck slowed. A young person with a hooded sweatshirt stood alongside the road hitchhiking. The driver, Skippy Mathers, was on his way to work at the canning factory just a few miles west. He was always early, as the banter with the co-workers was the highlight of his day. This morning, Skippy was doubly excited as the night before when taking his dog out for its evening constitutional, a four-point buck had wandered into the yard. His dog, Pinto, had an affinity for chasing anything that moved. Regardless of the size differential, Pinto ran towards the deer. The deer did not yield. Instead, it charged forward towards Skippy's dog, leaving him in a panic about how to deal with the situation. There wasn't time to think, yet alone react. Pinto stayed the course and jumped at the deer. The deer jumped back, then forward at the dog. This went on for several minutes, each taking turns chasing the other around the yard, only to turn and chase back.

"Damnedest thing I ever saw," Skippy said aloud, laughing so hard he nearly spilled his beer.

He couldn't wait to share the story with the day shift.

As he slowed, he tried to get a good look at the person in the hoodie but couldn't get a clear look at his face from the driver's side of the pickup. Reaching across the seat, he cranked the window down.

"Where ya' heading, partner?" he asked.

"Pine Hollows," a male voice answered.

Skippy sat back, waving him into the cab of the truck.

"Not headed that far, but can give you a lift to Madison," he said.

The young man in the hoodie climbed into the passenger side, buckling his seat belt. The truck moved forward.

"Got a name, stranger?" Skippy asked.

"Christopher," he answered.

"Just Christopher? No last name?"

His passenger said nothing, just stared ahead through the windshield. Skippy noticed the pallid skin of the boy when he secured his seatbelt, but thought better to mention it. This boy wasn't one for conversation. He wouldn't press. Besides, Skippy had to save up his energy for his own story about his dog and the deer from the night before.

"Okay, just Christopher, kick back and relax. My name is Skippy Mathers. Pleased to meet you."

The pickup truck continued down the road. Rows of dead cornstalks lined both sides, so deep into the acreage, it was impossible to see where they ended.

"Always wondered what farmers do with all those old stalks. I mean, I know they chop 'em down for next year's harvest, but what do they do with the old stuff? Farmer's market sells the Indian corn for decorations and cornstalks, but gotta be ten miles for every farm between here and Ohio full of them. Know what I mean?" Skippy was playing to a room of one.

Christopher said nothing.

As the truck neared Madison, the gate arm at the railroad crossing had lowered just up ahead.

"Damn, we were making good time too," Skippy grunted under his breath, fearing the delay from the passing train may cut into his story time with his co-workers.

Stopping the truck, he looked over at his passenger, attempting to engage him in conversation. The boy turned slowly to face him. Seeing his face for the first time, Skippy shrunk back against the driver's side door in terror. Christopher not only had pale skin, but solid, dark, soulless eyes. He reached across, grabbing Skippy's throat. Black mist seeped from the hitchhikers' eyes, permeating the air between the two. Tendrils of the mist invaded Skippy's eyes, nose, mouth, and ears before Christopher released his hold.

Skippy's head shot back, body convulsing momentarily before coming to rest on the seat behind the steering wheel. Skippy Mathers looked peaceful as black lines moved effortlessly beneath his skin through the capillaries on his forehead. Christopher leaned in close. A violent scream rang out from Skippy, which delighted his passenger. Opening his mouth unnaturally wide, Christopher inhaled deeply, drawing the black mist out and back into himself. Not a sound was heard except the train thundering over the tracks and the rhythmic buckling of the railroad ties.

The hitchhiker stepped from the passenger side of the truck, moving in a blur towards the train. In a singular leap, he jumped onto a ladder between two of the boxcars. Wherever the train was heading, it was also Christopher's destination.

A couple of minutes after the train passed and the gate arm lifted, a passerby alerted the police that an old man had fallen asleep at the wheel at the railroad crossing outside of Madison. When the authorities arrived to tend to the man, they discovered he was dead, skin shriveled around the bones like crepe paper. His driver's license stated the man's name was Percy Mathers, known to the locals as "Skippy." The most curious part, he looked at least ninety years old. He was twenty-seven.

Chapter Two

Colt, Emma, Kat, and Johnny sat at the dining room table of the Sturgess cabin. The table was beautifully crafted, as was most of the furniture in the homestead. Nearly all of it was made by hand, a skill Colt developed between hunts. When Emma became part of his world, she took an interest in it as well, immediately. Whether it was boredom from being out in the wild or a genuine interest, she showed an incredible aptitude for wood crafting. The interesting thing about Ms. Adams, she never made the same mistake twice. Her imagination was unbound, which resulted in exquisite pieces, beyond the simple patterns of construction.

Colt wasn't sure if it was a benefit of the elixir or that her fragmented memory created much more room for learning. In either case, she was a master artisan, persistent to the point with her perfection on a lathe, that the shop's generator could be heard in the wee hours of the night when they were working on projects. Frequently she would outlast her mentor who retired hours before she completed a work on the piece.

Every room in the house boasted of their individual or combined work. Eclectic, to say the least. Some pieces were ornate, others plain. It was that combination that made this simple cabin, which appeared that way from the outside, to be a shock on the rare occasion when visitors entered their humble abode.

Kat and Johnny appeared to be indifferent to the beautiful, hand-crafted walnut and pine furnishings.

"So, you two, what's been going on?" Emma asked.

Johnny sat quietly at the table, occasionally lifting his red devil mask, picking at the vegetable tray in front of him. Kat had her head down on the table, completely detached from any desire to converse. This was not the reunion either expected or hoped for.

"We were in quatertine," Johnny said unexpectedly.

"That's quarantine," Kat corrected him.

"You don't say?" Colt asked, hoping to get some semblance of engagement rolling.

Johnny continued. "Yeah, but Kitty Kat lied to the policemen."

Kat's head snapped up in anger, an emotion Colt had never seen.

"I told you; it was just a white lie. You didn't want those assholes digging up Aunt Rosie in the backyard, did you?" she barked at him. "You wouldn't have gotten that movie camera equipment of yours from the insurance money if I told them she was decapitated by an ash toker, now would you?"

Johnny pulled the mask down over his face and ran off to his assigned room for the weekend in a huff. Slamming a door Colt made before Emma was his woodworking apprentice. Emma stood up, visibly annoyed.

"You know, you two shitheads have been nothing but rude since you pulled up. Total disregard for other people's property, I ought to sock the both of you!" she said.

Kat stood up abruptly, nearly sending her chair to the floor. "Go ahead, bitch. Like I'm afraid of you!"

In under a second, Emma closed to her position, grabbing Kat by the arm, then slapping her across the face. Her fingernails left deep scratches on Kat's cheek. She, in turn, pulled her fist back to punch Emma.

"Enough!" Colt yelled. "I won't entertain this kind of behavior in my house."

Emma sat down in the chair Johnny just vacated. "You mean 'our' house."

Sturgess took Kat by the hand, leading her into the kitchen. Dampening a dish towel, he dabbed at the scratches on her face. That's when he noticed it. The blood. It wasn't red like it should be. It was dark. Darker than normal, nearly black.

He thought back to his theory of emotions being locked into a perpetual cycle following exposure to Olath's elixir. But Kat hadn't been the subject of his crown of thorns, force-fed the foul concoction poured down her throat or even exposed to it, or had she? He led her back to the table, sitting down next to her, making direct eye contact, which she resisted. Holding her face between his hands, she turned away in discomfort.

"Don't look at me like that. It gives me a headache," she said.

Colt released her face and sat back.

"Tell me about this quarantine of yours," he said.

"Do I really have to go into all that? It wasn't exactly a pleasant memory."

She stood, attempting to leave. This time, Colt grabbed her by the shoulders. In what was a spontaneous, yet calculated risk, he picked up the knife from the veggie platter, driving it into his hand. Blood flowed freely. Sturgess smeared the substance across her scratched face before his own wound healed. Kat paused, then fell to the floor kicking and screaming, which drew Johnny from his self-imposed solitude. Sturgess held her down on the floor while she convulsed. Johnny launched an attack on Colt, which Emma intercepted, sending the young man through the screen door, tumbling through the grass in front of the cabin.

"You good?" Emma asked Colt.

"Never better," he answered with a wink.

As Johnny dusted off the backside of his pants, he rose for a renewed attack, but was distracted by the sound of two approaching motorcycles.

Kat sat up slowly, following the unforeseen fit. Her head pounded like a war drum, but she was lucid for the first time in a while.

"Colt?" she asked.

He stood up, offering a helping hand.

"Sure am. The question is you in there, Kitty Kat?"

Standing, she brushed her hair back out of her eyes. "What? I mean, where? How did I get here?"

Colt glanced over at Emma, who seemed to understand what was happening, although she too didn't know how Kat Ellis came in contact with the elixir or if Colt had purged it completely. She saw how he brought Lizzy back to life with a similar technique, but it was risky, as there was no guarantee his restorative blood had the same effect on everyone. It was indeed a risk for him to try it on Kat. The result could have destroyed her or worse.

"You know, you will do that to me one day, so I don't die of decrepitude," Emma said to him.

"Interesting word. You'll have to explain that to me sometime," Colt replied.

In the moment's chaos, the approach of the motorcycles went unnoticed, or rather, ignored, as a far more important issue required tending to currently. Kat sat down at the table, picking up a few slices of bell pepper, crunching into them.

"Forgive me, stuff's a bit of a blur right now," Kat said.

"Take your time. But when you're up to it, I want to know about this quarantine of yours," he said.

She nodded.

Emma stepped to the screen door to see two people approaching, one male, one female. The male was helping Johnny up.

"Looks like your other two guests are here. Hope they are a little more on the friendly side," she said.

Christopher jumped from the train as it approached Doylestown, twenty-five miles out of Pine Hollows. He crossed the rail yard towards an access road when he saw another hooded figure. Carefully approaching her, he made that assumption about her sex based on physical build and a pink hoodie. Also, he felt a surge of power within that he only received from draining human life. Her back was to him, but she sensed his presence as well, turning to see the origin of the surge.

Looking down, beneath her feet were two bodies, drained of life, just like Skippy Mathers. She just fed, or whatever these shadow teenagers were doing. Christopher looked at her to see her face. Dropping the hood of her sweatshirt, she looked much like him: pale skin, solid black eyes, dark stringy hair.

"Hey, yinz two kids can't be down here. This is a switching yard, you'll get yourselves killed," one of two rapidly approaching men in work gear said.

Christopher held up his hand, the girl responded with the same gesture. Chattering at each other in an unknown language that sounded more like two squirrels than human beings, their fingers interlocked, spreading a rapidly expanding dark mist across the rail yard. The two approaching workers grasped at their own throats, collapsing to the ground. By the time their bodies hit a set of railroad ties, they had aged substantially. So much so, the impact with the ground shattered them to dust.

The girl smiled, "I'm Amanda."

"Christopher."

Amanda bowed her head. "Guess we need to find Matthew now."

"Yup. Any idea how?"

Squeezing his hands tighter, the dark mist returned to their bodies. "I have a pretty good idea," she answered.

———◆———

Jud Allen and Rhonda Coulter dashed up onto the porch, Johnny in tow. Wherever the motivation was to protect his sister, it had vanished. He bent over to pick up his devil mask that dropped from his head after Emma's blow sent him through the door. Rhonda held the door open for the two of them before rushing over to Jud's side.

"Howdy, Mr. Sturgess. Long time no see," Jud said, extending his hand for a shake.

Johnny rushed by him, reaching for Colt. Jud intercepted him, putting him in a full nelson, a similar grip John Paul used to subdue the four-armed behemoth in McNaulty's.

"Whoa, big fellah. Settled down, we're all friends here!" Jud exclaimed.

Huffing and puffing, attempting to break the hold, Johnny struggled as his sister placed her hands on his face, a method Colt had seen her use previously to calm her brother down.

"John Paul, listen and focus. Everything is okay now. Really. Colt was making me all better," she said.

Jud felt Johnny relax beneath his grip, relinquishing it. Rhonda hugged Kat and Colt before moving to Emma. She froze as if she saw a ghost.

"Heyas, I'm Emma. Pleased to meet you. Colt told me how you guys laid a real ass whooping on those things back in Kinston," Emma said, expecting a similar greeting the other two offered.

Rhonda just stared. Jud stepped between the two, shaking Emma's hand. He halted, as he had never seen anyone with white eyes before. Colt's eyes were always hidden behind the dark glasses. To them anyway. He saw no reason to be rude by staring.

"Hi, I'm Jud Allen. This is my wife, Rhonda," he said, handling the introductions.

"Pleased to meet you both!" Emma replied. She was happy that at least these two weren't as morose as the first arrivals.

Rhonda said nothing, but stayed focused on Emma, which made her a tad bit uncomfortable.

"Mr. Sturgess, I'd be most appreciative if you could point us towards the facilities. It was a long ride," Jud said.

Colt pointed to a door next to the living room. Jud headed in that direction, with Rhonda close behind. He went into the restroom first. Rhonda stood outside, leaning against the door. Emma turned to face Colt with a surprised look on her face. After a moment or two, Jud reappeared. Instead of going into the bathroom, Rhonda put her arm around him, returning to the table.

"What'd ya make of that?" Emma whispered to Sturgess.

Colt shook his head. "Don't know. Seem attached at the hip."

"Reminds me of those two freaks, Frick and Frack," she chortled, taking a long drink of lemonade.

Rhonda's behavior was strange. As was Kat's initially, and the jury was still out on Johnny. Whatever was affecting them, Jud seemed immune. So far. Colt sat back in his chair, looking at each of his house guests. Something was definitely different. Time changes character. He, of all people in the room, knew that. The discovery of the potential of Olath's elixir in Kat's blood stream gave him pause. She presently sat at the opposite end of the table; attention fixed on him. Kat hadn't uttered a word since her initial ones following Colt's special brand of healing. There hadn't been time for a full debrief, as Sarge would have called it, prior to the arrival of the Allens. His curiosity was also burning to know more about the quarantine. Were these four kids exposed to something he wasn't aware of through government intervention? It wouldn't be the first time as the Smoke Hunters referenced Agent Orange in subsequent small talk outside of their missions hunting ash tokers.

Rhonda and Jud took their seats at the table as Kat continued picking at the vegetable platter. Johnny sat quietly, also focused on Colt. His mask was back in place. Rhonda broke the tension with a debrief of her own.

"So much to catch up on. Where to start? I suppose —"

Emma interrupted her. "Don't you have to pee, too? I mean, it was a 'long ride.'"

"No, not yet. I'm good like that," Rhonda said, snuggling into Jud. "By the way, how long have you two been together?"

Emma snuggled into Colt, poking fun at Rhonda's over affectionate posturing. She was sure Rhonda didn't get it as she struck her as ditzy.

"Oh, about five years now, right darlin'" Emma answered, kissing Colt on the cheek.

He was not amused.

Rhonda jumped back in with her update. "That's outstanding. Sorry, that's a word I picked up from my husband. You know Jud joined the Marine Reserves after you left? Well, he had to turn eighteen first, which we both did while in quarantine. Thank god they brought those teachers in though, so we could still graduate on time. As soon as we got out of that hospital, we ran right to the Justice of the Peace at the Biggs Country Courthouse and tied the knot. Not our ideal romantic getaway, but made everything easier, especially for benefits and stuff. Doing the Reserves, Jud could study for the police exam, and a year later, became a deputy sheriff. I'm so proud of him!"

"With all that going on, surprised you don't have a couple of kids and another bun in the over," Emma said sarcastically.

"We are trying, no luck yet, but trying is the fun part, right honey?" Rhonda said, winking at Jud.

Emma rolled her eyes, motioning her finger in her mouth as if she were about to throw up. Unexpectedly, Colt stood up and walked into the kitchen. He stared outside the window at the blue skies dotted with white billowy clouds. Cumulus, he believed they were called. Rhonda Coulter was strong and independent. This giddy young woman in his home seemed the opposite. Standing outside of the bathroom was just plain weird. It was as if she would turn into a pumpkin if she wasn't in physical contact with him. Something had happened to each of them.

Not being in Kinston for the actual confrontation with the ash tokers and clowns, he wondered if being exposed to the burning elixir had affected them. Little was known about how Olath's stuff worked, other than the intel they gathered. The smoke sure had a negative effect on him. Doubling back on his theory of the strength of emotions at the time of exposure, was he seeing the next evolution of this madman's concoction? Both he and Lizzy were alive when they were force-fed the stuff. More questions than answers were surfacing. This was supposed to be a carefree weekend of bonding.

Then there was that little tidbit about Jud and Rhonda having difficulty conceiving. That one hit Colt between the eyes. It was the start of his story over a century ago. The singular desire of his own wife that brought evil into to their lives. An evil that would tether them to a madman named Ansel Olath over decades of death. Since then, he and Emma had built a good life together over the past five years. Was the nightmare of that night at Chooch's Farm ever going to stay dead and buried? He felt a hand on his shoulder. It was Kat.

"Hey. You okay?" she asked.

"I should ask you that question," he answered.

"Yeah. Felt like I was in a fog the past couple of months. Things have been a real challenge, but this was something different. Couldn't control my emotions and said things I didn't really mean to say but got a buzz off the emotional swings. Can't explain it."

"You don't need to. I know more than you can ever understand."

"Yeah, but I was a real bitch. I deserved that crack from Emma."

He smiled. "Yeah, ya probably did."

She punched his arm in jest. "You're gonna have to explain it all to me later. I'm still a bit out of it but noticed your accent has faded quite a bit, though."

"Yup, Emma's been schoolin' me. Guess her smarts are rubbin' off." He paused. "How about Johnny? Is he okay? What's with the mask?"

Kat glanced over at her brother, who was now watching the two of them like a hawk.

"Not sure. He found that in the cellar of the diner when we did spring cleaning. It's kind of been his thing ever since. I didn't find any harm in it, but he never takes it off. John Paul always did a bit of mimicking those he looked up to. If you remember, last you saw him, he had a cowboy hat and dark glasses."

"That I remember."

"I guess quarantine was rough on all of us."

"We'll need to talk about that in more detail. After lunch, of course."

Colt turned to his guests to inform them he was about to fire up the grill when he saw Emma with a look on her face he had not seen in all the time he knew her.

"Emma darlin' you okay?"

Rhonda stood next to her with her hands shielding Emma's eyes.

"Can't you see it, Jud? She looks exactly like Emma's mom. Not a little, not kinda, exactly!" Rhonda exclaimed.

Jud leaned across the table. His face went blank.

"What did you say your last name was?" he asked.

"I didn't, but it's Adams. Emma Adams."

Chapter Three

Rhonda snatched up her purse, rustling through it like a gopher digging a hole. Pulling out her wallet, she flipped it open, removing several photos from the vinyl inserts. She slid them across the table in front of Emma. Colt watched curiously. He wasn't aware of a connection between the three. Jud and Rhonda may have mentioned their friend during the adventure, but not by name. He picked up one photo from the table depicting Rhonda and Emma together at a sporting event. There was no mistake. It was the Emma they knew, except now she was older. Much older.

Emma picked up several of the photos, looking at each of them. Glancing to Colt for help, it was a look he had not seen from her in their shared time together. She was sassy and a spitfire. Seeing her helpless was disturbing. He wasn't sure what to say, yet how to explain the transformation and rapid aging. No one held the key to that mystery except the deadman the two of them slayed together in that parlor five years ago. He sat down slowly at the head of the table as Kat approached, also looking at the pictures. She stared at him for an explanation.

"So? What's these prove?" Emma said, placing the photos back onto the table.

Jud continued hovering from the other side of the table. He slid the photo back over to her. The picture sat between her hands. She looked down to examine it. In the photo were two women, a young Emma and an older woman who looked exactly as she did presently. Emma frowned before sliding it back across the table.

"Okay, what the fuck is going on? You two playing some kind of demented trick?" she asked.

"What happened after you ran off after I gave you that map?" Kat asked Colt.

Sturgess scooped up the photographs, shuffling through them.

"That's kind of a long story, Kitty Kat," he answered.

"We have plenty of time," Rhonda said.

Colt leaned his elbows on the table. "Emma was a young girl, sixteen, maybe twenty tops."

"Seventeen," Jud said.

"Fair enough," Colt said before continuing. "Seventeen. Olath took her from the carnival with a handful of others for whatever damn unholy purpose he was doing out at that farm. Instead of turning her into one of those ash tokers or worse, he tried some new elixir out on her."

"Correction, Lizzy did. She wanted a pet daughter," Emma said.

Although her words dripped with sarcasm, they weren't garnished with anger. Whatever connection she had to Elizabeth, it remained.

Colt nodded. "It was an experimental batch. Emma didn't have a choice; it was forced on her. Long story short, it transformed her in some ways. She's faster, stronger, learns like a sponge. Willpower of no one I ever met, but..."

Emma interrupted solemnly. "I'm growing older by the minute."

Sturgess addressed Jud and Rhonda directly. "Sorry, I didn't know."

The young couple sat back, staring at Emma, then at each other. The Allens broke out in tears in unison, crying hysterically.

"You have no idea how long we looked for you," Jud said through dark tears streaming down his face. Colt, Kat, and Emma noticed the tears.

They weren't clear, but a syrupy dark crimson color. Kat tossed them the same towel she had her wound tended to. Rhonda wiped Jud's face first, then her own. The two observed the streaks of color on the towel.

"I call 'bullshit,'" Emma snapped. "I don't remember either of you, yet alone anyone looking for me."

Colt squeezed Emma's shoulder. "You know your memory ain't all put together, darlin'"

"Stop using that old accent. Thought we worked through all that? Besides…"

An image crept in. Emma looked up at Jud, then at Rhonda.

"That shark book? And the Crimson Dolls?" She began singing. "What's holding you back boy, holding you back, boy. I got your back, boy!"

Pausing, Emma slammed her fists onto the table, sending the photo of her mother and her to the floor.

"…and it's gone," Emma said, tossing her hands in the air.

Jud and Rhonda inhaled simultaneously, falling back on the chairs unconscious. Johnny finally spoke.

"They're back to normal now," he blurted.

Colt looked over at him. He recalled Kat saying that Johnny had a sixth sense about things. What did he mean by "normal now?" Was this another aftereffect of the Kinston elixir exposure? The two of them were abnormally clingy. No married couple is like that after five years.

Sturgess moved Rhonda first, then Jud to the couch in the living room so that they wouldn't slump down on the floor. This was turning out to be one hell of a reunion.

Emma accompanied, standing directly over them, watching both incapacitated on the couch. She felt a twinge of remorse as she had gone through a similar ordeal with her experience in the herringbone parlor at Chooch Family Farm and Dairy. Wondering if she was that helpless at the point of injection of Olath's special elixir, the thought made her skin crawl.

"What did you mean they're normal now, Johnny?" Colt asked.

John Paul didn't answer, but slid the devil mask over his face, hiding from whatever conflict he perceived. Why he didn't answer was a mystery. Colt inhaled, peering over at Kat, who merely shrugged. His behavior was inexplicable, even to his sister.

Emma stopped staring. She had taken up a position between Jud and Rhonda, wiping away the tears with the moist towel. Examining the towel, the tears had faded from the dark substance to clear. Perhaps Johnny was correct in whatever special abilities he possessed to know the beyond.

Rhonda's eyes opened first. She sprung forward off the couch, hugging Emma with the love she had been missing for the past half decade. She loved Colt with all her heart, but there was an intimacy he couldn't provide, rather, wouldn't provide. He still viewed Emma as the young teen in the photos, regardless of her physical age. Then the promise to Lizzy to raise her as their daughter. That was a line he would not cross, although they had zero familiar ties. It was more of a mindset than anything else. Changing perspectives was as impossible as stopping the sun from rising.

Colt and Emma lived as a familial unit, more like best friends with all their work and time spent together, sharing a secret bond that nobody could fathom. Initially, a buzz spawned when the two went into nearby Apollo to get groceries, necessities, and/or general shopping sprees, which made Emma giddy. "When did Colt adopt a daughter?" Then, as time passed and Emma physically aged, the question became, "When did Colt get married?" It was their little secret which Emma delighted in as both possessed hyper-sensitive hearing, only she used hers purposefully to eavesdrop.

Rhonda stared into Emma's beautiful white eyes. She struggled to see her best friend in them, but it was her, nonetheless.

"I can't believe it's you!" Rhonda exclaimed.

Emma frowned. "Yeah, maybe. Not like I can remember stuff, though. It's like pieces of my memory pop in now and then. It's like somebody tore all the pages out of a phone book and scattered them around the room. Occasionally, I find what I'm looking for, but I don't have any clue how to bring it all together."

"I can help you," Rhonda said.

"How's that?" Emma asked.

"Simple. I can be your memory! We've spent at least ten years together. I know what you like to eat, the music you listen to, the clothes you wear, all of it," Rhonda answered enthusiastically.

Emma smiled. *What an interesting idea*, she thought.

Colt shared the same thought as he watched the scene unfold. It could help her reassemble a part of her life she assumed was gone to her. Unfortunately, there was the aging part, but he would suppress that for now.

Jud stirred, seeing the two of them sitting next to him. His head felt as if a pile of rocks collapsed on him. What was going on? Why did he feel suddenly awake, as if he were in a daze for however long? He searched his own memory for when the fog began, but he couldn't find an origin point. Abruptly, he stood, surveying the cabin. He stood to see Colt, Kat, Rhonda, a kid in a devil mask, and Emma's mom. Correction, Emma. Clearing his mind, he switched to the military bearing he gained during initial training in the Marine Corps. Deputy Sheriff Jud Allen quickly assessed the moment, using situational awareness that he learned at the police academy.

"I haven't felt this clear since…we left quarantine," he said.

"Speaking of which, let's talk about that," Colt said, "after lunch, though. Who's hungry?"

An Amish market carriage rolled up Pennsylvania Rural Route twelve, pulled by a large American saddlebred. The carriage was black, with an uncharacteristic, enclosed body resembling a stagecoach more than a traditional carriage. Tinted windows obscured any view of the driver or passengers. The only thing visible from the driver's compartment was the reins being controlled from somewhere behind a paneled wall.

As the carriage moved up the road, it neared two hooded figures hitchhiking in the grass. One wore a gray hoodie, one of smaller build wore a pink one. Their faces were as obscure as the operator of the carriage. Slowing as it approached the two hitchhikers, the carriage halted, and the passenger door opened. Christopher and Amanda peeked into the carriage to see a cloaked man holding the reins in a modified seat to permit navigating the vehicle without exposure.

"Need a ride?" the driver asked.

"Yes. We're heading to Pine Hollows," Amanda answered.

"What a coincidence. That is my precise destination."

Amanda entered first, followed by Christopher. After taking their seats, the carriage lurched forward. The two tried getting a better look at their host, but the cloak and hat he wore prevented any closer inspection.

Odd, Christopher thought, *this man doesn't dress like a typical Amish farmer.*

The carriage rode ahead with no conversation between the three occupants. It stopped after approximately thirty minutes. Amanda glanced at Christopher, their fingers interlocking. The dark mist rolled from their eyes towards the driver. He turned towards the two, breathing in deeply, then expulsing the mist. The two fell backward, choking, as the driver cackled with laughter. They grasped for the carriage door, but a locking mechanism slid into place, preventing their escape. Amanda looked up, extending a hand forward in panic towards the driver.

"My children, is that anyway to treat your creator?" he asked with a sly grin.

Christopher forced himself up, struggling to reach Amanda once more.

"I assure you; a second attempt will only yield disappointment and may bring about a premature demise for both of you. My patience is not what it used to be," the driver said with an air of menacing.

Amanda pulled Christopher back on the carriage seat as they both desperately struggled for even a molecule of air. Their skin shriveled, much like their victims.

"Much better. Just sit and relax. We have yet to retrieve your brother, Matthew. He is our next stop," the dark driver said. "Oh, and by the way, you may call me Kaleb Blackburn. We have a few tasks to attend to."

Steaks sizzled on the grill of the patio next to the Sturgess homestead. Fortunately for everyone, the inconsistent weather of the state offered mid-sixties temperatures with the surrounding tree line, cutting any wind chill that would have prevented an outdoor gathering. The reunion group was seated around the picnic table, also crafted by the hands of Colt and Emma. It may have been the most awkwardly exchanged conversation in the history of humankind. One person was cursed by a detached memory, two others who had just awoken from whatever strange slumber four of them were under up on arrival, one tended the grill and the final person sat quietly staring at the others through eye holes of a plastic devil mask.

The table was set with a variety of side dishes: potato salad, fresh tomatoes in olive oil with home-grown garlic, two loaves of sourdough made by Rhonda Coulter herself and the barely touched veggie tray that saw the unusual transformations of the guests. Whatever the overly affectionate, clingy bond that Rhonda had for Jud shared dissipated. Presently, her attention was fully focused on Emma, who was struggling with the amount of information Rhonda was pouring into her mind concerning their past. Jud added gravy, when needed, but sat back as third fiddle in the core dump of memory data.

Emma was frustrated. Her instinct was to run to Colt and make these people go away for a while. It wasn't as if she didn't want to remember. The prospect excited her initially with Rhonda offering to be her memory, but it was exhausting for her trying to process everything. To her, it was similar to gorging on something she wasn't fond of, but probably beneficial. The jury was still out on the beneficial aspect of piecing together a past.

Kat stood next to Colt wearing an apron that said, "kiss the cook." Although Aunt Rosie was the chef at the diner, Kat was no novice with culinary arts. Even if the canvas was "community grease" as Uncle Michael J. Babin called it. Handing the steak tongs over to her was a logical move. Colt tended the hamburgers with a spatula.

After loading up two serving dishes with grilled meat, Colt placed them on the table. After everyone filled their plates, the conversation he was dying to get to commenced.

"Okay gang, I wanna hear about this quarantine. Who wants to go first?" he asked.

Jud gulped down a mouthful of potato salad, then spoke up.

"I can go. Not long after you left, Rhonda and I started a grid search of Kinston. Moving from west to north was our initial pattern. We started in my neighborhood, of course. After a few days, a caravan of military trucks, along with unmarked emergency vehicles, swarmed the town. We got picked up and taken to Biggs County Memorial and put in the emergency ward for a few hours, then flown out to another hospital. No clue what the other hospital was. Did a little recon, but absolutely no identifying names, addresses, nothing.

"Long story short, we were pent up for about six months. They did every kind of test, drew more blood than I thought was possible. Stress test after stress test, which was kind of a blessing as it helped prep me for basic training. During our confinement, Rhonda and I came of age and got married as soon as we got back home." Jud finished his recounting of the quarantine with a forkful of steak. "Mmm. Excellent stuff."

"They debrief? Ask any question?" Colt asked.

"Yeah, a lot. Like every day, but I don't think they believed us," Kat answered.

"The food wasn't bad, but not like this," Rhonda added.

"How did they act when you told them what happened?" Colt asked.

"They were, what's the word, 'indifferent?' They just wrote everything down, then the psychiatrists came in. Said something about mass hysteria. Then the disease control guys. That's when the blood tests started," she answered.

Colt grunted, trying to zero in on the cause of their apparently altered states when they arrived.

"Did they treat you? Any medicine?" he asked.

The four guests all looked at each other, hesitant to answer. Kat spoke up.

"We're not sure."

"What'd ya mean, 'not sure?'"

"Well, around the half-way point, we were all herded into a room. There were two lines, just like boot camp inoculation drill. Step forward, get a shot. They had those air injector syringe hypos like Star Trek. Things were kind of foggy after that. Still functional, but foggy. But this is for sure, Mr. Sturgess. Seems like Rhonda and I were more reliant on each other, almost to the point of obsession," Jud answered.

"Got that right," Rhonda said. "Him going to Parris Island was the longest three months of my life. I was literally going crazy. Got a ticket to South Carolina and climbed on an airplane for the first time in my life. I couldn't see him, of course, but just being in the same state calmed me down. Well, a little."

Colt turned to Kat, facing her directly. She was tightlipped, but saw he was expecting a response from her as well. Johnny was devouring his plate of food, already dressing his second hamburger.

"Pretty much what they said, but..." Kat said, but fell shy of a full recounting.

"But what, Kitty Kat?" Colt asked.

"It's stupid, I really don't want to say."

Jud prodded. "C'mon, Kat. You're among friends here. It's not like we didn't battle four-arm monsters, thousands of ash tokers and Frankenstein clowns together. Seein' was believin' those couple of days."

Kat picked at a clove of garlic on one of her slices of tomato, sending it across the inner skin, placenta, poking it through a row of seeds until it disappeared somewhere on the plate below.

"I dunno. I started to see things. Like waking dreams. They weren't scary, but it was like an out-of-body experience that I was watching."

Emma shouted, "Clairvoyance? Ha! I remembered something!"

"Maybe, but it wasn't really like telling the future, but more like seeing a different present."

Finally, Johnny spoke. "Tell him about the dark guy."

"Dark guy?" Colt asked.

Kat shook her head. "That was somebody that John Paul saw in his dreams, or maybe for real. Johnny was taken to a different part of the hospital."

"He's my friend," Johnny said.

"Not sure if he's real or not, but he started talking to him when he was still awake. He's been wearing that mask since he found it in Aunt Rosie's Halloween stuff. According to him, it helps Johnny stay safe from the ash tokers," Kat answered.

"This dark guy have a name, Johnny?" Colt asked.

Johnny just shook his head no as he gobbled down a mouthful of Rhonda's bread. He never looked up from his plate.

"You said he was separated from the rest of you all?"

"Yeah. There was a group that went somewhere else, but they let us visit every day."

Sturgess pondered a plausible reason for the quarantine within the quarantine. What was different about Johnny? If they were indeed exposed, what was the result other than what he had already witnessed first-hand?

"Anything else peculiar go on during this quarantine?" he asked.

"Nope. One day, they just came in, put us on a plane and sent us back to Biggs County Airport. Put us up in temporary housing, awaiting placement. Rhonda and I left, rented a small house in Countryside with the..." he paused, clearing his throat, looking over at Rhonda. "Top Arnie gave me a reward for helping. I stashed it before getting picked up for quarantine. Was a bitch getting back to it as Kinston got quarantined too. Fences, guards, the whole nine yards. Then they leveled the whole town. Luckily, I snuck in along the railroad tracks before all that happened," Jud answered.

"Interesting. So, Kinston is no more?" Colt asked.

"Nothing left but a big parking lot overgrown with weeds. The buildings, streets, everything were all torn down. Still a barb-wire fence in and out, but they even collapsed the bridge into town and closed the exit ramp from the highway," Rhonda added.

"You can see it from the highway, but it's more of a mound of dirt and rubble," Jud said.

Colt sat back in front of a plate of untouched food, which Emma pushed in front of him to get his attention. In his previous travels, he had come across many abandoned towns, but none were ever razed, not that he was aware of, anyway. What was particular about Kinston? Other than the obvious size, it was still a tiny community. A part of him remembered Olath raving about some grand scheme involving an underground trolley line, but much like Emma's memory, the connection of relevance was elusive. He was barely alive at the time, with random electricity jolting through his heart to recall the details of the encounter.

"Enough chatter. I'm bored! Think I can go for a ride on one of those?" Emma asked, pointing over to Jud and Rhonda's motorcycles.

"You ride?" Jud asked.

"Does a bear shit in the woods? Of course, I do. Learned on the Harley he keeps locked up. He barely takes it out anymore," Emma said, pointing at the barn beside the cabin.

"Those are more trail bikes, a little more give in the column," Colt said.

Emma responded, wrapping her arms around Colt from behind, kissing him on the cheek. "Oh, don't be a party pooper! Wait. Are you worried about me? So sweet!"

Rhonda jumped up from the picnic bench with even more excitement than Emma did.

"Hell yeah, let's go, girl!" she exclaimed.

Jud also stood up, but Rhonda pushed him back onto the bench.

"No sir. This is a girls only ride," Rhonda said.

"But—"

"Girls only, Deputy Allen," Emma added.

Jud shrugged as he, Colt, Kat, and Johnny watched the two young women mount the pair of Honda CX500 Turbos. Colt yelled out for Emma to wear Jud's helmet that was hanging from the front hand clutch. She defiantly stuck out her tongue in jest before complying. The two sped off, spitting gravel in their wake. It would take some getting used to independent Rhonda again. The time in the haze where she was glued to his side could be annoying, but he didn't fall in love with her for that. Quite the opposite.

35

Colt began clearing the table with Kat's help. Jud pitched in washing dishes. Johnny retired to the couch inside with the bag he had been carrying since arrival.

"Reminds me of mess duty," Jud said.

Following clean-up, the four relaxed on the sofa in the living room. Jud picked up a newspaper that sat on the end table. Kat wandered around the living room, looking at the décor as Colt watched her. She floated, more than moved, taking in all the curios he had collected over one hundred plus years. Much like the way Colt did when first entering Rosie's tavern, Kat constructed the tale about the man by the things he displayed. Was a story lurking behind these things that lay hidden? In the center of the fireplace mantle, two tarot cards were mounted and framed: The king and ten of swords. She had gifted those to him upon his departure from Kinston. It brought a smile to her face and heart.

Kat Ellis had once told him that "he mattered." The obvious center placement of her offering, so prominent to everything else in his collection, so did she and Johnny. She turned to him, smiling.

"Shit," Jud spat out suddenly.

"What is it, Jud?" Colt asked.

"You have a phone, Mr. Sturgess? I must make an emergency call. I'll pay for any charges."

Colt waved over to the kitchen wall. "Over there, on the wall outside the kitchen. Don't worry about the charges. Slightly different calling from out here, though. Only one number. Dial zero, wait for the operator and give her the number you're calling. A little old-fashioned, I know, but we haven't quite caught up with things out here yet."

Jud rushed over to the phone, holding the newspaper as if it were the Dead Sea Scrolls. Following Colt's instructions, he was connected to the Biggs County Sheriff's Office.

"Hey, Molly, it's Jud Allen. Yeah, I know I'm supposed to be on vacation, but something just came up and why are you answering the phone? Moonlighting from dispatch?"

After a brief pause while she answered his question, Jud continued. "Need to talk to the Chief, pretty urgent. Yes, I'll hold."

Kat sat down on the couch next to Colt. Johnny opened the gear bag he was carrying around. Removing a super eight camera and package of film, it drew Colt's curiosity.

"What's that fancy contraption?" he asked.

"That's Johnny's latest obsession. After the destruction of the pinball machine, he found an old book about movies when we did our spring cleaning. Long story on how we came by the equipment, but he's gotten pretty good with it. Even edits. We didn't bring the projector as it's bulky and didn't want to impose," Kat answered.

"Another time, for sure. Like to see what he films."

Johnny joined the discussion. "My first movie was all the living stuff in the cemetery. Saw it when we buried Uncle Mike. Not in town though, as we can't go back. Got a graveyard stone for him and Aunt Rosie put behind the diner where you buried Aunt Rosie. I kept his badge. Thanks for that, by the way. Burying her and all. You did a good job."

Colt nodded. That had to be rough, but these two persevered through a nightmare that they would never have chosen. Victims of circumstance. How does one mourn for loved ones when they aren't permitted to set them to rest on their own soil, but what was most convenient in the moment?

One item adorning a wall of the cabin was a hook latch picture Emma had bought for him on one of her many shopping trips into town. It read, "I am not what happened to me, I am what I choose to become. Carl Jung"

It was appropriate for not only him, but all 6 of these wandering souls put on a path none expected by the fiend Professor Olath. It was just comforting to have such thoughts without the accompanying rage, which hadn't returned since that night at Chooch's farm. He wondered if that was one item that Kat noticed while perusing his collection. Colt's attention was drawn from his meanderings by something he heard. It was never his attention to eavesdrop, but his heightened senses frequently provided information not intended for him.

"Says here in the article, 'Percy Mathers, only twenty-seven years old, was said to appear to be a man three times his natural age upon discovery.' Sound familiar? Then the icing on the cake, 'the coroner made an initial statement that moving the body was problematic as the skin slid off the bones.' The article later said that the coroner has since retracted his initial statement. Sounds like a call is in order to Madison PD, eh?" Jud said into the phone.

Colt rose, walking towards the window that overlooked the porch. A sudden feeling that the women may be in trouble crept into him.

Chapter Four

Emma and Rhonda raced up sunrise hill, parked the motorcycles and sat down in two oversized chairs Emma and Colt built to watch both sunrises and sunsets. It was beautiful, with a sweeping view of the Allegheny mountains in the foreground, split by a feeder stream where they often fished. A gentle autumn breeze drifted over the two, causing a slight chill, but in the picture portrait of an afternoon, it went unnoticed.

"This is so great. Wish we could live up here all the time, too," Rhonda said.

"Why not? We have a few acres. Colt and I can help you build something."

"That would be heaven. But with our jobs and all, and my husband having to report for Reserve duty, probably just a dream right now."

"Tomorrow is not guaranteed. I'm walking proof of that. I could wake up and be a hundred years old," Emma said.

"Don't say that! We just reunited. We have to have more time."

Emma reached forward, plucking a dandelion from the ground. "Make a wish!"

Rhonda closed her eyes, then blew. The pappus caught the same breeze, drifting away between the rays of sunshine.

"What did you wish for?" Emma asked.

"I can't tell you, or it won't come true," Rhonda answered.

The two laughed. It felt great to Emma. This was the first time in a long time she had a friend outside of Colt. Something inside of her felt safe with Rhonda, like a genuine connection that wandered away unintentionally, then returned with bows and ribbons. She closed her eyes, leaning back in the chair, feeling the warmth and the chill at the same time. Opposing sensations, like the tug of war going on inside of her. The budding kinship versus the established security. Outwardly, she appeared like a middle-aged woman, but inside, she was still merely a twenty-two-year-old woman who had lost seventeen years of experiences to the crown of thorns in the herringbone parlor. Sure, she had an uncanny ability to learn, making fresh memories, but a major thing lacked that Rhonda and Jud shared.

"So do you love him?" Rhonda asked.

"Love who?"

"Colt, silly!"

The million-dollar question. How many times did she ponder this very question? What was love anyway? Not having anything to compare it to or even romanticize about except in the occasional novel she started but never finished. Emma found those syrupy offerings held very little reality, if not downright fantasy. At least her scrambled mind told her so.

"Of course, I guess. I dunno. Like I do, but there's like this dividing wall he put up. He thinks more of me like a daughter or a buddy. I mean, I look older, but I think he thinks it's skeevy to cross that line. Of course, I'm of age for stuff, and believe me, I've tried to get his interest. Last Valentine's Day, I surprised him with breakfast wearing nothing but that 'kiss the cook' apron on, but he yelled at me to dress properly. What does that even mean?"

"Wow, that must suck."

"Big time. I mean, forget about sex. I never even kissed him the way I want. That I do remember how to do! But, on the other hand, with all the hang ups I see and hear about relationships, it's kinda nice to just have a woman to man friendship without all the entanglements, if you know what I mean?"

Rhonda laughed at the last remark. "Well, kissing is pretty sweet. Glad you remember that."

"I would love to have sex just once before I die."

"Don't say that, it will happen. It's absolutely amazing. I've only been with Jud, but he sends my rocket to the moon."

"You're lucky. If only—"

Emma stopped, homing in on a sound, rather the sounds. In the distance, the sound of crackling fallen branches and crunching leaves drew her attention from the female bonding. Rhonda couldn't hear it but reacted to Emma's reaction.

"What?" she asked.

"Shh," she answered.

Emma stood up, moving forward towards the sound. Rhonda followed closely behind, eventually hearing the disturbance in the forest.

"Think it's a deer?"

"No, only two feet. Guessing a hundred twenty, maybe thirty pounds."

"How do you know that?"

"I just do."

Through a clearing, a figure emerged. Medium build, wearing blue jeans and a hoodie with some symbol neither recognized on the front. Emma was right about the weight. It walked like a boy, but with the hood synched up around the intruder's head, it was difficult to tell for certain. As it got closer, he lowered the hood. It was a boy, a teenager by the looks of it. His hair was a little more in the disco vein that most wouldn't get caught dead wearing in 1983. That fad had long passed.

"Can I help you, stranger? This is private property," Emma asked politely, but firm.

The boy returned his hands to his pockets after dropping his hood.

"Heyas. What's two babes like you doing all alone in the woods? Your bikes?" he asked.

The term "babes" didn't sit well with neither Rhonda nor Emma. Particularly Emma, who also wasn't fond of the strange boy's interest in the Honda Turbos.

"Actually, yes. Not that you answered my friend's question," Rhonda said.

"Chill babes, chill. Just makin' pleasant conversation. Either of you know where I can find a dude named Sturgess?"

This grabbed Emma's attention more than the continued use of "babe." She pushed past Rhonda.

"Never heard of him. Like I said, you're trespassing on private property...babe," Emma answered mockingly.

"That's a shame. Walked all the way up here, hoping to find him. Guess I'll just have to jack one of these sweet rides and head back to town," he said.

Emma crossed her arms defiantly, letting out a snicker. "Over my dead body, pencil dick."

The stranger's eyes rolled back, turning black. Baring his teeth to reveal a row of fangs, he raised a hand to strike her.

In a whirlwind of motion, Emma sprang forward with a direct blow to the boy's chest, sending him back into the tree line. He sat up, woozy, to see Emma standing over him. Spitting blood from his mouth, he attempted to strike her again, which she deflected, tossing him up into a nearby pine tree. She arrived first before he landed, balancing herself on a branch with the alacrity of a bird.

"Who are you and why are you here?" she snarled at him; white eyes glowing.

"Fuck off," he answered.

She flung him back to the ground, intercepting him once again before his head smacked into a large boulder. Smashing him to the ground, she stood above him, her foot on his chest pressing down ever so slightly, but with increasing pressure.

"What's your name, asshole, and why are you here? Last time I'm gonna ask," she warned.

Choking up blood that quickly filled his mouth, he spit out a solitary word, "Matthew."

Emma reached down, yanking him up by his hood, now sprayed with blood and covered in pine needles.

"Cute, Matt. Now get the fuck off my property...babe!"

Swinging her arm back, she tossed the boy forward, scaring a row of trees to their front, with the impact of his body ricocheting from the force. A final collision with a sapling surrendered his body to gravity with a thud.

Out of her immediate sight, Emma rushed forward, negotiating the various obstacles between her and the strange boy who threatened her and Rhonda moments prior. Arriving at the sapling, she witnessed the impact mark, but he was gone. Scanning the forest visually and listening beyond average human hearing, Emma fine tuned her search with other sensory receptors. Whatever way he escaped, Matthew didn't use the same noisy method as his approach.

What was he and why was he interested in Colt? She thought. Fuck, Rhonda!

Emma sped back to sunrise hill, hoping the boy didn't double around to steal the Hondas or worse. Entering the clearing, she let go a sigh of relief. Rhonda stood in the center of the hill, bright eyed with her hands over her mouth.

"You okay?" Emma asked.

Dropping her hands, Rhonda couldn't contain her enthusiasm. She hugged Emma, then grabbed her by the shoulders, shaking her forcefully.

"That was the coolest fucking thing I ever seen! You beat the shit out of him and talked smack to him while you did it. How'd you learn to do all this? I mean, you climbed that tree so fast, it was a blur and you balanced on it like Nadia Comăneci! Then you tossed him like a golf ball through the woods. Damn, girl!"

Emma blew on her fingers, dusting them off on her shirt. "Oh, I have a few tricks up my sleeve."

"But how?"

"Not sure, but pretty badass, no?"

"No! I mean, yes!"

Emma walked over to the motorcycles, mounting one. She waved over to Rhonda, summoning her to follow.

"We need to get back and tell Colt. Whatever that thing was, he wasn't human."

Rhonda nodded as the women sped off towards the homestead as fast as the motorcycles would carry them.

Colt sat on one of the dining chairs in the center of the living room. Jud had gone out to the porch, pacing, awaiting the return of the two women. Kat asked him about the last trip to Chooch's Farm. Reluctantly, he began the story when Johnny asked if he could film it. Since he had been quiet, not interacting at all with the rest of the guests, Colt agreed. What harm could it cause?

Johnny set up the camera and loaded the film cartridge. He went with tri-x black and white film. His creative sensibility felt this was a wonderful selection to capture the retelling of an immense piece of their story that only two of them knew. Colt attempted to relax. He'd never been interviewed.

"Just relax," Kat said, "everyone hates public speaking."

Colt remained apprehensive, as he hadn't shared what happened at the exact point of Olath's double-cross that cost him the life of his beloved Lizzy. Emotions were a funny thing. Mentally, one can be prepared to recount an event, but when it comes to physically doing it, somewhere deep inside, hidden emotions explode to the surface with the force of an erupting volcano. Cleaning up the aftermath can be a long, tedious process, but also can be the first step in healing. He had done this with Emma, but she never pressed further beyond the present. That he appreciated.

Johnny clicked on a lamp he commandeered from an end table for additional lighting. He looked through the viewfinder of the camera to see if he preferred it to the natural lighting from the porch windows. Deciding on natural lighting, he switched the lamp off. He nodded to Kat, then slid the mask back down over his face. Kat was to handle the actual interview while Johnny filmed. She cleared her voice to deliver the first question, clicking on the record button of a cassette deck. The film recording was silent. The audio portion of the production would have to be synchronized, if this film would ever see the light of day.

"I'm interviewing Colt Sturgess regarding his final trip from Kinston. Mr. Sturgess, can you explain what happened once you left the armory to the location on the map I gave you?"

This time Colt cleared his throat. "Sure. Rode my bike out to that location on the paper you had, Chooch's Dairy Farm, I believe. Pardon, memory ain't what it used to be. Got out to the farm. Thanks again for that. Solid directions. Went into a slaughterhouse, but I'll skip that part as it was pretty gruesome what I found. Lots of body parts hanging everywhere, being pumped up with Olath's elixir. Beat feet out of there in a rush only to be met by Lizzy, my wife, and Emma, who you met."

"Wait, your wife? She was still alive too?"

"Yup, sadly, she was under the same stuff Olath poured down my throat."

"What was that?"

"A potion, elixir, whatever you wanna call it. Poison, I call it. Same stuff the Smoke Hunters burned all over the town to draw in the ash tokers."

This aspect intrigued Kat. It was the first time he had mentioned it. Colt sent her and Johnny away before Lizzy and Emma appeared from the limousine. A wife, though?

"So, your wife was with Emma. All three of you were a product of this Olath character who had us prisoner in Kinston? The one who had John Paul hostage until…well…you cut off his arm."

"Yeah, but he's no longer with the living, not that he ever was, I reckon."

Johnny looked up, signaling Colt. It was a predesignated sign that they had under a minute left of the film.

Kat continued. "What happened next?"

"Well, I followed your advice. Caved into a crazy idea to let Olath transfer my blood into Lizzy so she wouldn't need...might skip that part for now. Anyway, Olath pulled a fast one, killed Lizzy. Then Emma and I finished off Olath after she burned down his sick operation."

Kat gasped. "He killed your wife? Right in front of you?"

Colt put his hands behind his head, staring off through the light of the front porch window. Jud had ceased pacing, which was a distraction. It was quiet except for the sounds of nature and two motorcycles approaching at high speed. The emotions must have hardened since that night as he experienced no flood, no eruption. They stayed quiet, dormant within him wherever he buried them. Johnny zoomed in on Colt's face, expecting some sort of reaction, but saw only the flecks of black in his white eyes.

"Yup, that he did, Kitty Kat. But...the rage is gone, for all that matters."

Johnny gave the thumbs up, sliding his devil mask back up over his head. Kat was sobbing.

"I'm so, so sorry. I had no idea—"

"Not your fault, Kat. My choice."

"But if I hadn't given you that map..."

"Then Olath would still be running around, killin' innocent people using body parts to make more monsters. We do what we must, and the wheel keeps turning. Right?"

This was the first time in all her years reading tarot cards that the practical application of divination lead to dire results in the flesh. A majority of the time, she provided her interpretation of the spread, never seeing the person again. Did they understand the reading? Did they follow any of the advice? Most importantly, how did it turn out? These were questions that tugged at her curiosity from time to time, but never to this extent.

This man who she had grown extremely fond of in a few scant days in Kinston, Pennsylvania, had lost his wife violently, she presumed, right in front of him. He had taken her advice at great personal loss, but he put an end to a great evil. She was right, Colt Sturgess was indeed the king of swords. Kat glanced down at the tape recorder. She held his record of pain in her hand. It was a powerful thing. Colt touched her gently on the shoulder.

A weekend of tears was not his plan when he invited the four out to his homestead, but maybe they were necessary. Much like their first encounter with the Smoke Hunters in the armory, everyone had a piece of the puzzle. At this moment, it appeared all of them were assembled, except one, Johnny. The mask thing was simply strange, but no more so than fishing goggles. Something was off though, particularly with his visions of a dark man who he categorized as his friend.

"Got what you needed, John Paul?" Colt asked.

"Yes, sir. Thank you, sir," he replied.

Colt reached out to shake Johnny's hand, but he responded by stuffing his in his pockets after reseating his mask. Sturgess recalled Kat telling him about John Paul Ellis' aversion to contact.

A nagging thought remained. Each of them was in an unusual state when they arrived. Whether from the exposure to the burning elixir or whatever the contents of the injections from the government doctors. Then there was John Paul. What was a norm for him though, only Kat knew.

Suddenly, the screen door burst open. Emma hated that, but on this occasion, it was she who was the guilty party. Rhonda was close behind; Jud held his ground in the doorway.

Rhonda almost leapt across the entryway carpet, brimming with adrenaline, she couldn't wait to recount the tale of their recent experience. Spitting out the details as fast as she talked, she didn't breathe until the last syllable was shared.

"She's so badass. Mr. Sturgess, there was this werewolf looking guy, maybe a vampire, I don't know what. He came out of the woods; said he was looking for you. Tried to take the Turbos, but Emma crash, boom, banged the mother fucker up into the trees, then down the trees, then through the trees. It was frickin' beyond rad. She's my new favorite superhero!" she finished with a big inhale.

Colt looked up at Emma, who was being squeezed to death by Rhonda. Emma acknowledged the occurrence with the bow of her head.

"Werewolf?" Colt asked.

"Said his name was Matthew, but not why he was intruding. I tried beating it out of him, but all I got. He had black eyes and big ass teeth, disco fever ass hair, needed a good bath, too. He stunk," Emma answered.

Colt glanced around at the rest of his guests. This was an unexpected development. He had planned a fun weekend of fellowship. Presently, with the appearance of this trespasser, safety was a concern.

"Where is this Matthew now?"

Emma shrugged. "Took off after him, but he disappeared. No trace. Shot back to sunset hill worried he may have gone back for Rhonda."

"Attacked you?"

"Didn't have the chance. I blinked first," Emma said.

Colt walked over to the door, taking the keys off of a hook next to it. "I'll be back. Gonna have a look around. Jud, guessin' you don't have an issue looking after things while I'm gone?"

Emma stepped forward. "What, I'm chopped liver? Chauvinist!"

Colt hugged her. "Now, you know me better than that. He's trained to protect and serve. Don't want you getting' in over your head. You don't know what that kid could have done to you, especially if he ain't a normal kind of human being, which you both claim he's not. Consider Jud your backup."

"Fine," she said, crossing her arms in a huff.

Colt went out to the workshop, which was actually a barn. He avoided calling it that, as the last barn he traveled to was used for anything but lairage. This one was multi-purpose serving as he and

48

Emma's woodworking shop, motorcycle maintenance, whatever they needed that required space. Emma had her own Suzuki dirt bike that she failed to mention to Rhonda, guessing she wanted to test out the Honda Turbo. Opening the front of the barn, Colt disappeared momentarily behind the door before roaring back out on his 1973 Harley-Davidson FL Electra-Glide.

The black Amish carriage pulled up in front of a tavern named Kelley's Irish Pub in the town of Apollo. Christopher and Amanda exited the coach first, followed by Kaleb Blackburn. They opened the door to Kelley's Pub, entering the establishment.

The small-town pubs always had a unique blend of low lighting, the smell of cigarettes and stale beer. This one had an additional odor. Copper. On first glance, Blackburn noticed the bar to be extremely untidy. Chairs and tables were flipped over, stains on the wall. He walked over to the closest wall with a smashed jukebox. An overhead light flickered above it. Touching the stain, he raised a finger to his lips and tasted it. Blood. Upon closer examination, he saw a severed head laying inside the upper cabinetry, spinning round and round on the turntable. His hooded companions remained in the doorway, watching as he continued into the bar area from the lounge.

"Lock it," he said, pointing to the door.

The two complied.

Passing through an entryway into the bar area, Blackburn walked through a curtain of green, clear, and red beads. At the bar sat a figure, drinking from a bottle. Three more bodies lay on the floor. Correction, two more and the headless body of the person occupying the busted jukebox. Pools of blood covered the floor that Kaleb had to navigate carefully to maintain footing. Before approaching the figure, he called for support.

"Amanda, Christopher, come to me," he said.

His two hooded travelling companions entered the room, stopping in front of the first blood puddle. They faced each other, chattering in their own unique language they used to communicate in the rail yard.

"Stop that. I told you I can't decipher that abominable sound," Blackburn said in disgust.

The figure at the bar lit up a cigarette before swiveling in his barstool to face them.

"Took you long enough. How long do you think I need to wait here?" he asked.

It was Matthew. The same Matthew that Emma had mopped up the woods with earlier. Blackburn stepped towards the young man, examining his face, which had blood splatter and deep scratches. Pulling him forward off the chair, he also saw two black eyes with pine needles imbedded in his hair.

"What, pray tell, happened to you?" Blackburn asked.

"Nothing. Had a tussle with a local out in the woods," he answered.

Blackburn lunged forward, grabbing Matthew's face. Circling his hands around his forehead and crown, his eyes were tightly shut. Matthew pulled away, but the grip on him was too strong. He felt his consciousness slipping away just as Blackburn released his hold on him.

"I told you not to go out to the farm on your own. That you would require our assistance for us to fulfill this contract!" Blackburn yelled at him.

"Yeah, well, fuck you, old man! I don't need some ancient asshole telling me what I can and can't do!"

"Who is the woman?"

"What woman?"

"The woman who handled you easily in the forest. The woman responsible for your black eyes and every other injury you are bearing. The woman who filled you with half of the pine needles in this part of the state protruding from every part of you?"

Matthew sat back. "Nobody. She's lucky I decided to take a powder, come back into town and wait for you all."

"Not from where we're standing," Amanda snickered.

Mathew shot up out of his chair. "What, you want next dibs?"

Christopher reached down for her hand. Their fingers interlocked, releasing the dark tendrils of smoke around their feet, expanding rapidly towards him. Jumping up on top of the bar, Matthew held his hands over his eyes and nose.

"Enough!" Blackburn yelled. "We cannot complete our task by in-fighting. We must pull our resources or failure is certain. That simply is not an option."

He sat down on one stool while the other three settled down to where they all stood together. There was a wildcard in the mix. Emma. This was unanticipated and required a shift in strategy. It was Colt Sturgess they were after, for reasons known only to Blackburn. How these three strange teenagers, two with unusual abilities, one apparently with none other than the ability to morph into whatever creature he was. Suddenly, that occurred to Blackburn.

"Give me your hand, Matthew. I won't ask twice," he sternly demanded.

Matthew chuckled, "Fuck you, old man. I can walk out of here right now and never look back."

One of the most challenging aspects of leadership is drawing the line of acceptability. Many traits comprise the qualities of a good leader. Most developed over time, but time was not a luxury in this situation. Often, pure intimidation worked wonders. Amanda and Christopher had already surrendered to that fear.

Calmly, Blackburn stood up, removing his hat, revealing a bald head. Upon dropping his cloak to the floor, a set of wings was revealed. He spun around to face the three, particularly Matthew. Blackburn's face transformed, as had his skin, illuminated by bright red glowing eyes. He smiled, revealing two rows of razor-sharp teeth. What appeared to be a hunch-backed, elderly man moments earlier, now stood something closer to a living gargoyle.

Cocking its head back, it let go a fierce shriek before lunging forward, grabbing Matthew by his throat. Flying straight back into the rear paneled wall of Kelley' Irish Pub, the creature known as Kaleb Blackburn pinned him with claws penetrating his skin. Matthew screamed out in agony. Twice today, the cocky mouthed youth was being accosted by an overpowering force.

"I told you; I wouldn't ask twice."

The creature flung him onto the floor into a pool of blood. Mathew humbly rose to his knees, while the creature returned to human form, walking gracefully over to the barstool, picking up his hat and retrieving his cloak. Backburn moved towards Amanda and Christopher. He stopped short, standing directly on Matthew's fingers. Another scream of pain.

"We have a slight problem. Your brother Matthew here has evolved past your current abilities.

He has acquired new ones, but without proper tutelage, he is worthless. We must adjust our plan and timetable. Tonight, we will approach the Sturgess home, acquiring the target. Anyone who stands in our way will be dispatched with all haste. The blonde woman may pose a problem. I have yet to address how that problem will be handled. She may serve as a potential asset, but only if she can be secured without incident," Blackburn said.

Matthew staggered to his feet after Blackburn released him.

"Is this your work?" he asked Matthew, motioning towards the lifeless bodies.

"Yeah. Kind of lost my cool after the woods thing. Needed to blow off steam, ya know?"

"Clean up your mess, then. Covering your tracks is not a variable that I had factored into this job. You've made quite a shambles, but maybe you may still serve a purpose. There's something I must teach you, but first, tidy up."

Colt searched the woods near and around sunset hill. He sat down momentarily, enjoying the same things Emma and Rhonda did earlier. It was one of his favorite parts of the property. Looking up, he saw a piece of torn clothing attached to a tree limb about twenty feet from the ground. He waltzed over to the base of the tree. Although he had superhuman speed, he was never one for climbing trees, not that the skill aided in the task. Jumping, perhaps, would suffice?

On the third attempt, he snatched the fabric from the limb. Examining it, he noticed nothing remarkable, just a simple swatch of cotton sweatshirt, but Emma was right. It stunk. More of a sulfur smell than body odor, although that was present as well. Colt tucked it into his pocket. He explored ahead a little through the woods before returning to the cabin. Staying vigilant, Sturgess moved forward along the path of destruction Emma had cut. The only footprints he detected were hers. *Odd*, he thought. Although if she was using him as her personal shot put, any others may well be undetectable. He pressed forward.

Back at the cabin, Jud summoned Rhonda to the front porch. In his hand, he held the article about the young man who was found near a railroad crossing outside of Madison.

"We have to go," he said.

"What? Now? Are you crazy?" she asked, not at all pleased with the request.

"Look, I know you're having fun with older Emma, but this has to do with the case —"

"Don't call her that. She's Emma. Our Emma. Why can't you get with the program on that?"

Jud held up the article. She snatched it from his hand.

"What's this?"

"Remember that couple I was telling you about a week ago? The accident I was called to out at Cooper's Gulch? This has a lot of similarities to the victims I discovered at that site."

"I thought you said it was just an accident?"

"Yeah, well, there are certain details that we don't release to the public."

"'The public?' I'm 'the public?'"

"No, of course not, but you know what I mean. This local case is too similar to be a coincidence, and I was the first officer on the scene. It's imperative that I investigate this."

Rhonda crossed her arms, frowning as she sat down on the top step of the porch. He sat down beside her.

"Listen, sweetheart. I know this is difficult. We talked about the commitments of the Sheriff's office and the Marine Corps Reserves. You were okay with both at the time," Jud said, hoping to draw the emotional pull of Emma out of the equation.

"'At the time.' Things have changed. I love you, Jud, but we looked for her for so long. To just up and leave the same day we all reconnected. Then there's the whole thing about the clinginess. Emma told me I waited outside of the bathroom like a dog while you peed!"

"I understand. We can come back next weekend if you want. Not like they are going anywhere."

Rhonda leaned back on her hands. She was going to get her way. They had just arrived for a three-day weekend. They were not leaving.

"Have you tried talking to her?" she asked.

"No. What's the use? She doesn't remember anything," he answered.

Something deeper was in play. She knew him better than anyone. His complete refusal to even converse with Emma was puzzling. Jud was sensitive, caring, and empathetic. It's what made him an influential leader, but more importantly, a good person. Rhonda emphasized that to him on the roof of the armory, yet with Emma, he was a rock. This was perplexing. Even when starting their search of Kinston following the eradication of Olath's army, it was Emma on which Jud focused their search. Not his family, but Emma.

"Go talk to her," she said.

"What?" he asked.

"Just go talk to her. If this all-important case of yours can't be solved by Tuesday morning, then fine, we'll leave. But I need you to understand that if you walk away without talking to your friend, correction, best friend, you'll regret it. I know you and how you feel. I also know how bullheaded you are if you have something going on inside you that you're not quite ready to deal with. You'll bury it until it eats away at you."

Jud crossed his fingers, then looked at his wife. Those big doe eyes that he fell instantly, madly in love with. She seldom asked him for anything. Rhonda Coulter Allen was a free spirit, handling anything she needed by just getting it herself. He was merely the sauce to her goose. If she had a reason to insist on this interaction, there had to be a purpose. After all, she had spent time with Emma. He had not.

Without saying a word, he stood up, walking across the porch through the screen door, careful not to slam it.

"Yes!" Rhonda whispered with a fist pump, when he was out of sight.

Turning the article over about the young man Jud referenced, she saw something on the flip-side that caught her interest, but part of it was torn off. She rushed into the house, looking for the newspaper. It sat on the table next to Johnny, who was fiddling with his camera equipment. Snatching up the paper, she sat down in a chair at the head of the table. Something about Johnny creeped her out from the onset. His devil mask wasn't helping her perception of him.

◆━◆

Jud found Emma in the living room wearing a set of headphones, plugged into a boombox. A stack of cassettes was piled on the table in front of her. He sat down, trying to get her attention.

Following non-commissioned officer school at Camp Lejeune, he approached his detachment first sergeant at the Reserve unit. Jud formulated a lesson plan on how to teach classes the Marine Corps way. It was called platform technique. He found it extremely helpful, as he wasn't exactly a skilled public speaker, but the instruction he received on it gave him extra confidence to address a group of any size. The first sergeant liked the proposal but informed him that the final sign-off would have to come from the detachment commander, Captain Cole.

Captain Cole had a reputation for being a hardass. This was a test of the young NCO's mettle. Jud prepared his lesson plan, then checked it, then double checked before the eventual presentation to his commander. The presentation went smoothly, although Captain Cole never telegraphed even a molecule of emotion during the brief ten-minute presentation. After leaving the office, Corporal Allen assumed it was a complete wash, but at least he tried.

Forty minutes later, he was ordered back to the office, greeted by the company clerk, who asked him for a detailed list of everything he needed for his period of instruction on the platform technique. Jud was also warned that he was not to spend a penny on supplies. If he needs something, just ask. That was a direct order from Captain Cole.

Looking over at Emma, he felt the stress of that entire situation anew, including the nerves and intensity. The big question was, why? If what Colt said was true, this was Emma. His wife, Rhonda, certainly had no doubts. Yet, his stomach was a swarm of butterflies accompanied by a pond of frogs in his throat. Maybe he could call up the lessons of the platform technique in a simple discussion with his friend. She looked over at him, smiling after he tapped on his ear for her to take the headphones off.

"Jud. Finally. I was beginning to think you hated me or something," she said.

He just smiled, struggling for a reference point.

"You have a ton of tapes, forgot how much you loved music," he said. It was a start.

"Oh yeah. There's a record club that puts inserts in the newspaper and in the mail. Crazy, if you ask me. One nickel and you get fourteen tapes. Just have to buy four more at the regular price in, I dunno, I never bought one at regular price, but they keep sending the offer. I have close to a hundred cassettes. Not sure what their business model is, but hey, helped my library," she said.

Jud shifted positions on the couch. He was uncomfortable and hoped it wasn't showing as prominently as he was feeling it.

"You still watch any monster movies?" he asked.

"Of course! We go to a drive-in outside of Pine Hollows, it's the next big town near here. Every once in a while, but not a big fan of slasher flicks. Those kids seem too stupid. Then again, I may have been too. Who knows?" she answered.

"You were never stupid. We'd call each other after church to talk about Chiller the night before. Sometimes, I'd even stay over, and we'd put up your dad's big camping tent, dig through the long extension cords from the Christmas box and plug in my portable tv. Wake up the next morning to your mom's strawberry pancakes. Those were the best."

"Huh, church, eh? Glad I'm over that shit," she said.

"That's all you have to say, huh? Don't remember any of that?"

She got up off the facing couch, scooting next to Jud, taking his hands in hers.

"Listen, I know this can be frustrating. Think of how I feel. Everything you just told me sounds absolutely awesome. I experience flashes, but I just can't put it all together. I'm sorry."

Jud pulled his hands away. Standing up, he walked over to the fireplace. On the mantle, he looked over a variety of trinkets, much like Kat had done earlier.

"You still read comics?" she asked.

He spun around to face her. Was this something she remembered, like the shark book?

"Rhonda told me you did but haven't in the past year or so. That's kinda when she knew something was up," Emma said, extinguishing his hopes.

"Yeah, well, some things you just outgrow."

"I hope not. I'd give anything to go back and undo all this. Kinda cool. Rhonda thinks I'm a badass, but what's the point, ya know?"

It was time for Jud to face a different type of Captain Cole. He returned to the couch sitting next to her. This time, he took her hands in his.

"Look, Emma. I know this is weird for all of us. Not sure what Rhonda told you, but we searched for you for a good week. The entire time we were battling those creatures, you were foremost in my mind. If there was a chance, we, no, I was going to find you. Had a map on the wall and everything. Then the suits came and took us away. Days turned into months, into years. Know what I'm saying? Then unexpectedly, here you are, except you're like twenty years older, as if the memory thing isn't bad enough," he said. Jud had taken the deep plunge into his feelings.

"I get it, it's just—"

"No, I don't think you get it. You can't! I had a whole life with you. Then it was gone. Everyone gets the whole grieving process, then the guilt of maybe not have done enough to find you. I mean, we got out of Kinston. Now, I'm supposed to just throw open the doors to my heart like everything is a-okay? You don't know why you're ageing and neither does Mr. Sturgess. We thought you were dead. Now you kick the shit out of a strange boy in the forest like a bionic Wonder Woman? What if I fall into this 'reunited and it feels so good stuff' and you wake up tomorrow super old or even worse? I lose you twice in one lifetime. Once was enough!"

He had his say and fulfilled his agreement with his wife. Now he needed time to think alone on the porch. Emma, too, had something to think about. Reaching forward for her headphones, she instead dropped them to the floor. Usually quick with a witty remark, there wasn't one for this situation. It was complicated, to say the least. Her and Colt, her and Rhonda, her and Jud. It was one thing to lean on the past, but an entirely different issue to have no past to serve as a conduit of shared experiences with those who you love, or rather, love you.

How interesting to reflect on that singular aspect of such a powerful word as love. Those details, together with another person who values you as much as themselves. Jud and Rhonda both looked tirelessly for her, even with the potential threat of Kinston not being cleared of the creatures that sent her to a destiny altered by the man she stuck a kitana sword into. Why is that a memory that she can see as clear as day, yet the ones hidden from her were provided by these two loving souls?

She sighed loudly. This was not the weekend they expected. Already replete with a handful of surprises. What was next? Rhonda ran towards her from the kitchen with a piece of newspaper in each hand.

"We gotta do this! It's tomorrow night. You have a costume you can pull together, rather, one you can help me pull together?" Rhonda asked excitedly.

Emma read the advertisement on the back of the article of Jud's with the missing piece added. It promoted a Halloween Party at the VFW in nearby Apollo. 7:00 p.m. - midnight, cash bar with a drawing. Showing the classic movie Halloween, then a dance with all you can eat chicken, meatballs and rigatoni and other local potluck delicacies. All proceeds benefit the local volunteer fire department. Costumes are mandatory.

"Hm…" Emma said.

"Just, Hm? I figured you'd go ape shit for something like this!" Rhonda said, disappointed.

"If you guys don't leave tonight hell yeah!"

Rhonda flushed with embarrassment. "Sorry you heard that. Didn't mean to be so loud."

"Don't you dare apologize. I'm the one who eavesdropped."

"So?"

"Yeah, that would be totally rad. We can even run into town, which is like fifteen minutes away, not sure which way you came. Maybe even ask Kat to go with us. She seems a bit out of it still. Hanging in her room since Colt left," Emma said.

"Done deal then. We're doing it!"

"What about, Jud?"

"Leave him up to me. We're going and he knows what that means when I press something."

Behind them, the screen door swung open. Colt stepped into the room.

"Bad news, ladies. Gather everyone up. Afraid I gotta ask you all to leave," he said.

Chapter Five

The Sturgess' visitors took their seats in the living room. Colt entered, sipping a glass of lemonade. He left his cowboy hat on the table. His hair had grayed considerably since Kat saw him last. She noticed immediately. Was he aging as well? Something else stuck out. Something she hadn't seen since the rooftop of the armory five years ago.

"I know we all planned this great weekend getaway, but those goin' ons with you and Rhonda, plus the fact your attacker got away without a trace, well, think it might be a whole lot better if we all stuck together for tonight. Then y'all should set off back home at first light," he said.

Emma sprung to her feet. "Nope. We have other plans. Halloween party tomorrow night at the VFW in Apollo. Starts at seven, ends at midnight, that is if nothing else is going on afterwards."

Rhonda stood up to join her reunited friend's opposition to his request.

"You know, Emma, you can be —"

"A real pain in the ass? Duh! But I can also be sweet as honey too. We made plans and it's not like that freaky kid is gonna come back around here. Pretty sure he learned his lesson on that last toss," she said pridefully.

"Yeah, besides, not like we don't have a super team right here. Unless you'd prefer us to be Colt's angels," Rhonda added.

Emma laughed, high-fiving Rhonda. Somewhere in her memory, she connected to the joke.

"I think Mr. Sturgess has a point," Jud chimed in.

"Of course you would," Rhonda said sarcastically. "You just wanna go back and pick up your case with the old people. Fine, you want to do that, nobody's stopping you."

Rhonda went over to her riding jacket, pulling out two sets of keys to the Hondas, tossing one set to Jud.

"Here ya go, but I'm staying!"

She crossed her arms; Emma followed her lead.

"Besides, Rhonda, Kat, and I were about to run into Secondhand Treasures in Apollo to do a little rack raiding for costumes," Emma said.

That caught Kat's attention, as she wasn't aware she was part of the plan. Glancing up at Colt, then over to the two girls, she was confused by the inclusion. Even throughout the Kinston adventure, Rhonda barely talked to her.

Jud spun the keyring around on his finger, not thrilled with his wife's posturing in the face of potential danger. Although, thinking back, this was indicative of her character and part of why he fell in love with her so quickly. It was more if he viewed the two of them as team Allen. Her quick reconnection with Emma, which he had yet to commit to, took a bit of an adjustment.

Emma reached down, grabbing Kat's hand, pulling her up to join their resistance troupe.

Something Kat had yet to divulge to Colt, or anyone for that matter, including Johnny, was her strange ability following the Kinston clean-up. There were the waking visions she mentioned, but an additional enhancement. When coming into physical contact with someone, skin-to-skin contact, a cascade of images would flash through her mind, occasionally emotions. They seldom made sense and she lacked a little white book that came with tarot decks to help her with any sort of translation. Kat Ellis had long passed that phase with her cards but relied solely on her intuition. This was something new she had yet to fine tune.

Emma's touch yielded a series of images connected to her. Whether it was past, present, or future, Kat didn't know. She wasn't familiar enough with the woman to interpret. The images, however, were lucid: Emma's face as a younger woman, Colt on a lab table, two lips kissing, some sort of large creature and swords. Lots and lots of spinning swords. The last image made her pull her hand away as that one elicited a reaction beyond the typical five senses. The unusual part of the vision, Kat could not feel any emotional connection from Emma to any of the images. In her experience, that was unique. Was this Emma's future or something else? It was the beginning of an endless puzzle.

"Oh, c'mon, Kat. It's a girl's day out, we'll have a rad time!" Emma said.

Kat smiled. A part of her was excited to do something other than monitor Johnny. She nodded her head excitedly, without checking Colt's disapproval. Colt cleared his throat, which Rhonda preempted the next round of objections. It was time to exercise her power that worked with most men she had ever met.

"Mr. Sturgess. We have two groups here, three men, three women, right?" she asked.

He said nothing.

"Emma has super bionic kickass kung-fu moves. Kat can see stuff in the future, and I charm the hell out of everyone. Now, you guys, on the other hand, have a super cowboy, a hard-core Marine and a monster slayer. Not sure what anyone is afraid of, but pretty sure nothing's coming through that door that's not gonna leave in an ambulance or coffin. The last thing we need is a babysitter or quarantined, again!"

Colt sighed. She had a point, several points. He just wanted to ensure everyone's safety, but there was always that wheel that dishes out fate, then keeps turning. In his last five years trying to squeeze into a normal life like a shoe two sizes too small, was this a valid fear or was it more of him trying to make up from some self-perceived guilt still lingered over decisions he made, both under the influence of his rage and his ability to summon it when needed? Regardless of how old he felt in relation to these five, they certainly were not children.

He turned to Jud, then Johnny. "You boys wanna go fishin'? Burnin' daylight but still a couple a good hour left."

Kat's Oldsmobile turned onto the main street of Apollo. It was a cute little town. One of those towns that people drive by wondering what people do for a living or is it a place to retire? The first building they passed was a corner pub with an ominous black carriage in front.

"Check that out," Emma said. "Wonder if that's like some kinda' hearse thingy for the party tomorrow night. So wicked looking!"

Passing by a Post Office to the left, grocery story on the right, Emma pointed out those are the places they get mail and groceries. As they drove down the two-mile stretch of Hunter's Way, the name they learned was the main street. Emma continued the tour with a home-town pride one would share with tourists. Across from the VFW, Post 1056, sat their destination, Secondhand Treasures.

Entering the store, giddy with excitement, the ladies were greeted with a broad smile from the clerk, particularly her favorite customer.

"Emma, dear, haven't seen you in a week. How are you?"

"Hey, Ms. April, doing fine as wine. These are my two friends, Rhonda and Katlyn."

"Pleased to meet you both!"

Not only was the shop keep's name April, but a double entendre of sorts as she was indeed Ms. April, crowned at the Summer Apple Festival in 1952 held annually in nearby Pine Hollows. Emma knew everyone's life story in town. It was kind of her thing, as she would put it, to talk while she shopped. Since Apollo wasn't exactly buzzing with activity on any day, people actually extended time to get familiar with one another.

"What brings you ladies in today?"

"Need to do some Halloween shopping for the party tomorrow night at the VFW," Emma answered.

"Oh, that should be an absolute blast. I may even drag out the hubby for that. Probably get him to dress up as a mummy, since all he does is sit around on that old recliner. Wouldn't even notice if I wrapped him up in gauze until dinnertime," Ms. April said.

Her response brought a roar of laughter from the girls.

"Well, I won't hold you up. You know where everything is. Have some Halloween stuff, not much, but some, on the back wall. As always, you need something, just ask."

"Thanks, Ms. April," Rhonda said.

Rhonda and Emma headed for the bargain rack; Kat drifted over to the Halloween wall. None of the three had any idea what sort of costumes to put together, but surrendered to their selections and collective imaginations. Rummaging through the various racks, Rhonda took charge, pulling out several selections, dragging Emma over to the full-size mirror affixed to the wall.

"Let's see what we have here," she said.

Holding various pieces up in front of Emma, each piece was evaluated, then dismissed until a striped off the shoulder top and leather miniskirt came up.

"Oh, me likes! Sexy pirate?" Emma said.

Kat turned to them from the Halloween wall. "I have a pirate hat and plastic sword over here!"

Rhonda snatched them from Kat's hands.

"Perfect!"

"Not quite," Emma said.

Flitting around the store, she found what she was looking for, a long red scarf hanging from a row of scarves. Wrapping it around her waist, she was pleased.

"How about boots?" Rhonda asked.

"Got those covered. I have the perfect pair back at the house. Went through a phase where I tried my sexier wiles on Colt, but no sale," Emma said with laughter.

Rhonda laughed at the thought, but the idea seemed to make Kat uncomfortable. Her reaction went unnoticed.

"Okay, your turn, Kat!" Emma exclaimed.

Buzzing around the racks, Emma looked at Kat, sizing her up, wondering what type of costume would fit the mysterious young woman she really didn't know very well. Rhonda offered a suggestion.

"She reads tarot cards. Has that, what's the word you used?" she asked Emma.

"Clairvoyance!"

"Yeah, that."

Kat stood helpless, smiling as her two new friends scoured the store for whatever it was they were looking to assemble. She was excited, as she had no idea what to wear. Not exactly being a fashionista, Ms. Ellis stuck to sweats and/or T-shirts with astrological signs printed on them. This was a rare treat, having two other women fuss over her. It was nice.

Emma returned to the scarf rack, pulling off the perfect selection. She then wandered back to a bar holding a selection of jewelry. Rhonda found the perfect dress. Enthusiastically, the two converged on Kat. Giggling, the young women moved Kat in front of the mirror, holding up their finds with great satisfaction.

"What do you think?" Rhonda asked.

The dress was black with tiny gold moons and stars on it. Emma held up a purple silk scarf and a long necklace adorned with stars and moons.

"I don't know. How's the scarf come into play?" Kat asked.

"I'll show you, hold still," Emma said.

Wrapping the scarf around Kat's head like a turban, she secured it around the back with a knot. She then double draped the necklace around her forehead. It fit perfectly without the need to adjust the chain.

"Voila!" exclaimed Emma.

Kat touched her face, staring at her reflection. She never considered herself pretty, but somehow this head wrap brought out the color in her eyes and the golden sparkle of the charms on the chain made her feel like royalty. Hopefully, the dress will fit. Rhonda rushed her into the fitting room. After a couple of minutes, Kat emerged.

"Wow, sister, you're pretty hot. Nice curves you've been hiding. Va-va-voom!" Emma said.

Kat rushed over to the mirror, excited by the response. Emma was right. She looked very sexy, seductive even. This was something new for her. *What would Colt think?* she thought.

"Well?" Rhonda asked.

"I frickin' love it!" Kat said.

Looking at the price tags, she was surprised at how inexpensive the dress was. She hoped the necklace and scarf were as well. Emma noticed her price checking.

"Don't worry about that. This shopping trip is courtesy of Daddy Warbucks," she said.

The three girls bounced up and down with joy. This was turning into the most fun shopping spree ever. Only Rhonda's outfit remained.

"Okay, Mrs. Allen. What are we going to do about you? Something to make your husband forget all about that stupid case of his," Emma said.

A mischievous grin spread across Rhonda's face, accentuated with a double eyebrow flutter.

"I have an idea, but not sure they have what I need here," she said.

"What ya have in mind?" Kat asked.

Rhonda shyly looked at Emma. Her idea may or may not have triggered a memory response. A question remained about the prudence of cracking the lid on that jar, but the costume was a great idea. It also could smooth things over with Jud, who was dead set about leaving.

"Probably don't remember, but when you guys watched Chiller, which Jud still does religiously, he always had a crush on Terminal Stare. Of course, he pretends like he doesn't, even gets embarrassed when I tease him about it—"

"Terminal Stare?" Kat asked.

"Yeah, one of the characters on the show. Sexy blonde hottie in a purple jumpsuit. Spectacular cleavage. Guess my memory isn't that bad," Emma said.

Rhonda nodded.

"Well, let's see what we got here. Hey, Ms. April, anything in the way of a purple jump suit or frizzy afro wig? Preferably blonde?" Emma yelled out across the store.

Matthew wandered down Hunter's Way, kicking an empty can. It wasn't any concern of his what kind of can it was. The walk was more out of frustration. He really wanted to complete the mission on his own at the Sturgess Farm. Playing third, possibly fourth, fiddle on this job wasn't to his liking. Then, of course, being tossed around, first by a woman, then by whatever Blackburn was, didn't sit well. If he wasn't so terrified of exactly what Blackburn was, he would have called it a day and taken a powder. The winged creature promised him something that exceeded money, he promised him power. More specifically, he vowed to train him, vowed to show him how to maximize his unique gifts. Unless taking an ass-beating was training, Matthew preferred just being on his way. That was no longer an option.

As he kicked the can a final time, it rolled on to the street only to be run over by the tires of a bus stopping for its hourly pickup en route to Pine Hollows.

"Figures," he said in disgust.

Peering into the window of a shop directly to his left, he saw her. The woman who mopped up the forest floor with him. The woman with the distinctive white eyes. He ducked down quickly, hoping he had gone undetected. Bear walking along the wall beneath the window, Matthew moved as quickly as possible out of the potential line of sight. Once cleared, he ran as fast as he could up the street, back towards Kelley's Irish Pub.

Upon reaching the door, presently with a hand-written sign that read, "Death in the family, back in two weeks," he continued around the side. Jumping down the steps that led to the basement door, he knocked three times, then two, then one. It was a pre-arranged code to permit access.

The door creaked open; he slid his wiry frame into the darkness.

"Matthew. What a pleasant surprise. I fully expected you to be miles away from here by now," Kaleb Blackburn said.

"You're not gonna believe who's in town," he said, out of breath.

"Do tell," Blackburn smiled.

* * *

"Purple's scarce these days, sweetie. All the kids are wild about some guy named 'Prince,' but wigs, I got you covered," Ms. April said.

"Oh, poo," Rhonda said. "Worth a shot anyway."

"Gimme a sec, hon."

Ms. April disappeared into the back stockroom. Kat and Emma continued browsing the racks for an alternative or something they could piece together similarly. Following her brief absence, Ms. April reappeared carrying a box, dragging another with her foot.

"These just came in from an estate sale, haven't had time to go through them and my good-for-nothing niece, god forbid she actually helped out around here, should have gotten them out to the floor already. Kids…" she said.

Rhonda grabbed the box on the floor, following along to the counter.

"First things first," Ms. April said, producing three curly headed wigs of various shades of blonde.

Rhonda snapped up the second one that was a sandy blonde color.

"Fuck yeah!" she yelled. "Oh, sorry, I mean, hell yeah. Oops, I mean—"

"Don't apologize. I call bingo on Tuesdays and Thursday over in Pine Hollows' Polish Club. I've heard worse, believe you me," Ms. April said.

Emma helped Ms. April pull the tape off the boxes.

"Fun thing about these blind bids on estate sales, never know what you're gonna get. Sometimes pay dirt, other times, shit," Ms. April winked at Rhonda.

The three scoured the box excitedly while Kat watched. There wasn't room for a fourth set of hands. That didn't dampen her enthusiasm for the hunt.

Rhonda pulled something out from the box, holding it up to show Kat.

"Hey, Kat! We found something for you. Do you have this one, Tarot of the Witches?"

Kat took the deck from her. The box was worn. She opened it up to examine the cards. They were in great shape. Upon a quick examination, the deck was complete as well. Closing her eyes, she attempted to connect with the energy of its past owner. She felt a warm, kind energy. That was a good thing. She would have to bind the deck to herself, of course, but it was not malevolent.

Looking down at the cards, she felt an infinite sadness. It had been quite some time since she did a reading for herself or anyone else. Why? She didn't know. Perhaps too many people close to her in her young life had passed on to the other side, or maybe she stopped believing in her practice. Whatever the lull in her divination, it felt welcoming, even restorative, to be holding a deck of tarot in her hands again after the long absence.

Peeling back the tape on the second box, what did Ms. April call it? Pay dirt!

"Well, look at that! A purple jacket. It's pleather, but still may work."

Rhonda plucked the jacket from the box, rushing over to the mirror. Emma and Kat flanked her.

"Bitchin,'" Kat said.

Rhonda sighed. "Maybe a little too small for the ta-tas."

Emma grabbed her by the arms, pushing her back to the fitting room.

"No such thing. You got it, flaunt it. Let's check that fit," Emma coaxed.

Moments later, Rhonda came out of the fitting room, wearing the wig and jacket. Kat reacted first, instantly, without thought.

"Wow. You're so hot," she said, almost dreamily.

Emma clapped. "Ditto! Just one thing." She zipped the jacket down to her belly button.

"Now that's Terminal Stare!"

Blushing, Rhonda pulled the zipper back up to the middle of her chest. "That may get a little too many stares."

"So what! These sodbusters around here need a little thrill. If it doesn't do it for Jud, you might need to check him for a pulse," Emma reassured her.

Rhonda looked for a second helping of reinforcement from Kat, who was staring at her.

"Yeah, um, just wow!" Kat said.

"Okay, cool then. If it's a little tight, whatever. I'm only twenty-two, right?" Rhonda asked.

"That's the spirit! I thought you were some kind of badass? Where'd this modesty come from, Mrs. Allen?"

Rhonda laughed. "Think it's the missus part!"

The three women howled with laughter. Only one item remained: bottoms to accompany the jacket and wig. Circling like vultures, the three women returned to the racks while Ms. April kept sorting through the two boxes. With no-holds-barred on selection, Kat snatched up a pair of purple shorts she found tucked away on a clearance rack. They had passed by the summer racks because of chilly weather, but why not? Pleather certainly would not keep Rhonda cozy.

Kat held up her discovery. "How about these?"

Emma rushed over, examining them as if the shorts were the Hope Diamond. Smiling, she handed them to Rhonda.

"Well?"

Rhonda grimaced. "It is October. Don't think I'd be too cold?"

"You're not gonna build a snowman! House to car, car to VFW. I'm sure they'll have heat on and you can ride with Kat. Positive she has a heater in her car. Let the boys freeze their yayas off," Emma said.

"Yeah, you can totally ride with me!" Kat said.

"Plus, not only do I have a pair of sexy boots, I have several pairs. Size eight?"

"Seven and a half."

"Close enough."

Emma led her shopping cadre to the front counter, removing a wallet from her purse. The grand total for the shopping trip for all three outfits rang up to four dollars and twenty-five cents. Kat offered to pay as the experience was exponentially worth more to her, as it was for Rhonda, but Emma insisted.

The last item Ms. April placed in the bag was the deck of tarot cards. "You girls read tarot?" she asked.

"My friend, Kat here does," Emma answered.

Kat smiled. "My friend," Emma called her. She liked that.

"You don't say? What ya charge, sweetie?" Ms. April asked.

"I don't know, like five dollars a reading?"

"Hogwash. You're selling yourself short, honey pie. Hold on just a minute, unless you ladies are in a rush? I assume you are all going to the Halloween shindig over at the VFW? That's what the shopping spree is for?"

"Sure are," Emma answered again.

"Great!"

Ms. April picked up the phone, holding it steady in the crook of her neck while she thumbed through a small notebook. Finding the number she was looking for, she dialed the rotary phone.

"Could use a little entertainment at that party. Usually just old-timers and vets flirting or pinching ass, pretending to feign ignorance. The deejay is stuck in the 50s and 60s. You can only take so much Bobby Vinton and Perry Como," she said, waiting for the other party to pick up.

The women watched curiously to see what she had in mind. Finally, her call was connected by the operator, then answered.

"Horace? This is April over at Secondhand Treasures. I said, April, oh you know who I am, put your damn hearing aid in." There was a pause. "Can you hear me now? Good! Hey, I got a question for you about the Halloween party. Yeah, of course tomorrow night, you celebrate it on more than one night?"

Ms. April rolled her eyes at the girls, who were all laughing, enjoying the conversation immensely.

"Look, I'll cut to the chase. Got an out-of-town girl here, from the city. She's a tarot reader and I thought…What's a tarot reader? Like a fortune teller with cards—"

Emma cut in, "She's a clairvoyant!"

"Yeah, a genuine clairvoyant. Predicts the future."

"Actually, it's more of—" Kat got waved off by Ms. April.

"You interested in having her reading her cards at the party? What?"

Ms. April covered the phone transmitter. "I swear, this old fool couldn't find either ass cheek with both hands. How he organizes this party once a year is by the grace of god."

She put the handset back up to her ear. "Okay, listen. She's standing here right now. Said she'd do it for fifty bucks for the night."

Kat's eyes widened, placing her hand over her mouth. She had never made that much money for a five-hour gig, three hours to be precise, as the movie time would cut into readings. Rhonda and Emma reacted with glee, embracing Kat.

"What'd ya mean you don't have that kind of budget? I know for a fact you get a cut from the…what? Thirty-five dollars? We'll take it. One more thing, she'll need a table with a tablecloth. A fancy cloth one, not those plastic ones you put out for picnics and Horace, it better be clean! Last time I attended a function was for McGreevy's wedding. The one at my table had old spaghetti stains on it. We're talking a famous clairvoyant tarot reader from the city here, no minor league stuff. What's her name?"

Ms. April covered the phone once more. "What's your name, sweetie?"

"Katlyn Ellis," she answered.

"Katlyn Ellis. Hell, I don't know how to spell it, think I'm some kind of dictionary? You're not thinking of giving her a check are you? Cash only. Oh? You'll put her name up on the sign, fine."

Kat wrote out her name on the back of the receipt from the shopping trip.

73

"K-A-T-E-L-Y-N. Yes, 'n' as in 'nincompoop.' One last thing, Horace, make sure you have a tip jar, just in case. Even though she's on the clock, can't deprive a pretty, young woman the right to earn a little extra, right? Oh, I don't know. You have those big jars of stuff for catering. Use one of those. Just not pickles. It will stink up the money, alright? Thanks, Horace, you're a doll. Kiss, kiss."

Ms. April hung up the phone, smiling. She had just negotiated a deal with the skill of a door-to-door salesperson.

"Okay, honey. Be there a little before 7:00 just in case there's some snafu, always is with Horace. I'll be over early in the morning cooking, so just look for me to show you the ropes," she said.

Kat nodded her head excitedly. What great fun this was turning out to be! She just needed to get back to Colt's place to brush up on her reading. A standard three-card would be best in case of a crowd. Celtic crosses took a lot of time, with much more complexity. Kat would have to fly solo as her tarot journal was back at the diner in Shermer. Not having touched a deck in quite some time, her intuition would serve as her anchor. After ten years, Kat Ellis knew the cards forward and backwards, but the safety blanket of the journal always served as a confidence booster, even if it was not required.

"Thanks, Ms. April. I don't really know what to say?" Kat said, still blushing.

"No need to thank me, hon. Just have a great time and come back to visit, ya hear?"

"I will. Promise!"

Scooping up their bags, the three young women exited the store, all three sharing the enthusiasm of the development. In front of them, parked horizontally across three parking spaces, was the black macabre carriage. Emma walked towards it, peering in through the dark tinted glass, but could see nothing, even with her unique vision.

"So cool. Wonder how they see out," she said.

"Oh, it's two-way glass, my dear. Perfectly clear from the inside," a stranger's voice answered.

Emma turned to face the strange man with glasses, a dark top hat, and cloak.

"The name is Kaleb Blackburn. Pleased to make your young lady's acquaintance."

"Yeah? This hearse, or whatever it is gonna be at the Halloween party tomorrow night?" Emma asked.

"Perhaps. Will you three lovely ladies be in attendance?"

"Yeah, with our husbands, and mine's a Marine. Just a general FYI, creepo," Rhonda said.

"A thousand pardons, ma'am. I did not mean to offend," he said.

"None taken. It's just the 80s, ya know buddy? Asking three 'lovely ladies' where they may be, especially strangers, isn't really cool," Emma said.

She took Rhonda's hand, Rhonda took Kat's hand, which drew an unexpected flush across Kat's entire body like stepping into a hot tub. The three scurried to the Oldsmobile. Something about the guy was skeevy, in Emma's parlance. The further distance they could put between him and them, the better.

Blackburn watched the three as the Oldsmobile pulled out of the parking lot, speeding up Hunter's Way. Amanda, Christopher, and Matthew stepped out from the carriage.

"What now?" Matthew asked.

"It looks like we're going to a Halloween party," Blackburn replied.

Back at the Sturgess cabin, Colt, Johnny and Jud had wandered down to the stream which cut through his property. Trout fishing was great, first thing during autumn mornings. In fact, it yielded breakfast that very morning. The afternoon, however, the sun was a little high and the fish were a little deep to tempt. However, the three gave it a valiant effort.

In particular, Colt watched Johnny. Each of his visitors showed up acting very peculiar, outside of the characters he knew them to be. Each of them returned to normal quickly, if there was such a thing with this group. Kat, by Colt's hand, Jud and Rhonda upon discovering who Emma truly was, which was still a bit of a shock to Colt. Of all the people who had survived Olath's purge, three of the only survivors in Kinston all had a past together. Although the probability wasn't beyond imagination, that one of them had been the recipient of the experimental elixir. Johnny was still a mystery.

If Colt's theory of emotions intensified at the time of exposure to the point of obsession, what was this young man's trigger? Hell, did it even have any effect? "Johnny only talks when he has something to say," Kat said their first night at the Allen house. That seemed to hold true, as he barely uttered a complete sentence since he arrived. Finally, what was the deal with the mask? Kat explained the origin, but why constantly wear it? This was the first time since they pulled into the Sturgess' driveway that he had taken it off. It was replaced with Johnny's fishing goggles.

Colt felt a little conversation starter would break up the boys' day out. Jud was obviously annoyed by Rhonda's insistence they stay when he desperately wanted to return to Biggs County Sheriff's Department to see if any headway was made regarding the clues he provided to the chief. Then there was Johnny. Who to tackle first with a bit of small talk? Since the fish weren't biting, perhaps he could get one of them to nibble on a little conversation. He tossed out some bait to the more elusive one.

"Johnny, how long since you went fishing last?"

Johnny kept his eye on the bobber at the end of the line, drifting downstream as fast as the current could carry it. Not the optimal rig for fishing mountain streams, but the act of fishing outdoors on a beautiful day, communing with nature, was more of the point than a fish at the end of the line.

"Five years, six months, seventeen days. Uncle Mike took me out for the opening of trout season. He's dead now, ya' know," he answered.

"Yup, reckon I knew that. Catch any fish that day?" Colt attempted to steer the question to more positive waters.

Johnny exhaled. "I caught three. Two rainbows and one brown. Thirteen, twelve and fourteen inches. All were over size limit, which is seven inches. Uncle Mike helped me more than fishing.'"

Colt was in awe of John Paul Ellis' ability to remember details with uncanny accuracy, despite his condition. Although he didn't completely understand anything beyond what the Babins had disclosed. Still, the sharpest minds had issues remembering what they had for breakfast the previous week.

"Sounds like a fine haul for a fishin' trip," Colt remarked.

"Yeah, but now I need to concentrate or may miss one," he said.

Colt supposed that was his cue to move on to Jud.

"How about you Jud? How's that comics collection coming along?" Colt asked.

Jud set his rod down. His concern with Rhonda being gone was more distracting than the glare on the water he was targeting. Walking over to a cooler that he packed for the trip, not knowing if their host was a drinking man, he brought his own supply of beer. Taking one out, popping the top, he returned to the creek side.

"Well, Mr. Sturgess, oh, don't mean to be rude, beer?" he asked.

Colt waved his hand, declining the hospitality.

"Sorry, we Marines like to have a beer or two. Unfortunately, haven't picked up a comic in years," he said, swallowing a mouthful of pilsner's best.

"That's a shame. Don't tell me you let your records collect dust, too?"

"Just no time. Between the deputy work and reserves, then Rhonda, kind of have most of my hours spoken for. Besides, there's an age you grow out of such things, eh?" He took another swig.

"I dunno, Jud. Seems like after all the years on the road for me, those are the kinds of things to grow into, not out of. Just one man's point of view though," Colt said.

77

Jud reflected on what Mr. Sturgess had just said. Why did he drift from those things he loved? During the clean-up of Kinston, he found what was left of the special, his bicycle, that he customized. It was to be his wheels until he could save up for a motorcycle. The remnants of that bike, he carried back to the bakery before setting off on the search for his family and friends. He never returned for it.

Maybe it was the two stops he made before arriving at the fair, the book and then record stores that hung in his memory as a reminder of the emotionally devastating events that followed. He didn't know, just that whatever things that made him love them simply evaporated with the inhabitants of Kinston. Many times, during initial training, he thought back on the strengths of his inked heroes to pull him through challenges that extended beyond his capabilities, particularly with teamwork. It gave Jud Allen something to think about.

In the distance, Colt heard the engine of the Ellis' car driving towards the cabin. His efforts at any bonding with the other men in the group had flailed like a fish out of water on a dock. Not sure why he had agreed with Emma on hosting this reunion, Colt grew to appreciate the opportunity of possibly getting to know these individuals that he shared a brief time with in hell. Not knowing if any of them even shared anything in common, what harm could it cause? Besides, it appeared as if the women were bonding. That was something.

"Time to go, fellahs. The women folk approach," Colt said.

Johnny reeled in his line, Jud retrieved his fishing pole and cooler, Colt led the way back to the cabin.

Chapter Six

After returning to the Sturgess cabin and enjoying an over excited conversation about the day's events, Rhonda and Emma took up residence on the couch, Kat sat at the table going through her new deck of tarot cards, Jud paced outside in front of the porch. On the way back, the three women passed by a farmer's market that sold two things: pumpkins and apple cider. They grabbed two of the largest pumpkins available and a gallon of cider. Johnny was fast at work on one pumpkin with a carving knife. Colt watched carefully to ensure the pumpkin wasn't the only thing being carved.

Rhonda sat behind Emma, braiding her hair. During the ride to Apollo, Rhonda divulged she worked as a hair stylist, taking exception to the term "hairdresser." It was too old-fashioned, and this was the 80s. Typically, Emma did her own hair and makeup, but not very good at it. Colt offered to take her into Pine Hollows frequently, but she never did quite grow accustomed to the stares her white eyes drew.

One memory that surfaced early on, back during her stay with Elizabeth in Delaney's Funeral Home, was the creature feature, Village of the Damned, about white-eyed children who controlled a village only to be eliminated by a bomb by the film's protagonist. How any of these emotional briar patches worked as the result of Olath's tinkering with human genetics, Emma had attached her own fear bomb to that memory. One of the few things that elicited that response from her.

"Everything okay with you and Jud?" she asked Rhonda.

"Copasetic," she answered promptly.

"You sure? He seems like he has a hive of bees in his bonnet."

"He gets that way. Anxious, you know? It's like the case with the old people he found that's driving him bonkers, as there are so many loose ends. It drives him crazy. After five years together, kinda get to know when to stay out of each other's way, and when to jump in with the emotional lifeline, ya know?"

"Yeah, I guess."

Unfortunately, it was only a guess for Emma. She and Colt are as close as two people could be. They shared everything, including a bed, except what typically went on in one. It was bearable at first, but as time went on, unquenched campfires became raging infernos. If it weren't for the age thing or the promise to Lizzy or the reemergence of Lizzy herself, maybe that aspect would be different. Whatever love was, she didn't seek it from anyone else, but watching Rhonda and Jud interact was shifting her perspective. Rapidly.

Even though it was creepy when they first got there with the bathroom thing, she witnessed intimacy. An over abundance of it, but to someone starving in the desert, how much was too much? Something else was going on. Emma was inexplicably attracted to Jud. If they had a past, she imagined what it may have been. Even caught herself daydreaming about it while trying on the sexy pirate costume. Her initial thought was, *what would Jud think?* Not Colt. This was the first time for such a shift in interest.

Yet, here she sat with her new best friend braiding her hair. She was his wife, not Emma. Sure, a pound of guilt danced on her moral scale, but it wasn't like she was thinking and feeling other things as well. Ignoring them was the right thing to do. When it comes to being human and understanding emotions, the right things rarely balance with desires.

"So, Jud said my mom was very nice?" Emma asked.

"Oh yeah, she was outstanding. Always did little things, you know, to make everybody feel special. Birthday parties, she made those take-home bags, but not with like junk and pennies. Gift certificates to Children's Palace. She was classy too, always dressed up. Wasn't a day I remember she wasn't beautiful, like you."

"I wish I could remember her."

"You will. That's what I'm here for," Rhonda said.

Kat was eavesdropping from the kitchen table. After the day they all shared, she felt like she was being left out. She took her mug of cider, placing the tarot deck back into the box. No point in studying further. It was more of an issue of confidence over familiarity. None of the seventy-eight cards had changed since she last did a spread. She joined Emma and Rhonda, except sat in the big comfy easy chair facing the two. They smiled as she adjusted. Kat hoped she wasn't intruding.

"How about my dad?" Emma asked next.

"Oh, he was so funny. I think that's where you get your natural smart assness from. He worked a lot and did the Jaycees with Jud's dad. The two of them together were like a comedy act. Everyone loved them."

"Jud was close with his dad?"

"He tried, but whatever it was, his dad kind of kept him at arm's length."

"That's sad."

Rhonda didn't elaborate further on how Fred Allen was the first identifiable person they came across murdered by the clowns in Kinston. If she were going to help Emma with her memories, planting new ones that were horrific would benefit no one. She also suddenly noticed Emma continued circling back to Jud. They were exceptionally close at one time. Rhonda wondered if emotions for him that Emma had suppressed because of her interest in him were surfacing. Then Jud keeping a football field length distance from Emma. Nothing was sexier than a man with a clear lack of interest. His agitation also seemed to be heightened. It was something for her to think about.

"How about you, Kat? What about your mother and father?" Emma asked, turning her head sideways as Rhonda continued with the braids.

Kat cleared her throat, taking a sip of cider. "Hm. My dad died when Johnny and I were young. Mom took us to school one day and we haven't seen her since. My adoptive parents were both killed by those things we all fought in Kinston. It's how we all met."

"Damn, I'm sorry girl, I didn't mean to—"

"No, it's okay. Really. Life is all about changes. It still hurts and I think about my dad and adoptive parents every day, but there are so many things to do and of course, Johnny, who is old enough to do his own thing, but since it's fallen to me, I guess it's my fate. I chose a long time ago to live and grow instead of wither and die. Loss is part of life, I guess."

"Wow! 'chose to live and grow instead of wither and die.' I love that. I'm stealing it," Emma said.

"It's all yours," Kat replied. "How about you, Rhonda?"

Rhonda blew a puff of air from her mouth, clearing a few loose strands of hair that had fallen on her forehead.

"Ha! Mine's simple. Dad died, Mom's a bitch. Disposition, unknown, and I'm happy about it."

"Rhonda!" Emma smacked her knee.

"No, it's true. Not into unearthing past drama. I'm pretty content with that thing out of my life. I vowed to never be the kind of wife or mother that she was. That is, if I ever become a mother."

"You guys trying?" Kat asked.

"Yeah, but no success yet. Trying is half the fun though, don't ya think?"

Kat and Emma both laughed, although some question lingered as to if either of them ever had sex. Kat must have, she kept emphasizing her age in the armory back in Kinston. Rhonda wasn't sure about Emma. She liked boys, but never shared whether she ever experienced it. If she had, Rhonda was certain she would have disclosed that experience minutes after it happened.

"Yeah, that would be the fun part," Emma said dreamily.

The way she said it made Rhonda wonder if Emma meant in general or with Jud. Either way, it made her giggle.

Kat grunted, then offered an observation. "Weird. Two of our moms we'd rather forget. The mom who was the coolest, and that's the one you can't remember."

Colt grew bored watching Johnny carving the pumpkin. Much like most of his other talents, they were sharp. Beyond what formal training teaches, the kid was a natural at anything Sturgess saw him do. While he was no kid by any stretch, John Paul Ellis' lack of communication skills sent a false message regarding his capabilities.

One pumpkin was nearing completion, as best he could tell, anyway. Not merely being carved traditionally, Johnny had sculpted meticulous layers within the pumpkin rind. Colt did not know what the face would reveal until he put the candle inside. Only the light would reveal its secret. Retrieving a couple of tea light candles from a bag in the pantry, next to the large candles reserved for power outages, Sturgess placed them and a pack of matches on the table in front of Johnny.

"Much obliged," Johnny said without diverting his attention from the pumpkin.

Colt smiled at his vernacular, which Emma had been teaching him to purge from his own vocabulary. Glancing around the room, everyone seemed to have created their own conversation pit, except Jud. He was the lone man out. Sturgess understood his desire to get back to work. He also sensed something a little deeper was in motion. That's when an idea struck him. The Harley.

The screen door opened at the edge of the darkness in the forest. Beautiful thing about living somewhat off the grid in a pine forest. The nights were dead quiet. No traffic, no hustle and bustle of people running around being stressed by whatever thing they reached for beyond what they already had. It was peaceful. Nothing more than the chill of night air, sounds from the nearby brook, and occasional coyote howls.

83

"Hey, Jud. Awfully lonely out here. Can I get you somethin'?"

"Thanks, Mr. Sturgess. Just thinking."

"You keep thinking that hard, I may have to re-sod the front yard before you leave," Colt said, leaning up against the porch post.

Jud stopped pacing. "Sorry, I walk when I think."

"Understandable. Let's see if we can put that to use. Follow me."

Colt led Jud over to the barn. He unsecured the padlock on the door, pushing it upward on the track.

"Emma keeps trying to get me one of those newfangled garage door openers but can't say I exactly trust my valuables being protected by a track of chain and batteries."

He walked over to a panel on the wall and threw the power switch. Two banks of overhead lights glowed gently, gaining in intensity as the minutes passed. The inside of the barn was more like an all-purpose facility, not only in size, but the stalls as well.

"When I first got this place, all that was standing was this old barn. Had a big Mail Pouch tobacco thing painted on the side. Can't say I was ever fond of the stuff, but reckon it was all the rave a few years back, at least enough to paint on barns. Saw more than I can count in my travels."

Colt walked Jud around the barn as he gave the grand tour.

"Kind of downsized it but kept some of the original features. Served a purpose, even though never did quite get around to think about farming again. Woodshop is on the far back wall. Table, saw, lathe, the whole thing. The stalls, however, kept those for the really important stuff."

Sturgess approached the first stall. There were four on the left side of the barn, each covered. Four across from those on the right side, open full of various materials.

"Got a guy out in Michigan that makes these storage covers. Some kind of integrated fibers with parachute material prevent rust. I don't get all that scientific mumbo-jumbo, just cheap to ship and do the trick. Was a big concern of mine with all the snow we get, but keeps them weather proofed, even with the occasional roof leak I gotta patch."

Lifting the first cover, he rolled out his motorcycle. The 1973 Harley-Davidson FL Electra-Glide.

"Damn, how could I have forgotten? Thought that was you when I first saw you, but in all the chaos, I never asked and we never seemed to be in the same place at the same time battling those gremlins," Jud exclaimed.

Just the sight of the machine pulled Judson Allen back five years earlier, standing in the parking lot of the demolition car. Three hits for a dollar, ten bucks you got to keep what you knocked off. The rider passing through on the motorcycle, this motorcycle, temporarily breaking his infatuation with the doe-eyed Ms. Coulter, now his wife. He stood less than a yard from the bike he had read about in so many magazines from the bookstore that no longer existed. Five years had passed, as had so many memories now bubbling to the surface.

"You know, I saw you ride through town. Didn't make the connection at first until the armory, but still couldn't be sure. I wasn't exactly the picture of confidence back then," Jud said.

"Men change. Sometimes for the better, sometimes for the worse. Where I'm standing, you took the better route," Colt replied.

Jud approached the bike with care, prowling around the outside radius of with the same scrutiny as Emma had the purple shorts a few hours previously. Colt chuckled.

"You can mount up, Jud. Can't hurt it. Take it for a spin if you'd like, although it handles a bit differently than that new fangled bike of yours. Just take it slow and easy. No light past the property line. Don't want to hit an opossum or skunk. They make pretty good speed bumps and take a week or so with lots of scrubbin' with buttermilk for the skunky types."

"Maybe in the daylight, wouldn't trust myself at night," he said.

"Fair enough, always tomorrow. I can take Emma's along for the ride. Been a few weeks. Don't want the seals and gaskets to shrink and crack. Know I'm being a mother hen, but gotta keep things running tip-top shape," Colt said.

"No, I absolutely get it. Looks like you made a modification or two?" Jud asked.

"Yup. Got tired of luggin' the saddlebags around, so I upgraded with a fiberglass saddle bag and tour pack. Still have space for my belongings. Now that I'm a homesteader, no need to go back and forth with the gear bag. Know what I mean?"

"Yeah, I do. Try dragging a seabag around everywhere you go. Not exactly my idea of convenience."

The two men laughed. Eventually Jud mounted up the bike, even started it. Talking at length about the benefits of the cycle, how it compared to other models and the unique characteristics of this one, time flew by. They even pulled the cover off Emma's bike and did a full once over review of the 1980 Suzuki PE 250.

Colt also fully restored a late model 1959 Chevrolet Apache pickup truck which sat under the third cover. He informed Jud that he had worked on it years prior to Kinston, or even meeting the Smoke Hunters. It was his passion project and where he learned most of his skills under the hood.

"Can't haul lumber and groceries on a bike," Colt joked.

As the moon rose in the sky, colored lights danced on the floor of the barn. Jud looked up to see a mosaic of an owl and a rainbow.

"That's beautiful. Odd place for stained glass, Mr. Sturgess. There a story behind that one?" Jud asked.

"I'll save that for another time, Jud. Let's head in," he answered.

Crossing the grass, the two were greeted by the two pumpkins Johnny carved. The flickering tea lights inside revealed his works of art. One very much resembled his devil mask in intricate detail. The other struck Colt as familiar, but he couldn't immediately place it.

"Shit," Jud said. "That's the face of the four-armed thing from McNaulty's."

Colt nodded, "Indeed it is."

Entering the cabin, Johnny was nowhere to be found. Colt assumed he had retired to his room for the night. He cleaned up well. There was no trace of pumpkin carving in sight. Someone had also cleaned the pumpkin seeds, soaking them in a saltwater brine with two cloves of garlic. That Colt could smell.

Emma had fallen asleep on Rhonda's lap. She was knocked out as well. Kat was curled up in a ball, still on the lounge chair. Obviously, the men's absence was not missed.

"Should we—"

"Nah, let them sleep. I'll get the spare blankets out. We can at least tuck 'em in."

Jud chuckled. "You didn't make those too, did you?"

Colt grinned. "Nope. But funny what ya' learn when you have nothin' but time on your hands."

In his guest room, Johnny sat staring at the darkness. Outside of his window, two faces peered in, chattering their teeth. He cracked the window. Black mist trickled in, surrounding Johnny. He smiled on the inside of his devil mask as he twirled around a maelstrom of smoke. Extending his arms, he spun faster and faster, feeling his body being lifted off of the wooden floor beneath him.

He was whole, powerful. Beginning to giggle, a voice came to him without a face.

"Shh," it whispered.

Johnny opened his eyes wide, tossing his mask to the floor. Slowly, his body lowered to the ground.

"My friends, where you been? I missed you," Johnny said to the darkness.

Chapter Seven

Morning came early. The sunlight breeched Kat's eyes as they flittered to greet it. Rising from her slumber, she slid on her shoes, grabbed her deck of tarot cards, then coat and quietly crept out the front door. She had one last detail before the Halloween party preparations began. It was also the first time since her father died she didn't check in on Johnny.

Wandering toward the sound of the gurgling brook, she hoped to find what she sought. The sun felt soothing on her skin. Kat absorbed its warmth, depositing her coat and tarot deck on the picnic table in front of the cabin. Deciding to kick off her shoes as well, the glistening grass welcomed her. The late October morning held off the November cold weather intrusion so far.

Even the autumn leaves were still dew kissed by the dawn, guiding her way to the creek.

The water in the stream was cold, but Kat didn't seem to mind, wiggling her toes in defiance of the temperature. She wandered slowly up the creek bank, half in the water, half out. It was cleansing, recharging her along with the polarity of the sun. So much happened the previous day. She felt fully alive, no, awake for the first time in a long time. Breathing deeply, she drew in the smell of pine, flooding her senses with more. That's what she wanted today. More.

Looking down as she walked, she picked up a smooth stone, then another. Examining each find along her route, she discarded the ones she didn't feel with a skip across the stream. Excitement accompanied each toss as the stones traveled further and further.

Kat Ellis was delighted in her solitude. After retrieving a third stone, all roughly palm sized, tumbled smoothly by the natural flow of nature, she stepped carefully out of the water. The dirt felt amazing beneath her feet, occasionally getting the bonus of squishy mud between her toes.

She paused, feeling as if someone were watching her. Taking a quick look around, she saw no one. The feeling remained. Shrugging her shoulders in dismissal, Kat flitted back to the picnic table where she had deposited her things. She hoped no one would interrupt her, for a little while at least.

Once she reached the table, she sat down, shuffling her new tarot deck. Even though it was only one of a kind from a thrift shop and not one she spent hours selecting, she bonded with it instantly. The Tarot of the Witches by Fergus Hall. Not that Kat considered herself a witch, wiccan, or pagan. Just someone drawn inexplicably to the metaphysical. On this deck, she connected immediately to the imagery. Distorted features and solid-colored backgrounds created a dream-like sensation that delivered Kat deeper into her intuition. The backs of the cards were simple lines resembling a diagonal plaid pattern. Those lines also tapped her gifts with varying widths, creating a three-dimensional appearance if staring long enough at them.

Following a final shuffle, she drew the first card, flipping it for the corresponding number that would dictate the next card drawn. It was the king of swords. She laughed out loud, knowing instantly who that was. She drew it several times previously, even gave him one upon leaving Kinston. Kat followed no particular spread for this read, just more of a trial run. She cleansed and bound the deck to her the previous night, before the conversation pit with Emma and Rhonda.

Counting out her next card, she drew the moon, eighteen in the major arcana. It was reversed. Before drawing the final card, a light breeze gently slid the cards from their resting place. Kat quickly grabbed them, placing two of the three smooth stones she gathered on top of each one. The third card she left face down, securing it with the last stone. This was her intention card. As she slid the deck back into the box, deciding not to draw a shadow card, it wasn't pertinent. That feeling of being watched crept in again.

"I hope I'm not interrupting," a voice came from behind her.

Kat turned around to see a young woman, probably around her age, in full fishing gear, waders, fly rod and all.

"Well, kinda," Kat said.

"Okay, then. I'll be on my way," the strange woman said with a unique accent.

"Wait! I don't mean to be rude; I was just in the middle of something."

"I totally understand."

The young woman peaked over Kat's should at the table.

"Tarot, huh? That's marvelous. I had a friend in A Level 2nd who used to read. Uncanny the things she would pop off."

Kat smiled, barely understanding what she was saying.

"That's a cool accent. Where are you from?" Kat asked.

"Originally, I was born in Camberley, United Kingdom. It's close to London. Dad was, well is, a diplomat in foreign service. It's where he met my mum. She's from Nairobi," she answered.

"Do you like her?"

"My mum, of course, who doesn't love their mum?"

"Sorry, stupid question. Just something we were talking about yesterday."

"Not stupid at all. You yanks talk about the strangest things," she laughed, shaking her head.

Extending her hand to Kat, she introduced herself. "Hi, my name is Corina Newton."

"Hi, I'm Kat…"

In her relaxed state, Kat had forgotten about her recently developing sensory abilities of touch. As their hands met, she felt instantly woozy. Her breathing became heavy. Instead of the familiar rush of images, her vision blurred. Attempting to clear her inner sight, she batted her eyes as if they were filled with sand. Not only did this not work, when she reestablished focus, Kat no longer found herself at the picnic table outside of the Sturgess cabin.

Panic ensued initially, followed by an overwhelming sense of calm. She was back at the creek in a deep pool of water. It wasn't cold like the stream she just ankle waded through. It was warm, almost like bath water. Her vision took on a soft focus, blurred around the edges. Barely touching the bottom of the pool, she felt the squishy bottom between her toes once more. She giggled, swirling in the water like a ballerina. It was then she realized she was naked. Instantly, she reacted, placing her hands over her breasts, hoping wherever this dream transported her, no onlookers accompanied.

Attempting to move towards shore, some force gently drifted her back to the pool. In the woods behind the creek bank, she heard the snapping of twigs. Someone was coming towards her. Fearing the discovery of her unanticipated skinny-dip, Kat sunk below the water-line, leaving enough room to see who it was while still able to breathe. She watched and waited.

Emerging from the tree line stepped Rhonda Coulter Allen, dressed in the purple outfit they had all had a hand in selecting. She stared directly at Kat, not breaking her gaze. Seductively, she lowered the zipper on the pleather purple jacket, letting it drop to the ground. Next were the short shorts. Shimmying her hips, they dropped to the creek bank beside the jacket. She, too, was now head-to-toe naked. Rhonda walked slowly towards the pool of water.

Kat Ellis was transfixed by the sight. What was going on? During the fitting, she was definitely attracted to her, but this was Jud's wife, and how did both of them get here? She was sitting at the table with her tarot cards seconds earlier. From the shore, Rhonda teasingly blew her a kiss, then dove headfirst into the pool of water. Kat's heart was pounding so hard, she felt it in her temples. She licked her lips as her mouth had suddenly lost all moisture.

Waiting for Rhonda to reappear in the water, Kat struggled to make sense of what was happening. Corina. Corina Newton. She had shaken hands with her. Was this some sort of extended vision and what did it signify? Suddenly, her thoughts were interrupted by the touch of a hand on her calf, another on her thigh, then her hips. She exhaled with anticipation. Whatever kind of dream this was, she wanted to indulge it. Feed it.

Most of her life was in service to others, especially her brother, more so over the past five years with only two of them and the diner. After the death declaration by the state that Aunt Rosie and Uncle Mike had died of natural causes following the quarantine, she had received a settlement which kept the Rosie's Diner open. With the news that neither were running the place anymore, customers dried up quickly. Kat even tried turning part of the place into a metaphysical shop selling crystals, herbs and doing tarot readings. The venture failed miserably. Thankfully, the Babins had long paid off the place so they had a place to live. The remnants of the inheritance were dwindling quickly, however. With all the handling of finances, Johnny, and a failing business, there was no time for herself, certainly not romance.

As the unseen hands reached her breasts, Kat closed her eyes tightly, biting down on her lip. The person she expected to see when she opened her eyes was Rhonda. Instead, it was Corina Newton, from Camberley, United Kingdom. She smiled at Kat, touching her face ever so softly. Kat looked back into her eyes with strange fascination, melting into burning desire. Having zero sexual experience, she surrendered totally to the moment, releasing all awkwardness.

Leaning in for a kiss while staying afloat, Corina smiled, raising a finger to her lips.

"Shh," she whispered.

Corina took Kat's hands, placing them on her breast while hers softly grasped Kat's hips, pulling her to her. As they embraced, Corina licked the moisture from Kat's lips. Kat slid her hand behind her head, through her dark curly hair, kissing her deeply, passionately. Corina's hands slid up and down Kat's back as bodies intertwined, spinning slowly in the October sunlight and warm pool, gurgling with the feeder stream supplying the only sound.

She left her mouth, slowly running her tongue down the inside of Corina's neck, along her collarbone, to her shoulder. Sliding her thigh between Kat's legs, Corina held her head as she responded, biting gently into her almond skin. Corina let out a soft moan. Kat rested her head on Corina's shoulder as she slid harder and faster along the length of her thigh with one hand on her hip, the other fondling her breasts.

Taking Kat's hand in hers, she guided it between her legs, using it to massage herself. Kat's head snapped up, staring once more into Corina's eyes, which stared back, penetrating her soul. Both women clutched each other tightly as their orgasms built to a heated frenzy beneath the warm water. As the moment of release neared, Kat locked her mouth on Corina's as they kissed fervently, inhaling each other, exchanging soul essence into one another. Kat screamed out in ecstasy.

"You okay?" A voice shattered the scene like a rock through a mirror.

Kat's eyes blinked, reestablishing focus. To her surprise, she was still seated at the bench near the cabin. Her face was flushed as she looked up. Corina sat next to her, holding a tarot card in her hand.

"You went a tad wonky. Just kind of frozen. Thought maybe you lost the plot on me for a second," Corina said.

Shaking out the shards from the sexually charged moment that had just collapsed, Kat looked at her, immediately blushing. It couldn't have been a daydream. The sensations were too real, so authentic. She was swept up in them, wanting to experience it again. Immediately. Harnessing her passions, she breathed in deeply, triggering the memory from a moment ago.

"Think I need some air," she said.

Corina threw open her arms. "All you need right here. We are outdoors."

Kat stood, walking away from the table. She was soaking wet and not from the magic pool. Looking down, making sure it wasn't showing through her jeans, she went through an anxiety drill she learned some time ago. Making contact with each of her fingers, she ran through the list. Identifying five things she saw. Next, she touched four things. Closing her eyes, she named three things she could hear, smell was a challenge. The pine was easy, followed by a faint odor of perfume wafting up from her hand. Corina Newton. Taste was the final grounding technique. The taste of her mouth on mine, she thought. Epic fail.

Whatever had just happened still pulsated inside of her. She wanted more. More than some illusion she unexpectedly experienced. Illusory, yet real in every conceivable way. That both were here in this space, fully clothed and dry, clearly proved otherwise. Taking a deep breath, Kat Ellis returned to the table, sitting beside her new friend, her new imaginary lover.

"Better?" Corina asked.

"Yeah, I think so. Just kind of wigged out a little. Too much fresh air and sunshine, I guess," Kat smiled at her.

"Oh, here's your card. Didn't have one of your rocks on it and the breeze nearly hoovered it away."

Corina handed her back the end card. It was the lovers, card number six.

⎯⎯⏴▬⏵⎯⎯

Colt appeared on the porch, stretching. He made his way to the two women sitting at the picnic bench. Tipping his hat, Kat grinned, expecting him to say, "top o' the mornin' to you, ladies." She was close.

"Mornin' ladies, don't believe I've had the pleasure." He extended his hand to Corina, introducing himself.

Oh no, what if he has the same experience when he touches her? Kat thought.

"Good day. Corina Newton."

"You're not from around these parts, are you, Ms. Newton?"

"Accent a dead giveaway, huh? No sir, I'm from jolly old England."

Colt glanced over at Kat, then back to Corina.

"What brings you out this way? Far stretch from England."

"That I am. My dad is visiting the state capitol, and I heard from one of his staffers this area is the bees' knees for late season brookies."

"Um hm," Colt replied with an air of suspicion. "Guessin' you're usin' a parachute adams or maybe a pheasant tail?"

She chuckled. "Not hardly, Mr. Sturgess. Those are spring drys, being late fall, no way you're going to coax them up from the bottom. Bouncing a thin mint or drifting a caddis fly is way more effective. Living out here with a stream running through your backyard, gobsmacked you don't know that."

Colt turned to Kat. "Girl knows her stuff."

Corina looked at Kat. "Oh, that was some sort of test?"

Tilting her head in confusion, Kat laughed uncomfortably at both of them.

"I don't know what either of you are talking about," she said.

Colt' tipped his hat again before taking his leave. "In a way. You two ladies take care. Sheriff Allen and I are going for a bike ride."

"So, what do I win?" Corina asked.

"Excuse me, ma'am?" Colt answered with a question.

"For passing your fishing test. What do I win?"

"Oh, that. Pardon if I was rude. Some strange goin' ons the past couple of days. Just makin' sure Kitty Kat here was safe."

"More than you can know."

"Good. Your prize is the hospitality of the Sturgess homestead. Any friend of Kat is welcome. Oh, and Kat, Emma will be up soon. She may need a hand in the kitchen, or she may burn it down."

Kat frowned. So much for my time.

Colt turned to walk towards the barn.

"Mr. Sturgess, anyone ever tell you that you are a dead ringer for Sam Elliot. You know, the actor? Loved him in The Shadow Riders with Tom Selleck."

"So, I've heard," Colt said, smiling, continuing back on task towards his destination.

Jud followed a few minutes later with a cup of coffee in his hand, catching up to Colt. He ran past the two women at the table, offering a half wave en route. Kat blushed automatically, recalling the start of her waking dream, or whatever it was. Her desire for Rhonda. She would have to work extra hard with the surrounding awkwardness in their company.

"Where were we? Oh yeah, here's your card."

Corina handed her the lovers card, which Kat put on the table next to the other two. Placing a rock on it, she looked nervously over at her. Could she possibly know what had just happened? Kat was a bundle of nerves.

"Sure you're okay, Kat Ellis?"

"Yeah, all good in the neighborhood. Just have to examine this spread and make sense of the connections," she answered.

"I like the lovers card. It's beautiful and intimate."

Whatever the emotional grasp that had taken control of her moments earlier, tapping into her deeper knowledge of the divination tool was akin to Jud's distraction by the Harley in the presence of Rhonda Coulter prior to Olath's invasion of his town. Of course, Kat did not know about that, but the sound of two motorcycles coming to life inside of the barn added an extra grounding component to the exercise she engaged in moments ago. Her spiritual connection pushed everything else to the side, awakening the knowledge she thought needed practice before the coming evening at the Halloween shindig. Effortlessly, she drew on her particular insight.

"Yeah, but it's not necessarily an indicator of love and relationships. It can be, it depends on where it lands in a spread. Like the card before it is the hierophant. That's a traditional way of thinking. You know, like the things you're taught. The experiences you have are basically following a path made up for you by parental figures, clergy, people you look up to. Always have a priestly figure on them, as we're all kind of brought up with religious backgrounds of some sort. Just accept the way things are, don't question the way they've always been. With the lover following, it's the next step. You've learned from your own experiences, setting a new set of traditions. Setting your own bar, so to speak.

"But here, it follows the moon reversed, which is always tricky. It can mean there's a game a foot—"

"That reference I know, Sherlock Holmes!"

Kat grinned. She was beginning to relax. Planting her feet back on terra firma with something she knows as naturally as breathing. It was the perfect distraction from her earlier departure into the warm pool of desire.

"Back to the moon. It can mean a deception of some sort is going on. Because it's reversed, means it will be discovered before the damage is done. Then again, like the lovers, it can also mean that even though times may fall in darkness, you're still whole and the beacon of hope."

"I like that last part. Much more positive."

"Yeah, me too."

Corina reached across the table, sliding the rock up from the king of swords. "How about this one?"

As she barely contacted Kat, the scent of her hair, her skin, everything rushed through her senses again, like a blast of wind. It was more than distracting; it was maddening. Everything she tried kept drawing her back to that warm mountain pool. Was this stranger a witch who had cast a spell on her?

"Um, that's Colt. It always will be."

"Mr. Sturgess? The Sam Elliot guy?"

"Yeah."

"Why is that?"

"Really long story. Maybe someday, if I ever see you again, I'll share."

Corina scooted next to Kat. The two bodies made contact again. Kat sprang to her feet, but she was too late. She had another orgasm by simply brushing up against this woman. Kat gasped as it caught her completely off guard.

Luckily, the appearance of the two motorcycles exploding from the opening in the barn provided enough of a diversion that Kat could collect herself. Walking around the opposite side of the table, she put a little distance between her and Corina before she had a heart attack from all the sexual energy engulfing her with every word, scent, glance, or touch of this woman from merry old England.

As the sound from the two motorcycle engines surrendered to the distance, Corina resumed the conversation, picking up the lover's card once more.

"Think I kind of like this one best," she said, planting a kiss on it. "Do you have names for your stones?"

"Excuse me?"

"Names? Like do you have names for your three stones, or do you just call them rocks number one, two and three?"

"Interesting. Never thought about that. Just followed my intuition this morning. Something in my brain told me to gather them. I mean, I knew it was a little windy when I left the porch, but it was my first idea as soon as I woke up. Cool idea."

Corina stood up, moving to the opposite end of the picnic bench.

"Go ahead, sit back down. That was your seat when I invaded your space. I feel I'm making you uncomfortable," she said.

"No, it's not that—"

"Rubbish. You nearly jumped out of your trousers when I chummed up to you a second ago. Go ahead. I'm really excited to see what you come up with."

Kat sat back down in her seat in front of the cards. Picking up the first stone, she closed her eyes, searching for her intention. Deciding to go with the first word in her head, she placed it.

"Love."

"That's one," Corina said, smiling.

Holding the second one close to her chest, she visualized Johnny placing it on the moon.

"Protect."

Corina handed her the last stone. What word would she select for the lovers? The word "sex" entered her mind, but she chose another.

"Friends."

Opening her eyes, Corina stood in front of her on the opposite side of the bench.

"Aces, I love it. Now you have your stones named," she said, reaching down to retrieve her fly rod.

That action surprised Kat.

"You're leaving?" she asked.

"I do have to get on my way, but thanks for the pleasant morning. I enjoyed it very much. Much more than you are even aware," Corina answered.

Kat shot up from her seat. "But wait. Will I ever see you again? Like, do you have a number or address or something?"

Corina reached down, picking up the "friends" stone Kat named, handing it to her.

"Do you believe in magic? I mean genuine magic, not the plonker stuff the guys in tuxedos and white rabbits sham with?"

"I guess so. Never really thought about it."

She walked over, placing the stone in Kat's right hand, covering it with her left.

"Katlyn Kat Ellis, you have abilities beyond anyone I've ever met. When you need me, hold this stone between your hands and focus on the lover's card. I'll find you wherever you are."

"How did you know my name is Katlyn? I never mentioned that?"

"Didn't you?" Corina winked at her, kissed her on the cheek and wandered back into the pines from where she came.

Kat entered the cabin. First order of business was a shower, then a change of clothes. Unfortunately, her plan got sidetracked seeing smoke billowing out of the kitchen. Rushing in, she observed Emma blowing on the flames that danced from the bottom of a frying pan of whatever she was attempting to cook. Colt was right in his assessment of her cooking skills, or lack thereof. Kat rushed to her rescue.

"Don't blow on it, you're only feeding the fire," she said.

Emma turned, tossing it into the sink, reaching for the spigot.

"No, not that either! You'll mess up the coating on the pan, maybe even crack it."

"Then what am I supposed to do?" Emma asked frantically.

Kat walked over to the sink, recovering the pan and headed back out the front door. She could tell by the black swirling oil in the pan, perhaps bacon was for breakfast? Heading over to the firepit next to the grill, Kat dumped the mess into the ash of past cookouts. Setting the hot pan on the grill to cool down, she skipped back into the cabin. Disaster avoided.

Emma was leaning up against the stove when Kat reentered the kitchen. She wore the face of defeat. Kat chuckled.

"It's not funny, ya' know. Think after all this time, I would know how to cook bacon," Emma said.

"Takes time to master it. No real trick, but it requires patience. Medium heat only and you have to stand over it watching. When the crackling sound slows down, flip it. If it smokes, flip it."

"That's a lot of rules for frickin' bacon!"

Kat tapped Emma's nose with her finger.

"Not everything gets cooked on high. Doesn't cook it any faster but will burn it faster."

"Thanks, Julia Child!"

The two girls laughed as Kat opened the kitchen window, turning on the vent fan above the stove to air out the kitchen.

"There's a fan? Huh, who'd a known?" Emma asked.

"So, what do you want for breakfast?" Kat asked with a hint of sarcasm.

"Guess bacon is off the menu, since that was the last of it."

Kat opened the refrigerator and pantry. "How about omelets and pancakes?"

"Look at you! You can do that? I mean, Rhonda said something about you working in a diner, but didn't make the connection. As you know, that's kind of my thing. Ms. Obliv!"

"Well, to be honest, I own a diner."

"Oh wow, that's so rad!"

"It can be."

Kat removed the ingredients from both locations, sitting them on the counter. She found another pan in the drawer beneath the stove, more fitting for cooking. Emma watched her preparation.

"Shit," Kat blurted.

"What?"

"I really need to jump in the shower real quick. Waded in the stream this morning, then wandered around barefoot. I hope I didn't track in any mud."

"Don't worry about that. You cook, I can clean. Not like I'm starving or anyone else is up. Go for it."

Kat crossed the kitchen, past the living room, down the hall. She peeked in on Johnny in the guest room. He was sprawled out, face down, snoring on one of the twin beds. Quietly, she closed the door. How he and Rhonda could still sleep with all the racket going on was a wonder to her.

Opening the bathroom door, she saw Rhonda in front of the bathroom mirror, wrapped in a towel, putting on makeup.

"Oh, sorry. Excuse me. Was going to take a quick shower," Kat said.

"No need to apologize. I can do this in my room. Didn't mean to hog the bathroom."

Rhonda gathered her things, brushing past Kat. She stopped in the doorway, facing her.

"You know, I had the strangest dream last night. Well, I think it was. Can't remember most of it, but you were picking up rocks naked. Weird, eh?" Rhonda asked.

Kat let out an awkward laugh. "Yeah, weird."

Sliding past her to the sanctuary of the bathroom, Kat closed the door and blew out a big puff of air. She was blushing so much, her cheeks burned. Staring into the mirror, she tried settling down, balancing heart and mind like the king of swords. What was this strange sexual energy permeating every cell of her body? Her dream was a little more explicit than just gathering stones. If a dream is what it was.

Stripping down, Kat jumped in the shower. Closing her eyes, she welcomed the cleansing sensation of the water. Within seconds, her thoughts drifted back to the warm mountain pool, Rhonda naked on the bank, then Corina. Kat's chest grew heavy, her breathing labored. The images danced in her head, along with the other sensations. Dizziness overtook her as she leaned one hand up against the wall to steady her balance. The images continue. Dropping the bar of soap to the floor, her hand slid between her legs. Kat moaned, whipping her head back, licking her lips. Another intense orgasm. She opened her eyes as the water streamed down her face.

"What the fucking is going on with me?" she muttered, spitting out a mouthful of water.

Reaching down, she retrieved the soap, blocking out any semblance of sexual sensations. *Ash trays, fuzzy bunny rabbits, burnt bacon, deer poop...* Kat substituted everything she could think of in a non-sexual nature to make it through the simple act of taking a shower. Drying off, she wrapped a towel around her body, one around her head. Leaving the bathroom, she knocked on the guest room to wake Johnny up. It was time and her clothes were in a suitcase in the room.

He stirred, looking up at her with haziness in his eyes. "Hey, Kitty Kat. Seen my mask?" he asked.

She was surprised. He hadn't addressed her by the nickname in quite some time. Truth be told, he barely spoke to her at all after quarantine unless he was hungry. John Paul Ellis shared the same culinary expertise as Emma.

Looking around the room, she found his mask lying on the floor. Picking it up, she felt a gooey black slime on the edge of the mask, veining towards the eyes. How odd, she thought.

"Not sure what you got on this, John Paul, but you need to wash it off. Pretty stinky too."

Snatching it from her hand, he looked at the front and back of the mask.

"What you see? Perfectly fine to me," he said.

"Right there, along the edges. That funky—"

Upon second examination, the mask was pristine. A few little cracks along the edges from age and wear, but nothing else.

"Huh," she said, surprised by the sudden disappearance of the substance that was present seconds earlier.

Kat picked up her luggage, rushing back into the bathroom.

"Katlyn Ellis, are you losing your marbles? Now I'm seeing things?" she asked herself in the mirror.

An hour passed with most of the group enjoying a hearty breakfast prepared by Kat. All hands were on deck for cleanup and dishes. Even Johnny helped. Emma and Rhonda retrieved the bags from Ms. April's shop, spreading their outfits on the table. Kat thought about dragging hers out to join in the fun, was even peer pressured to do it, but she needed some time to relax, processing the morning's events. Taking a seat on the front porch swing, she rocked back and forth.

It wasn't long after breakfast that Colt and Jud roared up the road, parking the two motorcycles in the barn. Kat wearily rose to her feet, anticipating two more meals to prepare. She was pleasantly surprised when Colt waved her off, informing her they had stopped at a small diner. Jud referred to it as a "choke and puke" to fuel up for the day.

Returning to the swing, Colt joined her with a cup of coffee.

"Got room for two?" he asked.

"Always."

Kat smiled. His company was always welcome. She felt safe with the old cowboy. Whether from the occurrence at Rosie's or some other reason, it was etched in stone. That thought had her reflecting on her selection of stones for the cards she drew. Colt, of course, was the king of swords, but the word she associated with him was "love." Johnny drew the protection stone. *Shouldn't they have been reversed?* she pondered. No matter, Kat Ellis drew the first word from her subconscious that presented itself on viewing the cards.

Did she love Colt Sturgess? If she brought her magic eight ball that sat on a shelf in her room back in Shermer, it may have told her "signs point to yes." That was a pipe dream. She also had erected a brick wall around her heart with all things pertaining to love. She lost enough. Sharing with the other girls the past day, they did as well, but Rhonda apparently rebounded nicely with Jud. Emma's relationship status was unclear. Five years with Colt, what was their actual deal? Relationships were so freaking confusing.

"Heard I missed one whale of a breakfast," he said.

"Nah, nothing fancy. Just some omelets and pancakes."

"No bacon?"

Kat chuckled. "Emma kind of overcooked that."

"That sure is a fancy word for burned beyond recognition," Colt said, smiling.

Colt stretched out on the swing, putting his arm around her. Cautiously, she put her head on his shoulder. With her sexual impulses running rampant, an omnipresent fear that whoever she touched would cascade into a whirlwind of desire forced a slight hesitation. She smiled as her head settled in. No flourish of desire. He remained a safe zone.

"How are things, Kitty Kat? We haven't gotten to jaw jackin' with everything going on. Got off to a poor start, but things seemed to settle down. Even pried Jud away from his case for a quick ride. Where'd your friend run off to?" he asked.

Her friend, Corina Newton. Things were beyond weird since she wandered onto the Sturgess homestead. Where she ran off to was a question that drifted across the back of Ms. Ellis' mind since she disappeared into the pines.

"Not sure where she went. Just a stranger passing by, I guess," Kat answered.

"Shame. Seemed like a nice girl. You two looked like you hit it off."

"I guess."

Kat struggled desperately to keep her mind off Corina as her urges were resurfacing. She stood up, moving to the porch banister, leaning against the post.

"Things have been okay, I guess, not so great on the diner front. Customers kind of took a powder after word got out that Aunt Rosie died. Can't run a restaurant without the star chef. I know my way around the kitchen, but I lack that down home charm that customers got with the meal. I swear, half of them came in just to bullshit with her," Kat said.

"I reckon that's true. From my bit of time with y'all, she was one of a kind."

"That she was," Kat paused. "Anyway, we tried some different things out. I even did readings and tried selling crystals. With the lack of customers, the space wasn't being used. But that went over like a lead balloon. So, we just get on the best we can. Probably have to take a job in the city at some point. The money is only going to stretch so far. Sure, I can get part time as a line cook. Lots of chains are opening these days that need those. Thinking the day of the hometown diner may ride off into the sunset."

"Hm," Colt muttered.

"Sorry, don't mean to sound depressing. Seriously, all good in the neighborhood, in the land of make believe, anyway. We're alive and I have new friends, so silver linings, right?"

Colt nodded before rising and heading into the cabin.

"Be right back. Need a refresh," he said.

Kat wandered off the porch. Her insides had returned to normal, mostly. All had reset to what they were when she stepped off the porch earlier, the sun and the grass and the smell of pines, nothing else. A breeze tickled her hair as she closed her eyes, concentrating on that third stone. Corina asked her if she believed in real magic. Was it possible to hold it between her hands and summon her from the woods? Drifting into the absurd, Kat wondered if Ms. Newton was a wood nymph or a fairy. Why not? They had encountered much, much stranger things. Colt's approach drew her back to the here and now.

He stopped beside her, handing her a worn sack, folded over and fastened with twine.

"What's this?" she asked.

"Let's just call it an early Christmas present," he answered. "Jud and Rhonda get one too, so it doesn't look like I'm playin' favorites, but figured I'd give you yours now so you can relax a little. You know, enjoy the rest of the weekend."

She tugged on the twine, wondering what it was. Unfolding the sack, she could see stacks of cash, mostly twenty-dollar bills.

"Oh, I can't take this. It's not why I told you that story," she exclaimed.

"I know, I know. But that's just collectin' dust. I'll never spend it all. Have everything I need right here. Please, Kitty Kat, it will help you and Johnny out. I implore you," he said. "Like that word, 'implore?' Emma taught me that one."

She wrapped the chord back around the satchel.

"I don't know, this is embarrassing," she said, wondering whether to accept the gift.

She didn't take the time to count it, but it was more money than she had ever seen.

"You didn't happen to knock over a bank or two in your hundred plus years of living, did you?"

That brought a roar of laughter from the cowboy. She never saw him laugh with that much enthusiasm.

"Can't say that I have. Although, can't say that I didn't think about it once or twice. A man with my abilities gets to thinkin' about all sorts of things in the wee hours of the night with one too many empty bottles of whisky at his feet."

Kat hugged him. He hugged her back. Her skin brushed his cheek as she released the embrace. No visions or images, or sexual eruptions. Just plain normalcy. What an absolute welcome state to experience.

"Well, thank you, sir."

He tipped his hat. "Pleasure is all mine, ma'am."

The screen door slammed behind them as Johnny strode forward.

"Mr. Colt. You have some black paint?" he asked.

"I may in the barn, Johnny. Let's go take a gander."

"I'd be much obliged," Johnny said, following close behind.

Watching the two walk towards the barn, Kat went over to her car, opened the door, tucking the sack under the driver's side seat. She would return later, before departing for the Halloween party, to move it to the trunk. Colt said he was going to give a similar gift to Jud and Rhonda but hadn't yet. She didn't want to create an awkward situation. After securing the satchel, Kat returned to the house. The pumpkin seeds still needed to be baked.

Colt led Johnny into the barn. In one stall on the opposite side of the vehicles, he had organized it by various types of materials. One had shelving with a variety of paints, both canned and spray. Glancing around the stock, Johnny saw it first. Retrieving the can, he shook it to make sure it was full and mixed correctly.

"Need any primer too, Johnny? What ya' plan on painting?" Colt asked.

"This," Johnny answered, holding up his devil mask.

Colt raised an eyebrow.

"You gonna touch it up? I have brushes. Red paint too."

"Nope, all black."

"Okay, then. Let's take it to the back corner. Have a sheet of plywood I use for varnish and paint. Good ventilation too, so we won't get high on the stuff," Colt said.

"I got it. Pretty good at painting. Ask Kat. I painted the front of our building with stars and stuff when she did crystals."

"Have at then, my friend."

Johnny took the can of spray paint out into the grass, making a bed of leaves before placing his devil mask on top. Shaking the can, he applied smooth steady strokes, covering the details of the mask. Why he wanted to do this was known only by him, but he was finally interacting and the usage of "I'd be much obliged" didn't go unnoticed. Maybe it was part of his Halloween costume for tonight's party, since he missed out on the shopping spree with the women. This must be his improvisation; another fancy word Emma had taught Colt.

Once he finished, Johnny returned the can to the exact shelf from where he got it. He even set it in the exact orientation it was before he removed it.

"Thanks, Mr. Colt," he said.

"Pleasures all mine."

Sturgess locked up the barn, then turned back to the cabin. He smiled on his brief walk, thinking about his initial apprehension in hosting this reunion. He welcomed Kat and Johnny anytime, but they had never accepted his offer to visit. Possibly from a shortage of funds, possibly from whatever hangover it left all four of his visitors with after their release from quarantine.

Jud and Rhonda he barely knew, but Emma insisted on them coming as well. Not knowing she had any connection with either and until a day ago, neither did she, he agreed. It would be nice to get to know everyone on a personal level, as they were all deprived of that in Kinston.

A day and a half remained until the four would head off, back to everyday life. He and Emma would resume theirs. With the party tonight, he thought about what the group could all do on Sunday. Halloween was actually on Monday, but his visitors would be gone by then. Discussing the options with Emma before they arrived, there were several activities they could do. Unfortunately for all of them, the choice had already been made, but not by their hands.

Chapter Eight

Sunset brought about light rain showers. Jud, Rhonda, and Colt moved the Honda Turbos into the barn beneath the protection of the tin roof. They stood under the stained glass, which currently remained dark, listening momentarily to the comfort of the raindrops. Rhonda retreated to the cabin to prepare for the party while Colt and Jud continued a discussion about how much daylight-saving time sucked with darkness covering the sky at 5:00 pm.

Sprinting for the porch, Colt used normal speed so as not to slide through the now soaked leaves and mud that denied any type of friction for superhuman momentum stops. Entering the front door, both men's jaws dropped.

"What do you think?" Emma asked in her sexy pirate costume she enhanced with extra sexy thigh-high boots.

Rhonda strode out of the bathroom, taking her place beside Emma, striking the terminal stare pose. The last member of Colt's angels, Kat Ellis, glided down the steps that led up to the master bedroom, stepping to the left of Emma.

"Wow," Jud gasped.

Colt tipped his cowboy hat. "Three fine fillies there," he said.

The three women struck a final pose before all laughing out loud. Bullseye. The exact response they were hoping for.

"Okay, now you two get to steppin.' Time's wasting and we need to get to the VFW and help Kat set up," Emma said.

Johnny sat quietly on the couch, fingers interlaced, wearing black gloves, a black cape, and the devil masked he had painted black.

"Pretty frightful, Johnny," Colt said.

Johnny nodded without a word. Colt turned to Emma.

"Well, didn't really plan on any disguise. This is more of your lady's shindig," Colt said.

"Now don't you start with me, Colt Sturgess. You either, Jud Allen. You both will put on some kind of costume and you both will enjoy yourselves this evening!" Emma scolded.

Jud looked at Colt and shrugged. "I don't have a costume. You?"

"I'm sure we can come up with somethin'. Don't want to disappoint the womenfolk."

Emma sighed. "'Womenfolk,' really? Thought we deleted that word from your vocab?"

Colt hit Jud in the chest. "Let's head upstairs, see what we can rustle up."

Entering Colt's master bedroom, Jud was taken aback. He expected more of a rough and tumble, sagebrush kind of décor, complete with wagon wheels, bleached cattle skulls and stuffed birds of prey. Instead, pink everywhere. Pink shag carpeting, bedspread, even the drapes on the four-post bed had a pink tinge to them.

"Have to say, Mr. Sturgess, a little surprised—"

"The pink, huh? Emma's decorating touch. She sleeps here more than I do most nights as I rise with sunup and she's up at the break of noon."

Jud chuckled. Then thought about the fact that they shared a room. One large king bed sat at the edge of the room.

"Oh? I assumed you two just slept together."

"A couple of days a week, but it's not what you're thinkin'. I'm old enough to be her grandfather. Can't quite get past that."

"Yeah, but we guys have needs."

Colt took out two cowboy hats from his closet, tossing one with sequins to Jud.

"My needs kinda turned to dust out on that farm years back."

Jud nodded. He wasn't sure what all happened at Chooch's Farm as he wasn't privy to the recording session with Johnny and Kat, but there were some things men just didn't talk about with other men. Prodding wouldn't work, neither would pressing the issue. The best thing the masculine ego accomplished in such cases was simply to drop the issue and mosey along, in Colt's parlance, anyway. Examining the cowboy hat, Jud reacted.

"You gotta be kidding me. Sequins and a big silver star. Really?"

"At least it's black. Emma's got a pink one in here, if you prefer?"

"I'm not even gonna ask!"

Colt chuckled. "Believe it or not, kinda light on my feet for an old-timer. Entered a dance contest down at the same VFW we're headin'. Won actually and advanced to the finals in Pine Hollows. Took second place," Colt recounted, with an air of pride.

"Well, I'll be. Never took you as a hoofer, Mr. Sturgess."

"Think I told a young man who kinda looked like you a few years back, seeing ain't necessarily believin'." Colt winked at him. "C'mon, can't keep the ladies waiting. Oh, one more thing."

Colt pulled a vest from another hanger, handing it to Jud, who shook his head vigorously. It was also covered in sequins.

"Let's go deputy! The show must go on."

"Fine," Jud said, sliding it over his shoulders.

Outside of VFW Post 1056, Ms. April was smoking a cigarette. She had already prepared three roasters full of hot sausage, meatballs, and chicken earlier in the afternoon. The buns had been sliced and Horace's wife, Florence, organized the potluck items that she collected up around town that morning. Food was set except for the few stragglers who always brought food late at the door. Ms. April could name them, even before the invitations were mailed, and the ad hit the newspaper.

It promised to be a good turnout if the rain didn't fall any harder. One thing that kept the citizens of Apollo home was inclement weather, which caused a tremendous problem with refunding tickets, putting a huge dent in the 50/50 giveaway kitty. As she finished up her smoke, Horace joined her under the awning of the VFW.

"What'd ya make of that?" Ms. April asked, pointing up the street at the black carriage with a single horse.

Horace removed his glasses, cleaning the lenses on his apron to get a better look.

"Beats me. Seen that carriage wandering around the last couple of days. Three kids and a coachman, I think. Haven't seen them at anybody's house. Figured they were sleepin' inside the thing," he answered.

Ms. April hit him over the head with her spatula.

"Horace Winston, that's the craziest thing you've said in a while, and you spit out some real humdingers. How could four people sleep in that little wagon?"

"Hell if I know, April. Just sayin' haven't seen them stray too far from it is all. Seen 'em at the diner?"

"No, but I actually work for a living. I don't have time to keep an eye on all the goings on in this town. That's for people like you."

"Yeah, well, I ain't seen nothin'," he said in a huff, turning around and heading back inside the VFW.

Ms. April considered another cigarette but remembered the two pies in the oven. She followed right behind him.

***

The women at the Sturgess cabin shared a good laugh at Jud's outfit, except Emma, who found it sexy. Colt opted for one of his fancier cowboy hats, non-sequined, but sporting a rattlesnake hatband. His vest was animal hide, and he changed into flat heeled snakeskin boots to match his hat. Emma smiled, knowing the flat heels meant he planned on dancing. They were quite an accomplished dance team, which she retold the story of the contest with far more detail than Colt just shared with Jud. One piece remained. Colt removed a small box from the corner of the mantlepiece. Inside was a silver five-pointed star badge. He pinned it on, holding his hand up to Jud.

"Interesting story behind this. Remind me to tell you about it later," he said.

Seeing the badge, Johnny jumped up, running to the back guest room. Joining the others, a moment later, he proudly pinned on his Uncle Michael J. Babin's constable badge.

"Almost forgot mine," he said.

Colt nodded, giving him the three finger Smoke Hunters' salute. Johnny returned the salute before sliding his black devil mask over his head.

Emma rushed over to the boombox, grabbing her large cassette storage box.

"Taking tunes?" Kat asked.

"Of course. You heard Ms. April; all they play is golden oldies. If I'm gonna get the old man here out on the dance floor, have to liven that party up a little," Emma answered.

Rhonda high-fived her.

"Just make sure you have some of those fellahs, The Time. Like that Minneapolis sound," Colt said. He was legitimately getting into the spirit of the party.

"Well, duh," Emma replied.

Rhonda turned to Kat. "You have all your stuff ready, Kitty Kat?"

Kat's cheeks flushed. Her heart raced, but she pushed it back, maintaining focus.

"I think so. Let me double check."

She walked over to the table, inventorying her belongings for the night ahead: The tarot deck, stones she collected, her outfit she was wearing, Mr. Horace would have a tip jar.

Did she just call me "Kitty Kat?" She did! Stop Kat, focus.

"I'll have to wing it without my journal, but check. Ready to go."

Rhonda hugged her. "Sweet! In that case, let's get a move on then."

I wish she'd stop doing that, Kat thought.

The group stepped out onto the porch; Colt locked up behind them. The rain was falling a little harder and steadily.

"Guessin' the bikes are out tonight. We'll have to take the truck and your car, if that's okay, Kat?" Colt asked.

"Oh, yeah. We planned on all going together, anyhow. Well, we girls and John Paul," she answered.

"Looks like you're with me, Jud."

"Great. The snakeskin and rhinestone cowboys ride again. Yee-Haw!"

Everyone laughed as they ran towards the barn. Within minutes, both vehicles eased out onto the driveway. Colt doubled back to lock the door. Emma rolled down the window of the Oldsmobile, popping her head out in the rain.

"Apollo, here we come!"

The Apollo VFW Post 1056 was the area's premier event center besides its weekly specials. One in particular was a pizza burger. A simple combination of quarter pound beef patty, fried pepperoni, mozzarella cheese, and a ladle of sauce. Well, it seemed simple. Whatever Horace and his crew used to mix in the beef was the secret. Some claimed oregano, others claimed fresh spices from Italy were among the flavorings. Whatever it was, people came from as far as Biggs County to savor the tasty burger. Tonight, however, there were no burgers on the menu.

Kat pulled her car into the first available space, Colt next to her. They were early by an hour, but true to form, the salty veterans who had purchased tickets the day they went on sale had already arrived. Forming different conversation groups, the men and women puffed on cigars and cigarettes, creating a cordon of smoke to pass through on the way to the entrance beneath the awning.

The Sturgess group moved towards the entrance, except for Johnny, who had his attention locked on something. Colt wandered over to see what he was staring at. Beside the building in the grass beneath a flagpole where old glory waved unencumbered by the falling rain sat an M-4 Sherman tank.

"Pretty sweet, huh? Wanna go take a closer look?" Colt asked.

Johnny pointed up at the sky, signifying the rain. Colt had nearly forgotten about the fishing goggles that Johnny crafted after a brief encounter with a splash of mud. Walking over to his truck, Colt opened the passenger door, reaching behind the seat. Retrieving an umbrella, he opened it, waving Johnny over. The two men walked hastily to get an up close and personal look at the tank.

Inside the VFW, the women with Jud in tow entered the main hall after wiping their feet on the mat, displaying the outpost's logo and paying the cover charge at the door, which included two free drink tickets. The door was covered in fake spider webs laced with little black plastic spider rings. Orange and black crepe paper streamers hung from the ceiling of the hall itself, with Beistle Company design cutouts taped to the posts and mini pumpkins on each of the tables. Cornstalks bracketed the restrooms with a male scarecrow adjacent to the men's room, a witch next to the women's room.

Kat was wandering towards the kitchen when Ms. April burst through the door, Horace Winston close behind.

"Katlyn Ellis, so excited that you made it and you're early. This old fossil is the post commander. To all intents and purposes, he's been the post commander since the Revolutionary War, Horace Winston," she said jokingly.

"Oh, come on, I'm not that old, April," he replied.

"How can you tell with your memory?" she chuckled.

Horace extended his hand to shake. Kat had prepared for any human contact with a pair of long stripper gloves, Emma called them, to limit as much skin-to-skin contact as she could in fear of interference with her readings. The visions could be helpful or a hinderance. Touching a bunch of strangers wouldn't cloud her intuitive gifts this evening.

"Well, April, you didn't tell me she was so pretty," Horace said.

Ms. April folded her arms. "See, I warned you," she said to Kat.

Kat laughed, then introduced her friends. Following the impromptu meet and greet, Ms. April led Kat over to a table at the far end of the hall between the restrooms, away from the speakers and music. Horace had fulfilled her request with a black tablecloth and an orange runner with embroidered pumpkins on it.

Ms. April whispered to Kat. "The runner was my idea. Brought it from the store."

Kat smiled. "Nice touch."

Kat took her place behind the table, removing her tarot deck, the three stones she gathered that morning, and a three-ring binder. The binder had all her notes on cryptids, not exactly applicable, but she didn't have her tarot journal. It would serve as a security blanket, at least until after the first few readings, while her confidence built. She exhaled, looking at the empty chair on the opposite side of her table. *Sure you're ready for this?* she thought.

From behind, Kat felt someone squeeze her left shoulder, but no images or sensations flooded her. It was Emma. Neither she nor Colt produced any sensory input to Kat. She wondered why.

"You got this. Don't be nervous, you're a pro," Emma reassured her.

"Thanks. That means a lot."

Rhonda waved, smiled and blew a kiss before turning to locate her husband. Of course, that simple, friendly gesture sent her into a frenzy. Focus, Kat! Focus!

If Colt and Emma were a dead zone on the emotional transmission band, Rhonda Coulter Allen would be a fireworks extravaganza. Why some people had that effect, while others did not, would take some reflection, perhaps knowledge beyond what she possessed. This also appeared to coincide with the appearance of Corina Newton. Maybe she had answers? Kat did not know how to find her again, so the thought was moot.

Colt and Johnny joined Emma and Rhonda, who were getting a grand tour of the facility. Jud wandered into the bar, sharing a beer with a vet, more than likely a Marine Corps veteran, swapping stories about boot camp. Emma made her intention known to crash the disc jockey table should the music invoke narcolepsy. That brought great joy to Ms. April, who made a pit stop to introduce her to the DJ, Bobby Onions, yes, his surname was Onions. Bobby welcomed her help with the music selection, even offering to set up a playlist order using the cassettes Emma brought to bridge transitions in and out of LP cues. She took a seat next to Mr. Onions as they drifted quickly into a musical discussion about where music was headed, dragging them out of the disco era.

Rhonda joined her husband at the bar while Johnny engaged in a preview of the food table, sneaking a pizzelle from one of the cookie trays. Colt found himself alone. Being one of the first groups to arrive, he moseyed on over to a table and sat down.

Hours passed with games, laughter, and dancing, accentuated by tons of food and drink. Emma cued up a few of her and Colt's greatest hits as the two put on a dancing clinic that even younger attendees were left speechless watching them perform. The cowboy and the pirate wench suddenly had a new fanbase. Bobby Onions urged them on for one more dance by boasting about them winning the previous year's dance contest to much younger competitors. Even Rhonda and Jud heaped applause to get their two friends back on the floor.

Kat was too busy with her readings to see what the commotion was about when the dancing was in full swing. Since the first party goers entered the building, she had a line. The mayonnaise jug that Horace had selected as a tip jar was so packed, people were pushing down the bills to stuff in more tokens of appreciation. Seeing the line, Ms. April kept shuffling food back and forth to ensure Ms. Ellis was being fed. Next to her sat a hot sausage sandwich with one bite taken out of it, a handful of chips, scoop of rigatoni and a chicken breast, all untouched. Kat had no time to even grab a forkful. Yet, Ms. April shuttled the latest offering, a plate with a variety of cookies from the cookie table.

Once everyone had passed through the buffet line, John Paul camped at the cookie table. An ample supply of samples greeted him, and he was committed to work his way through all of them. The thumbprint peanut butter cookies with the chocolate drop in the middle were his favorite but would not deter his goal of trying at least one of each of the others that filled two eight-foot tables.\Following the last swirl and dip of Emma to an old music standard, Colt retired to his table. Luckily, the hosts of the party provided lemonade for a public teetotaler like himself. Sturgess only had a sip of whiskey at home or on the road. Although Jud sneaked a shot of bourbon into one offering, Colt didn't object to. One wouldn't hurt. As he sat back, wiping the sweat from his brow, a stranger approached.

"Mr. Sturgess, I believe?" he asked.

"Depends on who's askin'," Colt answered.

The man extended his hand. "My name is Blackburn, Kaleb Blackburn. It is a pleasure to make your acquaintance. Do you mind if I join you?"

Colt shook his hand firmly, not sharing Kat's aversion to physical contact.

"Not at all. Pull up a seat."

Blackburn sat down. Colt looked the man over, from his dark top hat, shades, and outfit to the cane he carried. He was dressed more than costumed. In all his years alive, Sturgess developed a sixth sense about people, not literally, but with gut feelings. This man had him on high alert.

"Nice getup. Undertaker?" Colt asked.

Blackburn chuckled. "Heavens no, although I can see how one might perceive my dress as such. I tend to stick to anonymity, rather than stand in the direct sunlight of attention. I imagine that may be a challenge for you with the incredibly unique pigment, or lack thereof, in your eyes. Visually, pardon the pun, very striking."

Colt grimaced, abruptly knowing why he was having the initial reaction. The man reminded him of someone, particularly with his speech. Olath.

"So, what can I do for you, Mr. Blackburn?"

"Actually, Mr. Sturgess, the apropos question is, what can I do for you?"

"Afraid I don't follow."

"I represent a kind of consortium. This consortium is always seeking gifted individuals who demonstrate, shall we say, unusual abilities that the average man does not possess."

"You don't say?"

"Oh, but I do say. We have been watching you for some time now and believe you would be a superior fit for —"

Jud interrupted from behind Blackburn. "You okay, Mr. Sturgess? This guy's not causing you any trouble, is he?"

"Quite alright, Jud. Nothing I can't handle."

"Okay. Well, if you need backup, just give the word."

Jud wandered off, watching the table. He obviously had been enjoying the camaraderie with the veterans, more on point, plying him with generous amounts of alcohol. Colt smiled, appreciating the offer of help.

Blackburn continued where he left off before he was rudely interrupted.

"Charming boy. As I was saying, we, the organization, believe you would be an excellent addition to our very intimate circle of decision makers," he said.

"What precisely do y'all decide on?" Colt asked.

Blackburn leaned in, lowering his voice. Looking up over the dark glasses, Colt saw Blackburn's jet-black eyes. No sclera, no iris, just black. Grasping the handle of his cane, Kaleb Blackburn laid out his proposal in more detail.

"The human race is a frail system of mistake after mistake. Seldom growing, seldom learning. Certain structures are in place to ensure the prevention of its downfall, while providing beneficial motivations on the backend. Governments rise and crumble, holding allegiance only to corporate masters. Ineffective is an understatement. Wars yield profits, most humanity takes sides, much like sporting events. It no longer matters what atrocities the home team commits, as long as they win. Ideologies are as fluid as the short-sighted actors who play candidates on the political stage. And for what? Slips of paper, marred with ink of other men who have danced the dance of forbearers. Yet, the cycle has continued for millenniums."

"And you see me as one of these saviors of humanity?"

Blackburn laughed. "Oh, no. I see you as one who can give a shove every once in a while, or in your vernacular, a boot in the ass?"

"Still don't follow you, Kaleb."

"Simply put, in the real world, a small group of men and women control every single major event you read about in the newspaper or watch on your television."

"Sound like just another one of these teams you don't seem real fond of."

"Touché," Blackburn said, with a gentle clapping of his gloved hands. "The difference is, we aren't on a team. We manage all of them completely without their knowledge, which is why we can accomplish things only god himself dare attempt."

Colt's intuition was correct. This man sounded like Ansel Olath. Exactly like him and he harvested body parts to complete his perfect world vision with a twisted plan to take over the world with ash tokers, clowns and whatever other monsters he cooked up in his charnel house of horrors.

"Would you like to hear more?" Blackburn asked.

Colt paused before answering, taking a drink of his lemonade, ensuring Jud hadn't spiked this one and he was understanding this strange man correctly.

"Here's my problem, Mr. Blackburn. You see, when it comes to men like you and whatever group you're with, I find a thin line between fantasy and madness. Had an old sayin' back on the farm, 'a rattlesnake bite may kill ya, but they're no match for a thresher.'"

"I don't believe I follow you, Mr. Sturgess."

"That's alright. Simply put, although that snake may think he's got the upper hand because he naturally makes deadly poison, it ain't nothin' more than another stem of wheat to end up as feed someplace. Cycle of life, Kaleb, cycle of life. You either eat or get eaten, nothin' else matters."

"Interesting viewpoint. However, I may point out that the apex predator has no natural enemies."

That brought a roar of laughter from Sturgess. "That belief, Mr. Blackburn, is the thing that will get them eaten first."

Colt stood up, offering his hand. "I appreciate your offer, but I'm gonna have to decline. I reckon I prefer makin' my own way. What happens between now and then depends on how big of a thresher I run into."

Blackburn sighed, shaking Colt's hand. "A shame, Mr. Sturgess, but I understand. I can't say that my contemporaries will be pleased, but every man has a right to choose."

"Every woman too. Good evening, Mr. Blackburn."

With that, Colt walked over to the cookie table, joining Johnny in his search for the perfect confection. Johnny preferred quantity loading his plate with as much as possible. Returning to the table, he saw Blackburn still seated. Pulling his devil mask over his face, he approached. This man he knew. Taking Colt's seat, Johnny sat down.

"I know you," he said.

"Beg pardon?" Blackburn asked.

"You're my friend from my hospital. The dark man."

Blackburn reached forward, slowly lifting John Paul Ellis' mask. He gasped, then smiled.

"Well, if it isn't my friend, Johnny!"

"Yeah, that's me. Where ya been. Haven't seen you in a while. But seen your friends. They talk to me at the cabin."

Blackburn raised a finger to his lips. "Shh. We don't want to talk about that. It's our little secret. Okay?"

Johnny nodded.

Blackburn leaned in. "I got a favor to ask, my friend Johnny. Do you think you can do something exceptionally important?"

"Is it a top-secret mission or something?"

"Yes, as a matter of fact, that is precisely what it is. But you must promise not to tell another living soul. We have a deal?"

"Not even my sister?"

"Oh, no, especially not your sister."

Johnny looked left, then right to ensure no one else was listening, then he himself leaned in. Blackburn cupped his hand over Johnny's ear, whispering something that only he could hear. Nodding his head while Blackburn spoke, John Paul Ellis sealed the deal with a handshake, then returned his attention to the plate of cookies. Kaleb Backburn rose, heading for the door of the VFW. As he passed Colt Sturgess, he tipped his hat, then exited the facility.

Outside of the building, the rain had stopped. The smokers all moved inside since the party was in full swing. Blackburn sprinted across the street, entering the carriage. Slowly, the reins snapped on the back of the horse. It trotted down Hunter's Way, turning around and taking cover under a large oak tree.

"Guess you failed, pops?" Matthew asked from the back seat of the carriage.

He was squished against the far wall. Christopher and Amanda sat side-by-side next to him.

"Don't be so defeatist, Matthew. I never fail in my tasks, no matter how hopeless they may appear."

"I say we just smash in, grab the dude and get out of this godforsaken town," Matthew added.

"Like the mess you made in the bar?" Amanda asked.

That brought a snicker from Christopher.

"What's with the wonder twins? Do they do anything other than hold hands and bust balls?"

Blackburn turned to face Matthew. "I said, we wait. Patience is a virtue. We will do this as a team. It is the key to success."

"What does this stoner bring to the table, other than making a mess?" Christopher poked back.

"Silence! The anguish of working with youth! Within the hour, we will have accomplished our mission. Besides, I have a contingency plan in place that far exceeds any of your capabilities."

Chapter Nine

The party was winding down. Kat collected her things, sitting down at the table with Colt and Johnny. She felt somewhat guilty about the overwhelming take from the tip jar, which totaled one hundred fifty-nine dollars and change. When Ms. April came over with an envelope containing the thirty-five dollars she negotiated for Ms. Ellis' service as tarot reader, Kat asked her to take it as a donation, but Ms. April wouldn't hear of it.

Emma walked over with her cassette case, plopping it down on the table. Between her impromptu disc jockeying, Bobby Onions became more and more scarce as the night went on, and with all the dancing, she was exhausted.

"We've got one more dance left for the night, folks. Grab your partner and head for the dance floor. This is *Everytime We Kiss* by the Donnybrooks," Bobby Onions announced.

Rhonda came over, dragging Emma with one hand, Jud with the other, out to the dance floor.

Colt stood, taking Kat's hand.

"But I can't dance," she said.

"But I can," he answered with a sly grin.

Kat submitted, and the two danced. Jud swayed to the music, embraced by both Emma and Rhonda. Rhonda leaned in, kissing Jud naturally. Kat watched; her pulse raced. Without warning, Rhonda lifted her head, winking at Emma. Quickly they traded places. Jud continued the kiss, but it was different, softer, not as forceful. He leaned into the kiss with more passion. Arms slid around his neck.

Kat moved Colt so his back was to the trio. *Oh…my…. God!* She mouthed the words but didn't dare speak them, afraid to draw his attention to her reaction. Jud opened his eyes slowly to see that it was Emma he was kissing. He stepped back in shock, wiping his mouth with the back of his hand.

"What the fuck?" he asked with total agitation.

Rhonda reached down, taking his hand coaxing him back into their little group.

"It's okay, really. We talked about it," Rhonda said, smiling.

"Talked about what? Pimping me out to your best friend?" Jud fired back.

"Our best friend," Rhonda replied.

Jud stormed off, which caught Colt's attention.

"What's that about?"

"Emma just made out with Jud," Kat blurted.

She didn't know why she did it, but she did. Maybe it was that she was jealous of Colt and Emma's relationship, if you could call it that. Or perhaps it was her own burning desire for Rhonda, which she was completely unaware of. Not that it mattered. She was married. Married to a man that she just tricked her inebriated husband to make out with. As if basic human relationships weren't complicated enough, this four-some was a soap opera.

"Wait! Jud!" Rhonda yelled before giving chase, leaving Emma standing alone on the dance floor.

Colt walked over to her while Kat held her ground. Now, how was this little gem going to play out?

Looking directly into his matching white eyes, Emma let out a deep breath.

"Think I really fucked up," she said.

"Ya' think? Sure opened a can of worms, Ms. Adams."

That's all he said as he took her hand, leading her back to the table.

126

Outside of the VFW, Post 1056, Rhonda Coulter Allen opened the door, greeted by the chilly night air. Jud stood on the curb, staring up into the moonless sky. Rhonda approached with a lack of her normal confident self. She too had consumed her fair share of alcohol, but it was that thing she said, "we talked about it." In his line of work, that's called premeditation. That's what it was.

She stepped next to her husband, sheepishly sliding her fingers into the palm of his hand. He pulled away from her, then spun to face her.

"How could you do that to me?" he asked with more anger than wonder.

"Do to you? I thought having two chicks was every man's fantasy?"

"Not this man!"

He paced in front of her. She knew the pacing well. It meant Jud's thoughts were ricocheting around his head faster than he could speak. It was his way of slowing everything down, keeping emotions to a minimum, and developing a solution to the quandary. Most times she respected his method as it kept the focus on the problem, not how either may have mishandled it. This was different. She mishandled it. She and Emma were alone in that. Rhonda almost wished he would just yell and scream at her, letting it all fly, picking up the pieces afterwards, but it was not Jud Allen's way.

"I don't get it. Don't you love me?" he asked.

She moved in to embrace him, but he stepped back as if she had a toxic, communicable disease.

"Of course I do, with all my heart. You should know this by now. I live and breathe for you," she answered.

"Then why would you share me?"

"Excuse me?"

"You heard me, Rhonda. Why would you share me?"

She said nothing. She had gravely miscalculated the action.

Jud continued. "You said on that rooftop so long ago that 'you choose me.' That changed my life. That very second, that very moment in time. We were each other's first. Throughout that fuckin' quarantine, all we talked about was making it official the second we got out. I gave every molecule of my heart to you, and I thought you did the same to me—"

"I did, sweetheart. I mean I do. Every molecule."

"Then how can you want to share me with anyone for any reason? I'd kill a man if he laid a finger on you. You're my everything. Don't you know how deeply this hurts me? You don't give a shit if I bang your best friend. It's your best friend, Rhonda! That make it exponentially worse."

Rhonda dropped her head, looking at her rippled reflection in a puddle in front of the curb. Tears dropped from her eyes, causing more ripples. If only the rain would pick up again to wash the regret down the drain with the rest of the debris that had collected from the street.

"I don't know what I was thinking, okay? I just thought it would be all right. It drives me crazy knowing Emma is getting old, never even kissed a man—"

"You know that's not true. Just because she can't remember kissing a man doesn't mean she hasn't. Billy at the fair, Josh at Homecoming, Nick during Kennywood. We're not talking about kissing here though, are we? What did you all plan? Spill it!"

Rhonda hesitated, knowing the answer very well. Her silence told him the answer.

"A threesome, huh? Or did you plan on just sitting out in the next room waiting your turn?"

"I can't believe you just said that to me."

"Exactly. Now you know how it feels." Jud paused, trying to get things back on track. Emotions had crept in which he never permitted when handling stress. "Look, that whole 'we talked about it' shit is all fine and well between you two. But I am the missing piece here. You understand? Our superpower is that we deal with everything together. Shit, neither you nor I have any clue if she and Colt are knockin' boots —"

"They aren't."

"So what? Don't think he has feelings for her, regardless of how he handles himself. Christ, Rhonda, he's over a hundred years old and despite her appearance, she's only twenty-two. Did you watch them dance? The guy was beyond happy."

"We just thought—"

"That's the problem, 'we just thought' but from where I'm standing, you did little thinking beyond Emma's sexual tension. And what is the cost of that?"

Jud was finished for the moment. He stopped pacing, just stretched his neck. This was probably the worst way to sober up in the history of humankind. Looking at Rhonda, he took both of her hands.

"What now?" she asked.

"Still some talking to do. I suppose all that time in dreamland, following each other around like lost puppies, fucked up our judgement a bit. You and I have some stuff to discuss. Let's just hope that stunt of yours hasn't scorched some earth in the Sturgess household."

"I'm so, so sorry. I love you so much. You're my everything."

She hugged him. This time, he responded.

Most of the people in the VFW were packing up cookies in Tupperware containers they had lugged along for the party. It was the Pennsylvania thing to do. Judging by the excitement displayed by Ms. April, Horace and other post members, it was a stellar event. Ms. April was offering paper bags for people to stack cookie containers in for the trip home. Bobby Onions had stopped by the table to thank Emma for her help. Soon after he left the table, Jud reentered through the front door. Emma suddenly had to use the lady's room. Rubbing the back of his neck, he walked up to Colt.

"Mr. Sturgess, hate to ask, but—"

Colt had already expected his question, tossing Jud the keys to the truck.

"Just bring her home in one piece. Ms. Rhonda and the truck both," he said, winking at the young Marine and deputy sheriff.

"Thanks, I owe you one."

"Nah, you don't. What friends are for."

Jud turned and left the way he came but stopped to face Sturgess again.

"Um, sorry about that, well, you know…"

"Unnecessary, Jud. Kids will be kids. Hope you patch things up with the missus, though."

He nodded, still embarrassed by the indiscretion to make eye contact with his host for the weekend. Continuing across the VFW, Jud Allen exited the front door.

"Ladies and gentlemen, Elvis has just left the building," Kat joked hoping to ease any lingering tensions.

Colt just shook his head. Whatever young people thought and did anymore was anyone's guess. Sure, Emma's actions upset him. Although they didn't share an intimate relationship, they shared a relationship built on trust. What propelled her into the action she took with Jud's own wife was a real head scratcher. If he didn't know any better, he would think she was in quarantine, suffering one of the strange side effects that appeared to plague all of them on arrival. The bigger fear within him, and he thought about it since Kat's outburst, she had grown beyond him. Grown outside of their property lines. "Can't put a butterfly back in its cocoon," his father used to say. This was something deep down that he wasn't quite ready to face. Maybe it was time.

Emma came out of the bathroom, stomping towards them in a huff.

"I don't know why he's so upset. Could have been a really great time," she said under her breath. She had forgotten about Colt's hyper-sensitive hearing.

Sitting down in one of the folding chairs, she crossed her legs, no longer feeling like a sexy pirate. She hesitantly looked around the table at the remaining members. Colt broke the ice with a smile. Emma's security blanket had departed. Until Friday, he was comfortable serving in that capacity, but things had changed.

"You know, I can't help if I never kissed a boy and wanted to know what it was like," she said.

"How do you know you haven't?" Kat asked.

"Haven't what?"

"Kissed a boy?"

"I think I'd remember that!"

"Maybe, maybe not. Your memory isn't exactly reliable," Kat said before dropping the subject.

Emma scratched the top of her head, pulling off the silk bandana. She caused a real mess with two relationships. There was no denying that or her part in it. Why she and Rhonda even entertained the idea seemed foolish now that it had blown up in her face. She could choose any of a million other men on the planet, but the discussion of time sold her on the idea. Not knowing when her next aging bout would come on, while she was still relatively young and pretty, the idea had appeal. Who would want to have sex with her if she woke up one morning old and haggard? To die a virgin, or at least she was pretty sure she still was. Emma lacked a memory marker for that, although she was certain that was something she would be hard pressed to forget. Why it was important now, only fate knew.

"Guess in my rush to grab a piece of my past, I may have fucked up my friend's relationship. I suck," she said.

Colt finally spoke up. "Don't be so hard on yourself. Problem with chasin' down old memories. You forget about makin' new ones."

"Yeah, I guess. You're not gonna shoot me now, are you?"

"Thought about it but may not believe it, little missy. You're my best friend and it'd be kinda sucky without you burning down my kitchen," Colt said.

At that very second, Johnny sprung to his feet. "We gotta go!"

"What is it, John Paul?" Kat asked.

"We just gotta go!" He ran out the front door.

Kat looked inquisitively at Colt, then at Emma.

"Where'd he get that burr in his saddle?" Emma asked.

Kat shrugged. The three rose, heading for the door. Kat and Emma hugged Ms. April and Horace before following Johnny out on to the street. He was nowhere to be found.

"John Paul Ellis! Where are you? Answer me right now," Kat called out to him.

Walking up the street a bit, Emma saw a figure move under the streetlight.

"Think he's up there," she pointed.

From behind them, Johnny appeared, running straight for Colt, grabbing his hand.

"C'mon, I gotta show you something," he said.

Kat yanked Colt's arm in the opposite direction. Looking at her, he saw something in her eyes he had never seen from Ms. Ellis. Disapproval.

Colt called out, "Right behind you, Johnny. I'll catch up."

Johnny continued running up the street towards a towering oak tree. Colt faced Kat.

"What is it, Kitty Kat?" he asked.

"Something's wrong. His desire to leave so suddenly, but the big thing, he grabbed your hand. Johnny doesn't touch people. Anybody. He's never even held my hand. Even under heavy duress, he doesn't touch," Kat answered.

"What's going on? Some sort of trap?"

"I don't know. Just be careful."

"What ya gonna do?" Emma asked.

"Only one thing to do," he said, "spring the trap."

Colt, Kat, and Emma followed Johnny. As they closed in on his last seen location, they noticed the oak tree, but more prominently, the black coach with a single horse parked beside it, just out of plain sight. The streetlight was being deflected by the oak, cloaking in the night shadow.

Within ten yards of the coach, Colt stopped. The door of the coach swung open. Christopher, Amanda, and Matthew stepped out. Matthew walked ahead of the group with more swagger. As he cleared the streetlight, he stopped.

"Shit," he said, seeing Emma walk up next to Colt.

"You again?" she laughed.

"This your boyfriend that you messed up my pine saplings with?" Colt asked.

"Yup," Emma said, cracking her knuckles. She struck a fighting pose.

"Look, we don't want any trouble. Come with us, Mr. Sturgess, and nobody gets hurt," Matthew said.

He was the last one of both groups looking for another confrontation. Colt looked at the three teens, assessing the threat levels. The two in the hoodies, he wasn't certain what fighting skills they possessed. If they chose the one Emma easily handled as the spokesperson, the threat level was nominal. From Emma and Rhonda's retelling of their encounter with the lead boy, he was harmless. Well, at least Emma could deal with those two. What troubled him was the fourth.

Blackburn was nowhere in sight. Everything in his body told him he was lurking somewhere close. Closing his eyes, Sturgess focused on his olfactory senses. Colt searched for the distinct odor he detected in the VFW when the man sat down. It cut through the smell of the cigarettes, food and even perspiration. It was musty with a sting of sulfur. The smell revealed itself, but only a trace. Blackburn was in the carriage.

"You youngsters run along. Nothin' but trouble here. I already told your boss no sale on his offer," Colt said.

Matthew chuckled as he resumed moving towards them.

"Old man, you overestimate your talents against the three of —"

"Enough!" Kat shouted.

Dropping her bag, she raised her hand. A row of swords shot up from the asphalt, spearing Matthew through both feet.

"Fuck!" he cried out.

Toppling backwards, Amanda and Christopher caught him before he hit the ground, which would have sliced both of his feet off. Through the wall of blades, Matthew's supports locked hands.

"Whoa! How'd you do that?" Emma asked Kat in amazement.

Kat didn't answer, merely kept her hand steady, staring at the haphazard attempt to take Colt. She had fire in her eyes. Black mist

133

poured out from Amanda and Christopher, creeping towards Sturgess. Faster than the air could carry the deadly mist, it penetrated the obstacles, entering Colt's mouth. He choked, then coughed, expelling the mist from his nose. It retreated into the two youths, who shrieked in agony, grabbing their heads. They dropped to the ground. Matthew swung his arms around desperately in a wide circle to stay on his feet.

"Stop! You're hurting my friends!" Johnny yelled, grabbing Kat's arm.

The sword wall disappeared as quickly as it appeared. Emma leaped forward, grabbing Matthew with one hand, planting a firm fist on his kisser with the other. His body slammed back into the carriage with such force, the horse reacted with a snort, head and tail in a high position. The attackers didn't matter to Sturgess, but he didn't want the horse spooked. He used his speed to close the distance between Amanda and Christopher. The two dematerialized into thin air, then popped back in through billows of mist. Whoever they were, they were faster than Colt.

Moving to the right and left to him in a wildly choreographed fight sequence, they landed blow after blow on Sturgess. He had felt worse, even with the accelerated force, but he had to stop the assault, fearing it would turn on Emma, Kat, and Johnny next. Feigning injury, he hit the ground rolling toward the carriage, more specifically, the horse. In one super-speed motion, he mounted it, removing one rein from the bridle. Returning to the street, he waited for the two to materialize again. Kat watched curiously.

Emma's question to her was a good one. Not even Kat Ellis knew how she had summoned the sword wall. She reacted with a fleeting thought to protect the king of swords. Then they burst out. By the looks of the blood spouting from Matthew's feet, it was more than an illusion. They were as real as the dent in the side of the carriage his body made on impact following Emma's blow. She concentrated again, but nothing manifested.

Amanda took form first. With a spin, Colt began whirling the reign firmly in his fist in a vertical motion similar to the blades of a helicopter. She screeched an unearthly sound, reaching in the darkness for her companion. The audible cry for help was too late. As Christopher formed from the mist, he was caught up in the cyclone of wind scattering her into the night. His hand rematerialized, reaching for hers. Before they could interlock fingers, Colt's makeshift propeller dissipated both into the darkness of night.

Sturgess continued the whirlwind until he no longer sensed either of them. He held the reign firmly as he and Emma approached Matthew. Kat stayed back, holding Johnny. She had no idea what had gotten in him, particularly why he lured them all to this carriage. Those questions would have to wait until later. Colt loomed over Matthew, who was currently crying in pain, holding onto both of his feet. They were still attached. Thank goodness for minor miracles.

Colt tapped on the side of the carriage.

"You can come out now, Mr. Blackburn, or not. Prefer you just haul ass out of Dodge the way you came," he said.

The door of the carriage creaked open from the opposite side. Springing up a bit as the lone occupant exited, he wondered if there were more, as Blackburn was a slight man. Whoever just exited was considerably heavier by the reaction of the coach. Heavy footsteps rounded the back of the black painted carriage with a tinted front window. Clearing the back, Kat saw it first, letting out a gasp. Colt swung in that direction to see what caused her reaction.

Standing ten yards away was what could best be described as a living gargoyle: red glowing eyes, mottled skin, huge fangs. It smiled at them. Emma stepped behind Colt. The boy she could handle confidently. This thing, however, was a different story.

"I asked kindly, Mr. Sturgess, for your consideration. Now you leave me no choice," it said.

It was Blackburn's voice, but deeper, with a slight echo. He spread his wings, which were initially hidden by the shadow of the carriage. Colt moved Emma completely behind him.

Matthew laughed from his position, leaning against the carriage. "You're all screwed now!"

"Kitty Kat, take John Paul outta here, back to the car," he said.

"Not, so fast, Kitty Kat. What a charming name. John Paul and I have work to do, don't we Johnny?" it asked.

Johnny broke free from Kat's hold, running over to Blackburn. He pulled down his black devil mask, crossing his arms. Looking at the two, Colt realized what the mask was all about. Somehow, in some way, Blackburn, or whatever he was, controlled Johnny. But for how long?

Each of them had broken the strange spell from quarantine, except Johnny. Because he hid behind the mask and generally wasn't talkative, it was difficult to tell how he was affected. Not understanding all of it, the influence was suddenly clear.

"John Paul, step away from him," Colt said.

"No!" Johnny yelled defiantly. "Why should I listen to you? You left us three times. Everybody leaves me!"

"Johnny, he's using you! Wake up," Kat implored him.

"You shut up too. All you do is talk to me like a little kid," Johnny shouted back at his sister.

Kat cried, wishing with all of her heart that she could pull her little sword trick to help her brother, but it just wasn't happening.

"Shit," Colt murmured.

Thinking back on Johnny's actions in McNaulty's, Sturgess rushed Blackburn, lashing the reign around his throat, tumbling to the pavement. The thing took flight, but Colt reared back on the thing's head with the leather strap, causing it to spiral downward. That gave Kat and Emma enough time to seize Johnny, dragging him under the oak tree. Even with his strength fighting them off, he was no match for Emma.

Colt and Blackburn crashed into the grass of one yard facing the street. Continuing his assault, Colt swung Blackburn by one of his wings, propelling him into a utility pole, center mass, causing it to splinter. It collapsed on Blackburn in a shower of sparks from the mounted transformers.

Moving at top speed, he grabbed Emma, Johnny, and Kat, toppling them into the grass across the street. The large puddle the thing landed in was a potentially deadly electrical field. Hopefully, it was enough to keep Blackburn down for the count.

Throughout the neighborhood, lights flickered, then died all the way out up the block. The commotion drew a few Apollo residents out onto their porches to see the origin of the disturbance. Slowly the splintered utility pole trembled, then rolled over like an inconvenient log. The Blackburn gargoyle, or whatever he was, flapped its wings, slowly rising into the air. He shook his head, regaining its bearing, drifting towards the group of attackers. Colt braced for round two of the battle.

Without warning, a blast came from behind the group, then another. Blackburn howled in pain before one last ditch effort. It dove in towards Johnny, who was standing with outstretched arms. The creature grabbed him, flying off into the night, silhouetted by the light half of the half quarter phase moon that peaked out from the clouds. Colt spun around to see the source of the blast. There stood Horace Winston, reloading his shotgun. Sturgess placed his hand on the salty veteran's firearm.

"Hold up, old timer. He's got the boy," Colt said.

Horace nodded his head, then spit tobacco on the ground. "Fuckin' vampires."

Kat grabbed Colt's hand frantically. "We gotta do something! Chase after him or something."

Colt took off his hat, pondering the next course of action.

"Don't know where he's headin', Kat?"

She looked around for anything that may help. That's when she spied his mask on the street. Starting towards it, Emma grabbed her arm.

"Electricity. Remember?"

Kat pointed at the horse, which was still fine, standing on all fours. Emma released her. Picking up Johnny's devil mask, she felt the slimy tendrils covering it she previously thought she imagined. Kat closed her eyes, concentrating on her brother. Colt moved to her side.

"I see the air. They're still flying, but lower. The thing is hurt. Only one of its wings is flapping. It's following railroad tracks, but it's

137

dark, no details. I don't know how I know, but they're heading south. Dammit, dark again," Kat said with a measure of disappointment mixed with frustration. "Colt, help him!"

"I will, Kitty Kat. Promise."

"How might you be doing that?" Emma chimed in.

"He wants me. That's what this is all about," he answered.

"Um, over my dead body," she said.

Colt grunted, walking over to Mathew, who had finally shut his snarky mouth. Lifting him up from the ground, he held him by his hoody, pulling the drawstring around his face.

"Dude, really? Like your little team hasn't beat my ass enough?" he said.

"Where they headin'?" Colt asked. "I won't ask twice."

"Second time I heard that today. Look, I don't know, man. They didn't tell me anything. Blackburn's an independent operation. Don't say shit about the job other than the target."

"And what might your particular skills be, other than you seem to take quite an ass whoopin'?"

"I don't know. Seriously, bro. I was like those soul suckers you churned up, but we don't stay that way long. There's a next step. That's what Blackburn was gonna do, train me. I wasn't even getting paid. True deal. All I know is that my bones are rock solid. Your girl can give me black eyes, a busted lip and shoot fuckin' swords through my feet, but inside, I'm all good."

"Let's test that theory out," Emma said, grabbing Matthew from Colt's grip, tearing his sweatshirt.

She tossed him across the street into the large puddle where the transformer continued to spark. Matthew, who was so gleeful moments ago, convulsed atop the 200 kilovolt-amperes rain puddle. His screams cried out, ignored while the conversation continued.

"Boys right," Horace said. "We had a problem with their kind a few years back. Believe it was '68. They took up residence in the Kohlerload Mine. Soul suckers, that group was. Suck the life right outta ya, down to the marrow. Bones so brittle, even trying to move the dearly departed, caused the limbs to snap right off. Skin as dry as sandpaper."

"How did you deal with them? Think they're back in that mine?" Kat asked.

"Me and the boys formed a posse. Smoked 'em out. All that stake through the heart, garlic mumbo-jumbo you see on the late-late show, all nonsense. Nothing like a good twelve gauge. If you think they're headed south, darlin', sorry. Wrong way, but we'll check it out, just to make sure. Only one problem, that one was an ancient. Haven't run across one of those before. Not sure how to bring those down," he answered.

Up the street, a group of men approached. Horace stepped out to address them.

"Listen up, boys. Couple of vampires hit our visitors just now. Grab your arsenals. I'll load up my truck with extra gas I have for the genny. Meet back at the Post in fifteen minutes. Gonna take a ride up to Kohlerload to make sure they haven't come back. Mel, call the power company. Tell them some yahoos hit and run the phone pole and the transformers down. That'll get a service man out here asap. You all have your orders. Move out!"

Horace turned to Colt, pointing at Matthew, who was still making quite a ruckus. "What ya gonna do with that one?"

He looked over to see Emma standing ten feet away, throwing rocks at the boy.

"Emma, knock that off. Still may need him," Colt said.

Horace saluted, then wandered back down Hunter's Way towards the VFW. Colt made a mad dash, pulling Matthew out of the puddle without too much of a jolt to himself. Tossing him into the carriage, he turned his attention to Kat.

"Gotta ask, how'd you do that thing with the swords? I assume that was you?"

"Honestly, no idea," she answered.

"And the visions of them flying? Connection with Johnny?"

139

Still holding the mask in her hands, she showed it to Colt. He inspected it.

"What's this goo all over it?"

"So, you see it too? Thank goddess, thought I was going crazy!"

"Think this has something to do with it?"

"I wish I knew. Seems like stuff's happening to me I can't explain. Pretty sure it has something to do with those shadow people, though. Maybe how they controlled him?"

"Shadow people?" Emma asked.

"Yeah, I can show you in my binder."

Kat reached into her bag. Colt stopped her.

"Let's get you and this boy back to the homestead. Could use a professional investigator's eyes on this too. Maybe Jud's back. Streets ain't safe. Rather regroup at the homestead before I charge into somethin' I'm not real knowledgeable about," he said.

"Still think you're going to just up and surrender to them, then they'll hand Johnny over?" Emma asked sarcastically.

"Didn't say that. Need to game plan is all. More we know, the more we know," he answered.

"Well, that's pretty sagely, oh wise one," she said.

"What's gonna happen now? You two drive back in Kat's car. I'm gonna drive this here carriage back. When we get home, I wanna hear more about this mask and these shadow people. Jud can give this coach the once over," Colt said.

"What about me?" Emma asked.

"The boy's all yours. I'm sure once he comes to and stops droolin' foam, he might be more cooperative," he answered.

"Yes!" Emma said, pumping her fist in the air.

Colt grabbed Kat's arm gently. "Trust me, I'll do everything I can, but we'll knock all our noggins to do it. Won't be like Kinston. I ain't going anywhere."

She hugged him. Both she and Emma retrieved their belongings before heading back to the car. Colt climbed into the carriage. The tinted glass made seeing in the dark near impossible, even for his enhanced vision. With a stiff kick, he popped it out, retrieved it, tossing it in the back with Matthew. Reattaching the reign, he turned the horse away from the electrical disturbance, heading down Hunter's Way.

As he reached the corner facing VFW Post 1056, he saw Horace barking commands to his new posse. He would check in with them at first light. Kat and Emma pulled out as he followed behind in the carriage. Eventually, the speed of the car far exceeded that of the carriage. On the ride home, he remembered Johnny disassembling the Ferris wheel in Kinston.

"Damned shame," he whispered.

FRED TERLING

Chapter Ten

There's a reason people move into the deep pines of the mountains. They seek isolation. Isolation from the world, people, the chaos that is the infectious nature of humanity. Seeking solitude, many find something they searched for most of their lives…themselves. When Colt Sturgess first purchased his plot of land, all those considerations were a factor. Nearby, Apollo provided the occasional solace of basic human contact, but only when he chose it. Nobody came out to his homestead. Ever. Even his mail was delivered to a post office box in Apollo that he or Emma would retrieve twice weekly. It was their life. A welcome one following his encounter with Olath, his final farewell to Lizzy. Although he had built the cabin years prior, not expecting how events would unfold once he extinguished his rage, for the past five years, it was nirvana. Now, someone or something threatened that peace. For many, that was a justifiable reason to go to war. War to secure peace. That too was the way of man. Inexplicably, that irony suddenly tainted the soil of the Sturgess homestead.

Kat and Emma arrived from town first. Practically leaping out of the car, the two approached the cabin, Kat rushing in with her backpack. Emma sauntered behind after seeing Jud and Rhonda sitting on the porch swing by candlelight.

"Awkward," she whispered under her breath.

She had no distraction to pretend she didn't see them. What would she say? Was an apology in order or would she be impinging on their quiet time? The last thing she wanted to do was fan the coals if the two of them had slapped a bandage on the wound she played a part in inflicting.

Emma stuffed her hands in the pocket of Colt's duster he supplied before they ran off, as if that would provide a cloak of invisibility.

Reaching the first step, she glanced at them for only a second, but it was long enough to see both of them looking back at her. Time to take her medicine.

"Hey, um. For what it's worth, sorry, Jud. I can really fart out some bonehead ideas sometimes, ya know?" she said.

"Not entirely your bad, Emma. You had a dance partner on this one. It's all good. Don't want to get preachy and if I had a dime for every time I stepped in it with good intentions, we'd be rich right now," Jud answered.

She thought about saying more, but "shut up, Emma Adams" sounded off prominently in her head. Even discussing what had just happened in Apollo was something she didn't want to mention.

"Where's Colt?" Rhonda asked.

"Best if he fills you in on all of that when he gets here," she answered, promptly passing through the screen door into the cabin.

Entering the dining area, she found Kat thumbing through her binder, searching for something. Emma went over to the refrigerator, taking out a beer, then sitting down across from her.

"Doing some kind of homework?" she asked.

Kat's attention was so focused on the pages, she barely noticed Emma.

"What?" Kat responded.

"I asked if you were doing some kind of homework?"

"In a way. Signed up for this monthly newsletter a couple of years ago on cryptids."

"Is that a bug?"

"No. It's unexplained creatures that have been sighted. Like Bigfoot, Yeti, Werewolves, the Mothman, that kind of stuff. Mostly humanoid. Only a dollar a year, pretty good deal. Not saying I believe in all of them, but after you know what, my curiosity went into overdrive. Couldn't get enough of the stuff," Kat answered.

"Cool," Emma said, leaving her seat, scooting into the one next to Kat. Together, they leafed through the pages one by one.

"What are we looking for?" Emma asked.

"Shadow people. Strange humanoids that appear mostly at night. Ask for a ride or knock on your door asking to come in. Not a lot is known about them, but I remember reading about it in one newsletter."

"You keep them all together?"

"Yeah. Three-hole punch them and stick them in. I used to do the bookkeeping for my Aunt Rosie's business. Much more organized with that than my stuff, obviously."

Emma laughed. "I feel you."

"This is a bit of a clusterfuck. Knew I should have index tabbed these by name, but the newsletters only have a paragraph or two on each monster, so picking which one would only confuse any system I would have come up with. No excuse but going through it now trying to find stuff is a mess."

Emma sat back. "There a story about you?"

The question caught Kat off guard. "Pardon?"

"Are you in there? Like, the matron of sword summoning or something?" Emma asked.

Kat chuckled. "No, first time I did that. Still don't know how. If I did, that gargoyle wouldn't have taken Johnny."

"About that. How are you being so calm? I mean, I would lose my shit."

Kat stopped with the notebook, crossing her arms, thinking about that question. She didn't answer until she had an answer, reminiscent of her brother.

"I've been through a lot. It's like a boxer, you know. Get knocked down, get back up. First my dad, then my mom flaking out. Finally got settled with my Aunt Rosie and Uncle Mike, only to see her head lopped off by one of those big ash tokers. I grieve, of course, eventually. Think about them all the time too, but at this point I'm a little numb. Plus, I trust Colt."

"Good answer," Emma said, raising up her beer before taking another draw. "Be right back. Going to shed my pirate garb and hop in my jammies."

Kat returned to the binder. Several more pages in, she found what she sought. Popping open the spine of the binder, she removed the page, studying it carefully to see if it contained any more information than what she shared earlier about the shadow people.

Outside, the dark carriage finally arrived. Colt steered the horse directly in front of the cabin before exiting the vehicle, then securing the reins to the banister railing of the porch. Jud and Rhonda both stood up walking over to him.

"Just the man I was looking for," Colt said.

"Me?" Jud asked.

"Yes, sir. Need you to take a good look inside this thing. See if you find any clues."

"Clues for what, Mr. Sturgess?"

"Damned if I know. Big ugly, except with wings, not as ugly as the thing we faced in Kinston, flew off with Johnny tonight after we left the party."

Rhonda gasped. "Are you kidding me?"

"Unfortunately, darlin' I'm not. Creature had two forms. One went by the name of Kaleb Blackburn. Your police department might have some sort of record on him. Turned into a gargoyle after that. Like the ones on church roofs or those creature features of yours. Had a couple of kids with him, but they're gone. Well, except for one."

Colt walked over to the door side of the carriage, the one without the huge dent, reached inside, dragging Matthew out, depositing him on the wet grass.

"What's wrong with you people?" Matthew grunted.

"Who's this?" Jud asked.

"This is the —"

Rhonda stepped forward, completing Colt's answer. "The boy who Emma beat the shit out of in the woods!"

She raised her fist to him. Matthew scooted back in fear.

"Whoa, man! What the fuck kinda thing you got going on here? Angry women who hulk out, one who shoots swords out of her hands, an old man with bionic speed. What do you do, bro? I don't even want to know." Matthew held up his hand in defense.

Jud smiled. "I'm worse than all of them. I'm a United States Marine. You cross me, what the rest of them did to you will seem like a picnic."

Colt walked over to Matthew, lifting him up, slinging him over his shoulder.

"Like I said, not sure what I'm looking for. Anything that might be a clue. Sorry, ma'am, if I'm interrupting your evening. Kind of important. No clue where Johnny is. Even the smallest thing can be important," Colt said.

"On it, Mr. Sturgess," Jud said.

"Can I help?" Rhonda asked her husband.

He smiled. "Sure. Oh, Mr. Sturgess. Would really help if I had a flashlight."

"Junk drawer. Top drawer to the right of the sink. If it's not there, try the cupboard next to the candles. One or the other, I forgot where I put it after the last thunderstorm."

Rhonda ran into the house in search of the flashlight. She said "hi" to Kat as she passed her, then rummaged through the drawer until she located the flashlight. Not that she attempted playing subservient wife to make amends. Jud said their strength was together they made an unstoppable team. Even in the group of people with extraordinary abilities, the two of them were merely mortal. Yet side-by-side, they dispatched tens of thousands of ash tokers alongside an elite fighting team of seasoned hardcore soldiers. If a discovery awaited in that ugly carriage of death, the two of them would find it. Together.

Colt wandered down to the barn, opening the lock, flicking the power switch, and moved to the stall with the work materials. Matthew didn't make a sound slung over his shoulder. Whatever happened next, he probably would not like it. Pulling out a spool of baling wire and cutters, Sturgess returned the way he came, walking out to the backside of the barn. He flung Matthew onto the ground, then cut a length of wire from the spool.

"Aw man, what you gonna do with that?"

"Ever heard of being hogtied?" Colt asked with a mischievous grin.

"Dude, seriously?"

"As a heart attack."

Sturgess was only joking. He dragged the young man over to a fence post, securing his wrists with the wire.

"Wait, you're not gonna leave me out here, are you? Me and the sun don't exactly get along for too long," Matthew said.

"You don't say?" Colt asked.

Tugging on what remained of his three-quarter burnt sweatshirt and pants, Sturgess tore them off.

"Bro! You just can't leave me out here in my skivvies. There are ladies present."

"Imagine that," Sturgess said. "I guess you have until sunup for a real quick memory recall or your little pecker might just shrivel up like a breakfast sausage. Sleep tight. Oh, and one more thing, sport. Wouldn't try twistin' free from that wire or you might just find your hands on the ground."

Colt walked back to the barn, securing it before heading into the cabin. He found Kat disappointed at the kitchen table with several pages of her binder spread out in front of her. Emma sat beside her, reading a random page.

"This stuff is so cool! Did you ever hear of the skunk ape? First spotted in Apalachicola, Florida in 1811. I had no clue all these

148

different creatures existed. Well, maybe I did, but it's kind of cool relearning about them if I didn't. I mean did. Whatever," Emma said enthusiastically.

Kat obviously did not share in the excitement. The information she was looking for, she had come up short finding. Her body language telegraphed that.

"No luck, Kitty Kat?" Colt asked.

"Found the pages on the shadow people, energy vampires and wendigos, but just basic information that anyone could make up. Was hoping might be something in here to help. Guess I'm just grasping at straws," Kat answered in defeat.

Colt grunted, taking his hat off, setting it on the table beside her.

"I've got Jud and Rhonda searching the inside of the carriage, and our hostage out back is human bait, although he doesn't know it. Tied him up to a pole out back where the wind's blowin' south. He and his buddies, including Blackburn, all give off a strong whiff of sulfur. He comes back lookin' for him. I'll be waiting. First light, I'll check in with Horace at the VFW to see if they flushed anything out of the mines. Doin' all we can at the moment. Get some rest. Long day tomorrow," Colt said, attempting to reassure her.

Kat nodded, gathering all her papers together, stuffing them back into the binder, except for the one Emma was reading about the Canadian lake monster, Ogopogo.

"You can keep reading, just didn't want to be messy," Kat said to her.

Emma forced a smile, a bit distracted. She suddenly tuned in on Jud and Rhonda enjoying their search of the carriage together. What was that like? Sharing time with someone, even crawling around the floor of an eight-foot wagon, was enjoyable. She decided there was no longer any appeal in sea serpents, but back to her two friends. A twinge of jealousy sparked.

Until two hours ago, she and Rhonda were inseparable. Now she was back to her man. Emma felt outside, looking in. Why was that? Is this how relationships work? Then the kiss happened. What should have been a night to remember was suddenly a scarlet letter with her holding the needle and thread. The worst part, she apologized, carrying the bulk of the guilt. Finally, her tiptoeing into her own house, only to be forgiven by the object of her desire. Angst was quickly morphing into anger.

"You goin' to bed, Emma?" Colt interrupted her thoughts.

"Nah, think I'll stay up a while. Decent night. May just hang out on the porch. See what Jud turns up," she said.

"Mm, hm," Colt said with trepidation. "Just behave."

"Don't need to tell me twice," she said.

"I'm gonna wander the property line, just in case I get a nibble on my bait," he said, putting his hat back on.

"Sounds like a plan."

The moment Colt departed, Emma sashayed out to the porch, eavesdropping on the inside of the carriage.

Jud and Rhonda finished the inside of the carriage as best they could by flashlight. Daylight would provide a better examination. They also lacked adequate fingerprint gathering tools. Jud cautioned Rhonda not to touch anything where the previous passengers may have touched with their hands. She had the idea of using a makeup brush and powder when they returned in full sunlight to dust. It was a solid idea. They were sure Colt had some scotch tape somewhere to lift prints. He seemed to have everything else out in his barn. Deciding to call it a night, they passed Emma on the porch.

"Heading to bed. You up for the night?" Rhonda asked.

Emma took a large swig of her beer, then burped loudly. "Yup. Waiting for Colt to come back from his midnight stroll."

"Okay, well goodnight. Love you," Rhonda said, smiling.

"Yup. Tootles," Emma responded.

Jud said nothing, just followed Rhonda inside hand-in-hand. Emma waited for a few minutes before grabbing another beer. She decided that the rest of the six-pack was in order, three were left. Grabbing the yoke, she returned to the porch. Opening a fresh beer, Emma wandered out into the yard, leaving two unopened on the top step. There was frustration simmering in her. Inside of her, it felt as though something was trying to burst through her skin fueled by anger or was it disappointment fueling the anger?

Emma chugged the beer, then crushed the can, hurling it with all her strength into the pines. Tears streamed down her face. A voice came from behind her.

"You know I hate litter," Colt said.

Emma spun around to face him.

She hugged him, breaking down, letting the tears flow freely. "Oh, Colt."

He squeezed her tight. Her sorrow broke him. It was the first time he had been exposed to it. An instant melancholy washed over anyone who watched a person they considered a pillar of strength crumble. Emma Adams was strong, sarcastic, funny, patient, many things he was not. She'd been there for him, even saved his life. They built a life together, but she needed more. Inevitably, this day would come. Sturgess reflected on this earlier, but in her present state, it was clear the time was now. *Can't put a butterfly back in its cocoon.*

He led her back to the porch, reaching down for one of the remaining beers. Guiding her to sit next to him, Colt sat down. Emma spilled out her innermost traumas.

"It's just so unfair. Everyone gets to have a life. Mine was stolen by those fuckers. Inside I'm twenty-two, the outside just keeps aging. I'll die of premature old age before I even experience the things most people take for granted. Just once, I'd like to take an airplane trip somewhere, lay on the beach, watch a sunset without the thought of *will this be my last,* creeping in. I wanna learn how to cook, she chuckled. Maybe even have kids, raise a family. Fuck, Colt, I just wanna go out to a party with friends like tonight without botching it because I've lived enough experiences and made enough new memories that I know better than to consider sleeping with my friend's husband because she wants to offer him up as a pity poke!"

Colt inhaled deeply. The "pity poke" comment made him grin, but that was Emma, cracking a well-timed joke even in the maelstrom of sorrow. He glanced over at her. She looked even older than she had an hour ago. Not from aging externally, but from the beating she was taking inside. The two had discussed a solution, but it was potentially lethal. The possibility that Lizzy was so excited about, but never afforded the opportunity to try. Not by Olath's hand as planned.

"What ya wanna do, Emma? I love you dearly. More than a caretaker or partner. If our contingency plan is on your mind, I guess—"

"I don't know, and I love you too. With all my heart, I just need more. And I appreciate your maintaining respect for me. Although I joke, it probably would be weird if you and I flitted around her like Jud and Rhonda. I know I'm a pain in the ass and I'm hardheaded, but this time I really need that Colt Sturgess guidance like everyone else seems to rely on."

Colt swallowed down his last gulp of beer. "Knew this day would come. It's saying goodbye. That's the hardest part, kiddo. I've come to rely on seeing you every morning. Closing my eyes, knowing you'll be here the next morning. But I can't watch you in pain like a trapped animal either."

"Don't say that. It will never be 'goodbye.' I'll always be around. Just think, this weekend was meant for a purpose. I didn't know anyone I knew survived that town, yet alone two of my best friends. Maybe even one day, Jud and I can watch old monster movies together without the weirdness. There are so many parts of me I can feel sometimes, then they drift away. If I can really start over and truly put the past behind me..."

Colt rose slowly, taking her hand. "This could kill you, or worse."

"I know, but I'm already dying, except slower."

He nodded, leading her to the barn. Once inside, he drug two stools from the workbench to the center of the floor. Colt retrieved a piece of garden hose, cutting off a section, discarding the rest. Emma went to the corner of the barn where a small cover sat. Removing it revealed a trunk. She carried it over, placing it between the two stools. Sturgess joined her, sitting down, then opened the trunk. Inside were four sterile, sealed eighteen-gauge intravenous catheters. Jud was right, he had everything. These came courtesy of Emma's nimble fingers on visiting Ms. April in the hospital for her gall bladder surgery. She stole them for this very purpose. When she first suggested the idea to Colt, he quickly dismissed the ask as too dangerous, reflecting on what had happened to Lizzy. That wasn't his doing, however.

Colt handed her the piece of garden hose.

"What's this for?" she asked.

"Put it in your teeth and bite down on it. Not sure what this is actually going to do. My blood sometimes burst Olath's critters into flames. You were an experiment, so you're like me, one of a kind. No tellin' what's gonna happen," he answered.

Emma placed the piece of hose in her mouth, biting down on it. Colt tore open one of the four bags, removing the contents. He scooted closer to her, removing the safety caps from the needles.

Exhaling, he looked into her white eyes, possibly for the last time. "You sure?"

She nodded slowly, wiping away the last vestige of tears.

"Love you, kiddo," he said with tears in his eyes, which triggered hers all over again.

Emma leaned in for a hug, then sat back, wiping the tears from her own white eyes. He inserted the needle into his arm, then hers. In the tube between them, the blood slowly crept towards each other. They had been intermixed for the past five years; the next three seconds would wipe that all away. Colt Sturgess was letting go. Emma had a full life ahead of her, with a little luck. He, however, had chosen the ultimate sacrifice, returning to the solitude he had known for the past one hundred seven years.

Much like the two paths emerged in the fire of Chooch Family Farm and Dairy, Colt's blood surged in a spate of fire within Emma once the two met in the cold plastic medical tubing linking them beneath the stained glass on the barn's roof she helped him assemble. Her head shot back as the heat surged through her arteries, veins, and capillaries. She bit down hard on the hose, nearly biting it in half. The pain was unbearable. Emma's breathing became forced, like she had to remember to breathe, or she would suffocate. Her mind raced, dropping in and out of consciousness. Forcing her eyes open, she panicked at the sight.

Colt's concern was always Emma's safety with this completely unscientific, untested, hairbrained idea of theirs. It wasn't just Emma's idea; the thought had crossed his mind many times as well. If he could bring Lizzy back from the brink of death, more recently, cure Kat of the elixir's infection, could it restore Emma? Those were mere drops of blood; however, this was a full-blown transfusion. Through her clouded vision, it was he who she witnessed as the one in danger. Grave danger.

What Emma saw was Colt's ashen pale face, body slumped forward on the stool. His weight carried him slowly forward, crashing to the floor of the barn, dead center of the beautiful colors streaming down through the stained-glass mosaic on the roof. His ultimate tribute to a life he abandoned on that small farm outside of Carson City. Emma yanked the needle from her arm, kneeling to remove his as well. Blood streamed down her forearm, squirting from his. Pulling the needles from the ends of the tube, she wrapped one end around his bicep tightly to stop the bleeding. She made a mad dash to the barn stall with all the construction supplies. Grabbing a roll of duct tape and a piece of cloth, she returned to his side, crafting a makeshift bandage. It was less than hygienic, but bleeding out took precedent to infection. Not that his healing properties wouldn't destroy any germs that made the mistake of wandering into him.

Once he was tended to, she wiped the blood from her arm to repeat the triage. It was unnecessary. Her wound had already been sealed. Returning to Colt, she lifted his head. His eyes rolled back, unresponsive. She felt for a pulse. It was faint and very shallow. Sturgess' skin was cold to the touch. She began crying hysterically, rocking him in her arms.

"What have I done? Why? Oh, why?" she cried out to the sky.

Not that she believed in a higher power. How could something exist that brought forth such horrors as Olath, his creature making factory, limb harvesting and any of a thousand other blights on humanity that occurred daily? In times of extreme duress, however, for some primal instinct, people sought divine guidance. If this were the Emma Adams of thirty minutes ago, she would have laughed, making a comment about the false hope of desperation.

Colt shivered beneath her arms. He was going into shock. That was something she remembered. With ease, she picked him up running towards the cabin. Clearing the barn door, she stumbled, both of them rolling across the wet grass. Emma was moving much faster than before, although she didn't realize it in her current predicament. She wrote it off as clumsiness. Picking up Sturgess once more, she entered the cabin, hoping everyone had retired for the night. How she would explain this would have to wait. For now, getting him into bed with extra blankets was the primary task.

Inside the home they worked on together, she crept up the stairs to the master bedroom. She placed Colt on the bed, pulling back the sheets and top quilt. Tearing his bloody shirt off, removing his boots, she tucked him in. Retrieving more blankets from the chest at the foot of the bed, she piled them on. Emma climbed into bed, holding his head once more, brushing his hair with her fingers.

He'll heal from this. He always heals himself up, she thought. This was different, though. It was a little stick of a needle, nothing more. It was the co-mingling of the blood that had done this. All the time they worried about the potential effect of his on her, when it was she who carried the poison. Maybe water and meat would work again? It did at Delaney's funeral home. Gently, she laid his head on the pillows.

Down the steps to the kitchen she tiptoed, careful not to draw any attention, not noticing that her fuzzy pink pajamas were heavily stained with blood as well. Thankfully, she didn't have to thaw out raw hamburger or cook. There were still plenty of leftovers from the cookout. She grabbed one of the grilled steaks from the refrigerator, dumping out the pitcher of lemonade, filling it with water. Grabbing a knife from the block, she began slicing the steak in small pieces. Cutting so quickly, she nearly sliced one of her fingers off. This time, she noticed the speed increase. She frowned. That was unexpected.

Emma retrieved the pitcher of water, a plate of sliced up steak, and a kitchen towel. Back up the stairs to their bedroom she went. She approached him in fear of what she would find. His skin was still pale, but his breathing was visibly steady. Picking up the chair from her vanity, she sat down beside him, trying to get him to eat. He was completely unresponsive. Emma placed the water and steak on the floor next to the bed.

"Wake up, Colt! I need you! What am I supposed to do without you?"

She climbed into bed, putting his arm around her. Emma laid her head on his chest, listening to the barely audible heartbeat. Eventually, the receding adrenaline rush pulled her into slumber.

Jud was the first one awake the next morning. He had the plate number of the carriage and a name. It was only 9:00 am. Coffee first, then he would call Sheriff Dockerty with what he had gathered so far with an update. The flying gargoyle would be left out of the discussion. Following the call, he would test Rhonda's idea with the makeup brush and powder. The full sunlight would also help with a reexamination of the inside of the carriage. One thing that puzzled Deputy Allen was how to access the storage area. Those carriages were used by the Pennsylvania Dutch to take goods to market. There was a bench for passengers also, but always had space for goods.

Approaching the phone, he removed a business card from his wallet. It read "John Dockerty, Sheriff, Biggs County Sheriff's Department" with the number and address. On the other side of the card was Dockerty's home phone. It was Sunday morning. He hoped he could catch him before church. Picking up the phone, he dialed zero as Colt instructed him on the previous call, giving the operator the number. The phone on the receiving end rang.

Rhonda stretched, yawning, as she walked up behind him. Following the scene at the VFW, they drove around a bit, talking more. A few ground rules were put in place by both with a renewed commitment to always discuss any issues, no matter how off the wall, first before taking any action. Both had wounded hearts, typical of the day after a major fight, but this relationship was strong enough that eggshells would not be a distraction. She snuggled Jud from behind, hugging him while he awaited the phone to be answered. He smiled at her, mouthing the words, "good morning." Rhonda kissed his cheek.

"Mrs. Dockerty, good morning. It's Jud Allen. Yeah, I'm fine. The mountains are majestic. I hear you; you sound like your husband. He's always telling me how I need to take a few days off. Speaking of which, is he around? I have some news on a case. Sure, I'll hold on."

Jud raised his eyebrows at Rhonda, making a motion with his hand that he needed a pen. She ran over to the table where Kat's binder sat. Next to it was a pouch of pens and pencils. Retrieving one, she walked back to Jud, handing it to him. He held up the paper that he had written on, both the name Kaleb Blackburn and the license plate number from the coach. Sheriff Dockerty finally answered. Deputy Allen began his update.

"Hey, Chief, may have a break in that case. I have a plate number and name. I need Molly to check but wanted to run it by you first. What? Yeah, the case of the accident near Cooper's Gulch and the one at the railroad crossing outside of Madison. Huh? What's that?"

A few minutes went by without Jud speaking. He listened intently to whatever Chief Dockerty was saying to him. Whatever it was, it wasn't good. Rhonda could tell by the multiple expressions rapidly transforming from one to the next on her husband's face, none positive.

"I understand, Chief. Sure, I can wrap things up and be back in two hours. Sure. See you then. Goodbye." Jud hung up the phone.

"Two hours?" Rhonda asked. "What about all of this business with Kat's brother?"

Jud sighed. "Going to have to wait, love. The feds have apparently taken over my case and want debriefed immediately. Sheriff didn't even ask me what I had, just wanted me to come in asap."

"But what about Kat?"

"I empathize, babe. I really do, but that wasn't a request from the chief, it was an order. You can always stay —"

"I thought we discussed this at length last night. Together, remember?"

Jud hugged her. "Thanks. I love you."

"I love you more. Let's pack, I guess. We can check in with Kat and explain once everybody else is up."

Jud nodded. He hated abandoning a mission, especially one with such promise. More than that, he considered Kat and Johnny his friends. Then there was Colt, with whom he had recently bonded. He didn't want to disappoint the man when he gave him a specific task to do.

Emma opened her eyes. The sun was extra bright. She had discussed the idea of getting blinds for the room but had never gotten around to it. Sitting up, she turned her attention immediately to Colt. His back was to her. Everything in her body feared he was dead. Terror washed over her like a dam bursting as she slid her legs out of the bed, slowly walking around the footboard.

Cautiously, she approached him, stepping on the fork and dish where she set them the previous night. The plate was empty. Either he stirred in the middle of the night to devour a plate of steak or the raccoon they spent months trying to trap and relocate had returned. Leaning in carefully, she watched him breathe. It was shallow, but he was breathing. His body was hard at work healing itself, she hoped. Beneath his eyelids, his eyes shifted back and forth rapidly. Sturgess was dreaming. Emma let out a sigh of relief. He was still alive.

Temporarily relieved, she herself was famished. Still in her pajama bottoms, Emma wondered where she had gotten rid of the top, along with Colt's clothing. Somewhere in the house, pieces of bloodied garments lay. Hopefully, none of the house guests below tripped over them. Explaining what they attempted in the barn was going to appear extremely self-serving, particularly in the light of Johnny missing. Maybe it was. It was the timing that came into question concerning motivation.

Sliding on her bathrobe, Emma headed down the steps. As she approached the kitchen table, Jud gasped. Rhonda dropped her cup of coffee, which shattered on the floor, and Kat rose speechless, nearly in slow motion, from her seat at the table. All three stared at Emma with their mouths agape. She stopped, grimacing at the strange behavior.

"What?" she asked.

Rhonda ran to her, grabbing her hand, whisking Emma into the bathroom. Flicking the light switch, she pointed at the mirror. Emma turned, looking into it. Her face melted into the same expression as her house guests. She stared into the mirror, looking at a young woman she should have been at twenty-two years of age. The transfusion worked. She was herself again. Even the white eyes were restored to the crystal blue that she once had but possessed no memory of. Reaching her hand up to her face, the lines, wrinkles, age, all of it had been wiped away. She was Emma Adams once again.

"I don't understand," Rhonda muttered.

By that time, Jud and Kat had joined them in the bathroom. Jud examined her reflection. That was his friend who he last saw headed down the amusement row to work the high striker with Billy Ford. Emma Adams, his friend, who he spent the better part of his days searching for after the liberation of Kinston. Emotions he had long buried surfaced in a torrent. The same emotion he would not validate meeting the older Emma two days earlier. His knees buckled, tears flowing. Jud Allen was a mess. Emma knelt in front of him, throwing her arms around him. He squeezed back with all of his might. Rhonda joined them in a circle of sorrow. Or was it jubilation? Maybe, just maybe, the healing process could begin at last. The three of them were reunited finally, as if time stood still. Not even the previous night's indiscretion crept in. Kat just stood in the doorway, watching.

Kat returned to the kitchen; this was not her moment. She gathered her things, awaiting Colt, who was going to take her to talk with Horace Winston. It was time to get a move on. Not that she didn't feel happy about Emma's transformation or even questioned it. She had heard the story of Colt's final hour with Lizzy. However he did it, Sturgess restored Emma to herself. That she was certain, but Johnny was still missing. Once she had her stuff together, her intention was to return to Emma to inquire about Colt's whereabouts. She slung her satchel over her shoulder, turning back towards the bathroom. Nearly bumping into Jud and Rhonda, they intercepted her.

"Kat, we gotta go," Jud said.

"What?" she asked, shocked.

"He called his boss this morning and was advised not to do anymore on the case. The FBI took over and they want him to report immediately for a debriefing," Rhonda said, hoping to smooth over the disappointment.

"Fine," Kat said with a twinge of annoyance. "I need to see Colt."

Emma emerged from the restroom. What was she going to say?

"He's still asleep. He was up late —"

"I bet. Where is he, Emma?"

"Like I said, he was up late."

"Showering you in the fountain of youth, no doubt. Where is he, Emma?"

"C'mon, Kat. I know you're upset, but that's kind of unfair, don't ya think?" Rhonda asked.

Kat steamrolled past them, sprinting up the stairs. Emma watched her traverse the steps, wondering if she should stop her. If all went as planned, no explanation would be needed. She just hoped Colt would not have had any ill effects from the transfusion. That was not to be. Step by step, Emma followed Kat upstairs to the master bedroom. The time for any secrecy was fleeting.

Kat burst into the bedroom to find Colt sitting up, drinking a glass of water.

"Hey, Kitty Kat. Sorry, a tad under the weather this morning. Up too late, maybe one too many beers," he said.

Kat crossed her arms. He was lying. Emma entered the room. Sturgess' attention shifted to her. He looked at her intently, seeing Emma Adams as she was when he first met her alongside Lizzy in the town square of Kinston. A little older perhaps, but much like she was about two years into their life together. He smiled.

"Guess it worked?" he asked.

"I reckon'," she answered using the jargon she worked so diligently to cleanse him of.

"That's good. I just need a little rest before I get up and around. Horace can wait," he said to Kat.

"Jud and Rhonda are leaving," Kat proclaimed.

"His sheriff said he's ordered to return to headquarters. Something about debriefing to the feds," Emma added.

"The feds. You don't say? Wonder what they have to do with any of this?" Colt asked.

"Maybe Jud will find out and let us know?" Emma asked, not expecting an answer. It was more to quell Kat's disappointment.

"Wouldn't hurt to have a man inside," he said.

Kat sat next to him, placing her hand on his head. He was still cold.

"You look like shit. Didn't know you could get sick."

"Even the mighty fall to the common cold," he said.

"Sure that's all it is? Something didn't happen last night?" she asked, motioning to Emma.

"All's good in the neighborhood. Isn't that your saying?" he asked.

Kat smiled sheepishly.

"I have an idea. While you're resting, how about you and I pop into town to talk to Horace, Kat? Would give us something to do," Emma said.

Colt leaned forward, looking at the both of them. "That's a damned fine idea. Give me a bit to catch more shut eye."

Kat stood up, walking to face Emma. She touched her face, eliciting a puzzled look from Emma. Nothing. Both she and Colt produced no images, visions, or second sight when she came in physical contact with either of them. Whatever happened between last night and this morning, Emma's appearance may have changed, but from the projected psychic vision Kat could tap into, neither of them had it. Was it possible they were both devoid of souls, or maybe life energy?

She thought back on the sporadic images that appeared when she came in contact with Emma on day one. If they weren't her experiences, what did they signify? Were they actually Kat's and Emma was somehow an unexpected conduit of her own second-sight?

Either way, it was strange, but Emma's suggestion was not. It was sound. Whether she went with Colt or Emma, it really didn't matter. In fact, it may be more helpful to see Horace Winston with another pretty face. How he would react to younger Emma, though, was worth the price of admission.

"Okay," Kat said.

"Swell, I'll get dressed then, and we'll be on our way."

"May want to shower first," Kat said. "Pretty big blood smear on the back of your neck and in your hair."

"Shit," she said, rushing to the vanity to see.

The clothes may have been taken off, but hard to hide blood in strawberry blonde hair.

"Emma, sweetie. One thing. Give Jud and Rhonda you know what," Colt said.

"And Kat?" she asked.

"Already made that delivery," Colt answered.

Kat and Emma exited the bedroom after Emma put on one of Colt's cowboy hats to cover up the stain. Returning downstairs, Jud and Rhonda were seated on the living room couch. Kat approached them.

"Sorry, I was a bitch earlier. I have a lot on my mind," she said.

"Oh please, unnecessary at all. If anyone should apologize, it should be us for flaking out on you," Rhonda said, hugging her.

Even with all that was going on with Johnny missing, the embrace sent Kat's heart racing, her mouth dried. Every cell in her body trembled, wanting to knock Rhonda onto the couch, ravishing her hungrily.

Ash trays, fuzzy bunny rabbits, burnt bacon, deer poop... Kat cycled through her visual distractions to temper her desires.

Kat broke the embrace. "Colt said it might be good to have someone on the inside if you find out anything once you get back."

"Great idea," Rhonda said, turning to her husband.

Jud rose from the couch. "I promise to share what I learn, Kat. Seriously, I promise, even if I have to break confidentiality to do it."

Emma walked back into the room after a slight detour to pin her hair up under Colt's hat. She also did a quick wipe down of her neck with a washcloth, stashing it under the sink for later retrieval.

Rhonda and Colt continued staring at her in disbelief.

"Unbelievable," Jud said.

"You must explain all of this as soon as I get home. I'll call you later and we can talk, if you're here," Rhonda added.

"Totally, although it may be somewhat unbelievable," Emma said.

Kat snickered. "That's kind of becoming all of our thing, isn't it?"

Emma hugged her from behind. "Sure is, matron of swords."

They all shook their heads in agreement. From four armed monsters to gargoyles, none of these four people could have imagined the adventures they would share. It was a string that would bind them, reason with total acceptance. The four said goodbyes, exchanging hugs and promising to get together soon, talk even sooner with more frequency. Jud and Rhonda were only a phone call away, agreeing to hold the next get together at their house. Before they left, Emma stopped them.

"Hold up, you two. Colt wanted you to have something from us. What you're about to see, swear to secrecy. If you breathe a word of it, I'll be forced to track you down and kill you. Just kidding," she said.

Walking over to the mantlepiece, she moved her hand beneath it towards the fireplace.

"Damned thing. I can never find it right away. A-ha, there it is."

An audible click followed, then a slight creak.

"Open sesame," Emma chuckled.

She moved the bookcase, presently serving as her personal music cassette library, to the side. It was affixed to a set of hinges, revealing a secret room.

"Like the bakery," Rhonda said.

"Or Top Arnie's," Jud added.

Behind it was a door that Emma opened. Disappearing inside momentarily, she emerged with a sack, bound in twine like the one Kat received. She handed it to Jud.

"Colt really wanted you guys to have this. Don't open it until you get home. A little present from us to you. Merry early Christmas," she said.

"But —" Jud said.

"But nothing," Emma interrupted. "You want the old man to come down here and beat your ass? Marine or not, just take it."

Jud nodded. "Thank you."

The Allen couple mounted up the Honda turbos after securing their gift and overnight bags. As they sped off, Emma ran upstairs to get showered and changed. Kat waited for her on the porch, keys in hand. Emma skipped her typical hour of hair and make-up preparation to get the show on the road. She blew dry her hair, grabbing her pink rhinestone cowboy hat that matched the black one of Colts that he lent to Jud for the party. Tying her hair in a ponytail, tucking it up under her hat, she checked once more on Colt before heading back downstairs. He was fast asleep.

Meeting Kat on the porch, the two headed for the Oldsmobile. As it sped off, the sound of all the vehicles leaving drew the attention of Matthew, still tied to the post behind the barn. He watched anxiously as the shadow from the barn, currently keeping him safe, grew smaller and smaller as the morning sun rose higher in the sky.

Inside the house, the curtain on the second-floor master bedroom dropped. Colt watched as Kat and Emma drove to meet Horace in Apollo. Jud and Rhonda had also left. Slowly he stumbled toward his closet, putting on a fresh pair of jeans, shirt, boots and hat. It was a task; he was not well. Struggling to maintain his balance, Colt descended the stairs, using the banister as a guide. One foot, then the next, his descent down the ten steps forced perspiration to the palms of his hands, making the task even more difficult. His breathing was strained, as every small task was suddenly an insurmountable chore.

He stumbled to the desk beneath the window overlooking the porch. Sitting down forcefully, Colt removed a chain from around his neck. On it dangled Lizzy's wedding band and a small key. He removed the key before sliding the chain back around his neck. The key unlocked the desk. Fishing out a pen and piece of paper from the desk drawer, he removed a strongbox from the larger right bottom drawer. He began to write. Once finished, he slid the piece of paper into an envelope, addressing it to Kat and Emma. Next, he took out a few documents, signing each, returning them to the strongbox. He placed it back in the drawer, along with the envelope. Taking a deep breath, attempting to summon more energy, he relocked the desk, dropping the key on top of it so that it was in plain sight.

Standing, he moved to the door, exiting the cabin. Colt Sturgess walked forward out into the grass, patting the horse from the carriage on the head as he passed by the black carriage. Stopping, Sturgess turned around looking at his homestead. For years, he had called this home. It was a wonderful home, certainly where his heart was. With plenty of memories, his life was a pair of bookends, with the best parts being at either end. The stuff in between was a series of highs and lows, fueled by a rage he no longer had. It's been a good life, he thought. One last refrain remained to complete the ballad that was his life. Johnny Ellis must be freed. If Kaleb Blackburn wanted him, that's what he was going to deliver.

Starting towards the barn, he heard uncontrollable sobbing creeping from behind the structure. Matthew, the outcast. He had nearly forgotten about him. Summoning more of that same energy that enabled him to leave the house, Sturgess walked around to the back of the barn. Matthew looked up in fear, unsure of what was in store next.

"How's those feet of yours?" Colt asked.

Matthew looked up. Although he barely saw the man, even he could tell something was amiss.

"Man, what's wrong with you? Look like death warmed over, bro."

"It's your lucky day."

Colt reached down, untwisting the bailing wire, freeing the young man.

"Now skedaddle," Colt said.

"Where am I supposed to go? Can't exactly run wind sprints!"

"Well, let's see. I'm off to see your boss and the girls will be back within an hour. If you want tossed in the pines or stabbed again, feel free to hang around. But if I were you, I'd figure out the best way back to wherever you're from," Colt answered. "Oh, and don't touch the horse. That I'd take very personally."

For once, Matthew shut his mouth, merely shook his head in acknowledgement.

Colt wandered back to the front of the barn. It was still open from the previous night. He shook his head at Emma's carelessness, even if it meant she probably saved his life. Temporarily. The transfusion tube still lay on the floor between the two stools, faint blood stains beneath it. With some effort, he bent down, retrieved the trash dumping in a waste can at the rear of the barn.

Emma had always been a little sloppy with details. Jud, however, was more reliable. As expected, he had left the keys to the truck on the seat. Sturgess got into the truck, turned over the engine and crept out of the garage. Driving forward, he turned to look back at the home he and Emma had built. Would it be the last time?

Chapter Eleven

Colt drove slowly up the access road that led to his property. Swerving left and right, he found it difficult maintaining his concentration. Things were coming at him too quickly to process, although he was alone. All his senses were jumbling the data he was receiving. Attempting to shake it off, he pressed on. His vision zoomed in, then out, forcing him to slam on the brakes several times. This wasn't his best idea, nor could he trust Blackburn to release Johnny in exchange for him. The proposition had never been discussed. To further complicate matters, he did not know where he was going. Driving haphazardly on a back country road was one thing, but how would he navigate a major highway? A wayward insect flew into the windshield of his truck. He ducked instinctively.

Rolling down his window, Sturgess concentrated on the hood of the vehicle as if he were aiming it rather than driving. He pressed on, charting his progress by the reflections from cloud motion and the wind. Why he thought this was a good idea was anyone's guess, but a firm indicator of his mindset. Glancing momentarily in the rearview mirror, his eyes had faded from the vibrant white to a hazy yellow.

"They're all right. I look like shit," he murmured.

Somehow, he made it three quarters of the way up sunrise hill when he drifted off the road, slamming the brakes once more, missing a pine tree by inches. Throwing the stick in park, he sat reevaluating his decision. His eyelids flickered, then closed. Moments later a tapping on the door of his truck awoke him. It was Blackburn in his human form.

"I must say, Mr. Sturgess, you aren't looking well," he said.

Colt reached down on the passenger side of the truck, retrieved the same set of dark glasses he had worn in Kinston, putting them on as if they would somehow miraculously disguise his condition.

"Where's the boy?" Colt asked.

"I assure you; he is safe and sound. A shame, really, that our first meeting had to end in such a manner, but it was the safest way for me to escape that town alive while retrieving a bargaining chip. Is my young protégé well also? He appears to be missing."

"I cut him loose. Not sure where he's headin' but staying put didn't seem to be any interest to him."

"Ah, the youth of today. So fickle, so unpredictable. I had hoped for an exchange of sorts, but if he's gone —"

"Take me instead."

"Beg pardon?"

"I'll come with you, release the boy."

Blackburn grinned, looking back at the crest of the hill where two black sedans were parked. He motioned to them with his gloved hand.

"Finally, you have come to your senses. My associates with be very pleased."

"Just let me see the boy and I'll come with you."

"Therein lies the problem, Mr. Sturgess. My benefactor only considers a deal complete once my part of the bargain is delivered. Too many unknown factors where you are concerned. I deliver you, the boy goes free, and I collect my recruitment fee. It's simply how it is done. If you'd prefer, I can leave you here by the roadside and we can discuss it at a later juncture. Unfortunately, I cannot guarantee this job hasn't already been farmed out to an additional subcontractor."

Sturgess summoned up the energy to laugh. This creature spoke as if he were simply operating a typical, run of the mill lost and found venture except with dire consequences.

"Fine, your game, your rules," Colt relented.

Blackburn stepped back as two men with black suits, sunglasses, and black ties reached into the cab of the truck. For a moment, Sturgess' instinct was to fight back, but he made the deal, even before he left the cabin. This is what he sought. The two men in black slid a vest over Colt's head, fastening it under his arms with a series of buckles. Dragging him from the truck with care, they chair-carried him up the hill to one sedan, gingerly placing him in the back seat. A glass panel separated the two sections. Blackburn entered the opposite side of the back seat. Once he sat down, the doors locked.

"What's this?" Colt asked, tugging listlessly at the vest.

"That is merely an insurance policy. As I mentioned at that dreadful party, we have been following you for some time, fully aware of your unique gifts. That vest will send an electrical shock through your heart that will render you quite useless, perhaps even dead. Something you failed to acknowledge when you dumped me in that puddle."

Blackburn tapped on the glass divider with his cane. That prompt set both vehicles in motion. Slumped down in the seat, Colt stared out the window at the clouds drifting by in the blue sky, with the smell of fresh pine tricking in. He closed his eyes, drifting off once more.

Kat and Emma pulled in front of the VFW, parking in the same spot they had the previous night. Several trucks were lined up beside the building in the grassy area. They were here. Exiting the vehicle, the two rushed to the front door, entering the building. Emma grabbed Kat's arm.

"Um, this is gonna be a little weird, but they think I'm Colt and Emma's daughter," Emma said.

"What?"

"I aged a year or so ago. It wasn't exactly something that could be explained, so the older Emma, they think, is my mom. Since we really didn't plan that out, they already met me as Emma, so long story short, when they met the older version, they assumed I was Emma's mom.

"I guess that makes sense. Like I said, we didn't really think it through, so Colt introduced the older me as Emma too. So, they kinda of just started asking about 'junior,' if that makes any sense."

"Nothing about the two of you makes much sense, but let's go, junior," Kat said with a smile.

Emma laughed. "I guess you got me. I mean, rather got 'us.'"

Inside, six men were gathered around the coffee maker, talking and smoking. Horace saw the women first.

"Excuse me, fellahs. We have visitors," he said.

Horace gestured for them to follow him into the kitchen.

"Was expecting your pops, Junior. How's mom this morning? Guessing she may not be up yet. She was howlin' at the moon last night. Then with the vampire trouble —"

Kat interrupted. "Yeah, about that."

Horace offered them both a cup of coffee. They each refused. He sat down at a table that still had remnants of the party he hadn't tended to yet.

"Mine is clean. Not even any tracks, tire or otherwise. They're arrogant, not exactly cautious. Last time, easy to track them."

"So, this has happened before?" Emma asked.

Horace nodded.

"Excuse me if I'm a little out in left field, Mr. Winston, but those things didn't strike me as vampires, especially the kids," Kat said.

Removing a flask from his back pocket, he poured a shot into his coffee, taking a shot directly from the flask before returning it.

"See, the problem is with what Hollywood shows on the late shows. Nothing like what we saw in the war, which was the first time I saw soul suckers. They have stages. Lemme explain. Don't suppose either of you heard of Bastogne?" he asked.

Both women shook their heads.

"Didn't think so. How about Battle of the Bulge? World War Two?"

"Of course," Kat answered, hoping to move into the informational part of the story.

Working in a tavern for a good part of her adult life, she knew how veterans loved to tell stories. Not sure she believed half of them because of personal embellishments, everyone seemed to be the hero in their retelling. They were here for information. The sooner they got it, the sooner they could return to Colt with what they discovered.

"Bastogne was a wooded area outside of a town called Foy. I was with the 101st Airborne, dug in to probably the coldest, most godforsaken place on earth. Wintertime, you see. We were holding the line waiting for Patton's 3rd armored division to show up. Cut the krauts off from the supply lines. The executive officer was a good man by the name of Winters. Was a captain at the time, holding down a major's position. By day, we dug through the permafrost, making fox holes. At night, the Germans shelled the hell out of us sending splinters, limbs, hell, whole damn trees down on top of us. Next morning, clean up, back in the holes."

"What does all that have to do with these soul suckers?" Emma asked.

"Getting there, Junior, be patient. Anyway, second night while on watch, we took turns trying to sleep when we could, one man up, one down. Creeping around in the dark were a couple of figures. Thought they were Nazis that snuck over, trying to break our line. I shouted the challenge. They seemed to disappear into thin air. Didn't pay them any mind. Couple of fellahs nearby shouted over telling me to pipe down. I was just a lowly private first class, so I did what I was told. Next morning, a commotion over at my buddy's foxhole where I saw the shadow figures. Both guys were stone cold dead, life drained right out of them. The squad leaders all asked around to see if anyone saw anything, but I buttoned my lip. How the hell was I supposed to explain that, yet alone why my comrades in arms looked like skeletons wrapped in old butcher paper?"

"Did they ever catch the two?" Kat asked.

"Nope. But here's the funny part, what I remembered is the size. They were slight, like kids. Didn't see 'em again until Korea. Did a jump into Sukchon with a captain went by the name of Spiers. Crazy bastard with more courage that all of us combined. Was part rescue mission, part blockade. Pulled it off, but the Koreans killed all the prisoners, moving them out in boxcars before we landed. Long story short, moved south into the lowlands where we set up camp. Funny, all our intel and stealth, these damned kids would still find us somehow. One night, always at night it seemed, a group comes in selling pogey bait, offering to shine boots, that kind of stuff. Heard a scream. A group of us locked and loaded, heading to the disturbance. Was a fuckin' shame." Horace paused, visibly upset.

"What did you find?" Kat asked.

"Good friend of mine, George Shepard, guys called him 'Shep' on the ground with three of these kids, these things, hovering over his lifeless body, a kind of black smoke pouring into him. Once they spotted us, they turned to run, but we cut 'em down. That's when I realized these things weren't immune to bullets. What I saw outside of Bastogne was real. I wasn't crazy or losing my marbles from hypothermia. That's frostbite, you know."

"Okay, what about last night?" Kat pressed.

"I'm getting there, Ms. Ellis, I'm getting there. Fast forward to Vietnam. I was retired by then but heard stories. One man, Saul Cantor, saw some of the older ones while serving in defense of Long Binh Post. Part of his unit, led by this grisly old Gunnery Sergeant, took a squad out to hunt them. Top secret stuff, but after a few beers, one of their unit, kid they called 'Flower,' god knows why, told them stories about the bloodsuckers feeding on the bodies of the fallen, didn't matter which side, they liked the taste of it."

"The Redcatchers!" Kat exclaimed. "I met him."

"You don't say? Well then, you know what old Tech Sergeant Winston is telling you ain't a crock of shit."

"What about Apollo?" Emma asked.

"Good question, Junior. In '68, a sudden outbreak walloped us pretty hard of what people thought was anemia. The bastards were bleeding the town dry. Population used to be almost three times what it is today. A group of us vets set up a fire watch after swapping stories from different eras of service. We knew what was going on, but who could we tell? They'd think we'd just needed put out to pasture. On one of our watches, we saw them sneaking into town. Sniped a couple of them. The older ones can fly. Knowing they had to be close to just come and go as they pleased under the cover of darkness, we set out towards the abandoned coal mine, figuring that's probably the best place to start. Jackpot. Flushed them out with fire, the great equalizer, then picked them off like fish in a barrel. All said and done, thirteen, lucky thirteen of them dead."

"But you checked last night into the morning? Nothing there?" Kat asked.

"Sorry, darlin'. Nothing. Was hoping to find your brother, at least. The biggest problem is never seeing one like that one last night. He's a big one. Two shotgun blasts at point blank just pissed him off. Strong too, the way he just scooped up your brother, first time anyone seen that. If he headed south, like you say, could be anywhere. Lots of mountain and forest on this side of the state."

Kat wandered over to the window. Looking out, she felt the sun on her face through the panes. It was warm, soothing, yet her mind raced. What to do? It seemed hopeless. Colt was sick, Emma was trying, but what could she do with her super strength and Jud and Rhonda were gone? At least Jud could try to piece things together with his police training. She let out an audible sigh.

"Sorry, Katlyn. Wish I could be of more help. I can talk with the fellahs. Maybe strategize, find a different area to search." Horace said.

Emma reached out, shaking his hand. "Thanks, Horace. That sounds like a great idea. We'll head home. If something comes to mind, call us."

"Will do, Junior."

Emma approached Kat, taking her arm, leading her back out to the car. The two drove up Hunter's Way, stopping at the location of the previous night's assault. They looked around to see if anything was left.

The street had been cleaned, thanks to the power company that also had obviously worked all night replacing the utility pole and transformer. It was a dead end.

Jud and Rhonda made record time to Madison. Ironically, they hit the same railroad crossing where Skippy Mathers met his fate, except on the opposite side of the tracks. As their motorcycles idled at the crossing, awaiting the train to pass, Rhonda looked over at Jud. He stared straight ahead. Feeling her gaze, his mind bounced between a couple of minor details that were eating at him since he spoke with Sheriff Dockerty, who called him off the case. The sheriff had never done that, in fact, he encouraged out of the box thinking. It's why Molly joked with Jud about enjoying his weekend. Then the duty part of him weighed down his ethics like one of the boxcars speeding by. What if they were counting on him? Actually, they were. Colt asked Jud to inspect that carriage.

After the train passed, Jud revved the engine of his bike. Looking over to Rhonda, he said two words.

"Fuck it!"

Crossing the railroad tracks, he pulled a U-turn, Rhonda following. They headed back to the Sturgess homestead. She smiled beneath her helmet.

On approach to the downslope of sunrise hill, neither Emma nor Kat said much during the drive back. Speeding up the private lane, Kat suddenly slammed on the brakes, skidding across the road. Emma jerked forward. Her head impacted the windshield, causing it to crack. Feeling her head for damage, blood covered her palm. Panicking, Kat reached inside the glove compartment, digging out a stash of napkins from the fast-food place she and Johnny stopped by on the way up.

"I'm so, so sorry, just the truck. Colt's truck," Kat said, pointing to the left side of the road where he abandoned it.

Dabbing the wound on Emma's forehead, Kat expected more blood. As she examined it closer, she watched as the wound sealed itself. Kat witnessed this before on the couch of the Allen residence. Emma's sudden age regression, more specifically, how it happened literally overnight, became clear.

"He did this, didn't he?" she asked.

Emma shook her head affirmatively, with sheepish embarrassment.

Kat jumped out of the car, rushing towards the truck. Opening the door, she examined the inside. Keys were still in the ignition, window rolled down. Colt's cowboy hat sat on the passenger seat. Emma ran up beside her.

"You don't think —"

"I dunno what I think."

Stepping back from the truck, she looked closely at the ground. A thought occurred.

"If you have his healing powers, do you have his bionic sight now, too?" Kat asked.

"I don't know. Honest to god, didn't know I had anything other than —"

"Try. See if you can see footprints or anything." Kat said.

Emma looked down at the ground closely, then fell face forward, scuffing up her nose this time. Kat handed her the napkin after helping her to her feet.

"Whoa, that just made me crazy dizzy," Emma said.

"Okay?"

Kat wandered ahead up to the rise of the hill. Even she could make out two sets of tire tracks.

"Shit," she said under her breath. "We gotta get home now!"

"I'll take the truck," Emma shouted.

Jumping back into the Oldsmobile, Kat sped off to the cabin, Emma following. Once they reached the homestead, Kat parked, running into the house.

"Colt! Colt!"

She sprinted up the stairs and into the master bedroom. Inside the room, the bed was empty, sheets drawn back. Glancing around the room, Kat also noticed the curtain pulled back. Emma entered seconds later.

"What's missing of his?" Kat asked.

Emma began looking around the room. Opening the closet, she noticed a few items of note were gone.

"Pair of jeans, his everyday hat and boots, shirt, from what I can tell," she answered.

"How about his guns? Where's his guns and sword?"

"Downstairs, follow me."

The two women rushed down to the living room. Emma fished for the release switch to the bookcase and the secret door behind it. After opening it, the two entered the room. Gasping, tears welled up in Emma's eyes.

"What?" Kat asked.

"They're here, all of them," she answered.

"Fuck!" Kat screamed, running out of the room onto the porch. "Where are you, Colt? Can you hear me? Where did you go?"

She began sobbing into her hands. What was she going to do now? Everything had hit the fan all at once. What could a twenty-nine-year-old tarot card reader from Shermer, Pennsylvania do? Feeling way in over her head, she glanced over at the picnic table. Kat spun around, heading back into the cabin. Grabbing her backpack, she took out her tarot cards, shuffling through them until she found the king of swords, the moon and the lovers cards, removing them in that exact order, the same in which she drew them initially a day ago. In the front pocket of the pack, the three stones she collected that morning as well.

"What are you doing?" Emma asked.

"Maybe nothing, maybe everything," Kat answered. "I'll be right back. Stay here."

Out the door, across the porch, over to the picnic table, she ran. Placing the cards in the correct order, inverting the moon, Kat set the corresponding stones on top of the cards except for the last one. That one she placed in her palm, covering it with the other. She closed her eyes, concentrating on her, on Corina.

"C'mon dammit. Work. I've got nothing else to try," Kat whispered.

Breathing in deeply, she tuned into the sounds of birds, the smell of pine, the sensation of the wind on her skin. Nothing. She tried again, thinking harder. *How did I do the sword thing in town?* she thought. Colt was in danger. Emma was still here and Johnny. Those shadow kids and the loudmouth tied up behind the barn. What was different? Why couldn't she repeat it? Relaxing, she opened her mind, letting thoughts flow. Rhonda touched her. Fuck. Stop thinking about that.

"How can I be getting turned on at a time like this?" she muttered in frustration. "The pool. Corina."

Opening her eyes, there she stood in the flesh.

"You rang?" Corina asked.

Kat sprung to her feet, embracing her with all her might as tears streamed down her face.

"Yes, I need you. We're in so much trouble, and I don't know what to do!" Kat said hysterically.

Emma peered out from the kitchen window. Who was this woman and where'd she come from? She entertained the idea of going out to get a status check, but for once resisted her immediate impulse. If Kat had some tricks up her sleeve other than sword walls, it was best she stayed out of it. For now. Sitting down at the table, her adrenaline dying down, Emma tried shaking the guilt of the transfusion. Coupled with the state it left Colt in, she would never have asked him to do it. Ever. She would have rather died than put him in jeopardy. Hindsight is twenty-twenty, Colt once told her. Emma wasn't sure what that meant at the time, but it was lucid now.

"Stupid Emma," she said, cleaning up the scattered deck of cards, placing them back in the box.

"Settle down, poppet. I'm here now. Tell me all about it," Corina said.

"Where do I start? My brother got swept away by some gargoyle, ancient vampire or something. I summoned a wall of swords but can't do it again. We don't know where to look and our only hope, Colt, is missing and weak because he made Emma young again. I'm lost and can't handle anything other than having an orgasm every five minutes. How's that?" Kat answered hysterically, talking as fast as her mouth could spit out the words.

"Whoa, you have a bit of shambles! Let's talk about these swords first. What happened with those?"

Kat recounted the night before in explicit details, including the subsequent attempts to use whatever unknown powers of manifestation that she apparently possessed. Corina moved in closer to provide solace to calm her down, but Kat jumped back as if she just received an electrical jolt. The reaction startled Corina.

"Hey, now. I will not hurt you, ever, Katlyn. You must know this," Corina said.

"No, it's not that," Kat said, blushing.

"What then? You have me in a bit of a quandary."

Kat stood up from the picnic bench, putting space between the two of them.

"It's just…"

"Go ahead, spill it. If I'm going to help you, I need to know everything."

Kat spun around, slamming her hands on the table.

"If you touch me, I'm gonna cum! It's a non-stop thing since you wandered over here yesterday. It's maddening!"

"I see," Corina said, assessing the situation with a wry smile. "Well, that is certainly unexpected. This happens with me or anyone?"

Hesitating to answer out of embarrassment, Corina prodded her for an answer.

"Well?"

"Rhonda. My friend's wife, of all people. She doesn't even go that way, I don't think, but I can't help it. My attraction to you both is uncontrollable. I don't even need to come in contact with either of you. It's even thoughts of it that drive me nutso!" Kat answered.

"Hm. I may have cocked up," Corina said.

"Cock has nothing to do with it, I assure you."

Corina laughed. "No, it's an expression. How do you Americans say? 'Screwed up?'"

"You did this? Why?"

"Sit down a moment. It's time I come clean about something, so you're not so dodgy."

Kat sat down cautiously, still maintaining her distance.

"When I first sensed you, I felt a huge amount of energy, but it was being contained. Nice and tidy as if it were in a tiny box, but the power of it was like something I never encountered," Corina said.

"So, you weren't out here fishing?"

"Oh, no, I was. That part is completely true. But I was curious as to the source. I followed the trail and saw you gathering stones. I was gobsmacked that it was coming from a person. That just heightened my curiosity; hence, I followed you. Watching you with the cards, I felt the energy grow almost to where it was difficult sharing space, but I pressed on. Maybe I'm just a nutter, who knows? Curiosity begged, and I simply had to talk with you."

"What'd ya mean, energy?"

"Kat, you are a source of amazing power, but not conventional. When I sat down, I may have dropped a little cleansing spell to remove the block, basically releasing your energy."

"Ha! Then you are a witch!" Kat exclaimed.

"Not in any traditional sense. I'm not sure what I am. From a very young age, I knew I had gifts beyond what others did. It took a great deal of curiosity, diligence, reading and practice to understand them. You, of course, are aware of chakras, the centers of spiritual power in the human body?"

"Of course. That's old hat. I align mine before every reading."

"Good. It is the basis of my practice. I know it may be uncomfortable, but may I get close enough to you to try something? No touching, promise!"

Although hesitant, Kat agreed if it was going to help.

"Please, climb up on the table and lay back. Trust me, I just want to see what consequences I may have foolishly unleashed. Then we'll talk more about this manifesting of yours. That I've never heard of, ever, but it goes back to one of my original questions when we met about believing in real magic," Corina said.

Kat laid back on the cold slats of the wooden picnic table. Not even the morning sun had completely dried the moisture from the previous day's rain. Closing her eyes, she tried clearing her mind of everything. It would be a task with Corina kneeling beside her on the bench. A warmth shot through her entire body as Corina drifted her hands up the length of her, rather inches above it. As she drew closer, Kat could smell her hair. This brought back the vision of the two of them in the mountain pool, bodies intertwined, Corina licking the water from her lips. Kat sat up abruptly, nearly knocking her off the bench onto the ground.

"Stop," Kat commanded.

Corina stood up as quickly as Kat's reaction.

"Interesting," she said.

Spinning around on her behind, Kat scooted back to the bench, laying her head on her arms atop the picnic bench.

Walking away from the table, Corina stopped, staring off in deep thought. This energy she set free on a whim may very well be beyond her understanding. It wasn't in her to walk from a challenge, especially a complete unknown. *How does one ignore the existence of a dinosaur if they stumble upon one?* She mused. Kat was far from a dinosaur, she was a missing link, a new species on the evolutionary scale and she had discovered her. Beyond the scientific curiosity, which was downright rude, this was a living being just like her. Corina turned back around, returning to the table.

"Gargoyle vampire, huh?" she asked.

"Yeah, not that you believe me. If you knew my past, it would be totally acceptable, as I've seen things not even I would have imagined existed," Kat answered with her head still resting on her arms.

"I've seen things too, that many would consider rubbish, but I've met no one like you."

Kat looked up finally. "How so?"

"Let's jump back to the beginning of our conversation about chakras."

"Fine."

"See, everyone has a dominant, whether it be the root, sacral, solar plexus, heart, throat, third eye, or crown. Yours is sacral, sexual and creative energy, but it's off the scale. Stronger than any I've ever encountered. It's bursting out of you."

"Well, that explains a lot."

"Not really. It's the tip of the iceberg, so to speak. Question. What happened before you summoned those swords? Which, by the way, I've never heard happening in any way, shape, or form. I mean, I've seen magicians who defy reason and I'm no plonker."

Kat sat up, considering the question. She finally felt calm. No, she felt stillness.

"I just reacted when Colt was in danger," she said.

"Colt is the king of swords?"

"Yes. When I first met him, it was the craziest thing. I read him and kept drawing the same three cards repeatedly, even if I removed them from the deck. Even used a different deck. It defied any logic."

"And yet it kept happening?"

"Yes."

"Ever think that may have been your first manifestation?"

Kat looked perplexed. Did she herself continually replicate those three exact cards without realizing it? After all, it was unexplainable, impossible even.

"Never thought about it since that night."

"But you have no sexual attraction to him?"

"Well, maybe a bit. You saw him. It's not out of control, like with you and Rhonda."

"Okay, so just before that, did anything happen with Rhonda?"

"Um, kinda. She touched me in front of the VFW where the party was."

"How did that make you feel? Just that simple touch?"

"I nearly squirted in my pants. I needed to concentrate with everything in my body not to pass out."

"Wow, this is really running wild."

"You have no idea."

Corina focused on Kat, then closed her eyes. She tried connecting with her without touch. Kat watched her patiently, wondering what she was up to. Suddenly, she had the impulse to close her eyes as well. She was back at the pool. Opening her eyes abruptly, she hoped Corina hadn't sensed that immediate pull. The smile on Corina's face denoted she had.

"What's this pool I see that is dominating your attention?" she asked.

"Oh, that? It's really embarrassing."

"Um, you just confessed to nearly orgasming by merely touching your friend's wife. Think I can handle it."

"Even if it involves you?"

Corina grinned. "Especially if it involves me. But before you do, I want to try something, but it involves touching. I need to know the full breadth of your energy if we're going to channel it and settle it down. It's my fault that I let it loose, but by channeling it through the other chakras, we can make use of it. Spread it around, so to speak. Obviously, you manifested solid objects by merely reacting to a thought, inadvertently engaging the energy."

"But why couldn't I do it again, when I tried really hard?" Kat asked.

Corina reflected momentarily before answering. It was a solid question, especially with all the other unknowns Kat was presenting.

"My belief is by maintaining harmony with your energies, things can only manifest in a neutral state. Much like the autonomic nervous system. You don't think about breathing, your heart beating, digestion and, particularly to your case, sexual arousal, yet they all happen automatically. Your arousal sparks an entire subsystem of functions that produce, if my theory is correct, anything you can dream up. But something else is in play here. I think you have a gift that is at the highest level of functionality, but you lack the experience to use it. Think about getting a really cool sports car, but you've never even ridden a tricycle before. Without help, it just sits in the garage. What I think is going on is that you were wandering on foot and suddenly found yourself arse over tit behind the wheel of the car speeding down the freeway."

"Wow, you sound like some kind of scientist or something."

Corina chuckled. "Well, I am, but not in a traditional sense. Are you ready to try this experiment?"

Kat nodded with apprehension. Behind them, Emma came onto the porch, careful not to bang the screen door, taking up a seat next to the swing. She had grown bored in her anxiety or, more likely, her impetuous curiosity overtook her, much like Kat's impulses. Either way, they now had a spectator. Corina waved out of courtesy.

"Friend of yours?" she asked Kat.

"Yeah, but I don't have the same reaction to her."

"Interesting, cute girl. Wonder why."

Kat shrugged. "I guess it's like anything else. Everyone has different tastes. Not everyone likes chopped liver, not that Emma is chopped liver. She is beautiful, just not in that way. To me anyway. Besides, I'm not a whore. Not everybody turns me on, you know."

"Sorry, didn't mean it that way. What is her relationship to Colt?" Corina asked.

"It's really complicated and one of those unbelievable gargoyle vampire things," she answered.

"Interesting. As strong as your energy is, I get nothing from her or Sam Elliot. It's as if they were both dead, pardon that tosh, just get no energy from either of them."

"That may be more on point than you know."

Although the appearance of Emma and her energy analysis of both her and Colt were interesting, Kat was substantially more interesting. Corina patted the table with her hand. Kat took the cue, jumping up on it, stretching out once more. However, this time Corina climbed up as well, positioning behind her sitting with Kat's head on her chest. Immediately, Kat reacted, desperately pushing back the energy in response.

"Don't," Corina said. "Let it flow."

Kat huffed. "Fine, but if I make a mess, you're helping me clean myself up!"

"Deal," Corina said.

Kat closed her eyes, hoping to find something that would provide a modicum of control, regardless of Corina's request. *Ash trays, fuzzy bunny rabbits, burnt bacon, deer poop...*

Corina leaned in, whispering. "Tell me about the pond."

Retelling the experience, Kat trembled with desire. Corina touched her body, starting at the root chakra, moving to the sacral, just below her naval. She screamed out as her hands were singed by mere contact with Kat. Reacting, Kat sat up, but Corina implored her to continue. This was power beyond her knowledge. Her hands stung from the burns, but kept moving slowly up Kat's body, touching every chakra point, eventually reaching her head. Kat writhed with desire. There was nothing more she wanted to do than pin Corina down, taking her fervently.

"Stop for a second," Corina said.

Kat panted heavily. She crossed her legs, squeezing them together for added stimulation. Ablaze with desire, Kat Ellis didn't want to stop. She wanted more. Grasping Corina's calves, she ran her hands along her skin, beneath the cuff of her jeans.

"Seriously, Kat. Stop. I want to try something new. Keep your eyes closed. Think about something other than the pool of water. Concentrate on the wind, the sound of my voice and the touch of my fingers. I'm going to trace your chakra line. As I do, visualize moving your energy from your lower belly to the next point I touch. Okay?"

Looking up at her breathlessly, Kat offered a counterproposal. "I'd rather fuck you first."

Kat's energy was infecting Corina. She, too, was feeling a surge of uncontrollable desire. Could this woman project this energy as well? Placing her hands on her breasts, Corina began squeezing Kat's erect nipples, longing for her mouth. Grabbing her head forcefully, Kat kissed Corina recklessly.

"Whoa," Emma said from the porch, watching the scene play out. "Pretty hot. Should have made some popcorn."

Before relenting completely to Kat's passion, Corina broke the clutch, hazily getting up from the table. Kat leaned in behind her, running her hands between Corina's legs.

"Stop!" Corina yelled.

Blinking her eyes rapidly, the loud command snapped Kat Ellis out of her euphoric haze. She breathed deeply to lasso her cognition back to reality.

"Sorry," Kat said.

"It's okay," Corina responded, still shaking from the sheer ecstasy of the moment, an ecstasy that was simply indescribable.

"Damn, just when it was getting good," Emma murmured from the porch.

"Think I can get a drink of water?" Corina asked Kat.

"I'll get it," Emma yelled from across the yard. Her sense of hearing had improved.

Emma filled a glass of water from the sink, dropped a few ice cubes in from the ice tray and rushed out to the picnic table. She handed the glass to Corina.

"Thank you. I'm Corina."

"Emma. Emma Adams. Pleased to meet you." She turned to Kat. "Didn't tell me you had a girlfriend. Cool."

"She's not my girlfriend," Kat said.

"Really? Looked hot and steamy from where I was sitting."

Corina blushed, more from completely losing control than the inference that she and Kat were a couple. Her arrogance in believing she could channel Kat's power so easily was a total failure.

"Well, I'll get back inside. You know, to figure out how to find Colt and Johnny? Carry on," Emma said as she skipped back to the porch.

"Shit," Kat whispered.

Corina smiled, resuming her seat back on the bench across from Kat.

"Sorry, made a shambles out of that. Thought I had more control."

"You think you have a tough time with control? Try being me."

Kat refocused her energy. Emma was right. They were supposed to be concentrating on a way to find Colt, not a steamy make-out session. The situation was growing grimmer by the minute. This call for help to Corina wasn't her best idea.

"Don't worry about it. I just thought you could help. Didn't know where else to turn. My instincts screamed to seek you out," Kat said with a dash of melancholy.

"Me? Now that is interesting," Corina said, surprised.

"Yeah, how so?"

"If with all that's going on, your intuition told you I could help, then indeed I can. I just need to try something simpler."

"You really think? Let's try again then. I'm desperate here."

Corina nodded. Looking over at the bench on Kat's side of the table, she noticed the three stones. An idea popped into her head. She knew not to ignore such happenings.

"You used that stone as I told you?" she asked.

"Yes. It's how you came here. I think," Kat answered.

"Okay, let's try something else. Obviously, your battery is charged. Hold the stone for the king of swords. He is who you are looking for?"

"Yes. Well, both of them. Johnny's the inverted moon. I have a bad feeling he went after Johnny alone and someone or something intercepted him."

"If that's what your instinct is telling you, then it's true. Lesson one: you must trust those implicitly, like your high priestess."

186

Kat appreciated the tarot reference. "Exactly."

"Close your eyes again. Breathe deeply. Feel everything without thinking of me touching you. Now hold the stone for Colt and free your mind. He is a sword, the intangible, the wind. It can't be created or captured. Balance the impossible, the heart and mind."

As Kat squeezed the stone, feeling its smoothness, she envisioned Colt Sturgess. Much like the stone itself, he had been shaped by time, eroded by the wind and water to a smooth finish except, in his case, only a hundred plus years. He had been propelled by the fire of rage but changed into someone who knew inner peace for the first time. He evolved. Suddenly, the wind picked up, swirling around the picnic bench, gaining force in a radius around them. Corina struggled to maintain her grip on the table as the force of the wind gathered speed. Her hair blew about wildly while Kat sat completely still unaffected.

"Don't try so hard, poppet. Let it go. Permit the balance to release the excessive energy. The wind is yours and the king. Remember, the sword is two sided. It can cut its wielder as well as its oppressor," Corina said loudly over the building funnel of air. She was finding it difficult to breathe.

Kat opened her eyes to witness the sudden downburst. Was she doing that? Closing her eyes again, she let go as Corina had instructed. The wind died down to a gentle breeze. Corina took a deep breath of fresh air, stunned at the potential power of the young woman seated across from her.

"Listen, as your mind explores. You have unique abilities. Tarot cards, candles, crystals, herbs, they are all tools, nothing more. True mystics don't require them. It's much like dragging a ladder out into an open field to touch a cloud, ignoring that gravity no longer exists. If you want to touch a cloud, just do it. The tools are a security blanket...a crutch. They separate the gifted from the carny acts. Do you understand?"

"Yes," Kat replied dreamily, eyes still closed.

"Excellent. Now see what you saw when the vampire took Johnny."

"But that was last night, I couldn't possibly—"

"Don't think, see. Time is irrelevant in scrying. Infinite possibilities exist once something is in motion. Even a seagull can bring down a mighty plane if it flies into just one engine. Time is the same. We look at it in three facets: past, present, and future. What I just said in the present is now in the past. The next thing I say will be in the future and so on, repeating the cycle for infinity. The key is to take those three man-made terms and throw them out the window. Just be in the moment. Let loose, follow what you see."

Kat inhaled, visualizing the overhead view of the railroad track. The vision surpassed the point where she lost it the night before. Faster and faster, the vision progressed until the tracks were a blur, twisting and turning along the way at breakneck speed. Abruptly, it stopped. She gasped.

"What do you see?" Corina asked.

"A building."

"What kind of building?"

"A factory of some sort, next to the edge of railroad tracks. There's a river, no smaller, but bigger than a stream, more like a wide creek with lots of rocks on the other side. Black cars parked outside, but I don't see a door."

"Move towards the building."

Kat continued her mind's journey, drawing closer to the building. It was brick with boarded windows. *How strange*, she thought, *every single one is boarded up with pallets.* All painted black. Closer she moved towards the building. She sensed movement.

"There are men. In riot gear, like they wear on that tv show SWAT. Two, with guns," Kat said while continuing her mind trek.

Maneuvering her sight above them, she had a bird's eye view. Slowly drifting forward, she reached the front of the building. Ivy covered the sides and front. It looked like a door or entrance way laid dead head. Upon reaching it, she looked up. Framed with ivy was a rusted sign. It read, "Western Pennsylvania Transformer, Incorporated 1957." Kat's eyes snapped open. A broad smile replaced her despair.

"I know where they are! I know where they are!" she shouted.

Running around the side of the table, she hugged Corina.

"I found them! How did I do that?" Kat asked.

Corina produced a grin that matched hers. "I don't know. That was all on you."

"There was a sign. I could read it. Now I just have to figure out where this Western Pennsylvania Transformer is."

As the last word left her lips, the sound of two motorcycles roared up the access road towards the Sturgess homestead. Jud and Rhonda had returned. Kat watched as they pulled up in front of the barn, parking their bikes.

"That's my competition, huh?" Corina asked, grinning.

"Um, no, not really. I can't believe they are back!"

"The universe works in wondrous ways when you open fully to her. No rules, no control, just being. Remember that poppet."

Kat finally let go of the embrace. She noticed immediately that the contact didn't send her into sexual hyper-drive.

"C'mon, let's go tell the others what we learned," Kat said, taking Corina's hand.

"Um, I think it's better if I bow out on this one. The group energy you've all established is vital to what you are doing. I'd be disruptive."

"Oh, what do you English say? Bullocks! Learned that from Benny Hill. Besides, I need you to keep teaching me stuff or I may be the disruptive one," Kat reassured her.

"Perhaps next time. I have more studying to do. Your power has left me a tad knackered. Besides, we have unfinished business. I so want to find that pool and bring your fantasy to fruition in the real world," Corina said with a wink and a tease.

"But —"

"Go rescue your brother and the cowboy. You know how to find me."

Kat stood, shoulders slumped, as she watched Corina disappear into the brush.

Where the hell does she go? Kat thought. She can't just camp out in the bushes waiting for me to summon her with my magic rock!

She's real, that's for sure. Both Colt and Emma had met her. Jud and Rhonda approached.

"Any news? How's Colt?" Jud asked.

"Colt's gone, but I know where they took him, Western Pennsylvania Transformer," Kat answered.

Jud and Rhonda exchanged concerned glances.

"What?" Kat asked.

"Fuck. That's in Kinston," Rhonda sighed.

Chapter Twelve

Emma, Kat, Jud, and Rhonda sat around the dining table. There was trepidation about any type of rescue attempt. Coupled with their best intel came from a vision brought on by sexual energy. Hope was in short supply. Suspending belief in such metaphysical sources for non-believers may be the nail in the coffin for most, but this group had seen everything from ash tokers to gargoyles, so extending faith in Kat's abilities required little questioning. It simply was what it was. Besides, they had nothing else.

"What's the problem? Can't we just go in and see what's going on?" Kat asked.

"It's not that easy," Rhonda answered. "Don't you remember us saying it's leveled? No way in, they even blew the bridge. Hills surrounding the creek are graded down to an impossible slope. The debris nearly damned up the creek."

"Not so fast," Jud interrupted. "Difficult, but not impossible. I can draw a map. Let me think about it. I grew up on that creek, there are a couple of drains on the way to the plant. Depending on the damage from the demolition, they may still be accessible from the water. If we can get close enough where we aren't seen. Problem is, if guards are roaming around, probably on a scheduled patrol, stealth is gonna be the challenge."

"Screw stealth. If that's where they are, let's just storm the castle and get them," Emma added.

Jud smiled. "I like your attitude, but without a recon, no clue what we're walking into. Police backup won't happen. Whatever's going on in that old place, it's probably under the radar or fed controlled, which adds a whole other layer of complexity. I came back to help, but my job is fairly important."

"I understand," Kat said. "If you can help us make a plan at least, you don't have to go. Won't ask that of you."

"Oh, we're in. Just stating the obvious," Rhonda said.

Jud sketched a map on one page he tore from Kat's new notebook.

"We can slide along the bank. Night's probably best under the cover of darkness and all that. Would be easier if we had a raft," Jud said.

"Gotcha on that, Allen. We have rafts and a couple of kayaks out in the barn. Probably have to top off with the air pump. You don't think we live in the mountains on a feeder stream to a reservoir without water sports in mind?" Emma said.

Kat laughed. "What don't you have in that barn? It's like a K-Mart!"

The three women proceeded to the barn while Jud lagged. He was the strategist of the group and wanted to ensure the operation on his end was feasible. A renewed commitment fueled his drive to make this happen. After further reflection, he was ashamed that he left his friends in a bind after promising to assist them. His job was important, but the relationships he formed with this particular group of survivors were reflective of who he was at his core. Jud returned to reviewing what little intel he did have on the location.

On the opposite side of the transformer plant was rail access, but he wasn't precisely sure what obstacles were constructed to keep visitors out, as it wasn't visible from the highway. Creek approach was the best. After finalizing the plan, more like convincing himself of its feasibility, he departed to join the others.

Nearing the barn, he examined his team. Obviously, Emma knew how to handle a kayak, as did he. Rhonda and Kat would take the raft.

His wife had a crash course in rowing a couple of summers ago during a retreat with friends while he served reserve duty. Emma brought strength, speed, and confidence to the mission. Rhonda could hold her own, and he had both police and military training. Kat was the wildcard. From the retelling of the story from the night before, she possessed some sort of unnatural skills, but they weren't reliable. After running his five paragraph order the way the Corps had taught him, it was time to survey the equipment.

Entering the barn, Emma had pulled the tarp from the fourth stall on the left, one he was curious about but hadn't explored with Colt. Beneath it lay an assortment of outdoors adventuring equipment. Kat was right, that barn was like a K-Mart. Rhonda and Kat managed one kayak, taking it outside to the bed of the truck, while Emma took the second solo. The raft was next but needed inflated. Once Emma returned, the group removed it from the stall, loading it into the back of the truck as well, with a hand pump.

"No compressor?" Jud asked.

Emma shook her head. "No. Let's just say after our little adventure out at Olath's farm, neither of us wanted to see another one of those again. No worries, though. I can have this inflated in a jiffy once we get to where we're going."

Disappearing back into the barn, Emma returned with a length of rope to tie down the two kayaks and the raft.

"I've got something better," Jud said.

Walking over to his motorcycle, he removed several lengths of bungee cord from his saddlebag.

"Picked these up at Top Arnie's on my last trip. They have a million and one uses," he said.

Climbing into the back of the truck, Jud spent the next several minutes securing everything. When he was finished, the group returned to the barn to see what other useful implements they could find to aid in the mission. With luck, they would breach Kinston, go to the transformer plant, Jud could pull his deputy sheriff act and get

Colt and Johnny released. With additional luck, he would still have his job in the morning. Whether this rescue had anything to do with the bodies drained of life in the two cases, he hadn't a clue, but he was violating a direct order by not returning for a debrief immediately at headquarters. Nevertheless, he had made a commitment to his friends. That would be honored.

Retrieving a couple of flashlights, spare batteries and life vests, they started back towards the barn door when Emma suddenly froze.

"Problem?" Rhonda asked.

"Shh," Emma answered, slowly glancing towards the opposite side of the barn.

Whatever grabbed her attention, only she heard it. She homed in on the sound until locking in on it. With one super speed motion, Emma ran to the back furthest stall on the right, disappearing under the specially made tarp. A second later, a body slid across the floor of the barn.

"Fuck! What is it with you, girls?" Matthew yelled out.

He sat up dazed, still unable to use his feet from Kat's sword punctures the night before. Emma lifted him up with one hand.

"What are you doing here? You were tied up behind the barn, numbnuts?" Emma asked rhetorically.

"Who the hell are you? How many super-freaks live out here? You running a factory?" Matthew answered with more questions.

He had only encountered the older Emma. This younger version was new to him. Emma plopped him down on one of the stools she and Colt occupied the night before. Standing directly in front of him, she leaned in for maximum intimidation.

"It doesn't matter who I am. Where's Colt?" she asked.

"The old dude? I don't know. He took off in the truck after cutting me loose. He didn't want me to fry. Now I wish maybe that would have been a better idea."

"Oh, if it's sun you want, I can accommodate that, dipshit."

Emma grabbed him by the work apron he put on at some point that he found on the workbench. Lifting him off the ground, she moved to the barn entrance. Matthew raised his hands to his face, expecting to be launched out into the bright sunlight beaming through the door.

"Stop," Jud said.

Emma turned her head to face him quizzically.

"Set him down, Emma. Let me talk with him," Jud reinforced his request.

"Yeah, let the man talk to me!" Mathew echoed the appeal.

Rhonda nodded to Emma. Beyond all that had happened, Jud Allen was foremost an officer of the law. She didn't know it, but he was also brilliant with interrogations, uncanny even. That empathy that most believed would keep him from completing Marine Corps training served another powerful purpose. In the Biggs County Sheriff's Department, he was the one they brought in when they had a difficult suspect in the box. Confessions were his forte, which made anyone who knew him second guess any decision to bend the truth. Unfortunately, Emma didn't know that, however, she built trust with Rhonda during their brief reunion. With apprehension, Emma set Matthew back down on the stool.

"A moment?" Jud asked, summoning the three women out of the barn.

Once outside, he explained how he intended to conduct the interview, as he called it, with Matthew. Luckily, Kat had an ancient pack of Kools and a book of matches from the diner left over from Aunt Rosie in the glove box she kept for nostalgia's sake. Cigarettes were always a great icebreaker. He assured them the extra time may reveal what they would walk into. If they had confidence in this plan, he wanted consensus on how it would be executed. They all agreed. Jud reentered the barn, closing the door.

Colt's eyes fluttered open. The scene before him was workman like, sanitary. He found himself in an enormous room, possibly a warehouse, except that initial observation of sanitary rung true on several fronts. Other than so much white everywhere from the workers to the walls to the floors, it was so blinding it caused his eyes to water. Then there was the smell. Antiseptics like rubbing alcohol. Sturgess had never been in a hospital, but from tales he overheard in his previous eavesdropping while tracking Olath, this was what people described.

He heard stories like that at every stop. People found it imperative to share their ailments with others. Colt found it strange, but something he learned to endure in his quest for knowledge. Colonoscopies, hernias, gynecological exams, broken bones, stitches. He had heard it all. Something about being immortal, to this point anyway, the incessant need for people to discuss physical maladies was the strangest sort of bonding, yet effective. No matter the background of those engaged in conversations, the commonality was human frailty. As if discussing such things would somehow stave off the grim reaper or at least make them feel better about their own recent diagnosis. It was as if they traded such personal information with the ease of trading cards. "I'll swap you a cancer diagnosis for a case of stage two diabetes."

He breathed deeply, invaded by the smell of isopropyl alcohol. That he knew from using it to dissolve window frost during particularly brutal ice storms from lake squalls.

"Ah, I see you are finally awake," a voice said behind him.

An attendant turned the wheelchair around in which Sturgess was presently seated. His clothes had been removed, wearing only an over the head cloth garment. Adjusting his seat in the contraption, he winced as his ass stuck to the tackiness of the wheelchair. When the chair came to rest, he was face-to-face with Kaleb Blackburn.

───

Jud Allen sat down on the stool Emma used the night before in the barn. He handed Matthew a cigarette from the pack. There was a hesitation on his part to accept anything from any of the people on this farm. All they provided so far was excruciating pain of just about every kind.

"Nah, man, I'll pass. Probably got some arsenic or something in it, knowing you fuckers," Matthew said.

"Suit yourself," Jud responded, placing the pack and matches on the floor between them.

"What is this, bro? Some kind of good-cop, bad cop thing? You know I watched that stuff on tv, not falling for it."

Jud sat back on the stool, causing it to creak. He simply stared at the young man, bruised, and cut more from Emma's recent handling of Matthew.

"Nope, just trying to figure things out. My friend won't touch you again. I've seen to that. No threats, no violence. Not a fan of either," Jud said.

Rising from the stool, he walked casually around the barn. It was interesting how a couple of nights ago he was being shown the fleet of Sturgess' vehicles. Presently, it was an interrogation room. How things changed in forty-eight hours. Much like Kinston, the town he grew up in, was now a desolate wasteland harboring two of his friends in what he knew as an abandoned factory.

Emma drifted across his mind. Her sporadic memory. What was the use of having memories to hold on to for a place that no longer existed? Did they even matter anymore or was he now in the position of record keeper, a historian of the events that transpired, leaving it a pile of dirt between neighboring towns? Something to discuss with Rhonda at some point. They loved such conversations. Matthew broke his subconscious meanderings with the sound of a match striking. Jud continued to wander. It was part of the plan. People always had something to say if they felt ignored.

"So, why you bein' nice to me?" Matthew asked.

Still looking away from him, Jud picked up a strip of hose that had been discarded on the floor by the workbench.

"Oh, you know. Lost both my folks early but remembering my mom always saying you get more bees with honey than vinegar…or something like that," Jud answered smiling.

"All I know about bees is they sting the shit out of you."

The two shared a laugh. Jud returned to his stool.

"Think those are hornets. Most bees don't sting, well, unless you piss them off. Then they die right after. Guess it's the nature of some things. Instinct over prudence," Jud said.

"Yeah, I hear that," Matthew said, blowing a smoke ring from one of the Kools he tried.

Jud offered a handshake. "Jud Allen. Nice to meet you."

Matthew stuffed out the cigarette, wincing from stepping on it. His feet still hurt like hell from Kat's sword trick. He returned the greeting.

"Yeah, hey, man. Matthew Bristol, but acquaintances call me 'Opossum.' Never dug the name Matt. Always sounded like someone who stepped all over you. Not my thing."

"'Opossum,' huh? Unusual nickname."

"Yeah, well, I kind of like left alone. Not exactly a day tripper, prefer being active at night. Don't really stay in one place for too long to call anyone 'friend.' Never read a lot to come up with a more exotic name. Besides, in my line of work, after hours when the sun goes down is more productive."

"And what is your line of work?"

Mathew Bristol, aka Opossum, tapped another Kool from the pack, lighting it up, taking a deep draw. He then puffed out a few smoke rings.

"You the fuzz?" he asked.

"Actually, I am. Deputy sheriff down in Biggs County," Jud answered.

It was a calculated risk to disclose that tidbit of information, but if trust was to be exchanged, honesty was vital. Matthew blew a lungful of smoke off to the right of where the two men sat. It had worked. In a typical interrogation, suspects preferred blowing the smoke right in his face as a display of disrespect. That usually signaled to Jud it was going to be a tough road.

"That's cool. Appreciate you being straight with me, man. That's respect. I get that."

Jud nodded. The stage had been set. A tenuous bond of trust was forming, but he didn't want to press too hard yet. Matthew's backstory was a good entry point, since he willingly offered a few crumbs of information, along with his name. Jud recorded every word, every syllable this young man was tossing out.

"How'd you end up in this neck of the woods, so to speak?" Jud asked.

"Man, that's a story and a half. I'd get into it, but I'm thirsty as a motherfucker. Could use a jug of water. Nothing else. Don't do well with anything but water lately."

Jud rose, exiting the barn. Currently, he was in charge. A small show of goodwill by request would only deepen the trust bond. That was the end of what he would offer, however. A fine line had to be respected in conducting this interrogation. Much like offering a barking dog a bone, the command to "sit" must be rendered before passing on the treat. It denoted the animal's place in the pack. It worked wonders with humans as well.

The group outside moved to the porch. As Jud approached, Kat asked how it was going. He didn't respond to the question, simply retrieved a pitcher of water and a glass, returning to the barn.

"He's not being rude, he's just focused. Trust him. Jud's fantastic at this," Rhonda said.

Kat resumed waiting. Emma sensed her uneasiness.

"Hey, give me a hand, Kat. Let's stock up the artillery. Since Colt left all the hardware behind, let's load up the back of your car," she said, grabbing Kat by the wrist.

Reluctantly, Kat Ellis followed her into the cabin.

There's enormous value in gestures of kindness, even more so to a lost soul. Most times, the less fortunate prefer to be treated like everyone else. Not that Matthew Bristol was anything other than what he had presented so far. Details essential to the Kinston group's upcoming mission remained locked in his head for now. At least that's what Jud believed.

Returning to his stool, Jud handed him the glass of water. Taking the pitcher instead, Matthew drank the entire two quarts without pausing for a breath. Letting out a refreshing sigh, he placed the empty pitcher between the two of them.

"Thanks. I was drained."

Silence drifted in as a third party for the moment. Opossum just stared at Jud like he was an alien, sizing him up.

"What's your angle, man? Obviously not gonna run me in or you would have done that already. You called off the psycho chick from kicking my ass again. Seriously, what gives?" he asked.

Jud exhaled, never dropping eye contact. He let that silence set still a bit longer.

"We got a bit of a problem, Matthew. That gargoyle pal of yours—"

"Blackburn? He ain't no gargoyle. No fucking clue what he is, but the cat has powers. Like real powers. Gets in your head. Doesn't matter how far away. Not talking about like mind-control. He can take you places. Shows you things without being around, but you never really go anywhere. It's some sort of brain trip. I was just minding my own when he pops in. Every hour of the day. Wanted me to meet up with the others here. Don't know what his interest is in the old man, but that's his target. Guess he got him too as he left me out here high and dry, the fucker."

Jud relaxed a bit, processing the information. Colt was the target, but of what? Was it a revenge thing for Kinston or something else? Sturgess, of course, possessed supernatural powers, but who knew about that? The cowboy had spent over a hundred years stalking Olath's operation. He had disclosed none of the details or whose path he may have crossed. Perhaps vengeance wasn't Blackburn's goal, but something else.

"How'd you meet him? Blackburn, that is," Jud asked.

"That's a story and a half too. Not sure I have enough smokes for that one. I'll condense it like tomato soup as I'm guessing you want to go after his backstabbing ass. Here goes nothing. Jumped a train out of Louisville. Boxcars are how I get around. Anyway, dropped off at a stop down in Kinston. Wandered into town at night, of course. A big carnival of some sort was going on. Figured I hit a gold mine. Looked like the whole damn town was partying. Long story short, I rolled down the main street when all hell broke loose. Seriously, man, the craziest shit I ever seen. Little demons, clowns, the whole magilla just ripping through people. I ran my ass off."

Jud Allen knew this part all too well. He was at ground zero of the attack. This revelation piqued his interest exponentially, but he had to keep his poker face. A commonality was established that he did not expect. Although time was of the essence, mining Matthew's account from a different perspective became as important as Blackburn's whereabouts.

"Bro, I don't expect you to believe any of this, but I'm telling you. Never touch the wacky weed or any of that other shit. Keeping my wits about me is important. Been in the clink a time or two before. Not my idea of grand accommodations. I'll stick to boxcars."

"After the things I've seen lately, I believe everything you say. Please, continue."

Stuffing out the butt, Matthew lit up another Kool.

"Yeah. So, I found this big ass house a couple of blocks away. It was dark. Dumbasses always leave a key under the mat. True enough, there it was. I slipped in, went down to the basement and just laid low. Never put the lights on, just hung out, ya' know? Long story short, I must have crashed and burned, even with all the screams and shit. Never been so scared in my life. I'm a grown man, no shame in my game, but bro, I'm telling you, it was insanity with a bullet.

"Must have had a guardian angel, as nothing happened. Notta. I just slept until the sun crept in the next morning down the stairs. Woke up, checking out the house. Looked all prim and proper from the outside, but some freaky deaky people lived there, as the first thing I saw was something out of the Playboy mansion in the basement. Wall-to-wall pink fur, handcuffs, a table with whips, all shorts of sex shit. Sorry, never saw anything like that, thought it was pretty funny. Never know what goes on behind closed doors, eh?"

Opossum was drifting and Jud knew now was the time to press a little. The guy was a talker. That was good, but he needed to get at the more important details more than this house owner's proclivity toward sexual exploration. He smiled slightly as a lifelong resident of Kinston, wondering just whose house it was.

"So, I'm guessing you were around for the fireworks that night?" Jud asked.

"Hell yeah! How you know about that?"

"I am a Deputy Sheriff. We got calls."

Jud had to lie about his actual involvement. Key to questioning a person was never to give up any personal information, as the interviewee sculpted answers to what they perceived the questioner sought.

"Gotcha. Yeah, man. These soldiers stormed the town. Lit those fuckers up with tanks and trucks. Must have been a battalion raining down hell on the fuckers by the sounds of it. I wandered out, sticking to shadows, but didn't dare get close enough. I just heard all that firepower and the smoke. Damn the smoke. Something was on fire. Probably had flame throwers or something. Then it got all quiet."

"What did you do then?"

"Made a sandwich that I threw up a couple of hours later. Weird thing, now that I think of it, haven't really eaten much since then. Just not into it. Think it was that smoke. Wasn't normal, like oily. Fuck it, whatever. You asked a question. Next day, crack of dawn, some asshole comes riding around with a bull horn telling people to come out, all's clear. Umm, hell no. I stayed a few more days, scooping up all that I could, waiting for the coast to clear.

"Owners obviously weren't coming back, a nice caddy in the garage. I found the keys hanging in the kitchen. People are too predictable. Loaded up the trunk with silverware, they had the good stuff." Matthew paused, looking Jud over again. "Sure you're not gonna run me in? I'm talkin' too much."

"Promise. Just wondering how Blackburn fits into all this," Jud responded calmly.

"Oh yeah. Thanks too, about not arresting me. Not that there's any evidence. That was years ago, and I didn't quite get out of town with my take. As soon as I pulled out of the driveway, these fucking suits swarmed me like SWAT, even had choppers overhead. It was crazier than the night I jumped off that train. Cats were in those hazard suits, couldn't even see faces. Next thing you know, I'm in the hospital, getting forcibly showered and scrubbed with one of those brooms you sweep factory floors with. It was a total cluster fuck. That's where I first met Kaleb fucking Blackburn."

"In the hospital?"

"Yeah. Some kind of half ass quarantine. They didn't tell us shit, just lined us up. Blood test after blood test. X-rays, fingers up the bunghole, scrote squeezes, bro, I swear, I never been so violated. After about a week, they pull a bunch of us into a separate group, dragging us to a different part of the hospital. Doors locked from the outside. We ain't goin' anywhere. That's when the shots started and then more tests. Blackburn was always there, coming by, talking to us. As a group and by ourselves. It was a mind fuck; I've seen that shit before. Had an uncle in 'Nam told me about how some of those POW interrogations roll. Build up that trust, then use us for whatever the hell they have in mind. I wasn't biting. Then shit started hitting the fan. People started changing."

"Changing? How?"

Unbeknownst to Matthew, Jud was in that same hospital, but not in this group he was referring to. He remained with Rhonda as they lied about their relationship, telling the authorities they were married. Whatever was actually going on in the hospital, staff appeared to respect familial bonds. As for Kat and Johnny, that was a haze as to all the events that took place in quarantine. He didn't remember seeing them. Then the unusual character transformations. Could this be a new aspect of the mystery?

"Just changing. Some people went full tilt, foaming at the mouth, freaking out. They were dragged off; we never saw them again. Others well..."

"What, Matthew?"

He lit up another cigarette, staring off at the barn door. He had erected an unexpected wall in their conversation. Matthew confessed to being a petty burglar and transient, but whatever was confronting him on his memory's doorstep was fear. Jud saw it in his eyes. Even his posture stiffened. The talker suddenly grew quiet. Jud reached over, squeezing Matthew's shoulder. Slowly, Opossum turned to face him.

"I've experienced a lot of things. Knew as a kid, I didn't really fit in anywhere. Pretty decent home life, ya know? Glued to the tv most days. Not a whole lotta friends. Just needed to get out on my own. Skipped school one day, jumped the rails and off I went. That was about ten years ago. Learned a lot about myself and stayed out of the rat race of living. No offense, man, just not for me. Being controlled is a death sentence. That's what that place was. It was a testing lab, a prison. None of us had any say in what they were shooting us up with, or even why we were fucking there."

"I get it. I lost my whole family a while back. Everybody. Never had a car, rode a bike, paper route, bought comic books and records. That was my thing. Never occurred to me that maybe I should try to fit in. It was just my gig."

"Right on," Matthew said. "What happened? Seriously. You went from that to being a cop?"

"Yeah. Suddenly, after leaving that hospital, structure seemed like a good thing to fall into."

Jud just screwed up, dropping the fact that he, too, was in quarantine. Matthew jumped on that, literally up from the stool. He grabbed Jud by the hands, shaking them in adulation.

"You were there? Man, I knew something was familiar about you. Dude, you know then, you know I'm not full of shit! This stuff happened!"

Nodding slowly, Jud hoped he hadn't blown everything with his disclosure. He could have quickly recovered saying it was a different facility, but Matthew's reaction dictated Jud stayed on the course of truth.

Matthew sat back down, rubbing his chin, attempting to process a few things.

"You're not blowing smoke, are you, bro? I mean, you weren't with us."

"No, I was left in the other group, apparently. Yes, I was there."

"Well, fuck me to tears. Two birds of a feather, but you were lucky, believe you me. The shit that went down in that ward. When people started changing, the common thing was soul suckers. You didn't get to see that the night the old man and his woman kicked our asses."

"Soul suckers?"

Matthew rubbed the back of his neck. He was still holding something back.

"Yeah. People, I dunno. A fucking mist. Just poured out of us, I mean them…"

This time, Matthew slipped. Of course, Jud caught it.

"…the mist has a way of going into somebody else. Drains the life force. They look like goddamned mummies when you're through until you learn to just take little sips. It's a mind-fuck too. Not quite on Blackburn's level, but once you're in, it triggers some kind of fear thing. I don't know how to explain it other than that. The mist feeds off of scaring the shit outta people. The higher the better. Until you learn how to control it, you can suck someone down to dust. Real wicked shit. They tried it on the old man, but something about him really fucked them up."

That was it. The link between the three bodies drained of life. Three that Jud knew about, anyway. His case, the investigation, was tied to Blackburn and his companions. That was the "who" of the case, but the "why" remained. Were the couple outside of Cooper's Gulch part of this scheme, or just unfortunate victims of a feeding? Then, the man found by the railroad tracks outside of Madison. What was the connection between them and were there others?

"What happened to you?" Jud asked.

"Figured that out, huh? Yeah, I was one of them. When they moved us because the ones they couldn't control were causing a big problem, I wasn't fucking going along with the program anymore. I used it to get out. Got as far away from that place as I could. May have sucked for the people I hurt on the way, but I wasn't going to a bigger bird cage."

"Any idea where this 'bigger bird cage' is?"

"Nope. Just got woken up one night with Blackburn in my head, talking to me, no, commanding me. Tried ignoring it, but like I said, the cat has powers. I can't do the mist thing anymore. Blackburn said that was just the first stage of what comes next. He was supposed to show me more if I helped with the old man, but that didn't go too well from the get-go."

Matthew crushed out his cigarette, picking up the empty pitcher. A solitary bead of water rolled into his mouth. He held it out to Jud, who retrieved it. Time for a refill if they were to continue.

"You know, your boy bought all the way in. Too bad Blackburn flew off with him. Maybe he could tell you more."

That caught Jud off guard. For the first time, he broke his detachment.

"My boy?" he asked, confused.

"Yeah, man. The chubby dude with the mask. You know, they had to tell you. It's why you're asking questions, right? To find where Blackburn took him and the old man?"

Johnny Ellis. He was talking about Johnny. Matthew detected the surprise on Jud's face. Not that it was hidden.

"Oh, shit. You didn't know? Sorry, man. He was in on this all along. The boy was the trump card, the ace up the sleeve, the inside man. The other two with me and Blackburn were his direct line to the man himself," Matthew disclosed.

Jud sprang to his feet, rushing out of the barn.

"Hey, where you goin'?" Matthew yelled out behind him.

Jud ran over to Kat immediately.

"Were you and Johnny separated at the hospital in quarantine?" he asked.

"Yeah, but why do you ask?"

"When?"

"Like right away, but I got to visit him almost every day."

"What's going on, babe?" Rhonda interrupted.

Jud paused, looking at the group. He dashed over to the cabin, refilling the pitcher of water, then retrieved a quilt from the couch. Heading back to the barn, Emma, Kat, and Rhonda watched, still trusting his process without further questions.

Returning to Matthew, he handed him the water, tucking the quilt around his back.

"What's that for?" he asked.

"Going to run a quick errand. I'll be back later. In case nighttime hits first, it can get cold out here. If you run out of water, there's a hose around the side of the house. I'd offer you better accommodations, but not mine to give," Jud said.

Matthew nodded. Jud headed back the way he came. Opossum shouted out.

"Hey Jud Allen, you're pretty square in my book. Thanks, man and sorry."

Jud turned back to face him. "Sorry about what?"

"You know. If you were in that hospital, you're infected too, like the rest of us. Hate like hell to see you change into whatever, but it happens to all of us eventually," he answered.

It was the first time Jud considered that. They were let go. Free to carry on their lives after a brief stay. Maybe they were just a control group. That was the strange, out of character reactions they all endured following release. Hopefully, that would be the extent of the change

Opossum spoke of, that they were cured by the strong emotional response of seeing Emma for the first time since the incident. Whatever the reason, certain people were taken away to Matthew's group, perhaps for another reason, a biological reason. This was not the time to ponder ifs and buts. He needed to find Colt and Johnny with his ragtag team of warriors.

He rushed towards the truck, where Kat stepped abruptly in front of him.

"You going to tell me what's going on and why the questions?" Kat asked.

"I think Johnny's in a lot more trouble than we thought. Pretty sure Colt's with him. We need to roll out now," he answered.

Rhonda jumped in the pickup truck with Jud, Emma joined Kat in the Oldsmobile. They sped off on a mission back to Kinston. Would it be their final one?

Chapter Thirteen

"You probably have so many questions, Mr. Sturgess?" Blackburn asked.

Colt shook his head with a sarcastic smile. "Not particularly."

Blackburn circled Sturgess like a hawk over a field inhabited by a single mouse. His fingers were crossed, index fingers steepled, pressed against his lips. His eyes searched for something that he could not find. It frustrated him, but that would be the last thing Kaleb Blackburn would let creep into his face. The man who could transform into a gargoyle held a stoic gaze, as if he truly were composed of stone.

"I must confess, I'm somewhat at a loss. Probing a subject's mind is typically child's play. You, however, are a void. As if you are not living," he said, sliding a chair in front of Colt.

"Subject, huh? First time I've been called that," Sturgess said.

Leaning forward, Blackburn took Colt's hands into his.

"I hoped to gain an insight into your past, but since that doesn't appear possible, let me share mine," Blackburn whispered.

Colt's head shot back in a spike of indescribable pain. For a moment, he felt as if he would have to force a breath on his own. Slowly, he exhaled. No longer in a wheelchair in some unknown lab, he was surrounded by darkness. A large moon appeared, then a cemetery. He detected movement on the far side of a row of crumbled gravestones. A shadowy figure stepped from a large decaying stone shaped like an angel. It was Blackburn. Black top hat, long coat with an enormous sword on his shoulder.

He motioned Sturgess to follow, which he did. Whatever this vision was, Blackburn was manufacturing it. Escaping the scene would be fruitless. Colt heeded the gesture to see what his captor wanted to show him.

Across the cemetery lay crumbling ruins. At an initial glance, this place preceded him by a century or two, maybe more. Following Blackburn into the ruins, he kept a close eye on the specter. Was he going to deliver a strike in this place out of time? If he did, would this mean the end of him in reality? Then the matter of John Paul Ellis' release. Sturgess moved ahead of Blackburn into an antechamber. Greeted by gothic architecture with large stone gargoyle capped columns, it presented all the ornate trappings of a cathedral. If the decorator originated from the depths of hell. Blackburn joined him just inside the entrance.

"This is my story. My origin. After being infected with the blood plague, I was dropped here. Ages before Olath or you or anything, for that matter. I was bitten by what was later coined as a vampire in modern folklore. My creator led me to this sanctuary, but an immediate problem emerged. It was already inhabited by other creatures of the night," Blackburn said.

Colt's vision blurred suddenly. When he regained focus, Blackburn was swinging wildly at dozens of creatures emerging from catacombs. In his hand, a jeweled broadsword. His speed was comparable to Sturgess as he dispatched the attackers with a similar alacrity as Colt did with ash tokers. The humid, stagnant air hung in the tomb, causing the blood spray to drift momentarily, transforming into a crimson mist before dissipating. Even the moon behind him appeared to glow blood red.

As the last creature fell, Blackburn grabbed it, sinking his teeth into the thing's throat. Draining it, he flung it unceremoniously to the corner of the room like an empty beer can at a picnic. He wiped his mouth, then pivoted to Colt. Blackburn held the broadsword in front of him.

"This. This was my initial power. Have you heard of the sword of Damocles, Mr. Sturgess?" he asked.

Colt shook his head negatively.

"Cicero wrote a parable in 45 B.C. Not to drag out a history lesson, Damocles was envious of King Dionysius, his power and wealth. Dionysius offered Damocles the throne to experience the benefits of being a king, which he welcomed. At one point, Damocles noticed a large sword suspended over his throne, held up by a single horsehair. This is when he abruptly decided he no longer wished to be king. The moral of the story, of course, is there is always looming danger when holding a seat of power. Even John Kennedy used it in a speech regarding nuclear warfare. I, however, took it another way. Seizing the sword adds a greater level of fear and obedience from subjects. Courage is what Damocles lacked. Courage to seize the sword and have it all."

"There's that word again, 'subject.' I reckon now you're gonna demand my loyalty to a mythological sword?"

Blackburn roared with laughter. "Hardly. Look around you. Riches are as far as the eye can see in the darkness; your gifted eyes have no such limitations. This is only a small part of this structure. I left it all behind. In time, I grew to appreciate there are greater things than money and power. Those who flail on the world stage for either or both are merely marionettes, easily swayed to dance for a pittance when so much more to gain is just fingertips away for the willing. To accept the simple meaning of Cicero's tale is to accept a message meant for sheep."

"Mmm, hmm," Colt responded.

"That's all you have to say? I granted you a glimpse into something beyond any other's experience and you utter nothing more than a grunt?"

"Where's the boy?" Colt asked.

"Aha! You get it. A tiny fragment, but you understand," Blackburn answered, clapping his hands gleefully. "Very well. Let's finish your purpose."

Blackburn dropped the broadsword, clasping Sturgess' hands once more. The dizziness rushed in, followed by the darkness and labored breathing. Blinking his eyes rapidly, the light from the laboratory returned, followed by the face of Kaleb Blackburn.

"I hope you didn't mind the brief trip down memory lane. It's much easier if the other participant has a two-way receiver, so to speak. You appear no worse for the wear," Blackburn said.

Colt remained silent as he shook off the disorientation. He wasn't sure of the extent of Blackburn's powers, especially if he couldn't detect the obvious. Colt Sturgess was dying quickly. The healing ability would have immediately triggered on any outside pain stimulus. Hell, he couldn't even catch his breath from whatever Blackburn had just done. However, there was more. His equilibrium was off, strength was what one would characterize as feeble, his eyesight was failing and that was just what he could feel. Whatever plan they had for him in this factory, laboratory, whatever it was, it had better happen soon if Johnny had any chance of freedom.

"Better?" Blackburn asked.

"Let's just get on with it," Colt answered.

"But of course," he paused. "Just one more thing. I'd like you to meet a few old friends. Just as a courtesy to them."

Blackburn wheeled Colt into an examination room. On the other side of a large glass observation window was an adjacent room. Colt squinted to see what filled the room. It appeared to be large, cylindrical clear glass tubes. Much like test tubes, but these ran from floor to ceiling with a girth large enough to fit a human body. *Human bodies,* Sturgess thought.

An attendant and assumably a doctor entered the room. Blackburn threw a switch on a panel that lit the tubes up. His perception was correct. They were indeed human bodies. Sturgess forced himself to stand, leaning against the glass window, looking into the room.

The room was wall-to-wall with rows of tubes stretching from floor to ceiling, with several tanks running parallel to the encasements mounted to the ceiling. The tanks had multiple pipelines feeding the individual glass prisons. It was something out of a horror movie. Like the limbs hanging from the ceiling of Olath's charnel house, except this operation was neater. Cleaner. As if someone had taken the madman's ideas and improved upon them.

"Notice anyone familiar?" Blackburn asked.

Perusing the room, the first person he saw was Sarge, then Flower. Both were naked, submerged in a clear, thick fluid like lab specimens. To their left, two more familiar faces he left for dead on the main street of Kinston five years earlier. When they noticed Colt looking through the window, each tapped on the confinement chambers from the inside, followed by big smiles and simultaneous waves. Frick and Frack were both alive and well.

"I see two of them are quite happy to see you," Blackburn snickered.

"What in the name of god is going on here?" Colt asked in disbelief.

"Don't worry about your friends, Mr. Sturgess. They are alive and well. That fluid they are suspended in is an experimental liquid oxygen solution to slow down aging, increased cell reparations, a myriad of uses that I won't bore you with. They are comfortable, feel no pain whatsoever. We provide a modified opium derivative that keeps them calm, happy even."

Colt turned to face each of them. The implications were obvious. They turned the remnants of Kinston into subjects.

He shook his head in disbelief. "You fellahs are running some sort of futuristic ghoul lab. Like that bastard Olath, but all hi-tech like with government backing and unlimited resources. Leave it to the feds to take something horrific and turn it to profit."

"Never profit. Remember the sword of Damocles. Oh, almost forgot, your friend Olath is with the others as well," Blackburn said taunting.

Colt grimaced. "Bullshit. That son of a bitch is anything but a friend. Nothing left of him but ashes at last check."

"Maybe so, but he kept meticulous journals over the centuries that we found in the one building that you didn't destroy, the farmhouse. More specifically, the farmhouse basement. It's why we searched so diligently for you, Colt, or should I call you, Patient Zero?"

Blackburn took Colt by the arm, guiding him into the confinement room. He no longer possessed the strength to resist. Stopping in front of the tube next to Frick and Frack, two black, slimy chucks of something floated around in the fluid. The one chunk had a grayish leg that had grown from it, the other was more rectangular. Atop the shape was a distorted oval stump. As it turned in the fluid, Sturgess observed several malformed teeth, an oversized eye and charred ear. It was hideous.

"That is your old nemesis, Professor Ansel Olath. The doctors here attempted early infusions of Solution X, a jug of a remarkable liquid we retrieved from the twins here to your immediate left on their attempted escape from the farm you leveled. I beg pardon, I continue to assume it was you that were responsible for its demise since you are the only survivor of that operation. The only one we are aware of. Although I understand from my young protégé, Matthew, that you have a female companion of extraordinary abilities and, of course, the girl who commands swords at will —"

"Leave them out of this or you die here on the spot and this hell on earth goes up in a ball of flame. You know, fire and I are old friends."

"That's what I understand. You have my word. Besides, my contract was for you and you alone. I don't wander outside of purpose unless I desire it. I've spent enough time on this errand tracking the survivors. You were the last piece. Within you lies the secret to all of this here. A shame really that you are nothing more than a common laborer with a singular focus. We could have accomplished anything," Blackburn said.

The man Colt assumed was a doctor emerged from the room behind the glass observation window.

"Enough with the tour, Kaleb. Your work here is finished. Take the..." The doctor stopped, then cleared his throat after finding the correct description that wouldn't offend. "...take your payment and leave. I'm going to need the space down below. Nobody can tolerate the smell anymore."

Blackburn bowed, releasing Colt's arm. Sturgess braced himself on Olath's tube to prevent himself from falling. If it wasn't for his dire predicament, Sturgess would have found irony in the use of the container for his own stability. The doctor noticed the unsteady posture overcoming him. He looked into both of his eyes with an examination penlight, following a quick check of Colt's heart with a stethoscope. Looking up, concerned, he addressed Blackburn.

"You sure this is Colt Sturgess? The man in Olath's journals?"

"Of course. He nearly sent me to the great beyond single-handedly in Apollo. Why? Is there a problem?" Blackburn asked.

"Your self-importance must be blinding you. This man has every sign of a person going into cardiac arrest!"

The doctor and his attendant carried Colt back to the examination room, placing him up on the table. Blackburn followed before being stopped by the doctor.

"Go now. It's time for me to go to work."

Colt reached out towards Blackburn. "The boy...you promised."

Blackburn nodded. "Indeed. I am many things, Mr. Sturgess. One is a man of my word. Until we meet again."

Kaleb Blackburn tipped his hat, leaving the examining room. He walked through a security door, down a ramp to a cargo elevator. Pushing the grating up, he stepped onto the platform and pressed the button to take him to the level below.

"I'm coming, my children. The time is finally here," Blackburn said as he descended to the sound of machinery.

Emma, Jud, Kat, and Rhonda arrived at the entry point, Hawthorne, a small-town bordering Kinston. Jud drove the solitary street through the center of town, glancing down the access road to a barbed wire fence which separated Hawthorne proper from the east side of what was formerly Kinston. A singular surveillance camera was mounted on top of a utility pole twenty yards from the obstruction. Jud continued down the street, turning the small two vehicle caravan around in the parking lot of Four-Star Pizza. Heading back in the direction they came; he made a left turn at the water pump station next to the creek they would travel to Western Pennsylvania Transformer. Parking out of sight alongside a brush pile and old railroad ties, the team stepped from the vehicles.

Jud reached into his jacket, removing his police credentials, sliding it on the dash of the truck.

"What's that for?" Rhonda asked.

"Well, if anyone comes by and sees the truck, this should be deterrent enough to keep them moving along," he answered.

"Oh, really. You don't think they'd smash the window, grab it and head off to use it for whatever reason?"

After considering the objection, he agreed, retrieving the badge.

"That's why I married you. You're way smarter than me," he said.

"Not smarter, just, well, you know…"

He leaned in and kissed her before assembling with the rest of the group.

The night was bitterly cold, even for the next to the last day of October. Whatever respite the day's sun had provided all weekend, it retreated behind a cold front with malice. Fortunately for them, those nights typically yielded a crystal-clear night sky. This was no exception. The moon would help them on their blind navigation down Rogers' Mill creek should Jud's childhood memories fail them. Although only in the waning crescent phase it would have to be enough.

Kat, Jud, and Rhonda unpacked the back of the truck, carrying the kayaks to the water's edge while Emma tended to inflating the raft with a foot pump, a task she accomplished in under a minute. After Jud and Rhonda geared up with Colt's revolvers and bandoliers of speed loaders, Emma retrieved the Kitana. The oars were Kat's responsibility. Jud and Emma took the lead in the kayaks, Rhonda stuck with Kat in the raft.

It was a tight fit. Rhonda sat behind Kat, nearly straddling her, and they embarked in the inflatable vessel. The body contact caught her off guard.

Ash trays, fuzzy bunny rabbits, burnt bacon, deer poop…

Rhonda Allen sensed her uncomfortable shift.

"You okay? There's nothing to it, really. You paddle on the right side of the boat; I go to the left. If we need to turn, I'll let you know and only one of us will paddle. Pretty easy, peasy actually," Rhonda said.

"Mm, hm," Kat responded, trying to push back her automatic reactions that Rhonda was completely unaware of.

The three craft drifted into the current of the twenty yards wide waterway.

"Everyone ready?" Jud asked.

The group signaled in various ways that they were.

"Here goes nothing," Jud said as they began the three-mile journey downstream.

Back at the Sturgess homestead, the sun had long surrendered to the skyline. All was quiet. Suddenly, a scream disrupted the tranquility of the solemn surroundings. Momentarily, silence settled in again, only to be ripped with an unnatural screech. The sound came from the barn.

Whatever was taking place within was torturous, violent even, based on the disturbance. As quickly as the sounds began, a force blew the barn door off its hinges. A dark form shot up into the air at an incredible rate of speed. Just below the clouds, it stopped. Hovering. Hunting. The creature had a grotesque face, large ears with enormous wings that glinted in the moonlight.

Turning its head left, then right, it searched through glowing amber eyes. Sniffing the air, its ears twitched, searching, seeking prey. What that was precisely, only it knew. Drifting forward, its wings flattened to maintain altitude. Abruptly, it turned, staring into the night sky. The creature had found the object of its search. In a quick motion, it shot across the top of the tree line, heading south.

Along the western side of the state, a small object pinged on radar screens of air traffic control towers. They didn't last long enough to get a location fix as it moved at such an extraordinary speed, there was simply no way to track it. No reports would be filed as the readings were written off as flocks of birds or equipment malfunctions. If they saw the origin, nobody would believe it anyway.

Colt laid still on the examination table. The quicker this was over with, the sooner he could get Johnny back to his sister. If Kaleb Blackburn could be trusted. The fate of the other men he had met in Kinston five years earlier, now encased in glass tombs, would not be his goal this night. His own tank was nearly out of fumes. Wherever their destinies would end would not be by his hand.

Then there was Johnny. How he would get back to the Sturgess homestead was anyone's guess. Maybe Emma, Kat, Jud, and Rhonda could help? They didn't even know where he was. The last time he saw all of them was before he departed his farm.

A shame really, he thought. *Was just beginning to know those kids.*

"Dammit, what the hell is going on here?" the doctor shouted, rising from his seat after running multiple slides through the electron microscope.

"What is it, doctor?" his attendant asked.

"I've reviewed these journals, cover to cover for the better part of the past four years. Everything indicated this was the man, patient zero, but instead of finding the secrets to immortality, I have nothing more than a slide of fucking decaying cellular walls. This man, whoever he is, will be dead in under an hour. How he still lives is a mystery!" he answered, frustrated.

Colt smiled. Whatever the secret was to his century plus of life, with all his enhanced abilities, would die here with him. The cycle of madness was over. Storming out of the room, the doctor stopped suddenly, spinning back around to face the assistant.

"Get a vial of Solution X and hurry. We've run out of time," he said.

"But doctor —"

"I said now!"

The junior assistant sped off to retrieve the mysterious Solution X. Colt had a good idea what it was by Blackburn's mention of it. He also had an equally good idea of what this doctor was going to do with it. The only thing that remained was to see what effect it would have, if any.

The transfusion between him and Emma was a disaster for him. As with all Olath's experimental elixirs, the results were unique to the person who received it. It was fool's folly to expect a duplication of results unless the identical conditions were met with the identical genetic match. Not similar, identical.

He had done his own research, as curiosity tugged at him on how he survived. Basic interest demanded some sort of explanation. A paper was published in 1953 by Franklin, Watson, and Crick on deciphering the actual substance of DNA. Why would a rancher with an affinity for vengeance be concerned about such intellectually lofty pursuits? There simply had to be an answer. The same answers many seek when filling churches on Sundays. Colt Sturgess preferred libraries. Why this doctor seemed oblivious to genetics was confounding. Then again, people put in charge aren't necessarily the most qualified. Another lesson he had learned from his travels across time.

The attendant returned, handing the doctor a small case with a single vial of dark liquid. Retrieving a syringe from a cabinet, the doctor drew back the plunger. As the leading ring drew to the rear, the barrel was filled with liquid. He approached Colt.

"This may sting a bit," he said.

"Doctor, I must protest. We have had no success with this solution except madness," the assistant warned again.

His warning went ignored as the doctor injected Sturgess with the fluid. Colt's eyes rolled back into his head as his body convulsed. Both the doctor and assistant rushed to secure his arms to the table with binding straps. With maximum effort, they succeeded. A heavy breath left Sturgess' lungs as his body relaxed.

Once everything was calm, the doctor went to work, taking four new vials of blood and scraping several skin samples. He removed a case, placing the samples carefully in foam slots designed to hold the vials. Standing back, wiping his brow, the doctor sighed.

"Let's see if this has any effect. If not, we start back at square one with another who was affected. I'm going to get a coffee. If there's any change, no matter how slight, call me. Understood?" the doctor asked.

"Yes, doctor," the assistant answered.

"Oh, and never question my authority again or you'll end up out on your ass. Am I clear?"

"Yes, sir."

The doctor took the case of samples, leaving the examination room.

Colt drifted into a deep sleep, following the convulsions. He saw the proverbial bright light. As he approached it, a silhouette appeared. It was Lizzy. His Lizzy with her arms wide open. As Sturgess embraced her, he shot backward to the familiar visions. Olath, the fire, Kinston, the pile of ash beside him in the mad professor's parlor. Lizzy took his hand again with the crown of thorns mounted on her head. He glanced at her, but something was off, something was different in hindsight. Emma appeared. Sweet lost Emma. He sensed her somehow. Then Kat, Jud, and Rhonda. They were drifting down a creek in the darkness. If only he could hold on for just a while longer. The king of swords welcomes such challenges... He knew those words. Did he have one last ride left in him? Colt tried to rouse himself from the dream state, but to no avail.

***

"Wait!" Emma yelled out.

The rescue group had passed the half-way point of their trip when they stopped at her command, drifting only by the gentle current of the creek.

"What is it?" Jud asked.

Blankly, Emma stared ahead. She was seeing something, feeling something that was beyond the others. She began paddling furiously.

With her enhanced strength, the motion sent her kayak ahead of the others swiftly.

"Colt's in trouble. We gotta hustle!" she said.

Kat frowned, concentrating. She was perplexed why she could not sense the same element of danger. The raft turned in a circular motion as her pause while Rhonda paddled sent the inflatable turning in one direction.

"Kat! Wake up. We're spinning," Rhonda said.

"Oh, sorry."

Righting itself by the oars moving in concert once again, they closed quickly on Jud's position, but Emma had moved quite a distance ahead. As they finally approached her position, Jud reminisced about the old days fishing from the banks of the creek. Memories that were swept away by time, events, and the bulldozers that leveled his town. Their town. The only constant companion on the trip so far was the ugly chain-linked fence topped with barbed wire forty yards to his left.

Kinston was always a welcoming town. The kind of town in Norman Rockwell paintings. All that remained was dirt and rubble. It was shocking to see it up close for the first time since they were whisked off to quarantine, then his subsequent retrieval of Top Arnie's gift. Something about where anyone was born that has an indelible tether to the heartstrings. When there's nothing left, that bond is severed.

He saw Emma stop at the dam of concrete and steel. The remnants of the West Main Street bridge into town. It was far more of an obstacle than appeared from the highway. This was going to be a problem breaching. As the group caught up, each of the watercraft took a horizontal position against the obstruction.

"What now?" Rhonda asked.

Emma climbed out of the kayak, grabbing onto a piece of rebar protruding from the concrete. Pulling herself up, she slipped, falling into the icy water.

"Fuck, that's cold!" she screamed, reaching for Jud's hand.

Steadying herself, she grabbed a chunk of concrete, propelling herself to the top of the rubble. Naturally, the rest of the group did not possess her abilities. They would have to wait for a different solution.

"Stay here," Emma shouted.

"I don't think we have a choice," Jud shouted back.

Emma stepped on a larger piece of the collapsed bridge vaulting to the top of the graded embankment. She looked around for something she could use to get her friends to the top of the rocks. Whoever the construction, rather destruction, team was that leveled the town, they did an excellent job. Approaching the fence line, she observed the vegetation overgrowth that had swallowed the former town of Kinston. In the distance, she saw the lights from a solitary building. That was the transformer plant, their destination, she surmised.

Emma looked at the fence, wondering if that would suffice. The fence poles would do the job, as long as her friends below could hang on. She certainly possessed the strength to lift them. Stepping towards the fence, she grabbed onto the links. A loud crack, then a jolt blasted her backwards onto her backside. No one from her party saw the attempt as they were out of sight line, but they heard it.

"What's going on, Emma?" Jud called out.

Sitting up dazed, she looked down at her hands, which were smoldering with burns in the shape of the links she grabbed. Instantly, they faded.

"Fuck. Electric fence. Should have known," she mumbled. "Stupid Emma."

She stood, turning towards the group. "All good. First idea didn't work out."

Looking back at the fence, Emma ran towards it, vaulting over the eight-foot obstruction with plenty of room to spare. Once on the other side, she engaged her speed towards an outcropping of ruins about two-hundred yards from the factory. She crept up slowly over a portion of the wall that remained intact from the demolition. Kneeling, Emma looked forward towards the factory. She waited, surveilling the structure for any activity. Two guards wandered up a flight of concrete steps past a patch of trees. Waiting for them to make a patrol circle, they instead retreated down the steps after a minute.

"Can't wait to see what they got going on in that place," she whispered. "Not making transformers, that's for sure."

Standing, Emma entered the ruins of the building. She found something familiar about the place. Reaching into her fractured memory, all that emerged were fish sandwiches, whatever that meant. She, of course, preferred steaks. Big ones. Wandering around the darkness of what was left of the building, she bumped into a billiard table. She pushed it, but it was heavy. Really heavy. Emma reached under one edge to lift it. Waist high was the best she could do. Half a ton appeared to be her limit. Letting go of it, it thundered back to the floor.

"Well, that's not gonna happen," she said.

A sound caught her attention. Emma moved towards the back of the building. Stepping outside, she saw the origin. An American flag. Old glory. Tattered, yet still waving gently in the breeze. Somehow, it was spared the bulldozer's wrath, as was the building it flew in front of. More importantly for her, she spied a rope attached to it. Unwrapping the rope from the cleat, she lowered the flag. Unhooking the flag from the halyard, the roped was still attached at the top of the pole, which frustrated her. With a firm tug, the finial snapped. The remaining length of rope fell in a coil on her head. She looked back at the pole.

"Lucky you gave way. I was perfectly willing to pull you down," she said.

Speeding back toward the fence line, she wrapped the rope around her shoulder, folding up the flag. Emma couldn't just leave it on the ground. Jud would know what to do with it. Once more, she jumped the fence, slid down the embankment and navigated her way across the rocks towards her friends below. Tying knots every foot or so in the rope, Emma tossed the loose end down to Jud. He cinched it around his waist quickly and grabbed on to the closest knot. She tugged one, shooting him up to the top of the obstruction in one mighty heave, nearly sending him over the other side.

"Sorry," she said, grinning.

"No worries, get Kat next. Rhonda knows how to steady the raft," he said. "A little gentler this time, eh?"

She nodded, repeating the same process for Kat, then Rhonda. The four stood atop the remnants of the collapsed bridge.

"Where do we go?" Rhonda asked.

Emma motioned them forward to the edge towards the slope of the embankment.

"Shit," Jud uttered.

"What?" asked Emma.

He pointed off in the distance towards the factory. Slowly approaching were a set of headlights. Someone in the passenger seat was sweeping the area with a spotlight.

"How'd the hell they detect us? Wonder if it's just part of the patrol." Jud said.

"Um, I may have accidentally tugged on the fence, which may or may not still be electrified," Emma answered sheepishly.

Jud sighed. "So much for the element of surprise."

They all squatted instinctively, watching as the headlights drew closer.

"My screw up, my fix. C'mon Allen, I have a plan," Emma said.

Stepping to the edge of the rubble, Emma extended her hand. Reluctantly, Jud followed. She put his arm around her shoulder, hers around his waist, then leaped forward across the embankment to the base of the fence. Another jump and the two landed on the other side of the fence.

Jud rose slowly, unprepared for the sudden movements.

"So, what's your plan?" he asked.

"Just stand here in the middle of the road, um, well, weeds, where the road used to be. Flash that badge of yours when they stop," she answered.

"Where are you going?"

"Don't worry about that. You're just a distraction. I'll take care of the rest."

"A distraction, huh?"

She winked, blowing him a kiss, then disappeared in a blur of speed. Jud sighed. He guessed it was as good a plan as any.

On the rocks, Rhonda and Kat watched patiently. Scooting forward a little, Rhonda sought a better view. She slipped, falling down the twenty-foot pile of concrete and rebar. Screaming out just before she hit the water, Kat reached for her, but it was too late. Instinctively, Kat raised her arm. A gust of wind passed over, meeting Rhonda's entry point into the icy, murky water. The wind built to gale force, pushing a wall of water to the right of her location, channeling it away from Rhonda. She looked up in time to see Kat drifting down towards her in her own surge of air. She was flying.

Rhonda stood up, wincing. On her right calf, there was a large open wound. A piece of rebar caught her along the lower right calf during her accidental tumble. Kat reached down, offering her help.

"Fuck, how could I be so clumsy?" Rhonda said, grimacing through the pain.

"Don't worry about it. I do far stupider things all the time," Kat replied.

"Hey, how are you doing this Moses thing? Can you hold it?"

"I think. Let's just move as fast as we can to that pipe. I can see it from here. Put your arm around me, just hop. We'll make it together," Kat said.

Rhonda complied. As they moved forward, the wind moved with them, pushing the current to the right side of the creek. Moving carefully along the sediment, there were still rocks covered in moss to contend with and the occasional carp, which Kat swept into the current with an additional flick of the wrist. As they reached the pipe, Kat noticed a set of concrete steps running next to it, something Jud failed to mention. That was probably the way he intended as a point of entry. Kat stepped up on the first one, then the second. Rhonda was obviously in pain. Even the hopping was labored. Reaching the fourth step, the two sat down. Releasing her hold on the wind, water splashed back towards them like getting splashed by a huge mud puddle. The two drenched women looked at each other, bursting out in laughter. Why not? What else could go wrong?

It was at that moment Kat realized that her reaction to Rhonda's touch wasn't the typical, sexually fueled reaction. She was unsure why but tucked that nugget of wisdom away for further discussion at a later point in time with Corina. Those nuggets were beginning to pile up. For now, Colt was in trouble according to Emma, as was Johnny, according to Jud. They were within sight of the Western Pennsylvania Transformer factory. In minutes, they would have to confront whatever awaited them. She tended to Rhonda when a sweeping light from the vehicle above broke her reflections. Although out of sight of the intruders, instinctively they still ducked just beneath the pipe. Kat looked down at Rhonda, who was turning pale. She had lost blood. A lot of blood.

"Hurry, Jud and Emma," Kat whispered.

"Halt. Who goes there?" The passenger in the patrol jeep yelled the challenge.

Jud held up his hand, with his deputy sheriff badge in the right hand.

"Deputy…I mean, Agent Humptyfrats from the Bureau. Out conducting spot security response drills," he answered.

The guard climbed out of the jeep, keeping his M-16 rifle covering Jud while the driver approached.

"Humptyfrats, huh? Didn't you get the word from the top to stay clear of here?" he asked.

Whatever Emma was planning, he hoped she would trigger the trap immediately. This guard wasn't buying his military jargon, but it was the only thing he could come up with on the spot. With all his advanced planning, Deputy Jud Allen needed to work on improvising under duress.

Before he could answer, a blur of motion swept past him. The armed guard's head abruptly met the hood of the jeep. That was his cue to deliver a right cross to the driver. Both guards slumped to the ground.

"Was wondering when you were gonna show," Jud said to Emma.

"Don't they teach you anything in the Marines about patience being a virtue, Allen?" she asked, with a hint of her unique brand of sarcasm.

Jud surveyed the area.

"Well, looks like we have transportation. Think you can get the girls now?"

"Sure, on my way!"

"Oh, wait. I have an idea."

"Another one? Aren't you full of them tonight?"

He pointed down to the unconscious driver. "Yeah. How fast can you strip this taller one?"

She smirked. "All the way down?"

"Nah, down to his skivvies. Just need the uniform."

In a blur, Emma moved along the man's body. Within five seconds, she tossed a pile of clothes at him. "Fast enough?"

"Yup!"

Emma turned to vault the fence, but stopped short, turning to Jud. She removed the folded-up flag tucked away in her coat, tossing it to him.

"What's this for?"

Emma shrugged. "I dunno. Didn't want to just leave it. Figured you'd know what to do with it."

He nodded. Emma jumped the fence while Jud stripped down, dressing in the guard's outfit.

Leaping back on the rocks, she was surprised to see that neither Kat nor Rhonda was present. She looked downstream, panicky that they may have tried to climb the hill, only to have fallen into the creek. The collapsed bridge served as a dam, with large quiet pools at the base of the structure. However, rivulets of water swirling in the pools denoted water still flowed beneath it. That meant undertow. She began descending the rubble when movement up ahead on the shoreline caught her attention.

Emma vaulted back to the fence line, which caught Jud's attention.

"Problem?" he shouted over to her.

"Don't think so. Just looks like our girls made it downstream a bit. Better haul ass and get that jeep back to where you think the pipe is," she said.

Running along the fence, Emma used her hearing to zero in on Kat and Rhonda's location. She reached the cracked concrete steps that ran next to the pipe. The descent was a little tricky on the first few steps, but exponentially easier than the bridge debris. Emma made it to where the two women sat. Immediately, she saw Rhonda was in distress.

"What happened here?" she asked.

"I fucked up and fell in. Scraped my leg pretty bad. Kat was amazing. Parted the creek like the Red Sea. It was awesome," Rhonda answered.

Kat and Emma exchanged glances of concern. Moving towards Rhonda, Emma drew the kitana she had strapped on her back.

"Whoa! You're not going to chop her leg off, are you?" Kat asked.

"No. But you can't tell Jud what I'm about to do. Don't know how he'd react, as you guys don't seem to be affected by the Kinston shit. Promise?"

Kat nodded; Rhonda was too delirious from blood loss to answer. Emma ran the blade across her palm, slicing it open.

"I saw Colt do this once. Hope it works," Emma said, examining Rhonda's wound.

Blood congealed in her hand as she grasped Rhonda's leg. Ringlets of crimson smoke rose from the damaged limb. Rhonda screamed out. Up the hill, Jud heard his wife's cries of pain. He slid on the combat boot without tying it and jumped in the jeep. The tires screeched as he pulled from the vegetation up onto the remnants of West Main Street, heading towards where Emma told him to meet her. Slamming the brakes, Jud leapt from the front of the jeep before it came to a full stop. Rushing towards the fence, Emma landed in front of him with Rhonda in her arms.

"What happened?" he asked, taking his wife from his best friend's arms.

"They had a minor accident, but she'll be alright," Emma answered.

Jud laid Rhonda down in the back of the jeep, looking for a sign of an injury. The bottom right pant leg was torn and covered in dried blood. He tore the denim back to examine the skin, but no wound, no scar, nothing. Slowly, he turned to Emma.

"What did you do?" he asked.

"Nothing. Well, maybe something. Look, she was bleeding out and no telling if there was any infection. You'd rather I help or let her die on the hill?" Emma answered defensively.

Before he could answer, a burst of air grabbed his attention as someone drifted over the top of the fence, landing softly on their side. It was Kat.

"Think you can show me how you do that sometime?" Emma asked.

Kat just smiled. Unapprovingly, Jud shook his head while propping Rhonda up in the back seat. She was still out of it from the blood loss.

"Am I the only one around here without superpowers? I mean, I read comic books for the better part of my life and here I am, plain old Jud Allen."

"Yeah, but we love you anyway," Emma answered playfully.

"Okay, we're here. Let's go get Johnny and Colt," Kat said.

The crew piled into the jeep. It drove forward. Nearly to the Western Pennsylvania Transformer factory, a large object flew over them, close enough to tassel their hair around.

"What the fuck?" Emma shouted.

"I didn't do that," Kat said.

The three looked around before continuing. Whatever it was, it was gone now. Or was it?

Chapter Fourteen

The winged creature from the Sturgess homestead sat perched atop the transformer factory. Still and silent, it appeared like another stone guardian on any gothic architecture. Watching two men in black suits below talking about the past Sunday's football game while smoking cigarettes. From the left, a sedan sped up an access road, leaving a trail of dust.

Peculiar, it thought. *Didn't know about a road in for vehicles.*

Upon seeing the car, it leaned further over the edge to get a closer look at a row of cars parked adjacent to the loading dock of the factory, long assumed vacant. Those too had to be getting in somehow. The sedan pulled up to a ramp that led to the rear of the facility. Two more men in black emerged from the front seat, opening the back doors. Two people exited the vehicle, with similar shock vests that Colt was fitted with prior to his arrival. The four walked up the ramp, with one man in black leading, the second trailing, both passengers, an older man and woman between them. As they reached the door, the trailing escort pushed the older man. He reacted.

"Now, I told you, son, you'll get no trouble out of us. If you keep pushing me though, I don't care what kinda hai karate they taught you, but I promise I will disarm you of that pea shooter and stick it where the good lord split ya," the man said. It was Arnold "Top Arnie" Phillips.

The creature above chuckled at the old veteran's defiance. Although it did not know who he was, there was respect for his attitude. As the four disappeared through the back entrance, it went back to surveilling the area. Multiple targets were on the creature's radar. Patience was its current companion. Temporarily. A few scores needed to be settled. It would wait all night if need be.

Inside the factory, Top Arnie and his wife, Martha, followed the lead man down a corridor to a sealed door. Placing his hand on a glass panel, an infra-red scanner cycled from top to bottom behind the glass, obviously verifying the man's clearance. A buzzer sounded as the door clicked open. The man led them through the door while the trailing guard returned to the outside.

"Told you to watch your mouth, Arnie," Martha whispered as they walked.

"Nah. If they wanted us dead, they would have just shot us and dumped us in the trunk. These are G-men, if you haven't figured that out, love bear. They need us alive for whatever," he said.

The three walked through the strip door curtains into the main area of the building. To their right, they saw the glass containment tubes holding the bodies.

"Holy baby Jesus! What's going on in here?" Top Arnie asked, stunned at the sight.

Martha put her hands over her eyes, seeing all the floating, naked bodies.

"They're none of your concern," the man in black said. "Just keep moving."

As they passed the large glass window of the examination room, Top Arnie stopped. He knew the man strapped to the table. Where? He had to think about that momentarily. The old-timer had been around multiple wars, twenty-four years of service and the daily flow of customers. But he knew this man distinctly. Suddenly, it hit him.

"Sturgess? That you? Damn, you got yourself in a pickle," he said, tapping on the glass.

The man in black approached Top, grabbing him by the arm.

"We need to keep moving. I have orders to take you directly to sterilization immediately —"

Top Arnie looked at the young man before pushing past him to the door of the examination room.

"Son, first off, you ain't sterilizin' shit. I been shooting blanks for the past twenty years. Secondly, I eat concertina wire and piss napalm every morning before I start my day. If you're gonna shoot, do it now. Don't try hitting your little shock treatment, either. Disconnected those on the way here," Top said, taking Martha by the hand leading her into the room after removing both of their vests, dropping them on the floor.

In front of the building, Jud approached the main lobby entrance with the jeep. He hoped the uniform would be enough of a distraction to get whoever may be tending the front desk to permit access. If security was posted in the lobby. He really didn't know what to expect once they arrived. The plan got them this far, with a bit of improvisation. From this point on, everything would be improvised.

Rhonda sat up, slurring her words like someone fairly intoxicated.

"You should've seen Kat, honey. She called up the wind outta nowhere. Really saved my ass," she said, or what it sounded like she said.

Jud turned to Emma. "Ready?"

Emma sat transfixed, just staring straight ahead. Her eyes glowed an intense white, even brighter than when they first met her as the older Emma Adams.

"Emma, you okay?" he asked again, shaking her slightly on the shoulder.

"Something's wrong. Like totally wrong," Kat said from the back seat.

Without warning, Emma snapped out of her daze. "Everybody out, now!"

Jud scooped up Rhonda in his arms. Kat exited the jeep to the right side. Emma hopped behind the steering wheel, throwing the jeep in reverse. Punching the accelerator to the floor, she drove the vehicle through the front double glass doors, skidding into the lobby. A guard at the front desk ducked down behind it after seeing the headlights of the jeep plowing through the entrance to the building. Peaking his head above the desk, Emma had already leaped behind him, delivering the same blow she had to the guard with the M-16. He dropped to the floor.

One level below, the impact of the jeep breaching the entrance shook the walls, automatically triggering a containment lockdown. The doctor looked up from his microscope only to see Top Arnie, Martha and the man in black entering the room. He reached for the case of samples, slammed it shut and ran out of the laboratory the same way Top Arnie and company had just arrived. Within ten seconds, all interior doors would be sealed, only accessible from the outside. Once the lockdown was in full effect, nobody was getting out.

The night shift of twelve technicians, including two janitorial staff, ran for the closer east wing door. Five made it before the doors magnetically sealed. They were trapped. Even the doctor's assistant didn't make it out, returning to the examining room. However, a surprise awaited him.

Colt Sturgess' eyes opened from the sound of the chaos. Wherever he had been in his dream state, he was now awake. Fully awake. He effortlessly pulled free of the bindings. When the assistant returned, he grabbed him by the wrist. Not with enough force to break it, but enough to instill fear.

"What's your name, young man?" he asked.

"Patrick. Patrick McDonough, sir," the assistant answered with a quivering voice.

"Okay, Patrick McDonough, pleased to meet you. First things first. I'm gonna need my clothes."

"Yes, yes, sir."

"Don't run off now. I got another job for you, then we'll all get outta here safe and sound. Deal?"

Patrick nodded nervously. After Patrick left to retrieve Sturgess' clothes, Colt turned to see Top Arnie and Martha.

"Damn. Top Arnie? Haven't seen you in forever and a sunrise," Colt said.

Top shook Sturgess' hand, "I'll be a striped lion. Last person I thought I'd see here was you."

He pivoted to Martha. "This is the fellah I told you about. Super speed and all. Colt Sturgess, this is my one and only, as in the only woman fool enough to put up with my cantankerous ass."

Martha extended her hand. "Pleased to meet you, Mr. Sturgess."

"Pleasure's mine ma'am."

Top Arnie turned around, peering out the observation window.

"What's the sitrep? Any idea why these G-men came out, commandeering us in the middle of a perfectly good October night?"

Colt scooted to the edge of the examination table, recounting his understanding of the situation. At least the room was soundproof, as the alarm blaring outside of it was becoming a distraction to his sensitive hearing. The strobing red lights weren't helping either. He was on death's doorstep a half hour ago and to wake up to this chaos was unnerving. Then there was the mystery of the blast one story up. He continued with the debrief awaiting Patrick's return before investigating.

Outside of the factory, the doctor ran down the back entry ramp. The creature grinned. Whatever the disturbance was around the front of the building, it was pleased it held its ground. He was one of the prime targets.

Swooping down, the creature charged the doctor, lifting him from the earth with its large talons. The two smoking guards stopped their rush to check on the sound of shattered glass, turning to fire at the thing. It turned on the two men, diving towards them, severing the heads from their bodies with a single swipe from its claws. Once more, up into the night sky, the creature flew upstream to the location of the collapsed bridge. Spiraling up in the darkness, it stopped three hundred feet above the pile of rocks that once welcomed visitors into the town with open arms and hearts.

Pulling the doctor up to face it, the creature locked its ember eyes onto his. He screamed out in both pain and terror. Whichever was greater didn't matter at that moment. Vengeance was the dish being served, and it was icy cold.

"You don't remember me, Doctor Franks, but I'll never forget you," the thing sneered in a deep, growling voice.

"What...what are you going to do with me?" Franks asked, petrified.

"Ever hear of it's not the fall that kills you, but the landing? Guess what?"

The creature grabbed the case the doctor had handcuffed to his wrist, which he cleaved off with a flick of its talon. Doctor Franks screamed, spiraling downward towards the debris until eventually hitting the rocks, splattering like a water balloon. Target number one, neutralized. Rotating back towards the factory, the creature watched as a handful of workers ran from the east exit towards the row of parked cars. Whatever was going on inside the building was worth a watch. It flew back to the transformer plant.

<hr />

Jud, Kat, and a woozy Rhonda entered the lobby. Shards of glass crackled beneath their feet. It reminded Jud of the encounter at McNaulty's. The three ducked under a collapsed support beam that had previously held the roof in place. Sparks sporadically showered down on them like confetti.

"Ta-da!" Emma proclaimed, tossing her arms in the air in triumph. Barely keeping his wife standing on her own, Jud had enough.

"Nothing to celebrate, Emma. If you haven't noticed those alarms blasting, just let everyone in this building know we're here!"

"So what? All this sneaking around —"

"All this sneaking around? Are you fucking kidding me? FUCK!"

Rhonda looked up at her husband. He seldom dropped f-bombs, if ever. He was pissed.

Jud continued. "For your information, the sneaking around is so we could fucking breach this supposedly abandoned building as covertly as possible. We don't know who's in here, what they're doing or anything! The first Marine Division could be on the next floor, fully armed, and we wouldn't have a clue! Do you think a factory that hasn't been occupied in the past ten years deserves surveillance cameras, armed guards? How about an electrified fence that your impatience alerted them to our presence? You very well may have put Colt and Johnny's lives in further danger with your stunt."

Emma broke eye contact with him. Looking up at the ceiling, she crossed her arms. Her demeanor just added fuel to Jud's fire.

"And another thing, you crash this jeep into the lobby? You could have killed that guard if the crossbeam didn't give way. He's not an ash toker, or clown, or gargoyle, or one of those shadow people. That man is punching the clock like most of us do. We're here to rescue our friends! When did you decide murder is part of our mission? Does that apply to anyone in our way? Fuck, Emma, use your head!"

Silence dropped on the group like the remnants of the lobby ceiling above them. Emma stepped forward into his personal space.

"Yeah, well, Colt is in big trouble. Johnny probably is too. We need to get in as fast as possible. Tiptoeing around ain't my style," she said defiantly.

"Your style? Do you hear yourself? We came back to help you; to help Kat. It's probably going to cost me my job that I busted my ass to get. Excuse me if I thought we were all in this together. I don't understand your strength or speed and I certainly don't get Kat's skills, but I trust them. Wanna know why? Because I trust my team. I don't need to understand what supernatural abilities you all have. Just accept them. But when one goes rogue and threatens the safety of the rest, then it's a problem. My wife, your best friend, could have died because we had to separate from them to react to something you did. Don't you understand that?"

Emma paused, turning her back to him. "You didn't like me from the get-go…"

"Don't play that card, Emma. Next to Rhonda, I've loved no one more than you…"

He grabbed her, spinning her around to face him again.

"…And you're not getting away with playing martyr. There are consequences to every action. Look, one of the most important leadership principles I learned in the Marines was to know yourself and seek self-improvement. I do it daily. If I'm not working on myself, I'm missing out. You weren't in Kinston. We succeeded in taking back our town because we did it together. There was stuff that none of us ever did before, yet we trusted ourselves and one another. I know you only remember fragments of your life before then, but fuck Emma, you always put others first. It was part of who you were, part of who you are."

Letting out a heavy sigh, Emma touched his arm.

"Okay, boss. I may have been acting a little impulsively. What do you want from me?" she asked.

"Simple. To pull off this impossible rescue, we need to act in concert, like a human body: unit integrity, mission objectives, no weak links in the chain. We're in the home stretch, no more hot dogging," Jud answered.

"Fine. I'll play my position. You need me, just yell."

Nodding, Jud looked around the lobby. There was a door to his left, a facing door to the right.

"Any clue where to go next?" Rhonda slurred.

Both Emma and Kat answered in concert. "Down."

Jud hurried to the door on the left. Peering through the small window, he observed steps going down. This was the door. He pushed on it, but no success. Noticing the glass panel on the wall, he touched it. The infrared sensor scanned his palm up and down before an audible buzzer sounded. One of two lights to the right of the panel lit up. Red, signifying no entry. Glancing around the shattered lobby, he looked down at the unconscious guard.

"You're up, Emma. Use that hulk strength of yours. Can you bring the guard over here, gently please? No telling what your headbutt to the desk did to the guy," he said.

Gingerly, Emma picked up the guard, cradling him in her arms like a baby. She walked slowly towards him, stepping over chunks of collapsed ceiling. Reaching Jud, he placed the guard's hand on the glass plate. This time the light turned green. The door buzzed and unlocked. Jud held the door for the others as they made their way down the steps to the lower level.

"Should I leave him?" Emma asked.

"No. May be other security panels," Jud answered.

At the bottom of the stairwell, another sealed door obstructed forward progress. The sound of people banging on it from the other side echoed in the corridor. Jud motioned Emma forward to repeat the process.

"Let's hope he has access rights to this level too," Jud murmured.

The unconscious guard's hand did indeed grant them access. Before they could enter, a rush of remaining night shift employees flooded through the narrow door, nearly knocking Rhonda over. Kat caught her, moving them out of the way of the fleeing workers. The last one through addressed Jud.

"Don't want to go in there, buddy. Containment breach of some sort. We're all getting out of here," he said as he ran up the stairs.

They all were aware of the breach. It was not nuclear, biological, or chemical. It was Emma's impatience, ramming a jeep through the front door. The group entered once the coast was clear. Their jaws dropped seeing the rows of human test tubes. Banks of computers lined the walls for as far as the eye could see along the back wall down into the rest of the factory floor.

Jud's father, Fred Allen, had worked here briefly when it was an actual transformer plant. Many of the residents of Kinston and the surrounding area did. He had been here with his dad occasionally, but it looked nothing like this. This was more of a futuristic laboratory, which further deepened the mystery. What the hell was going on here?

"Do you want me to keep carrying Sleeping Beauty here?" Emma asked.

"No. Unless we're not in the right place yet," Jud answered.

"We are," Kat said.

"Then you can put him down."

"Where?"

Jud turned, looking at the door, wondering if it was one way in, no way out. He pointed down at the frame of the door.

"Doorstop, if need be," he said.

Emma placed the unconscious guard where instructed.

"'Doorstop'? Thought I was supposed to be more compassionate," she said under her breath.

———————

Colt was pulling on his second boot after ordering Patrick to kill the alarm system when Kat and Rhonda entered the examining room, followed by Jud and Emma. Emma rushed Colt, taking his face in her hand. His eyes glowed white, brighter than before.

"Thank god you're alive. I was afraid you were gone forever, and you're all healed again!" she said, tears streaming down her face.

Colt chuckled. "Yeah, darlin', this old codger is still kickin'. Touch and go for a while, but I'm kinda like a cockroach."

"I thought I killed you with that transfusion. You looked so pale, so sickly."

240

Colt stood up, patting her on the back. The transfusion did nearly kill him. Whatever Olath had injected her with, it infected his blood. However long he had with Solution X, he wasn't sure, as it was drawn from him in the first place back at Chooch's Farm. Whether these scientists tampered with it, only they knew, and the doctor was long gone. Patrick was still in the room with them, however, but Sturgess had other plans for him before he would let him join the others outside.

"Well, well, well, the gang's all here," Top Arnie said, interrupting the reunion.

"Top, great to see you again," Jud said, shaking his hand rigorously.

"Same here, Jud, although you don't come out to see old Top Arnie anymore. Afraid I'll put you on KP? Just bustin' your balls, Corporal. I've been following your progress in the papers. Proud of you, son."

"You know about all that?"

"C'mon, Jud. I've known you since you were a kid. Of course, I do."

"What are you kids doing here? More curious, how'd you find this place? Hell, I don't even know where we are," Sturgess asked.

Emma moved to the side, revealing Kat.

Kat interrupted with a hug of her own for Colt. "Where's Johnny?"

Colt rubbed his chin. "Not sure, Kitty Kat, but I got a pretty good idea. Gotta take care of somethin' first. Top and me been discussing a plan."

Sturgess turned to Patrick, who sat silently in the chair at the electron microscope station.

"Patrick, front and center," he said.

Patrick sprang to his feet, running over to Colt.

"Son, I need you to do something for me, then you're outta here. However you do it, let those people out or I will," Colt said, pointing to the glass containment units.

"You can't. I mean, there's a procedure. It's all computer operated. If I just open them all up, half of them will go into cardiac arrest. They can still breathe in containment, but the narcotic needs to be drawn back incrementally and the body temperatures must be raised individually, or they could go into shock. Then the whole brain stimulation engrams to restore autonomic functions back to normal. No two are the same and it must be done individually. There's more but —"

"How much time?" Top Arnie asked.

Patrick walked over to a control panel that glowed with a series of individual numbers from one to thirty-two. Next to it, he picked up a clipboard, lifting the first page, reading the second.

"Within first to last is a range. Like I said, each one is individually set, based on system parameters —"

"How long, Patrick?" Colt asked more forcefully.

"Anywhere from two minutes and two seconds for the quickest recovery module to ten minutes and twenty-nine seconds for the last," Patrick answered.

"Well then, you'd better get to work. Just two exceptions. Those happy-go-lucky assholes on the end, leave them be. Dump the pieces in the unit next to them. Will make damned fine kindling."

Colt was referring to Frick and Frack and what remained of Olath. He turned to Top Arnie. "You sure you got this?"

"In spades. I'll recruit the Sarge and Flower too, once they're out of those contraptions," he answered.

"Let the boy go with the others too once they're free. He didn't give me any problem."

"Roger Wilco!"

Rhonda approached Jud, still woozy. She put her arm around him.

"You okay, babe?" he asked.

"I guess. Better, but I feel like if I don't eat and get something to drink, I'm gonna die," she answered.

"Is there anything to eat here? A vending machine? Refrigerator? One of those water dispensers? Anything?" Jud asked.

"Um, yes. In the break room on the opposite side of the locker room," Patrick answered.

"Everything alright?" Colt asked.

Jud glared at Emma, who turned away.

"Yeah, I think so. Just need to get Rhonda fed," Jud answered.

The non-verbal exchange between Jud and Emma did not go unnoticed by Colt. A myriad of possibilities ran through his head that Emma may have done. She was strong-willed and impetuous. He only hoped she had done nothing that may have infected Rhonda as well. Emma possessed unnatural abilities but lacked the experience to use them. Even in the hundred years that passed, Colt still hadn't mastered many of his. The last thing he wanted was for her to be spreading Olath's contamination. This was the main reason he was so hesitant to pull the trigger on the transfusion, which obviously reverted her to herself, but at the price of his own life.

Colt started for the door when he stopped, turning back to Patrick.

"Those fancy jumpsuits you all wear and those shoes. You got more of 'em? Don't want these poor folks wandering around buck naked in the cold outside."

"Yes. We're required to change out every shift. The gear locker is down the hall to the left before you reach the locker rooms. Hazmat jumpers and static resistant shoes. Towels too."

Colt motioned for Jud and Rhonda to follow him. The three set off down the hall.

Outside on the roof, the winged creature watched as the lab workers scattered down the steps to their vehicles. Its next target wasn't among them. Growling, it dropped from the ledge onto the roof, pondering the next move. Whatever was happening inside the factory, the object of the creature's vengeance raged on. It could feel him, sense him, get inside of his mind like he had intruded on so many others. Deciding to wait a little longer, the creature had another curiosity tugging at it. The departure of the cars.

There was no visible way in or out of the factory other than the railway. The bridge was collapsed; the town surrounded by electrical fencing and a gate cut off access from nearby Hawthorne. Yet, it watched as several cars sped down the access road. The same access road it observed the men in black arrive from with the wise-cracking elderly couple. Flapping its wings, the creature took flight, following the small caravan of cars speeding away from the facility.

Following at an unobservable elevation, it hovered a half a mile down the access road. The lead car stopped at a checkpoint being serviced by two more guards, except these were dressed in military uniforms. Unlike most secured operations, this one lacked a guard shack, only a five-ton army truck. After a few minutes of discussion, the lead car turned right into a tree line. No road was visible, but vehicle after vehicle followed until they had all departed, reappearing a few hundred yards east of the checkpoint.

This perplexed the creature, further fueling its curiosity. Drifting slowly over the treetops, it finally saw through the subterfuge. In the woods, an abandoned railroad trestle stood, crossing a narrow section of creek. It had been reinforced and paved to act as a makeshift bridge, completely undetectable through the dense brush. Drifting down for a closer look, an Army Corps of Engineers stamp was painted on a ramp leading down from the other side of the structure. The creature glided forward until it reached another gate. This one was secured with some type of locking mechanism it wasn't familiar with.

Perhaps a remote device operated it, like a garage door opener? It thought.

Whatever the case, a twist on the apparatus immediately rendered it permanently open. The creature grinned at its strength. Turning to take flight once more, its arrival wasn't as stealth as it assumed as a rain of bullets showered down on it. Ricocheting off its body, the creature spun around to deal with the attackers. Flying forward, the creature cast both from the top of the trestle in one quick motion. Wherever they landed was of no concern. The threat was extinguished.

Flying back over the checkpoint, it saw the guards were no longer in attendance. Obviously, they were the origin of the attack. The creature landed to inspect the five-ton truck, more specifically, the contents. The back of the truck was empty. Examining the cab, nothing but a satchel filled with extra uniforms and a field jacket. Instinctively, the creature grabbed the satchel, once more flying upward into the night sky. It made haste back to the factory.

Colt and Jud returned after several minutes with stacks of silver, hermetically sealed packages. Rhonda found more than enough to eat as the night shift abandoned dinners they brought for the shift. Not only did she clean out the refrigerator, but downed half of the jug at the water station. Her color had returned, and she seemed more of herself again, commenting on how one container of lo mein was pretty good, although cold. Colt watched her closely, recalling his incident at Delaney's funeral home with the raw ground beef and bucket of water. Emma had done something. Hopefully, residual effects weren't on the horizon.

Emma and Kat were in the containment area of the lab helping the subjects who had already been released from their fluidic prisons. Tearing into the packages, they dried each one with the procured towels, helping them to get dressed. Martha Phillips took the natural lead in the operation.

Once Sturgess saw everything was well in hand, he motioned for the Kinston group to follow him. Top Arnie yelled out as they walked toward the freight elevator Blackburn used.

"You said this goo is liquified oxygen, huh?" he asked.

Colt didn't answer, merely smiled. Top Arnie returned the smile with a wink.

"Whatever it is you're gonna do, you got about twenty minutes, thirty tops, before it gets warm in here," Top said.

245

"Understood," Sturgess answered.

Colt led Emma, Jud, Kat, and Rhonda to the freight elevator. Jud put his arm around Rhonda, looking down at her. She nodded and hugged him. Slowly, the elevator climbed to their floor. Silence settled in. No one knew what awaited them below, but they were about to find out.

The elevator stopped. Colt threw open the gate and they all stepped onto the platform. Emma tossed out a well time joke to break the tension as the elevator descended.

"Next stop, ladies' lingerie and fashions," she said.

Chapter Fifteen

The group moved cautiously from the freight elevator. They stood looking at a back wall full of crates, boxes and the smell of cleaning solvent, flanked by two forklifts. Several rows of empty pallets stacked eight feet high sat in the immediate front.

Navigating the short maze to the center of the floor, Jud executed a quick visual reconnaissance. Appearing to have only two directions to explore, he motioned to where he knew the loading dock to be. The other direction was a hall exit to the side of the building. How deep this floor ran was anyone's guess. Colt moved into the lead position, arriving at the same conclusion as Jud. Glancing up, he noticed the crossbeams supporting the floor above. The same floor that Top Arnie and company were about to set ablaze. Once more, time was a factor.

"Johnny! John Paul Ellis, where are you?" Kat called out.

Banks of UV lights suspended from the ceiling swayed gently, but no other response. Reaching the center of the vast room, the smell hit them.

"What in the mother-of-pearl is that funky ass smell?" Emma asked.

The odor was extra strong to both her and Colt, particularly with their fine-tuned senses. Emma did everything she could not to lose her lunch. Reacting with less sensitivity, Jud, Kat, and Rhonda pressed on. Their progress was halted as a figure approached from the darkness. It was Kaleb Blackburn.

"I should have known all the commotion above was your doing, Mr. Sturgess. Ah, I see you've brought friends," he said, stepping into the light.

"Where's the boy, Blackburn?" Colt asked.

"In good time, in good time. First, I have been pondering our encounter outside of that dreadful little town. You got the better of me —"

"You mean he kicked your ass, and you flew away," Emma interrupted, crossing her arms smugly.

"Yes, quite. I'm guessing this is your team? The ones who dispatched my young protégé so handily?" Blackburn asked rhetorically.

Colt turned around, looking at his rescue team. Emma with his kitana, Kat with her backpack bejeweled with stars and moons, Jud and Rhonda with Colt's revolvers and bandoliers of speed loaders. Each of them stepped forward alongside Colt Sturgess. Like Jud said, "no weak links…"

"Actually, this is my family," Colt answered.

This brought an exchange of smiles across the group.

Sturgess knew Blackburn was fishing or delaying. Either tactic meant he was up to something. Colt continued to peruse the area. Trusting Blackburn's word was never a consideration. Sturgess suspected another act in this play, a hidden act. After the last encounter with Olath, that much he had learned about trust versus expectations. Besides, nothing seemed to go easy where this crew was concerned.

"You're stalling, Blackburn. I'm only gonna ask one more time. Where's the boy?"

"I sense your impatience. Very well, then. A rematch, if you will. Equal footing this time, since I am more prepared to adapt to your gifts," Blackburn said.

Slowly he removed the huge greatsword he revealed to Colt in his vision. Rushing towards Sturgess, he raised the weapon to strike first. Calmly looking over his shoulder, Emma had already expected the need, tossing the kitana to Colt. As Blackburn brought down the mighty weapon, Sturgess blocked the blow with his own. As the two swords clashed, the men stood inches from each other, eyes locked. A metallic sound pinged from the floor, then again in less than a second later. Blackburn grinned.

248

"I apologize, Mr. Sturgess, for destroying your well-crafted weapon. As I told you. This sword was forged in the fires of hell," he said.

"Funny thing about hell, once you survive it, realize that it ain't all that it's cracked up to be. You see, Kaleb, you got to show me your little story, but you don't know mine. Especially this sword, which isn't based on a myth.

"Helped this Japanese fellah by the name of Koji Otsuru a while back. Havin' issues with a railroad foreman. I resolved it, then moved him and his family out to a plot of land of their own. Didn't ask for anything as it's not why I did it. But simply the nature of good folks to return a favor. Turns out, Koji was a descendant of Sengo Muramasa. Now I'm sure he ain't as fancy as your Damocles, but a damned fine swordsmith. To wrap up this brief story with a bow, this is his best work. The way he explained it, sixteen folds in the blade which makes it, forgive me, not real good at math, but sixty-five thousand layers of forged steel. Moral of the story, you may want to check yours because, frankly, Kaleb, pretty sure that wasn't my sword piece that just hit the floor."

Blackburn broke Sturgess' gaze, looking slowly up the blade of his sword. Midway up, he saw it was indeed his broadsword that had broken in half from his attack. Tossing the remainder of his weapon to the side, he roared with anger, followed by a deafening screech as Blackburn transformed into the giant gargoyle thing. Knowing he would have to act decisively, Colt flipped over the creature's shoulder as it morphed, bringing the Otsuru blade down vertically with all his strength, severing Blackburn's right wing completely off.

Again, the creature screeched, but this time it was the sound of pain. The sound of agony. Like a cornered animal, it swung full force, toppling Colt to the ground. Rising slowly, Jud and Rhonda jumped into the fray, emptying six round each into the creature's chest. It fell backwards, blood spraying from where its wing used to be and the twelve tightly grouped bullets. Sturgess reached up to grab the creature's leg. Emma rushed it with her superhuman speed, clawing at its left wing. That attack gave Jud and Rhonda time to reload.

With a single wing flap, Emma was tossed backward. A support beam broke her fall as she slumped to the ground, unconscious. Jud took aim, but the creature was one move ahead, seizing Colt with its talons, sinking them deep into his chest. Attempting to go airborne, Blackburn spun in circles, unable to maintain lift. It dropped Colt to the floor in a crack and a thud. The thing landed, flailing back and forth between transformations, unable to maintain either. Finally, it fell to his knees as a one-armed Kaleb Blackburn. Blood soaked the surrounding floor. Kat noticed Colt was in a similar situation, except he was prone.

"This…isn't over…yet…" Blackburn said, forcing each word out with maximum effort.

Blackburn closed his eyes in deep concentration. Kat and Rhonda rushed out to tend to Colt. Jud checked on Emma, who was still unconscious. Out of the darkness from where Blackburn emerged, the sound of skittering and footsteps echoed across the sealed concrete floor. The indescribable odor was the first thing to hit the open air. One by one, other creatures appeared, all humanoid, all with various unnatural deformities. Some had multiple appendages, others looked like science experiments gone awry. As they filed in, they encircled the Kinston group. Jud lifted Emma into his arms, moving to the center of the room where Colt laid. If this was going to be their last stand, they would greet it together. Spitting blood from his mouth, Blackburn had one irrevocable act of defiance.

"Attack, my children!" he yelled before collapsing to the floor.

The creatures moved slowing in cadence, closing the circumference of the circle they formed around the group. Kat looked over at Rhonda, who was taking aim at the incoming threat.

"Sorry, Jud. My turn," Kat said.

Grabbing Rhonda by the front of her shirt, she kissed her. Slowly at first, Rhonda's eyes were as large as silver dollar, certainly not expecting a kiss in the middle of this showdown. Resistant to the action, she felt a burning travel from her toes to her head. Rhonda's hand slid along

Kat's cheek as she returned the kiss passionately. Desperately. She had surrendered to it. That was the fuel to fill Kat's battery. It wasn't necessarily sexual contact as much as the surrender, although the sexual energy held the power for her to conjure whatever her instincts desired.

Emil Ludwig, the German–Swiss author, wrote, "The decision to kiss for the first time is the most crucial in any love story. It changes the relationship of two people much more strongly than even the final surrender; because this kiss already has within it that surrender." For Kat Ellis, Ludwig's words were more of a prophecy in this instance.

Kat released Rhonda, stepping back towards Colt, who she would protect with her life. Rhonda stood frozen, unsure what had just happened. More specifically, her reaction to it. The creatures charged forward, only to be knocked backward by a significant wall of wind encircling them.

Bending down, Kat retrieved the Otsuru sword. Effortlessly, she slowly raised it to her waist. Looking down to the floor, then raising her head, her eyes glowed so brightly that they appeared to illuminate her skull. Kat let out a deep breath as dozens of rows of duplicates of the sword manifested out of thin air in a vertical position around her. Raising the Otsuru blade straight up over her head, her body rose from the floor.

"Duck," she said to Jud and Rhonda.

They complied with Jud covering Emma's body in the event she regained consciousness before whatever was about to happen played out.

Kat's body spun as the wall of wind collapsed around her. Faster and faster, she spun, as did the summoned swords except in the opposite direction. The creatures watched in awe, lacking direction from a leader. Blackburn found a final modicum of energy propping up on his remaining elbow.

"Dammit. I...command you...attack!"

Dropping the sword into a horizontal position, the manifested blade followed suit. The creatures rushed forward. Kat drove the blade of the sword in her hands straight down, splitting the concrete. The summoned blades launched outward, intercepting the mob of mutated creatures. Unnatural screams filled the room, as did odors. The things were beheaded, limbs cleaved, others hacked off, bodies impaled from the force of the launch onto crates, boxes, a few even made it to the back wall.

Raising her arm once more, she sent another volley to the left, then the right. When nothing moved, she stopped. Looking down at Jud and Rhonda, she nodded confidently. Their faces were blank, flushed even. Emma sat up groggily.

"What I miss?" she mumbled.

Kat walked slowly forward. Regally as if she were going to be knighted by the queen. She looked for Blackburn. He was no longer on the floor in front of her. On a wall beneath a bank of UV lights, she saw him hanging from two swords that found the mark. Waving her hand, all the manifested kitanas disappeared. Kaleb Blackburn crumpled to the floor. Kat approached him with the same dignity as her stride.

"Where's my brother, motherfucker?"

No answer was forthcoming, as Kaleb Blackburn was nothing more than a nightmare, forever extinguished by her hand. Pulling him up by the lapels of his suit coat, his skin dissolved to dust, pouring out of the arms of the garment. Only his skeleton remained. Kat dropped it to the floor. By this time, Jud, Rhonda, and Emma joined her side.

"He's gotta be down here somewhere. Colt was here. Blackburn was here. This is where Colt led us," Rhonda said with reassurance.

"Let's look around," Jud added.

"How is Colt doing?" Kat asked.

The group of four moved towards Sturgess when the floor shook. A brief pause followed, then it shook again. The next thing they had yet to deal with was getting closer to the other side of the wall behind the crates to the right. Bracing for the next offering in Blackburn's twisted arsenal, they formed a line. Kat picked up the Otsuru sword, holding it at the ready. Suddenly, the boxes in front of them exploded, sending wood and glass particles hurling towards the area they chose for their last stand. Instinctively, Kat summoned a wall of air that redirected the fragments, but the force of the explosion sent them careening backwards.

Jud and Rhonda were the first to see the thing. It was huge, larger than the behemoth the group faced in McNaulty's. Jud took aim, as did Rhonda. Emma and Kat regained their equilibrium to see the sight next. Black mist swirled from every opening on the monster's face, cascading around the thing's body as if it were dancing to some macabre symphony that only it heard. Breathing heavily, it looked at each of the survivors of the Kinston invasion. Fixating on Kat, it pointed.

The unsightly thing bellowed from the depths of hell. "You killed my friends, Kitty Kat. Now I kill yours!"

"Johnny? Oh my god, Johnny!" Kat screamed out.

Whatever Blackburn did to Johnny, this is what he had become. Maybe it started in the quarantine, maybe over the past day. In any case, her brother stood in front of her, frothing at the mouth. Easily two tons of rage on the warpath. It rushed towards her, causing the ceiling to fragment. Chunks of concrete rained down with every step he took. Jud instinctively fired.

"Jud, no! It's Johnny!" Kat yelled.

Jud stopped the volley. Emma stepped forward.

"I don't give a shit who he is. Didn't like him before, sure don't now," she said.

Johnny raised his fist to strike. Emma shot around the black of him, slew-footing the creature, sending it to the floor in a thunderous crash, causing more of the ceiling to crumble. Unknown to all of them, one of the support beams buckled as well. Kat strode towards Johnny.

"John Paul Ellis, listen to me —"

"No, you listen to me, Kitty Kat! You killed my friends. You don't want me to have nice things. Mr. Blackburn warned me about people like you," he said, sneering.

"Blackburn used you, Johnny. He put that thing inside you."

"Shut up! They're my friends too, and I'm keeping them safe from you."

Rising, he charged once more towards them. Kat raised both arms, summoning a cyclone of wind surrounding Johnny, much like the one earlier that protected her and the others. This one restrained him. With a little luck, he would wear himself out trying to breach it so she could calm him down. He swung madly at the containment field, making it grow large and spin faster.

"Stop, John Paul! The more you resist, the bigger it grows. I won't be able to control it," Kat shouted the warning.

As the cyclone built in intensity, it drew in the fragments of wood and glass from the explosion of boxes he presumably caused. It was now a swirling debris field as well. Johnny reached forward, trying to free himself from the wind funnel. His arm pierced the wall of the swirling air, only to be met with shards of glass and splintered wood. He screamed out as the flesh was stripped from his bones. Staggering back, he roared. Faster and harder, the cyclone spun. Kat dropped her arms, hoping to free him, but the windstorm encircling her brother grew in intensity. She no longer controlled it. His rage did, and he was a prisoner within it.

"Johnny, stop! Please, for Uncle Mike and Aunt Rosie, please stop!" Kat screamed, trying to be heard over the growing sound of the tumultuous swirling air.

Johnny roared again, slamming his undamaged fist onto the floor repeatedly. The shockwave knocked the team off balance, but more importantly, the crossbeam collapsed. Emma used her speed and strength to grab Kat, Jud, and Rhonda, whisking them away from the danger into the safety of the opposite hallway. Unfortunately for Johnny, an anvil sized chunk of concrete fell straight down the middle of the funnel, drawn in by the counter spin. He fell to the floor. The cyclone disappeared.

A familiar voice yelled from the floor above through the gaping hole caused by Johnny's anger.

"You all okay? What the hell's going on down there?" It was Flower.

Kat ran out of the hallway to the left, with Emma in tow. Jud and Rhonda cautiously returned to the center of the room. Johnny's hand was the only thing identifiable protruding from a pile of rubble. It was white, fingernails blue. Something shiny was in his hand. Kat bent down to see what it was, but Emma interceded, pushing her back.

The black mist circling Johnny's body crept out from beneath the concrete obstruction. Searching for a new host, it crawled towards Emma.

"I got this one, since I was out of commission for the gargoyle fight. Hope this works," Emma said.

The black mist seethed around her feet, up her legs, torso, neck until it reached her mouth. She breathed in deeply. The black entity entered through her nose and mouth until it was no longer visible. Her eyes turned jet black as her head jolted back. Several seconds later, Emma raised her head slowly. Opening her eyes, the black dissolved to the familiar glowing white. Forcefully exhaling, the entity flowed from her nose and mouth, screaming, formless, poisoned by the very solution that kept her alive. It attempted to reassemble, but turned to embers, scattering up into the air like the remnants of a campfire.

"We're ready for the last phase up here. You done with your mission objectives?" Top Arnie joined Flower, looking down into the hole from the floor above.

"Yeah, we're good, old-timer," Emma yelled back.

"Well, you wanna amscray then. This place is about to heat up in a hurry," Top said before he and Flower disappeared from the fissure.

"You two better get over here. Better hurry," Jud said from behind them.

Kat retrieved the item from Johnny's hand after checking his pulse for the last time. It was Uncle Michael J. Babin's constable badge. Turning to Jud's position, she noticed the concern on his face. Stepping away, Kat saw Colt in a similar pool of blood as Blackburn. She rushed to his side. Jud and Rhonda stepped back, giving Emma and Kat their time alone with Colt. They knew him best. It was their time with what they knew were his final moments. Emma knelt beside his right side; Kat assumed the left. Each took one of his hands. They were cold, unresponsive.

"What are you doing? Heal already!" Emma shouted at him. "We didn't pay you any mind, figuring you'd jump back in the fight once you were able. Now do it. C'mon, you old goat, we took care of everything for you."

Kat squeezed his hand. First Johnny, now Colt laying here lifeless. She pulled his shirt to one side and gasped. He had two enormous puncture wounds caused by the talons of that vile winged creature named Blackburn.

"Hey, King of Swords, time to wake up now. Can you hear me?" Kat said, hoping a soothing delivery would be more effective than Emma's bluntness.

His eyes flickered as he coughed up a mouth of blood. Kat wiped it away with a remnant of his tattered shirt. Looking at Emma, he forced himself to talk.

"Look at you. All grown up, but still a shit ton to learn," he said.

"Why are you just laying here? Heal and get up. Those jarheads or whatever they are upstairs plan on burning the place down. Can't carry you out like this, but I will if I have to," Emma said.

"Not this time, darlin'. This was a one-way trip from the get-go," he said.

"What do you mean, 'a one-way trip?' You were just fine a minute —"

It suddenly dawned on Emma. The transfusion, the sickness, the unresponsiveness. This was his last mission, his final ride off into the sunset. He was here to secure Johnny's freedom at the cost of his own.

"Fuck! I did this! If I hadn't insisted on the transfusion —"

"Shush, Emma. You did nothing of the sort. My choice, remember? Without me, doesn't happen. I'm past old. My best days were behind me half a century ago, but I need you to know, the past five, with you, were the best of my life. You have all that to look forward to..." Colt faded from consciousness.

"But why? What kind of shitty sacrifice is this? For me?" Emma yelled as tears streamed down her face. "Why?"

Kat reached across, softly grasping Emma's hand. "It's called unconditional love."

Sobbing uncontrollably, Emma's head fell on Colt's chest.

Sturgess opened his eyes, turning what was left of his focus on Katlyn Ellis.

"...and you, Kitty Kat, I wouldn't have found myself outside of that pit of hate. You challenged me to be better, to be myself again. You freed me. Don't know what else I can say about that, but...I love you dearly."

Kat's eyes welled up with tears. "You can't go. I've lost everything. I have nothing left."

"Funny thing about losin' stuff. Means you found it in the first place. Cherish every minute."

He summoned enough strength for one last movement, reaching up, touching Emma's face.

"Only regret is I don't have more time for one last dance, although I suppose this was it. I love you more than fresh pancakes and coffee, Emma Adams. Now go be you. Don't waste this gift. Oh, and... key...desk..."

With those ultimate words, Colt Sturgess took a deep breath, exhaling slowly. He was gone.

Emma screamed out, bringing down another section of the roof.

"No, no, no, you can't leave me alone! I have nobody now. No past, no future. You were everything to me, Colt Sturgess!"

Jud and Rhonda stepped forward. Rhonda took Emma's hand.

"That's not true, you know. You have us and we have each other. The Kinston crew. At least it's a start," Rhonda said.

Jud took Kat and Emma's other hand. Kat completed the circle, taking Rhonda's hand. Together, they formed an unbreakable bond around the body of Colt Sturgess. Like most ballads, his would end in tears.

"We can't just leave him here," Emma said.

As if on cue, his skin turned to dust, pouring like sand through the frame of his skeleton onto the floor of Western Pennsylvania Transformer turned government funded ghoul lab slated for destruction in a few moments.

"Of course," Emma said sarcastically.

Jud reached into his jacket, pulling out the flag that Emma gave him. "Think this will do?" he asked.

Emma nodded as they each took a corner, draping it over the man who brought them together for the weekend. None of them could have expected how that weekend would have played out.

Looking up, Jud noticed smoke drifting down towards them from the ceiling opening.

"Think it's time to go before we end up on the wrong side of that blaze," Jud said, leading the crew towards the back hallway out of the factory.

Kat paused momentarily, saying a last farewell to her brother, John Paul Ellis. Fear washed over her mind. What if he were in the control group and separated from them because they weren't physically or mentally able to endure the treatments? Blackburn obviously was the custodian of rejected experiments. An interesting perspective she would have to ponder at a later point in time. The room was filling with smoke. Running to catch up with the others, something called to her. Rather her instinct. It was more powerful than the typical intuition that drifted through her mind.

Approaching the flag shrouded skeleton of Colt Sturgess, she bent down, retrieving his skull. After blowing off the dust, she tucked it away in her backpack with Johnny's badge. She didn't know why she was compelled to do it or even why such a morbid act, but time for reflection certainly was no longer on her side. A glimmer of gold also attracted her attention. It was Colt and Lizzy's wedding band on a chain. She retrieved that as well. Feeling a twinge of guilt about grave robbing, Kat ran forward to catch up with the others, the group stood on the inside of the exit door. Only one problem. It was still locked.

The creature remained perched on the top of the roof when another wave of survivors ran down the ramp, followed by the older man and his wife. This group all had hazmat jumpers on and funny looking slippers. Where they were going, it didn't know as all the cars were gone except for one government vehicle that was intended for the doctor who presently no longer required its services. The creature also grew concerned, as it no longer shared a link with the reason it was here. Picking up the satchel of clothes, it dropped over the side of the building undetected.

The subjects from the glass cylinders all huddled together in the parking lot, seeking guidance from the man and woman who freed them. Top Arnie exchanged a few words with Martha, the Sarge and Flower, on what to do next. Behind them, fire flickered behind the boarded-up windows. It wouldn't be long before those wooden slats aided in the destruction of the facility.

A lanky figure in ill fitting military utility trousers, bare feet and a field jacket sauntered towards them. He approached Top Arnie. Top examined the strange dress on the young man, who he assumed was a young man by the scratchy facial hair. The rest of his face was covered by the hood of the field jacket.

"Help you, son? Picked a bad time for a midnight stroll, especially with no shoes," Top Arnie asked.

"Actually, pops, I'm here to help you," the stranger answered.

The Sarge stepped between the two. "Listen here, kid. We got no money, so just keep movin' along. Damned drifters," he said.

The boy pushed Sarge back, knocking him to the ground.

"I wasn't talking to you, fucking GI Joe. Mind your place and know your role. I'm talkin' to the old man here."

Sarge jumped to his feet, but Flower grabbed him, holding him back.

"That's right. Get your boy to keep you from an ass whoopin' like you never had," the stranger taunted him.

Top Arnie put his hand up, calling the Sarge off. They were in a bind, and he knew it. Soon, rescue units would be on the scene in response to the fire. Whatever shadow government entity was running the lab would follow soon after. Unless they wanted to end up back in the human test tubes, they had to get out of the area as soon as possible.

"What'cha got, young man? Don't mind the Sarge. He's been pent up in goo in a glass jar for who knows how long. Ornery son of a bitch right now. Luckily, we got out of dodge just in time. Problem now, we don't appear to have motor transport waiting for us," Top said, hoping to defuse the situation.

The stranger looked around Top Arnie, locking eyes with the Sarge. He would not be bullied ever again. If this is where he started, so be it.

The Sarge dusted off his jumpsuit. "Yeah. What the old man said. My bad, sorry."

Still maintaining eye contact with Sarge, the strange young man offered a way out.

"If you head down this access road about half a mile, you'll find what you need. An army truck sitting next to the tracks, fully gassed up, keys in the ignition. Can't see the road, especially now, but it's there. Old cracked up pavement, but it leads to a trestle that's been paved. The ramp on the other side takes you out. The security fence is active, but I took care of the gate when I wandered in. It's your ticket to freedom. Just have to punch it."

Top Arnie patted the stranger on the arm. "Thanks. You'll be in our prayers tonight," he said.

"Don't do me any favors," the stranger said, walking away back the way he came.

As he passed the Sarge, he growled a deep, unearthly growl, then was gone disappearing into thin air.

"Well, what do ya make of that?" Flower asked.

"Setup or a trap, maybe," Sarge answered.

"Only one way to find out. Let's go," Martha added.

"And that's why I love you," Top said to Martha, kissing her on top of her head.

Top spun around to address the Kinston refugees.

"Alright, folks. I know your limbs aren't quite fired up yet and your brains are a little scrambled, but we gotta move and now. Fall into to some kind of gaggle fuck of a formation and follow me!"

Top walked to the front of the group, leading them in the direction the young stranger directed them to go. As they made their way down the access road, Sarge turned to look back at the blaze, swallowing the building. He could have sworn he saw the silhouette of a skinny boy with no shoes holding his middle finger high in the air.

— • • —

Inside the corridor of the storage level of Western Pennsylvania Transformer, Emma pounded on the door, but it stayed firmly sealed. She had put several dents in it, but the magnetic locking mechanism held firm. No glass panel on the wall to hand print their way out, not that any security officers remained for the task.

Smoke encroached on the safe space Kat created, continuing to send the toxic fumes backwards with gusts of wind. Unfortunately, every burst also cost them clean oxygen necessary for breathing.

"Fuck!" Emma yelled. "Anything you can do?" she asked Kat.

"Not without completely using up our air. Plus, it doesn't work like that. Things just kind of come to me and I react," she answered.

"Well, this would be a great time to react!" Emma said.

Jud looked up at her, shaking his head. Rhonda had succumbed to the evening's events and lost consciousness on his lap. Whether it was the method in which Emma fixed her, the battle, or the decreasing availability of oxygen, it didn't matter. None of them had much time left if they couldn't find a solution to this conundrum.

Emma resumed pounding on the door. Leaning against the wall, Kat passed out, sliding down to the floor. Jud gingerly laid Rhonda on her side, stood up, and helped Emma with the door. Inevitably, both ran out of energy and breath. Leaning against the door, sweat dripped down Jud's brow. He looked into Emma's white eyes.

"You know, I don't hate you," he said, cracking a smile.

"I know you don't, just here to make your life a little more difficult," she said.

Wiping the sweat from his forehead, she kissed it.

"Let's give this door one last go, shall we?"

Before they could spend the effort, the door began to buckle and squeal. Some enormous force was being exerted from the outside. The center of the steel door folded, being torn off. Emma and Jud fell into the chilly night air, breathing it in deeply.

"What the fuck?" Emma wailed.

Grinning down at them was a huge, winged creature with ember eyes. Emma jumped to her feet, swinging blindly at the creature, who grabbed her wrist.

"What's with you? Like really," it growled.

She struck the thing in its chest with her free hand. It laughed before sending her tumbling across the parking lot. It looked down at Jud.

"Where are the others?" it asked in a deep, hollow voice.

He was speechless, pointing back inside the door. The creature stepped over him, lifting both Kat and Rhonda from the smoke-filled hallway. It flew up, carrying them to a safe spot behind a row of railcars. Emma stood up, unsheathing the Otsuru sword.

"No, Emma!" Jud yelled. "It's helping us!"

The creature swooped in, grabbing Jud, then Emma before she could object, softly landing where it had taken the others. Jud rushed over, checking on Rhonda first. Her breathing was forced, no longer rhythmic. He began mouth to mouth to clear the smoke from her lungs. Emma checked on Kat, who had roused when she touched her wrist. Everyone waited patiently as Jud worked on his wife. They had lost enough tonight.

Happily, after a few tense moments, Rhonda began coughing, spitting out a black substance. Collectively, they held their breath. Each witnessed similar substances in the encounters with all varieties of creatures. Stirring, she sat up.

"What? Sorry. I just…"

Jud hugged her tightly.

"Afraid maybe we lost you, lover," he whispered.

"Can't get rid of me that easily, Deputy Allen," she replied groggily.

"Umm…" Kat said, pointing at the huge gargoyle who just served as their benefactor.

Jud helped Rhonda up as they all stood quietly, awaiting the next move from the creature. A loud explosion rocked the area on the other side of the rail cars. Leaping forward, the creature shielded the group with its wings from the flying debris.

The roof collapsed on the building as the fire reached the liquid oxygen tanks. It burned hot and steady to the point the team could feel heat surging across the tracks beneath the box cars. The fire raged high into the air, reaching towards the same moon they used to guide them to the structure.

"There's a car around the side. I moved it behind what was left of a VFW. I can take you. Best way out, unless you want me to fly you out. Not sure how you even got here," the creature said in its deep voice.

"Who are you?" Emma stepped forward with the obvious.

"Oh, yeah, right? Sorry…" it grunted.

The creature lifted its wings, then lowered them, transforming into their former captive, Matthew Bristol, or as his acquaintances call him, "Opossum."

"Son of a bitch should have known," Jud said, shaking his head vigorously.

"Yeah, sorry about that, man. Was kind of waiting on Blackburn, but don't sense the asshole anymore," Matthew said.

"Kat took care of him and all of his minions."

"Damn. Bad scene. Those people didn't ask for the shit they did in that hospital. Would have liked to take the fucker down myself, but if he's gone, guess that's cool."

Kat cleared her throat a few times, attempting to gain Matthew's attention. He finally looked over at her. She nodded her head down, shifting her eyes from his down.

"Dude, she's trying to tell you your dicks hanging out," Emma finally went with the direct approach.

He immediately covered himself with his hands.

"Sorry, left what clothes I had up on the roof and haven't quite gotten the hang of switching over with clothes like Blackburn. Guess that wasn't my smartest move today. Toast by now," he said, blushing.

Along the highway to the right, the sounds of sirens led a caravan of flashing lights of emergency vehicles in the distance.

"Probably wanna leave about now. Like I said, I can fly you out, or you can take the car. I just wouldn't advise headlights. No telling who else is inbound. This was a fed facility, you know. Where'd you guys park?" Matthew asked.

"Hawthorne. Behind the water pump station. We have to breach that gated fence, though. The entire line is electrified, apparently," Jud answered.

Matthew laughed. "Not anymore, bro. Not anymore. Took that fucker out, just for the hell of it."

Jud glanced over at Emma, Kat, and Rhonda. All that remained of their team. Where would they go from here? He and Rhonda at least had a life together, although he may no longer have a job. He sighed out loud.

"What's the matter, man? Didn't get your boy out? How about the old man? I noticed they're not here."

"Yeah, more victims of something that started five years ago. Just wish I could have done more to help. Kat has all kinds of powers and Emma, as you know, is our mini hulk. Then there's me and Rhonda. We're just here for the ride with a couple of guns," Jud answered.

"Bro! You're shittin' me, right? I'm here partly because of you. Seriously. You might not have all those crazy superhero things goin' on, but you talked to me straight up, with respect. Nobody ever did that. Then, you come back with water and a blanket. You didn't have to do that, you could have just took off. They might have the muscle, but you got the heart, bro. Don't sell that short," Matt said.

"Why don't you two get a room already?" Emma said.

"Shut up, Emma!" everyone said in concert.

"Thanks, Matt, appreciate it." Jud extended his hand for a shake.

"Uh, yeah," Matthew said, holding himself with one hand, his other hand up. "Sorry dude, like I was holding my junk…"

Regardless of his objection, Rhonda stepped towards him, shaking Matthew's hand, then hugged him.

"Since no one else said it, thanks for saving us," she said.

Matthew nodded, appreciating the lack of any pretense on Mrs. Allen's part.

"Plus, looks like you got a splendid wife. Don't fuck that up, man," Matthew said.

"Never."

"One more thing," Matthew said, reaching down for the briefcase with the doctor's hand still attached to one side of the handcuffs. "Sorry, didn't have the key."

Emma took the case. She opened it. The others peered in, examining the contents: three test tubes labeled, "Sturgess, Colt" with a series of numbers that made little sense to any of them and several small jars with what appeared to be skin samples floating in clear liquid. Dumping the contents on the ground. Several of the items smashed on impact. What remained intact was crushed under her foot.

"Enough of this bullshit. It stops here," she said.

As the flashing lights grew closer, the sound of a helicopter joined the chaos. It was time to leave for good.

"Where'd you say this car was?" Jud asked.

"I know, let's go," Emma said, pulling on his arm.

Matthew shook his head, laughing. "You really are a piece of work. Hold tight."

Transforming back into the gargoyle, he lifted Kat and Emma first, flying around the burning factory, depositing them on the ground, then returned for Jud and Rhonda. Once they were all present, each one jumped into the car that Emma had already started.

"Thanks again, Opossum, appreciate it," Jud said before climbing into the rear seat.

The creature leaned towards the driver's window, tapping on the glass. Emma rolled the window down.

"Sorry, fucked up your barn door. I'll head that way in a minute to help fix it. Gotta drop a few phone poles across the road to delay those fire trucks and whatever else is headed your way. Should buy some time," Matthew said before shooting straight up into the sky.

Emma pushed the accelerator to the floor, speeding off through the vegetation that was at one time Main Street, Kinston, Pennsylvania. Jud leaned forward to give any directions if she needed. Since she had no memory of the time before the town was leveled, he could play navigator. She didn't need help as her unnatural vision saw not only what was directly ahead of them but also what was further in the distance.

Jud sat back, taking Rhonda's hand. She looked more like her normal self than she did all evening. Kat leaned quietly against the front seat passenger door, thinking of Johnny, running thousands of "what if" scenarios through her head. *Why have extraordinary abilities if you can't save the ones you love?* She thought. Then again, there was plenty for all of them to think about.

Every single one of them had lost everything. Their families, their town, everything. Only Emma had the luxury of not being able to remember the events, people, and places that were vital in shaping who they were, rather who they are. "You have us and we have each other. The Kinston crew," Rhonda said back in the factory. Maybe that was something. At least a shred of something left. Corina factored in too, wherever she was.

Finally, something went off without a hitch as Emma cleared the open fence that separated Hawthorne from Kinston. She stopped the car as it reached the first intersection. Jud directed her back to the water pump station. The car and the truck were untouched. Back in the truck, Jud and Rhonda, the Oldsmobile, welcomed Emma and Kat. Emma took the keys, however, as Kat was certainly in no shape to drive.

Both vehicles pulled out onto the highway headed north towards the Sturgess homestead. On the way, they passed a convoy of emergency vehicles and black sedans. More helicopters filled the sky en route to the blazing transformer plant. It was no longer any of the Kinston crew's concern.

FRED TERLING

Chapter Sixteen

After arriving at the Sturgess homestead, Jud, Kat, and Rhonda wandered exhausted inside the cabin. Although each had issues to consider, collectively adrenaline had bottomed out. Like zombies, they shuffled across the porch, entering the door. Emma headed over to the barn to assess the damage caused by Matthew's gargoyle form.

The barn door had been blown off the track, most of the door was in disrepair. Entering the barn, Emma hit the light switch. Inside, everything was still. No noise, no flurry of activity that she and Colt shared in renovating much of the house and creating furniture. It was empty. Color from the stained-glass dome illuminated the center of the barn where two lone stools sat. This was where the beginning of the end took place. Tears fell from Emma's white eyes. For the first time, she felt what it was to be alone. Truly alone.

Her heart was shattered, yet the morose emotions washed over her as quickly as her body healed flesh wounds. What was happening to her? Maybe whatever process that healed her body also healed her emotions. Even outside of the transformer plant, she was wise-cracking moments after Colt had died. First were the memory recall problems, now the inability to sustain any honest emotions. She felt numb, tired. Was this the wondrous life she had ahead of her? A life that Colt Sturgess willingly sacrificed himself for.

Footsteps behind her interrupted Emma Adams' thoughts.

"Hey," Matthew said.

Emma turned to see him emerge from the darkness. She was pleased it was him and not the gargoyle. Although fear wasn't in her repertoire, the thing gave her the willies.

"I see you found some clothes?"

"Yeah. Midnight run to Hills Department Store."

"Don't they close at nine?"

"I guess. Not really one to follow set schedules. How I got the nickname, ya' know?"

She smirked. "Nice taste in music, anyway."

Besides blue jeans and Converse high tops, Matthew sported a Van Halen t-shirt.

"Yeah, loved the first album, although I don't exactly have access to a tape player on the road."

"You could always steal one," Emma said, laughing.

Matthew didn't find the joke that amusing. It fell flat. She sensed it immediately.

"Sorry, I can say stupid shit sometimes."

"No worries. I guess it's kind of what I do. All I know, really," he said, looking around awkwardly. "How'd you know all that? Only Jud was in here when we talked about stuff."

Now it was time for Emma to be awkward. She pointed at her ears.

"Super sensitive hearing. I eavesdrop, even when I don't mean to," she said.

"Ah, cool. Like the bionic woman."

"Yeah, something like that."

They stood momentarily in silence. It was bonding, but uncomfortable. Neither knew how to talk one-on-one with the opposite sex. Not that there was a mutual attraction. Matthew considered Emma smoking hot, but she hadn't decided on him yet. He certainly wasn't the type any woman would be into. Lanky, facial stubble in random patches. If Colt looked like Sam Elliot, Matthew "Opossum" Bristol resembled Shaggy from Scooby Doo. His chosen occupation and preference as a drifter didn't add bonus point in the plus column either. Still, with some work...

"Well, should we get to work on this door?" he asked.

"Sure. Although hate to keep the others awake with the sawing and pounding," Emma answered.

Matthew thought for a second. "I have an idea. Don't really need to pound if you don't mind me bringing out my friend for a while?"

"The gargoyle? What the hell! Help me gather lumber from the last stall on the right, should speed things up. Just watch your step. Don't need you to bring the roof down on us."

He started to undress.

"What the hell are you doing?" Emma exclaimed.

"Duh, the big guy is slightly larger than me, if you hadn't noticed. It would suck if I shredded my new threads. Just turn your back. Not like you haven't seen it already."

Emma turned her back, laughing. It seemed some emotions were readily accessible.

Inside of the cabin, Rhonda immediately raided the leftovers in the fridge from the cookout. Kat and Jud stood in the dining area watching intently as she ate burger after burger, stripping two cowboy tomahawk steaks down to the bone. She filled up glass after glass of water from the spigot until she let out a mighty belch.

"Oops, sorry," she said sheepishly.

"You sure you're okay, love?" Jud asked.

"Yeah. Not sure what's come over me. I'm just so hungry suddenly. Maybe because we missed dinner?"

"Rhonda, sweetie, you devoured the contents of the refrigerator at the transformer plant," Jud reminded her.

"I did? Oh yeah, guess I did," she said.

Setting the glass in the sink, she breezed by Jud, grabbing his hand.

"Coming to bed?" Rhonda asked with a wink.

Jud shrugged, following his wife.

"Good night, Kat," he said, leaning in to kiss her cheek.

The Allen couple retreated to their assigned bedroom for the weekend. Jud ducked into the bathroom to wash up. By the time he entered the bedroom, Rhonda was fast asleep, passed out across the length of the bed. He pulled her still damp clothing off and tucked her in. Sitting down in a rocker in the corner of the room, he gazed out into the starry sky.

It happens to all of us eventually, Matthew said when Jud questioned him. What was in store for them, or had they been the fortunate ones to have escaped the effects of Olath's elixir? The two of them stood at ground zero of the smoke from both it and the burning bodies of the ash tokers. If he could will it away with a thought, he would without hesitation. That singular line, that singular thought, intruded his mind like the very plague itself. Intruded was a significant word, as he didn't want it to think about it.

Looking at the existing light glowing on his wife's face, the panic intensified. If anything happened to her like his dad or Johnny or Colt, would he have the perseverance to push on without her like Kat and Emma were now expected to do? Maybe he was just exhausted and hungry himself. Pushing the fear aside, he refocused on Rhonda's face. Nobody could ever love someone so deeply as he did her. With that image, he too drifted off to sleep.

<hr>

Kat sat on the couch, clutching her backpack. She was afraid to open it to retrieve her three mementos from the transformer factory. It would signify closure, the end of the two last vestiges of love she had in this world. To see them would bring the grim reality that they were gone, crashing down on her like the fragment of concrete on her brother. Instead, she leaned forward, picking up Johnny's camera bag.

Removing the contents, she laid the camera down, holding onto a film cartridge labeled "Colt's interview" in Johnny's handwriting, more like scribble scratch that only she could decipher. She smiled, thinking about that. No matter how hard she tried, or Aunt Rosie threatened to unplug the Gorgar pinball machine until he practiced his schoolwork, he always wiggled out of it somehow. Usually with some chore that needed done when Uncle Mike was around. Maybe that's what Colt meant about having found something to lose it. She probably wouldn't get the film processed because of those two words etched on the label. There was no rush to decide.

Crossing her legs on the couch, Kat got comfortable. With a cleansing breath, she opened her backpack. First removing the badge, placing it among Johnny's other possessions from the camera bag. Next came the skull.

Again, she questioned herself about why she took it. On face, it was a grotesque action, not to mention disrespectful of the dead. The desire to take it perplexed her. Holding it up to the light, she examined it with the same fascination as Hamlet.

"Alas, poor Colt, I knew him, Horatio," she said in jest.

Dropping the skull on her lap, she sobbed. "What kind of sick fuck am I?"

In her backpack, next to the tarot deck she purchased from Miss April, the three stones she picked up from the creek bed vibrated gently. Wiping the tears from her cheeks, she opened her backpack again.

"What the..."

The three stones were glowing, in addition to the subtle vibration. Removing them one at a time, she laid them on to the coffee table. Each glowed with a different color. She marked them to remember what each corresponded to, as the stones were very similar in appearance. The king of swords glowed blue, the reverse moon glimmered amber, and the lovers radiated red. Placing her hand on each, the first two were cold, but the red one was hot to the touch. What on earth could this mean? The vibration slowed; the light faded.

"No, don't go out. I need to understand!" she shouted at the three rocks.

The lights faded out, with only three smooth rocks on a table in front of her. Afraid the others might see the skull of their friend propped up on the table, Kat tucked it away in her backpack. *Maybe Corina would know why I had to take it?* she thought.

Corina. It was only the second time she had thought about her since they departed the farm to find Colt and Johnny. Leaning forward, she snatched the lovers rock from the table. She still had not come clean about what word she associated with it. Laying down on her side, she clutched the rock to her chest, completely forgetting about the last thing she took from the factory, the wedding ring. She looked up at the door, fully expecting Corina to walk through at any second. Kat watched and waited, eventually falling asleep.

Emma and Matthew fixed the barn door in record time. It was more than fixed; it was improved. Offering a couple of suggestions from what he observed on the doors of freight cars, they enhanced the durability and ease of opening based on that design. His experience of rail car hopping paid off. Once they had the door mounted, both stepped outside of the barn to check out their handy work.

"Pretty fucking sweet," Emma said, raising her hand for a high five.

Matthew instinctively ducked. Laughing, Emma grabbed his oversized creature hand, lifting it up to complete her original gesture. The monster laughed with a deep, guttural guffaw. With large strides, it momentarily disappeared behind the door, reemerging as Matthew Bristol.

"Better?" he asked.

"Much," she answered.

The two walked over to the picnic bench after securing the new barn door and turning off the lights. Matthew picked up a satchel of his own that he stowed in the bed of the truck.

"Whatcha got in there?" Emma asked.

"Just picked up a few things shopping. Ya' know, man things and smokes, of course."

"Nasty habit."

"Yeah, maybe, but gotta have at least a couple of vices."

He peeled open the end of the carton of cigarettes, firing one up. He breathed in deeply, blowing out smoke rings. Emma watched him curiously. How could something so harmful bring such joy?

"Lemme try one," she said.

Matthew laughed as he tapped the end of the pack, producing a fresh coffin nail. Handing it to her, he lit the end.

"So how do I do this? Just puff on it?" Emma asked.

"No, that's a cigar. You breathe one of those suckers in, you'll be coughing blood for a week. Just purse your lips a little and breathe in, but not too deep as you're a virgin," he answered.

"A virgin, what in the fuck —"

"I mean with smoking. Geez, lighten up, mini hulk," he said. "But while we're on the subject, are you?"

She punched him in the arm, sending him off the table and into the wet grass.

"Wouldn't you like to know?" she said, holding the smoldering cigarette between her fingers with a teasing smile.

Yup, Opossum was growing on her. Taking a deep breath, primarily because he warned her not to, she bent forward gagging and choking.

Laughing hysterically in his own human voice, Matthew got up from the ground, motioning for her to put her arms in the air. She complied.

"What's that do?" she asked, still coughing uncontrollably.

"Nothin', just wanted to see if you'd do it," he answered with a huge grin.

Emma flicked the cigarette at him. "Asshole."

"That I am, Ms. Adams," he said with a bow.

After her coughing ceased, he sat back down.

"So, now what?" she asked.

Matthew stared off across the field of the Sturgess homestead, rubbing his chin.

"Million-dollar question, eh? Don't really know. At first, all I could think about was righting a couple of wrongs. Found out when I changed and flew out of the barn, I could tap into Blackburn's brain like he had mine. Intrusive shit, ya know. Like he was soul raping me whenever he wanted. Then that fucking doctor who put everything in motion. I saw him too, through Blackburn's eyes. I figured two birds with one stone, know what I mean?

"Then I get there. Decided to wait, cool off. Saw the old couple giving the men in black shit made me laugh. Doc comes running out. That was the first bird. He's nothing more than a bloodstain and a memory on that demolished bridge. Then a funny thing happened. I saw all those people running out of the building. Kinda felt a kinship, the need to help. Be a good guy for once. I mean, with this power, I can make a wishlist of anyone who ever shit on me and rain down terror on their asses. But why? More than likely, they never knew I existed in the first place, or even cared. Why waste it?

"I thought about your boy, Jud. Compassion. That kind of nailed it for me. Took my eye off the ball long enough for you guys to take out my primary target, but you know what? It's all cool because the old-timer and his old lady came out with people they held as prisoners. People like me. Instead of revenge, I picked helping them. Might sound corny, but it's what I did. In this form, of course. Some asshat gave me shit, but the old man called him off before I changed my mind. There's always going to be some jerkoff, no reason for me to turn up the volume and be a bigger one. Fuck that noise.

"That's when I heard you guys pounding on the door. You ain't the only one with Jaime Sommers hearing. The rest is history. As for your question, kinda wanna see the world a bit, but on my terms. Used to just follow the breeze, survive, but never lived. Think that's what's next for the Opossum."

He had finished with the last draw of his cigarette, casting it to the ground, stamping it out. Retrieving it, he looked for an ash can. Emma took it from him.

"You know, mini hulk, you could always come with. Start fresh. I can carry you at night. Still no clue what the sun will do to me," he said.

Emma chuckled. "Nah, thanks, but I have a shit ton to handle around here, now that Colt's gone. Don't think I could ever leave this place. Too much of us is here."

"Suit yourself," he said, picking up his bag. "Need to turn your back for a sec while I change, if you know what I mean. Sun will be up soon; I need to head west to stay ahead of it. At least until I test it."

"I'm good. Like you said before, ain't nothing I have seen before," she sniggered. "By the way, not fond of Opossum as a nickname. You are aware they eat garbage, right?"

"Ever seen my diet?"

They laughed together as he stripped down, transforming into his gargoyle form.

"Well, what is it?" the creature asked.

"What is what?"

"The new nickname!"

"Oh, how about gargoyle boy?"

It rubbed its chin like his human counterpart. "How 'bout gargoyle man?"

Emma roared with laughter. "Done deal!"

The two shook on it.

"Who would believe it? Emma Adams and a fucking gargoyle fixing a barn door!" she said.

"Sure you've seen stranger things in your brief life," he said.

"That's for certain, and then some."

Gargoyle man nodded to her for a final time.

"Until next time, tootles, Emma Adams," he said, blowing her a kiss before ascending into the sky.

Emma let out a loud sigh, glancing across the farm. Melancholy drifted in, then dissolved as quickly as it appeared.

"Fuck! Can't even feel a moment of sadness, then it's gone. These are my emotions, goddammit!" she yelled to no one.

Standing up, she strolled across the property, touching everything. The barn, the fence, the grass, the posts on the porch. Finally, she ran her hand down the screen door. Looking down, the pattern on her hand disappeared, much like her sadness. Not having the full breadth of the human condition was maddening. Memories were snapshots in time to savor the wonderful moments, lessons learned from the bad. Those were scattered, and she had yet to unlock the mystery of how to reassemble the puzzle pieces. Just over twenty-four hours ago, she could at least feel. Now only happy-go-lucky emotions remained.

Entering the cabin, she saw Kat fast asleep on the couch. Jud and Rhonda had to be asleep as well. How she envied them. At least they were the only normal ones of the little Kinston crew. In all her wild imagination, she could never have guessed just being regular people would be so amazing. She wondered if she ever was.

Trudging up the stairs, Emma hesitated to enter the master bedroom. Fuck it, she thought, marching ahead. Swinging open the door, she turned on the dresser lamp. There it was. The bedroom, their room. Where she slept every night for the past five years, beside him. Beside Colt. She had the rest of the house to choose a room, but here is where she felt safest. Tucked under his arm, or spooning beside him, it was her comfort zone. Their comfort zone.

She sat down on her side, gliding her hand across his pillow. Picking it up, she laid down, clutching it. His smell was still permeating everything. The pine hair gel he would occasionally use before going out for functions, particularly dance contests she teased him about. Closing her eyes, she desperately sought that comfort to draw her into slumber, but it wasn't coming. Sitting up, she cast the pillow aside.

"Dammit, Colt Sturgess…"

Tears dripped down her cheeks, dropping onto the bed. At least she had that moment before they stopped altogether. She sat back against the headboard, glancing around the room. Far from a conventional relationship, it worked for the both of them. They were living proof that a man and a woman could live a carefree coexistence without getting bogged down in demands of a romantic relationship or a significant age difference. Just two best friends doing everything together without ever even having a molecule of boredom between them. Now she was alone.

The key! She had forgotten about the key. Quietly, she tiptoed downstairs, careful not to wake anyone. Approaching the desk, she saw it sitting on top. Nothing else, just a solitary key. Unlocking the desk, she discovered Colt's note directing her to a strongbox in the bottom drawer. Emma retrieved it, walking back upstairs with the same caution she exercised coming down.

Jumping on the bed, she opened the box. The letter contained instructions for the disposition of the farm, vehicles, land, everything. Her hand trembled as she went through the legal documents, one by one. When did he have time to do this? That's when it occurred to her he had taken care of many of the details long ago. He didn't expect to live forever. Who does? This was simple, sound financial planning. The last note, the one Colt scribed the morning before leaving, was the last thing she opened as it was in the desk drawer, not the strong box. That was the one that drove the dagger through her heart. It wasn't so much what he wrote, but the timing. It was the morning after the transfusion while she and Kat were off in Apollo talking to Horace Winston at VFW Post 1056.

"He knew, dammit! He knew…"

What she knew was far simpler. Her assessment was correct. The transfusion brought about his demise. Whatever went wrong with Colt Sturgess was finalized in that thin rubber tube. Somehow, her blood poisoned him during the transfer. An unfamiliar emotion washed over her. That emotion was guilt. Unlike her sadness, this one was hanging around and would, for some time. His letter never mentioned a word about it. It was full of kindness and love, Colt's trademark since releasing his rage in that far away funeral home where she force-fed him half-frozen ground beef. Maybe it was self-pity or self-actualization. Whichever case it may be, they were interchangeable at this point.

Emma crumpled up the note, squeezing his pillow again. That damned smell of pine. She would miss it. She briefly considered what Mathew the gargoyle boy said, rather the gargoyle man. He was off to see the world on his terms, not what someone else expected of him. Colt also spoke to her about starting her life anew. Emma stuffed her face into the pillow, sobbing uncontrollably.

After an hour, she finally stopped.

Rising from the bed, she walked over to the closet the two shared, reached into the back of it behind the rows of clothing. She hauled out two suitcases they bought for a cruise, but never went on. Emma Adams suddenly had work to do. She began packing. Colt's pillow and canister of pine scented beard oil were the first things placed in the suitcase. Next, she took documents, one by one, from the strongbox. Not being able to find a pen, she started signing each of them with an eyebrow pencil. Two went unsigned, those she tucked back in the box. After the documents were tended to, Emma returned to the closet.

"Too many choices," she said aloud.

She spent the rest of the night narrowing those choices before dawn broke through the windows, signaling that her time was up. Emma lay down, finally exhausted. Her adrenaline roller coaster reached an abrupt stop. Looking back at the bed, she chose not to impinge on the last memory of it. The last memory of him. She curled up on the floor in the fetal position, falling asleep in seconds.

Everyone slept in the next morning except Kat. She woke up at the crack of dawn after just a couple of hours of sleep. Wandering out in the frigid morning air barefoot, Kat wasn't bothered by the cold rather, she found the dew on the grass refreshing. She carried the three stones in her hand as she approached the fence separating the property from the field behind it. Leaning against a fence post, she welcomed the sun on her face. Across the field she watched, staring as if awaiting someone only she expected to arrive. Minutes turned into an hour. Finally, her frustration boiled over. One at a time, she hurled each of the three stones out into the pasture in different directions. Sighing, she had no more tears to cry.

Jud and Rhonda were the next two up. Rhonda sauntered toward Kat. She smiled.

"Good morning, or well, not so sure how good it is after last night. How are you feeling?" Rhonda asked.

That would probably be the question of the day and Kat Ellis hadn't really prepared a canned response. A tangle of emotions triggered back and forth inside of her. The odd thing was, she didn't feel fragile as she expected. Other than losing the last two members she considered family, Kat felt somewhat empowered. What she had done to Blackburn, and the creatures didn't emote any pride, more curiosity than anything. Nothing more than a flight of fancy that entered her mind that she acted upon. Much like manifesting a pizza when hungry or a pitcher of lemonade on a hot summer day. It was as natural as breathing.

Instead of answering, Kat shifted the focus back to Rhonda.

"Question is, how are you feeling? You totally pigged out last night. Like twice," she asked.

"Oh, that. Not sure what that was all about. I'm so stuffed, pretty sure I was going to purge when I woke up. Don't think I'm going to eat for days," Rhonda answered.

"Yeah," Kat said, returning her attention to the open field.

"I have a question. Kinda awkward, but…"

"The kiss?"

Rhonda nodded.

"You're wondering if you're a lesbian now because you enjoyed it?"

Rhonda nodded again, blushing this time.

"No. No need to worry. It's kind of how I charge up my abilities, powers, whatever you want to call them. I give off an energy that's like a super sex magnet. Best way I can explain it. Kind of sucks people in. You're safe," Kat said with a smile, hoping to quiet Rhonda's mind.

"Oh no, I wasn't implying anything wrong with it. In fact, I think it's really cool you're so comfortable with it. It was just…you know, Jud."

"Your marriage is fine, Rhonda. But if you ever have any of those kinds of feelings outside of my sphere of influence and want to talk, I'm just a phone call away."

"Thank you so much!"

Rhonda hugged her, kissing her on the cheek. Kat smiled at her, thinking how beautiful she was, inside and out in the morning light. It was then that she realized that there was no uncontrollable reaction on her part. No need to summon the fuzzy bunnies. *Intriguing*, she thought. Had Kat Ellis developed some sort of control through last night's experience? Yet another thing to add to the list to ponder later.

Rhonda took her hand. A slight tingle, but nothing beyond reason.

"Let's go. Jud wants to say goodbye. He's anxious to get back to work as soon as possible. So freaked out about his job. I told him no way he'll get fired, he's too valuable to the force, but you know him well enough now, the last boy scout."

The two walked back towards the cabin when the sound of the screen door slamming preceded the appearance of Emma. She was lugging two large suitcases, a makeup bag slung over her shoulder and a carry all type bag in her teeth. Rushing towards the truck, the two women ran to help her with the load.

"Where are you going in such a hurry?" Rhonda asked.

"I'll tell you all in a minute. Plus, I have parting gifts," Emma answered.

The three women placed the luggage in the bed of the truck. Emma picked up the Otsuru kitana that Jud had left the night before.

"Sorry it was out here all night. We tried, but couldn't lift it," Rhonda said, referring to the sword.

Emma stopped, turning to Rhonda. "You know, you apologize too much," she smiled, then hugged her. "Colt said it was balanced especially for him. The sword guy made it specifically for his weight, height, and strength. Measured that with sandbags and a rope. Don't ask, I didn't get it either."

Holding the kitana, she thought about leaving it, but what it symbolized beyond the man was how she remembered him. Opening the cab of the truck, she gently placed it on the seat of the passenger side.

"It has a really sweet blue velvet cover. Need to grab that from the safe," Emma said, rushing back to the house.

Kat and Rhonda exchanged glances, wondering if their friend had lost her marbles. Why the sudden rush to leave? Emma reappeared less than a minute later with the long sword cover trimmed with gold tassels in her hand.

Blue, how appropriate for the glowing rock of the king of swords, Kat thought.

Jud wandered out to join the others with a cup of coffee in hand. His curiosity was also stirred watching Emma buzzing around the inside of the house.

Emma slammed the truck door and approached the Kinston crew.

"Where's the horse and carriage?" Jud asked, taking a sip of coffee.

The group turned towards the barn. Indeed, it was gone. Emma walked over to where it was parked, and the horse was temporarily stabled along the back fence line. A flapping piece of cardboard caught her attention, pinned to the wall of the barn. It was a torn box cover from a carton of cigarettes. Walking over to it, she snatched it from the wall. On the underside white portion, a message was scribbled.

Hey, mini hulk. Came back to pick up the horse and buggy. Since it was Blackburn's, figured it belonged to me. If not, well, you know what I do. Anyway, even though it has a big ass dent in it, thanks again for that, smiley face, probably be a good sunshine test. Although I know a cat who buys horses could be a little flash money for the trip out west. Keep cool, Gargoyle Boy...

"What is it?" Rhonda asked from across the way.

"Oh, nothing. 'All good in the neighborhood' as Kat says," she answered.

With a smile etched on her face, Emma folded up the note, stuffing it in her back jeans pocket before returning to the group.

"Okay, obvious question. What the hell are you doing and where are you going?" Rhonda asked.

"Couldn't sleep last night, too jazzed with energy, bummed out, but excited at the same time. Weird things are going on inside me. I can't grieve," she said.

"That's called PTSD, Emma. It takes time. Before you do anything rash, you should probably—" Jud didn't get to finish before Emma interrupted.

"Maybe, but being surrounded by all this won't help," she said.

"But —"

" — but nothing. Minds made up. Colt wanted me to live, explore, start my life. If not now, when?"

"It's just..."

Emma grabbed Jud, hugging him. She appreciated his concern. It was her earmark to act sporadically, impulsively. He himself scolded her for it the previous night.

"Shut it, Allen! I love you for caring, but this isn't a sudden decision. Colt and I talked about this years ago. It's why he got a copy of my birth certificate for that same building you work in. I have my driver's license so I'm all legal. Just a few loose ends left that you're all going to help me with," she said.

"Us? How can we help?" Rhonda asked.

"Be right back. I have one last thing to get," Emma said, dashing towards the cabin.

Jud, Kat, and Rhonda huddled up, whispering about the mental stability of their friend. It's not like any of them could stop her, physically or otherwise. Her will was stronger than her muscles. If she was dead set on exploring, what could be the harm? Besides, she always had a home to come back to.

Emma sped back to the group with a Halloween tote bag.

"Ready for Wizard of Oz time?" she asked.

Everyone shrugged. They were a captive audience. What choice did they have? She reached into the bag, drawing the first envelope. It was marked, "Jud."

"Front and center, Marine!" she said, saluting him.

Playing along, he stepped forward as if he were in formation.

"For outstanding leadership in the certain face of death and keeping my arrogant ass in line, I hereby award you one 1973 Harley-Davidson FL Electra-Glide."

Emma dropped the keys in his hand, giving him the envelope.

"The pink slip is in the envelope, signed over to you by the owner, one Colt Anthony Sturgess."

She saluted him again.

"What? Are you crazy? That bike is priceless. I mean, I'm flattered, but I dunno. Wow! I can't accept this," he said, attempting to hand the envelope back.

"Sorry, buster brown. Already signed over title and fuck what it's worth. Colt wanted you to have it said so on his final note. You are now the lawful owner. If you're concerned about the value, sell it."

"No, no, that's not what I meant. I would die before I even dreamed of selling it. You don't understand. I saved up forever —"

"Yeah, yeah, saved all your paper route money for that shitty motor-cycle that was broken down from Kaplans. I remember," she said, not realizing her memory recall.

"Wait, you remember that?"

"Told you, Allen, bits and pieces surface. Guess something about you that makes them pop. Now, are you going to say thank you, or are we gonna argue about this all day? I would like to get on the road before next Tuesday."

"Yes, well, thank you. If you ever want it back —"

"Next!" Emma yelled out. "And you're welcome."

Jud stood staring at the keys in his right hand, the title in his left. Rhonda hugged him, knowing what the gesture of thanks meant to him. It was a dream machine to her husband. She recalled how it was the only thing that distracted him from her at the fair. How impressed she was with his immersive knowledge of it.

"Rhonda Coulter Allen, I summon thee!" Emma said, continuing with the pomp and circumstances.

"Me?"

"Yes, you! Get your cute little ass up here."

Emma handed her the same two items as Jud.

"One 1980 Suzuki PE 250. This is my present. Don't mind the eye pencil smear, it's all I had to sign with. I know it's not as cool as Jud's, but it's a hell of a lot of fun, as you know," Emma said.

Rhonda teared up, hugging Emma tightly.

"See, Jud, this is the appropriate response," Emma said, sticking her tongue out at him.

Rhonda ran over to Jud, dangling her set of keys. He was still in shock.

"Guess we'll be coming back next week with a trailer for pick up, schedule permitting," Jud said.

"Bullshit," Emma said. "I already packed them up on the bike trailer. Just need a small favor, if it's okay. I can hitch up to the truck and follow you two home. Maybe hang out for a day or two before I set out for parts unknown. You know, see how the other half lives."

"Of course, yes, we would love that," Rhonda said excitedly.

"Cool," Emma replied. "Let's get it hooked up."

Jud and Rhonda walked towards the barn. Jud still had reservations but surrendered control. Whatever was going on with his friend, it made her ecstatic. Taking only makes some people happy, whereas giving has the same effect on others. Right now, that was the best medicine. Emma turned facing Kat.

"Wait here. Best is yet to come. I'll be right back," she said in a low voice.

Emma didn't need any help to hook up the trailer, but it was part of the theater of the moment, like watching loved ones open Christmas presents. Once the hitch was secure, Emma prompted Jud and Rhonda to gather their things. "Burning daylight," she said.

The two complied, packing up belongings, taking one last look at the cabin before departing. So much happened in the past four days. It was difficult to process, but they were used to it. However, this time around, it would be by their choice. No hospitals, no quarantines, no doctors, no Blackburn, just the two of them. Standing just inside the front screen door, Jud turned to Rhonda.

"Ready for the next chapter?" he asked.

"As much as I ever was," she answered.

The Allens mounted their bikes, awaiting the final word from Emma.

Kat returned to the fence, watching the moment unfold. As strange as it seemed, it appeared a happy ending was in store for those three. She sighed with a touch of anxiety as Emma walked towards her. Kat assumed she was going to be asked to leave next. After all, if Emma was leaving and Colt gone, she would have to lock up. With a little luck, Emma would let her stay for an extra day or two. Unlike the others, she had nowhere to go except an empty diner with no customers.

"Hey, Kitty Kat," Emma said.

"Hey. I was gonna ask, and it's totally cool if you say no, but...mind if I hang out for a couple of days? I mean, I really don't have anywhere to go and, well, I still have a lot of emotional baggage to unpack. This is the perfect place to unwind, you know?"

A long pause ensued before Emma reached into her bag with a key ring of multiple keys.

"I'll do you one better. How about I just give you the cabin?" Emma asked, breaking her stoic expression into an ear-to-ear grin.

"Excuse me?"

"Not to get all Willy Wonka on you, but yeah. All of it. The cabin, the barn, the fence, the property, which is twenty-three acres, by the way. A bit of a pain in the ass to cut, but riding mowers are a blast. Oh, and all the stuff in the barn too, just in case."

"What?" Kat remained speechless. A couple of motorcycles was one thing, but a complete farm?

Emma laughed. "One condition. When I get back from my walk-about, we're roomies. Colt left it to both of us. I guess he figured that way I'd actually get my ass out in the world and explore. Don't worry, no mortgage, bills are minimal. Ms. April can guide you through those. Everything's paid off. A few simple instructions on the generator and we have a handyman. Everything you need to know is in here," Emma said, producing a large manilla envelope. "Well, what do you say, queen of wind and kick ass swords?"

Kat just stared at Emma, utterly shocked.

"I'll take that as a yes," Emma said, placing the envelope in Kat's hand, squeezing her fingers around it.

"But —"

"But nothing. You saved all of us, big time. Totally sucks about Johnny and Colt, but like he said, 'get out there and live your life.' We have a deal?"

Kat nodded, sobbing hysterically.

"Cool. By the way, dry those tears. Don't wanna have puffy eyes for your visitor," Emma said with a wink.

"Visitor?"

Emma took Kat's shoulders, turning her slowly around. Walking across the field towards them was Corina Newton. Kat's initial reaction was to run across the field, smothering her with kisses, but she pivoted to face Emma, giving her an enormous hug.

"Remember now. If you have any issues, talk to Ms. April. She can help. Take care, Kitty Kat. See you soon and I love you."

They were Emma's last words as she hugged Kat, then engaged her super speed to reach the truck. Kat watched as Jud and Rhonda led the escort away from the Sturgess homestead, now the Ellis homestead. Turning to face the meadow, Kat dreamily walked to the wooden fence. Corina had arrived.

"Hey, poppet. Miss me?"

Kat nodded, half-smiling. Certainly not the welcome Corina expected.

"Oh, things didn't go well. I'm so sorry. I just figured watching you and your mates, they had," Corina said.

"I guess, half and half. We survived, but Colt and Johnny didn't make it. I tried my best. No, we tried our best, but we were too late."

Kat turned around with her back against the fence post. Sliding down the length of it, her bottom hit the wet grass. She sighed.

"Mind if I come over?" Corina asked, with a backpack of her own slung over her shoulder.

"Sure," Kat said, lackadaisically.

Corina ducked under one of the fence beams, joining Kat on her side of the fence. Frowning, Corina hoped she could emulate the ray of sunshine warming Kat's hair, but whatever happened since she last saw her, cut deep. Really deep. Kat broke down, embracing her in a bear hug, tears flowing freely.

"Oh, goddess, how am I going to go on? I've lost everyone who ever mattered to me, everyone. Nothing left. I am totally alone. So much has happened. I'm numb. This doesn't even seem like reality half the time."

Kneeling in front of her, softly, lovingly, Corina took Kat's face between her hands, wiping the tears from her cheeks. As their eyes met, Corina smiled.

"I know it's not the same, but I lost a puppy once. Pop said something I've reflected on, even to this day. He said, 'Corina, don't weep. To lose something, you had to have found it in the first place.' I know it's not much comfort —"

"Wait, what did you just say?" Kat was shocked.

"About the puppy? I loved him so."

"No. The part about losing something!"

"Oh, yeah. 'To lose something, you had to have found it in the first place.' It's true, you know. Cherish those memories."

Kat didn't respond. She leaned back against the fence post, staring across the field, fully expecting the ghost of Colt Sturgess to ride up on a phantom steed. Those were the exact words he used. Not similar, not sounded like, but the exact words. Although she had done the books for Aunt Rosie and Uncle Mike's business, she couldn't calculate the odds of the same words uttered by two different people in a matter of hours. Another sign or just fate reinforcing a much-needed message in such a dark hour?

"What? Was it something I said? Bullocks, sorry if I said misspoke," Corina apologized.

"No, all good in the neighborhood."

Kat brushed backed her tears as a slight breeze rippled through her cropped blonde hair. Did she just do that, or was it nature's way of telling her everything was going to be okay? Colt's message for Emma to make the most of her life could be meant for her as well. All of them, really. She glanced over at Corina, forcing a smile.

"That's better," she said.

They embraced again, but properly, as if meeting for the first time. Corina noticed the embrace immediately. It was firm and welcoming, but Kat wasn't all over her. The rampant sexual energy had dissipated substantially.

"I see you've gotten a handle on the sacral energy thing," Corina said with a sly smile.

"Yeah, I guess so. Kinda figured out how to load it up and pull the trigger when I need to. If you only could have seen what I did with it."

Snapping her fingers, a gust of wind kicked around the two of them. Kat winked.

"Oh, showing off now, huh?" Corina laughed. "I came back to attempt in whatever limited capacity I can to teach you what I know but seems like you got the drop on me. Maybe you can show me a thing or two."

"That the reason for the backpack?"

"Like you Americans like saying about our dear literary creation, 'no shit, Sherlock!'"

Kat laughed as she took Corina's hand, who pulled her up to her feet. Kat slowly led her back towards the cabin.

"How about we teach each other? I think we'd make a pretty good team, and you must tell me where exactly you go when you leave. Can't be hanging out in a tent in the bushes somewhere. It's too freaking cold at night."

"Deal! But…you may need these," Corina said, reaching into her own pack.

One at a time, she handed Kat back her three stones that she tossed in the meadow earlier. She examined each one closely to see the small marks were etched on each of them, ensuring they were the same. Taking them in her hands, each glowed the same colors as the previous night. That caught Corina off guard.

"How…how are you doing that?"

"I don't know, was hoping you could tell me. The more important question is, how did you find them? I gave them a pretty good toss."

Corina leaned in, kissing Kat's cheek. "Did I fail to mention I'm a witch?"

"Ha! I knew it!"

The two laughed as they continued to the front of the cabin, crossed the porch, passing through the screen door. Kat held it so it closed softly.

From outside the cabin, the sun continued its northern ascent. Cardinals flocked to the bird feeder at the edge of the porch. The dew dissolved from the blades of grass. In the distance, a feeder stream from the Allegheny mountains gurgled over slick rocks protecting the native trout lying low along its bed.

Inside the cabin at the center of the Sturgess homestead, the background of nature's canvas, the voice of two lovers intertwined on a singular card of divination, began a journey scribing their next chapter.

"I have so much to tell you. You won't believe what I did. I hardly believe it myself."

"Can't wait to hear, poppet. First, tell me about this pool…"

Epilogue

Channels rapidly switched on a television screen mounted to a wall. The channel surfing halted when two large red words caught the interest of the person controlling the remote. The words dissolved to a man sitting at a news desk in a dark suit, sporting salt and pepper hair.

"This is an update on the fire still burning out of control at the former Western Pennsylvania Transformer plant. Sources are now telling us the blaze may be fueled by an underground gas leak. As you know, this is now the third day the fire has been burning. Hazmat teams have been on the scene attempting to ascertain the source of blaze, but fire teams could not access the actual site, which has been reduced to ash and rubble. Their initial attempts, as first reported here, were delayed because of the collapse of several utility poles believed to have been toppled by the blast itself.

"Authorities have reiterated that there is no chemical danger from the smoke to nearby communities. The factory, thought to be abandoned years ago, has been reported by authorities to be currently used as a staging location for construction vehicles working in the former town of Kinston to clear brush and debris for potential redevelopment. Work crews who fled the scene cannot be reached for comment. The two individuals who were found wandering the railroad tracks when rescue vehicles arrived remain in critical condition at Biggs County Memorial Hospital. They are not expected to survive due to the severity of burns.

"We will bring you more information as this story develops."

The television clicked off.

293

"Liar, liar —"

"— pants on fire!"

Frick glanced over at Frack, awaiting a response to the double entendre of the joke. He just shook his head. They continued the odd habit of speaking back and forth, Frack completing Frick's sentences.

"I'm bored."

"Me too."

"When do you think —"

"— they let us outta here?"

Both shrugged. Their syncopation was finally beginning to resume after two days. The first day, the two were completely unconscious. Looking down, they examined themselves, wrapped in sterile gauze.

"I look like —"

"— a mummy."

They each began tearing at the wrappings on the same limbs, in the same manner at the same time. One by one, the bandages unraveled, dropping the stained remnants to the floor. A nurse entered the room to administer medication and record vitals. When she saw what the two were doing, she retreated to the corridor of the intensive care ward.

"Doctor! Doctor Brady! They're awake and tearing off bandages."

Doctor Brady rushed into the room to be greeted by two portly patients with pink skin like newborns, completely hairless, including their eyebrows and lashes. He moved to the bedside, examining each one. Touching the surface of their skin, it was soft, supple, not the charred flesh barely covering bones a scant three days prior.

"What is this? I've never seen the like," he said, mesmerized by the impossible speed at which his two patients had healed.

"Nurse, call Doctor Livingston at once. I don't care where he is or what he's doing. Get him here, stat!" he yelled.

A little over an hour and a half hour passed before Doctor Livingston entered through the doors of the ICU. Doctor Brady intercepted him at the nurse's station.

"This better be good, Alex. I was just about to start the back nine at Meadowcroft. This is my first day off in three weeks," Livingston barked.

"Really? It's almost dark," Brady answered.

"Why do you think they put headlights on golf carts?"

Brady shook his head with a smile. "Suit up, Roger. You will not believe this."

"What?"

"Why do you have to be such a pain in the ass? Just get on your scrubs."

"Because, my dear Doctor Brady, I'm the best burn guy in the tri-state area. I can afford to be."

"Not anymore, you're not. In fact, what I just saw, there may no longer be any need for your services."

Doctor Livingston's curiosity had been piqued. He washed up and changed over into his surgical scrubs. Returning to the nurse's station, Brady led him down the hall to the specialized burn care unit of the intensive care. Entering Room 101, Livingston gasped when he saw Frick and Frack sitting up in plain hospital gowns.

"Sorry Doctors, I put those on them as they were just sitting naked giggling at each other. At least they've settled down. Somewhat," Nurse Hopkins said.

"We want —"

"— Ice cream!"

Frick looked at Frack. They both winked at each other at the same time.

"You scream —"

"— I scream!"

"We all scream —"

"— for ice cream!"

They finished the volley by saying the last line together. Frick and Frack roared with laughter. Livingston glanced over at Brady.

"Is this some kind of joke? If so, I'm not amused. Where are the actual burn patients, Alex?" Livingston asked tersely.

"This is them! I had nurse Hopkins run them down to X-Ray, look here," Brady said, switching on the x-ray review panel on the wall.

He held up the first set of images, then a second. "There they are. The bullets are still lodged in each of their heads. How either isn't dead from those is still a mystery, now this."

Doctor Livingston frowned before turning back to his two patients. Wandering over to them, he examined them both closely. Their legs were still wrapped. He motioned to Nurse Hopkins, who handed him a pair of mayo scissors. Snipping along the line of Frick's leg, Frack giggled. Livingston removed the gauze, raising both eyebrows in astonishment at the sight. The same pink, soft flesh greeted him.

"My turn!" Frack said, clapping his hands together.

Livingston repeated the process on the other twin with the same results.

"Can either of you boys explain this?" Doctor Livingston asked.

Frick and Frack both looked confused by the question. No answer was forthcoming. Brady summoned his colleague back towards the door and out into the hallway.

"Well?" Brady asked.

Livingston pondered a while; arms crossed with his chin in his hand. He walked over to the nurse's station, flipping through the chart. It was simply baffling.

"Where to even begin? We obviously need to start with a battery of tests. Everything. The kitchen sink on these two. Of course, we need to keep this strictly confidential, that extends to the staff as well," he answered.

"Naturally. If this recovery is biological and we can isolate it..."

Livingston patted him on the back. "Exactly what I was thinking. No limit to where we can take this discovery. That's why it's absolutely imperative we keep this contained in that room. Nurse Hopkins, you trust her?"

"No reason not to, but I'll have a word with her."

"Reassure her that her job depends on total secrecy. We'll treat this as a new admission. This way nosey techs won't question it. Won't take much to pronounce the previous patients deceased, not like they were expected to survive. Plus, no identification and no inquiries after three days."

"Exactly. Okay, I'll go talk to Hopkins. Since you're the expert, why don't you handle the twins?"

Livingston picked up the file, reentering Room 101. Within moments, a loud disturbance burst from the room. Brady rushed in to see Doctor Livingston lying dead on the floor, his head turned completely around. Frick and Frack tugged the intravenous needles from their arms, sending the poles across the room barely missing Nurse Hopkins cowering in the corner of the room.

"What in the name of god is going on here," Brady muttered.

"No —"

"— more—"

"— TESTS!" Frick and Frack both yelled the last word in unison before charging Doctor Brady.

Brady met the same fate as Livingston, but by Frack's hand this time. The two turned slowly, looking down at Nurse Hopkins. She covered her face, trembling uncontrollably with fear.

"Where can we —"

"—get some ice cream?"

The nurse held up her shaking arm, pointing back at the door. "F-f-first floor. N-next to the lobby."

"Th—"

"—th—"

"—ank"

"—you."

The two exploded in laughter. They weren't making fun of the nurse's inability to spit the words out from sheer panic. It was more a celebration of cleverness in responding. After pulling off the monitor sensors, a series of alarms sounded at the nurse's station. Frick and Frack exchanged glances, rushing out of the room. They bumped into a nurse on the way in, pushing her across the shiny, waxed floor into the desk of the station.

The two pink, hairless men walked out of the doors to the ICU and down the hall, past the elevators to the exit door leading to the steps. Frack pointed up to a numbered sign next to the door.

"Three!" he said proudly.

"I can —"

"— read, stupid."

Frick tittered into his hand.

"If you could read 'stupid' —"

"— you'd be a genius!"

Both chuckled maniacally. They continued down the steps, holding the railing as their feet were still wrapped, causing them to slip.

Back in the intensive care ward, two attendants helped the nurse laying at the base of the nurse's station to her feet.

"What happened?" one of them asked.

The nurse rushed into Room 101, letting out a scream as she entered.

"Call security! Somebody, call security! Now!"

Frick and Frack reached the first floor. They walked into the snack bar, sauntering up to the counter where a cashier stood. She was a young volunteer candy-striper who gave them an odd look. She had seen strange things on her shifts, but nothing like these two pink skinned, hairless men in hospital gowns with their bottoms exposed.

298

"We want —"

"— some ice cream."

Frowning, she hesitantly pointed over to a freezer case at the rear of the tiny shop. Frick and Frack moved hastily to it. Opening the case, their eyes swelled with joy at the assortment. Rifling through the selections, each of them made choices, several choices, placing what they couldn't hold into the front of the hospital gowns. That action produced a full view of their genitals. Shuffling their feet towards the door, the candy-striper called out to them.

"Hey, you need to pay for those," she said.

Frick and Frack snickered, tearing into the first chocolate Scooter Crunch sundae bars. With a mouthful of ice cream, they both pivoted towards the young girl.

"Put it on our tab —"

"— Room 101."

They laughed, shambling into the lobby, headed towards the front door. What they ignored during their ice cream raid was the announcement of a Code Blue over the hospital speaker system. Walking carefree into the lobby, Frick and Frack came face-to-face with two police officers who had just dropped off an overdose victim. The officers already responded to the announcement. Securing the front entrance was of utmost importance in keeping the assailants confined to the hospital while security conducted its sweep.

Frick and Frack did not know they were walking into a blockade.

"Stop, and get down on the floor," one officer shouted, pointing his stun gun directly at Frack.

The two looked at each other, ice cream dripping down their chins. They looked at one another, then kept walking. The officer fired the stun gun. His aim was true as the two darts hit Frack in the chest, releasing the 50,000 volts of electricity. Frack shook, falling to the floor. Frick looked at him full of curiosity, then fell to the floor as well. The two police officers exchanged glances, wondering why Frick took a dive too. Whatever the reason, both were cuffed and led out to a police cruiser. The attending officer radioed the security station to inform them the suspects had been apprehended.

"Yeah, we'll take them down to county lock-up. Crime scene investigators are en route. They'll handle the site details," the officer on the radio reported.

"Roger, that. The coroner inbound too? We have two bodies here, over," the voice on the radio replied.

"10-4. Should be here shortly. Have someone standing by and secure the area."

"Roger, out."

Frack was semi-conscious. It took both officers to get him into the back of the squad car. Frick just followed along as if nothing had happened, climbing in the back seat next to his twin. After closing the door, one officer addressed the other.

"And here you thought it was going to be a quiet night."

The officers got into the squad car, put on the flashers, and sped off down the road. Ten minutes from the county jail, Frack was aroused from the effects of the shock. He sat up, still disoriented, glancing around the moving vehicle.

"Where...where's my...ice cream?" he said completely by himself.

Frick tilted his head confused.

Crossing a set of railroad tracks, the police car continued around a bend through a tunnel. Reaching the other side, a limousine sped past them, forcing the squad car off the road, down an embankment, and into a tree. The two policemen were knocked out cold from the collision. Frick and Frack sat up slowly, looking at one another. At the crest of the hill, they saw the door of the limousine open. It was too dark to see who had stepped out of it. Hopefully, someone was coming to help.

Inside the car, they heard a loud thud on the roof, followed by two footsteps. A figure dropped from the top of the squad, opening the back door.

First, Frack was pulled out by his feet, then Frick by his wrist like a naughty child. Still cuffed, the figure reached around both, snapping the chains binding the cuffs together. Frick and Frack rose slowly, dusting the front of the hospital gowns off with the same hand. The two looked up as the figure stepped from the shadows, illuminated by a streetlight. Both twins' jaws dropped in utter surprise.

"You?"

"But how?"

"We thought —"

"— you were dead!"

"We saw it —"

"— through the —"

"— professor's eyes."

They were right, yet there she stood. Elizabeth "Lizzy" Sturgess in the flesh.

"Oh, please, boys. You don't think me stupid enough to put my trust in that buffoon's hands, do you?" she asked rhetorically.

Both shook their heads "no," with a touch of fear sprinkled with a dash of terror. She bent down, grabbing two paper bags, tossing them to Frick and Frack.

"Now, I need you to get dressed immediately. We have work to do. First order of business, find my daughter…"

The Kinston Crew will return in Gods and Necromancy.

Author's Notes

I'm really proud of this one. Two years ago, I challenged myself to do something I'd never accomplished, write a full-length novel. Since then, it has been an open door of ideas. This novel, in particular, was a fully blind write. Meaning, I wrote this book with none of the typical planning, storyboards, and only a handful of notes. Opening a blank document, I went for it. If there is a message here, it's just go for it. Being a creative can be an immense challenge as a typical person doesn't quite get the burning need to manifest things out of thin air.

In smaller writing pieces, particularly news columns, it was effortless to pour emotions and feelings into the articles. To do that in a much larger work was the real challenge. This aspect of writing was something I dreamed of doing. This being the second in the series, I believe I accomplished that, which is my second message. Be you, let your heart represent your work. It's okay, there are others out there dying to connect to real, raw emotions.

With Ballad…, I really wanted to examine the complexity of relationships, specifically the survivors of the Kinston event. It's a deep dive into the personalities you met in Olath's Bride. You meet them in book one, but at the fast pace and separation of the characters, their actions are predicated on survival, not kinship. Now that they share a common past, I felt the need to toss them into the deep end with one another to see how they mesh. Of course, friendships aren't necessarily easy, and relationships are twice as messy. Then there is the addition of a couple of fresh faces and survivors whose fate didn't quite follow theirs.

Thank you again for supporting my work. Sorry to leave you with such a cliffhanger. Well, maybe not. See you soon with more from the Kinston Crew.

About the Author

Fred Terling lives in Canonsburg, Pennsylvania with his wife, Lori and their dog, Poe. Fred has written over the past several decades in the fields of marketing, print journalism, politics, and professional ice hockey. Ballad of Colt Sturgess is his third full-length novel with his fourth, Gods and Necromancy, slated to release in December of 2023.

When not writing, Fred works in the community as Board President of the Mental Health Association of Washington County and Vice Chair of the Greater Canonsburg Area July Forth Celebration, Inc. He is also a Marine Corps Veteran.

www.ingramcontent.com/pod-product-compliance
Lightning Source LLC
Chambersburg PA
CBHW050701290626
47170CB00016B/2539